My Cousin's Cousin

My Cousin's Cousin

Susana Cory-Wright

Copyright © 2024 Susana Cory-Wright

The moral right of the author has been asserted.

Apart from any fair dealing for the purposes of research or private study, or criticism or review, as permitted under the Copyright, Designs and Patents Act 1988, this publication may only be reproduced, stored or transmitted, in any form or by any means, with the prior permission in writing of the publishers, or in the case of reprographic reproduction in accordance with the terms of licences issued by the Copyright Licensing Agency. Enquiries concerning reproduction outside those terms should be sent to the publishers.

This is a work of fiction. Names, characters, businesses, places, events and incidents are either the products of the author's imagination or used in a fictitious manner. Any resemblance to actual persons, living or dead, or actual events is purely coincidental.

Troubador Publishing Ltd
Unit E2 Airfield Business Park,
Harrison Road, Market Harborough,
Leicestershire LE16 7UL
Tel: 0116 279 2299
Email: books@troubador.co.uk
Web: www.troubador.co.uk

ISBN 978-1-80514-440-3

British Library Cataloguing in Publication Data.
A catalogue record for this book is available from the British Library.

Printed and bound in Great Britain by 4edge Limited
Typeset in 11pt Minion Pro by Troubador Publishing Ltd, Leicester, UK

In memory of Alicia de Villapadierna (1961–2018), for Jonathan who has always given me the space to write, with gratitude and love.

And for all victims of domestic abuse, especially those who feel they do not have a voice; that there is shame in speaking out; that it is safer to stay silent.

I like for you to be still: it is as though you were absent,
and you hear me from far away and my voice does not touch you

As all things are filled with my soul...
You are like my soul, a butterfly of dream,
and you are like the word Melancholy...

And let me talk to you with your silence
that is bright as a lamp, simple as a ring.

Extract from Poem XV by Pablo Neruda

Domestic abuse, also called "domestic violence" or "intimate partner violence", can be defined as a pattern of behavior in any relationship that is used to gain or maintain power and control over an intimate partner. Abuse is physical, sexual, emotional, economic or psychological actions or threats of actions that influence another person. This includes any behaviors that frighten, intimidate, terrorize, manipulate, hurt, humiliate, blame, injure, or wound someone. Domestic abuse can happen to anyone of any race, age, sexual orientation, religion, or gender. It can occur within a range of relationships including couples who are married, living together or dating. Domestic violence affects people of all socioeconomic backgrounds and education levels.

(https://www.un.org/en/coronavirus/what-is-domestic-abuse)

1

Ino
Winchester
April 2017

Ino's heart was pounding so irregularly, and with such force, that she couldn't breathe. But even the terrible suffocating feeling was important; vital, even, to the little mind game that she played with herself. Increasingly, it became the only way she could get Calypso to school at all; the only way she could get through that brief hour, the one in which Ino pretended to be someone else. Not that it was such an act of imagination – there were so many selves to her past that she could pick and choose from; she could mix and match. Sometimes she imagined herself as one of those cut-out dolls Calypso had never much enjoyed, the ones where you kept the body, but added different outfits and hair pieces. Somehow, though, they always ended up looking impractical and weird. It was the only time she was grateful for having had such a peripatetic upbringing. Sometimes, for example, she was the McGill student again, Canadian born and reared; other times she was the fifteen-year-old innocent who had left home one summer to visit a family in Spain she hadn't known existed until then. But more often than not she was just a wife and mother living in yet another country that was not the land of her birth. And this morning, because she was running even later than usual, she'd not had time to camouflage the damage to her face.

As the lights turned red, Ino slammed on the brakes, bringing the car to a shuddering halt. Loose papers, a pen and a roll of sticky tape shot from the glove compartment with surprising force, but then she knew that a single box of tissues could have the impact of a brick if thrown from a car travelling at speed. A sobering thought, and one she had no right dismissing even as the hubcaps scraped the kerb. With her right foot hovering over the accelerator, Ino strained towards the mirror. She flipped open the tube of concealer she kept in the well between the seats and began frantically dabbing it under her eyes. Perspiration ran down the back of her neck, her forehead glistened, and her heart felt as though it might leap through her silk blouse. Adrenaline coursed through her whole body. She had to put on her face by the time the lights changed. She had to. This too was part of the game. Daddy Yankee was, rather unhelpfully, seductively crooning 'Despacito' on Radio 2. She turned him down.

There – red was giving way to amber. Any moment now it would be green… but no, wait! The lights were still red *and* amber. There was still time. Her hands began to tremble. *Any minute now, any minute now.* Her right eyelid twitched uncontrollably. Concealer wasn't going to be enough. Not today. With trembling fingers, she prised open the chichi double powder compact, winkling out the tiny sponge. The girl at Boots had said it was just the thing to disguise dark shadows. If the problem was only dark shadows she'd be laughing. Ino tilted her head to one side, pulling her long hair free of the chiffon scarf that had become entangled with her seat belt. If only she could wrap it round her face. If only she could wear a burqa. For a moment her wide, shocked eyes stared back at her. *How has it come to this?* they seemed to ask. *How?* She puffed out her cheeks, wincing in pain as, in her attempt to plug the cracks, she'd only succeeded in brushing across gossamer-thin scabs. Blood seeped onto the sponge.

She flexed her foot, ready to hit the accelerator. If she could just make it through the lights having applied her make-up, she told herself, everything would be all right. She dropped the tube on the floor, not minding that it rolled under the seat, leaving a sticky trail in its wake. With one knee wedged under the steering wheel, she ducked down, rummaging for a tissue. The contents of her handbag spewed onto the floor. Unhooking sunglasses from other objects as though severing tentacles from an octopus, she emerged breathless just as the lights turned green. Her foot smacked the pedal and the Mercedes SL shot forward triumphantly. And so too did the volume button. *'Tengo que bailar,'* reverberated through the car. There was nothing 'slow' about it. The Spanish lyrics were scrambling her brain.

"Shit!"

"*Mummy!*" screeched Calypso. The child's small foot gave a protesting kick against the back of Ino's seat. Never mind the contents of the car, or Puerto Rican rappers, Ino had not given her *daughter* a moment's thought.

"Sorry, sorry," muttered Ino; then she cursed as she narrowly avoided hitting a car. Her heart was still pounding, her armpits soaked with perspiration. What was she doing? What was she doing driving Calypso *anywhere* when she was so upset? *Driving* full stop? Her thoughts were thin spikes, like so many pickup sticks, randomly skewering emotions. She gripped the steering wheel; hands slippery with sweat. The beat in her head was getting louder. She couldn't cope, that was the truth of it. She simply couldn't cope, and the physical pain was blinding and sobering in equal measure.

"Mummy, you're driving too fast!"

The timbre of Calypso's childish voice was brisk, but her eyes were round with the sudden realisation that her adult mother was imperfect. Ino's own eyes slid guiltily away. With sinking heart, she understood that she had entered that fallible no man's land where a parent falls irredeemably from grace and things are never quite the same again.

"I know," Ino muttered.

She *did* know. She *was* driving too fast. Ino lifted her foot off the accelerator (gently this time) and, catching her daughter's eye, smiled feebly, feeling her lip split as she did so. Calypso's return glare was uncompromising. Ino concentrated on the road. On some subliminal level, was she somehow *willing* them to have an accident?

"Mummy?"

"Yes?"

"Mummy, why do you keep looking at yourself in the mirror?"

Ino's gaze flicked to her daughter, whose legs were stretched out straight in front of her, rigid with tension. "Just checking," she muttered guiltily. "The road."

A lie. Ino felt a hysterical giggle rise in her throat. Just checking, to be more accurate, that the colossal wallop Archie had dealt her the night before was exquisitely, beautifully unchanged. Clearly, oversized sunglasses weren't going to cut it; barely detracting from the raspberry-pink splodges concentrated around her left eye. She tried to examine her face objectively. More defined were the indigo-blue and purple broken veins underneath the socket. The eye itself was so cloudy it was hard to make out its original colour. The small cut on her upper lip seemed to have widened too, so that when her tongue flicked round her teeth, she tasted blood. As if on cue, Daddy was purring more love which only added to Ino's mounting hysteria.

She mumbled something about smudged mascara, but Calypso only stared back at her, making her feel ridiculous and even sorrier for herself than she already did. Calypso's feet once again dug into the back of her seat. Ino tried to stem the rising irritation that in a few seconds could take her from calm to flustered. 'Despacito' was now a low hum. If only she could take things *despacito*. She would try. She really would. She tapped the steering wheel in time to the reggaetón pop and then sang along, the words coming effortlessly.

"What does it mean?" interrupted Calypso, just as Ino was at last feeling a little calmer. "Is it Spanish?"

"Yes, it is!" said Ino delightedly. "It *is* Spanish."

"But what does it mean?" There was a tightness to her daughter's tone which Ino recognised. Calypso was becoming impatient.

"Well…" said Ino, taking a deep breath. "'*Quiero respirar*' means 'I want to breathe'…"

"We all want to *breathe*," said Calypso, unimpressed. "What else?"

Ino mumbled something about necks. Listening to the rest of the lyrics, she realised how inappropriate they were for a small child.

Calypso was frowning. "That doesn't sound right, Mummy – why would anyone want to do that?"

"When… when people are in love…"

"They breathe in necks?"

"No, not exactly. Er… sometimes."

"Is that what happened to *your* neck?"

Ino met her daughter's eyes in the mirror. *No, Daddy was probably trying to break mine.* She mumbled something about having a reaction to… soap. *To your father, more like.*

"Doesn't sound very nice."

It's not! Ino was wondering how she was going to extricate herself from this particular line of inquiry when Calypso rushed on.

"I'm Spanish too, aren't I, Mummy?"

"Yes, you are, darling," said Ino overenthusiastically, in her relief.

"Which bit? Which bit is Spanish?"

"Your grandfather – *my* father – was Spanish. So that makes you a quarter Spanish, because a half of a half is…?"

Calypso looked blank. "You're awfully clever, Mummy," she observed at length. "I mean, you don't *sound* Spanish. You always speak in English."

"Thank you, darling," said Ino, amused. "That makes me feel very happy."

"But not *that* clever," countered Calypso amending her earlier comment.

"Oh, why's that?"

Calypso didn't answer, and a moment later there was a thud as, one by one, her shoes flew onto the seat beside her.

"Oh, darling, you haven't taken off your shoes!"

"Mummy," said Calypso, fidgeting in her seat.

"Darling, don't kick," said Ino.

"Mummy."

"Calypso! I said, don't kick!"

"*I* was only going to say that you aren't very clever at putting on mascita."

"Mascara."

"Mas… whatsit – doesn't it go on your *eyes*? Celia's mother never gets mascita—"

"Mascara."

"Celia's mother never, *ever* gets m-a-s-car-ra-ra on the side of *her* face. Her eyes are always just beautiful."

Well, bully for Celia's mother, thought Ino, feeling childishly annoyed. What would that so-and-so know about anything anyway? Except of course she *did* know, which was precisely the problem: knowing everything she possibly could about Ino had become her special subject.

"I mean, you have beautiful eyes too," said Calypso, as if the thought had only just occurred to her. "Sometimes. Not when they're all runny, though. Or gloopy."

Gloopy? And for some inexplicable reason, Ino felt like crying. She wanted to be a child again, with a mother who cared; who would shoulder all this worry. She flicked the indicator, hurtling onto the dual carriageway. Cars seemed to be flying at her from all directions. The music's beat was everywhere too along with the sexual nature of the words.

Good God, thought Ino as the song ended abruptly on a particularly erotic note. The sound of car horns ricocheted round her head. Someone beeped. Ino jumped. "Jerk!" she hollered.

"*Mummy!*" hollered Calypso in return.

Doubly startled, Ino was sharper than she intended. "*Calypso!* Don't do that! You scared me!"

There was an indignant sniff. "Mummy, *you* scared *me!*"

Ino overtook in the slow lane, her whole body hunched over. She *must* focus; she *must* concentrate. Only a little while longer, a little further, and Calypso would be at school within the hour and she'd have peace. *Only a little longer...*

"Do you *like* your eyes gloopy, Mummy?"

"What?"

"I said," said Calypso, enunciating carefully, "do… you… like… your… eyes… gloopy?"

"I heard you, Calypso."

"Then why did you say, 'What?'"

"I didn't mean—"

"Do you prefer them gloopy?"

"No, not really."

"Then why—"

"Why, what?"

There it came: another well-aimed kick in the kidneys.

"Why?" repeated Calypso.

Ino prayed they weren't going to start a sing-song of 'whys' for the rest of the journey. "Calypso, please! Mummy's trying to concentrate."

Calypso flopped back in her seat. In the mirror Ino could see her daughter's plump shoulders moving up and down as she tried to scratch her back.

"You look like Baloo," she said affectionately.

"Baloo's a bear," said Calypso sceptically. "I'm just a little girl."

"So you are," agreed Ino. Her daughter's school dress had ridden up and was tucked into her knickers, and she fiddled with a sock. If Ino didn't get her to school soon, Calypso would have completely stripped by the time they got there; a favourite trick of hers.

"*All* I was going to say, Mummy, is why are you wearing your dark glasses if you're trying to concentrate?"

Valid question, thought Ino, *and out of the mouths of babes...* but answering it was exactly what she could not do. She could not tell this babe that her father had a fondness for beating up her mother whenever the drink was upon him – or even when it wasn't, as was so often the case these days with Archie. Just thinking about her husband made Ino tense. It was her turn to rearrange her clothing as she tugged at her skirt, pulling on the seat belt to make herself more comfortable, her eyes fixed firmly on the road. Ahead of them, the chalk grassland with its abundance of musk orchids, butterflies, Iron Age hill ramparts and the buried remains of a Norman chapel rose above the horizon. There was a crispness to the air – spring in all its expectancy hung suspended in the fresh breeze.

Ino changed lanes again, but carefully this time, exiting at the next junction. At the roundabout she turned towards the village, which wasn't really a village but a small cul-de-sac; a one-lane hamlet on the outskirts of the city. Calypso's school was located at the entrance to this 'village', and because there was no through road, congestion at drop-off and collection was always intense. The only way Ino could deal with the headache of parking was to arrive extra early, but even a few minutes' deviation from the usual departure time was enough for the traffic to accumulate. The school ran a one-way drive-through system which worked efficiently enough. Ino planned to drop and run. What she didn't want to have to do was to accompany her daughter inside and thereby have to negotiate the 'piranha pit', which was what one of the other mothers dubbed the school quad. Ino had never managed to quash the sensation that hundreds of eyes were always watching her.

Luck, as it happened, was not on her side, and already cars were parked haphazardly on the road in front of the school entrance. Mothers scampered back to their waiting vehicles, mouthing a "Sorry!" as they revved their engines and departed. There was the familiar sound of car doors slamming; parents greeting each other – the usual cheerful, happy exchange of contented people going about their daily routine. Or so Ino imagined. She gritted her teeth. As a result of all this 'happy' bustle, there wasn't a space to be had; nor could she squeeze into the 'drop and go' queue. Ino had to drive almost to the end of the lane before finding a place to park. Ordinarily, she loved this time of day: the air saturated with dew and the scent of early flowering syringa. There was the cooing of wood pigeons, the clink of bottles as always late, the milk float delivered its round – in short, the comforting sounds of a village sleepily quivering awake.

"Come on, Mummy!" said Calypso, unclipping her seat belt.

Ino flipped the visor mirror, wincing at her reflection.

"You look scary, Mummy," said Calypso helpfully, her breath hot in Ino's ear.

"Grrr!" said Ino, and Calypso jumped, giggling.

"You're a witch!" said Calypso happily.

"And I feel like one too!" sang Ino, feeling anything but lighthearted. She slid over to the passenger seat, keeping her head low, and opened the door. Calypso followed, scrambling into the front before bouncing onto the pavement.

"Right, let's do this," muttered Ino, striding purposefully ahead, sunglasses at the ready.

But Calypso remained rooted to the spot. "Mummy!" she called after her.

Ino turned on her heel. The painful tic in her eyelid had begun anew. "What? What is it?"

"You've forgotten my shoes!" Calypso was wriggling her toes, enjoying the sensation of standing on the pavement in stocking feet. And for a moment a tiny voice in Ino's head stopped her, warning against further impatience. *Remember this, remember this...* the voice cautioned. It wouldn't be forever, this moment: her little girl looking so very sweet in her red-and-white striped summer dress and red felt blazer, her straw boater spinning in her hand. Enjoying such a simple thing as being shoeless on the pavement.

"So I have! Silly me!" said Ino with a smile in her voice, if not her heart. She unlocked the car, ducking into the back. One of Calypso's shoes was wedged under the seat in front. She retrieved the shoe, the long chain of her necklace becoming wrapped round the handbrake as she did so. She emerged flushed and panting. Ignoring the questioning look of a passing parent, she hunkered down, hiding behind her daughter.

"Mummy, you will, won't you?" said Calypso.

"I will what?"

"You will make sure Oreo has enough water?"

"Mmm?"

As Ino fastened her buckles, Calypso imprisoned Ino's face in her chubby little hands. For a moment Ino was lost in the sensation of having her young daughter caress her; their roles reversed.

"Poor face," said her daughter in her child's matter-of-fact tone of voice. And then she stopped her caressing to repeat sternly, "*Won't* you?"

Ino nodded.

"Promise?"

"I promise." Ino got to her feet, groaning inwardly as her knee creaked.

There was another tug at her hand and Ino made a mental note – a *conscientious* note – to do that as soon as she got back. No matter what happened, she *must* leave water for Oreo. She still remembered the last time she'd arrived home after being out all day to find the poor creature squeaking in a truly pathetic fashion. She didn't want to think how close it had been to expiring completely, and she never, *ever* wanted to relive the fish tank episode. No, she would go straight home after this and put out the water bottle so as not to forget. She would set the alarm on her phone directly. *Ahora mismo.*

Ahora mismo? Heavens, where had *that* come from? Yes, her father (the father she had never even known) was Spanish, but that side of things was well and truly dead and buried, so to speak. *No pun intended,* she thought morosely. It was a long, long time since she'd thought about him or Spain. *Ahora mismo* indeed! It must be that wretched pop song flicking on the Spanish switch in her. Ino stumbled ahead. She could hardly see where she was going, but she didn't dare remove her dark glasses. She didn't dare show her face. Not after Calypso's form teacher had asked her only a few days ago if everything was okay at home. *Okay?* Where to even begin with such a question? With such a word? She grasped Calypso firmly by the hand, as much for her daughter's benefit as her own. But Calypso pulled against Ino, deliberately dragging her feet so that the tips of her shoes scraped the concrete.

"Don't!" said Ino sharply. "You're scuffing them!"

"I know, but, Mummy, you aren't listening! Will you make sure?"

"Yes, yes," said Ino. "Don't fret. Your rabbit will have lots of water."

Calypso's lip began to tremble.

"Oh, what is it *now*?" said Ino.

"You're not talking in your *kind* voice." There it came again: that thin little warble. "You've got on your nasty, cross, grown-up voice." Calypso took a big breath before adding, "Like you always do."

Ino's antennae were uncomfortably pricked. "Like I always do?" she echoed. She felt even smaller than her daughter; small and alone. She tightened her grip.

"Ouch!" protested Calypso. "You're hurting me!"

"Oh, darling," said Ino, her own voice cracking. "I don't mean to, really I don't, but we must get a move on."

In response, Calypso seemed to dawdle even more slowly, unhurriedly tracing imaginary patterns with the toe of her shoe. With every scratch to the leather, Ino's nerves jangled. She could have screamed or cried – both, preferably – and just as she opened her mouth to vent her frustration, Calypso began to hum, her little cheeks puffing in and out with the effort. She pushed the hair out of her eyes. Taking another breath, she half-sang, half-spoke the words "*You can't hurry love…*"

Ino froze. "What was that?"

Calypso's eyelids flickered. "*You can't hurry love,*" she repeated, robot-fashion, and then, noting her mother's surprise, sang more loudly, emphasising every fourth word. The result was slightly off-key, slightly odd. If Ino hadn't been so completely astonished, she'd have found the intonation quite hilarious.

"Wow! That's amazing," Ino managed at last. "Wherever did you learn that?"

Calypso smiled delightedly and continued half-chanting, half-speaking the words. "Daddy sings it."

"*Daddy?*" echoed Ino, nonplussed. And she knew Calypso didn't mean it as in 'Yankee'. "Does he?" She'd never heard Archie sing anything at all. Ever.

"Yes," said Calypso happily. "When we go to the pu…" She stopped short.

Ino's eyes widened. "When you go to the *pub*?"

Calypso nodded. "He said not to say."

I bet he did. Ino paused to wipe her glasses, massaging the bridge of her nose. She touched the edge of her eye. It felt half-closed. "Children aren't allowed in pubs," she volunteered mechanically.

"They are in this one. There are go-gos," added Calypso helpfully, referring to her baby nickname for goldfish as though this would somehow make her presence in a pub acceptable.

"Go-gos…" repeated Ino.

"That's all right, isn't it, Mummy?"

Ino did a double take. The mention of goldfish would always conjure up the day Archie had bought Calypso her first pet. A visit to a nearby pub had sparked Calypso's desire to keep fish; any fish. Ino, Archie and Calypso had all gone for a walk over the little bridge behind the pub. Or, to be more precise, it had been a very little walk over an even tinier bridge. Calypso – a wriggly, plump, eighteen-month-old bundle of perpetual motion – was not the kind of child to be held placidly in anyone's arms. Ino could have handled the occasional twist and turn but Calypso was constantly jigging at a fast trot and/or bending from the waist down so that Ino was terrified of dropping her in the water. Ino was fraught and exhausted after only five minutes, whereas Calypso was super energised, pointing animatedly to a school of trout.

On the way home, Archie had had the inspired idea of buying Calypso a pet fish. Drunk by now, he had careered into the parking lot at Marwell Zoo. With promises of "Won't take a minute, back soon!" Ino had naively believed that Archie would be just that: back in a minute with a small plastic bag of water containing a single fish in his hand. But he was rather longer – more like a couple of hours longer – having decided to take a detour via another pub he'd scrambled over fields to reach (a pub not at all visible from the road), while Ino fumed in the car, waiting. He'd also taken the car keys, preventing her from driving away. When he eventually did weave his way back, it was in the company of the four store assistants required to transport the enormous fish tank. The dozen dazzling but temperamentally mismatched tropical fish spent the journey home busily consuming one another, until by the end of the week there was only one left.

Well, that narrowed things considerably, thought Ino, brought back to the present. Would it be peevish to ask if 'Daddy' went on his own? It was bad enough that he took Calypso.

"We like goldfish," said Ino brightly instead. "It's okay," she added, noting her daughter's glum expression. "Let's talk about something else. I did like the way you sang."

Calypso continued to scuff her shoes, with an intermittent sniff thrown in for good measure. They stopped in front of an unassuming little thatched cottage opposite the school. Its chronically shy owner (Ino imagined a kind of Boo Radley) never appeared but always left a special display for the children. Calypso could press her nose against the window without even standing on tiptoe to see the collection of Easter bunnies, china eggs and tiny doll-sized furniture arranged on the shelf. Invariably, Ino had to practically drag Calypso the last few yards to the school playground – another kind of fish bowl whose waters were just as treacherous; its aqua life just as predatory.

Ino scanned the yard, breathing an outward sigh of relief at the sight of the usual group of working mothers. These neatly attired civil servants, lawyers, doctors and army officers delivered promptly and retreated, Ino imagined, to the seclusion of silent, well-ordered offices. She spied the lady farmer and her wife, the stonemason. Then there was the charming bookbinder who seemed to have a perpetually startled air about her, the journalist, and the sous-chef at the local Michelin Star restaurant. Thankfully these mothers were too busy to gossip, but there was a smaller group of stay-at-home mums who had lots and lots of time to linger in the yard. In fact, for these mothers, drop-off and pickup bookended otherwise empty days. These were the mothers Ino was afraid of bumping into now.

Ino shimmied past the two lookalikes, Linda and Amelia – different at a glance, if only in height. These two fiercely competitive fashionistas prowled the playground, parading their exquisite clothes and dressing primarily for each other. Today they stood talking quietly, identical YSL straw bags (long sold out to the hoi polloi) rolling off muscular wrists. But they were harmless, as were the Slovakian bombshell and the Canadian divorcée, although the latter two were generally avoided by the other mothers, feared by the fathers and dreaded by the staff, given the one's overtly sexual overtures and the other's propensity to weep at the drop of a hat. Another group – the do-gooders; members of the Parents' Association who were always the first to volunteer for committees, welcome newcomers to their year group or organise volunteer groups at school fundraising events – huddled by the school office, ready to pounce the minute it opened.

Ino waved with one hand, keeping the other close to her face, but they barely looked up as she scuttled past. They were far more interested in the arrival of the overweight same-sex couple Lynn and Julie, whose tiny, diminutive daughter Fran was allegedly capable of striking terror in the hearts of her sturdier classmates. Ino didn't quite believe it, although Calypso was adamant that Fran really was terrifying. All Ino could see was a small, blonde, perfectly formed little creature in possession of the teeniest feet she'd ever known on a child and a truly beatific smile. "But you don't know, Mummy," Calypso often said to her. "You don't know."

This was certainly true, but Ino was also happiest *not* knowing. She would have been especially happy not to be told on a daily basis, for example, just how many times her house alarm had been activated. By accident. And by Marion of all people – Celia's mum; she of the perfect make-up. As a secretary at the local police station, Marion seemed to have access to all kinds of information including just how and when and what had triggered Ino's clearly overly sensitive security system. A day rarely went by that Marion did not greet Ino with an "Oh, Ino, your alarm went off today at 9.15am, were you aware?" Or "Oh, Ino, you'll *never* guess what your Calypso has been up to today!" *No, I can't, but I'm sure as all hell you're going to tell me.* And now, as if from nowhere, somehow just sensing that Ino was near, Marion popped up directly in front of her, an immaculately turned-out Celia lumbering behind her. Calypso scowled at them both.

"Hell's bells," muttered Ino.

"Well, hellooo," said Marion in that carefully modulated and affected tone that always irritated Ino. "A little jumpy, are we?"

No more than usual, thought Ino, *and always, always when I see you.* But she kept her head down, taking longer than was necessary to check Calypso's book bag and then fluff out her hair so that it fell on the right-hand side of her face.

"I should tell you…" began Marion, pausing for effect, but when Ino responded with silence she continued anyway. "I should tell you," she repeated, "that I've been hearing all sorts about Dormer Cottage." She ran small, narrow fingers along her fake Birkin. In fact, everything about her was bony and artificial, thought Ino. Counterfeit goods inside and out. She was too shrunken to be pretty, too *prickly*. It was especially true today, with her freshly dyed jet-black hair, white skin and thyroid-deficient eyeballs. Ino suppressed a giggle. She was a dead ringer for Michael Jackson.

"I know," agreed Ino, keeping her head lowered and concentrating on Marion's narrow, childlike foot, not dissimilar to the child Fran's. What was she, a size *three*? "Every spider sets off the alarm these days, never mind the rooks and the magpies—"

"Oh, it's not the *alarm*," tinkled Marion. "Not this time."

Ino could feel Marion's popping-out eyes rake over her body, scanning it for any clue at all as to the provenance of her clothes. *Well, good luck with that,* thought Ino. El Corte Inglés was where she'd bought this suede jacket, and it was older than the combined ages of their daughters. There it was again: that reference to another life. El Corte Inglés was one of Spain's John Lewis-type department stores, with a name that literally meant 'The English Cut'. Ino smiled at the irony.

"Something funny? Wanna share?"

"Er…" *Not really.* Ino didn't dare meet the penetrating look she felt certain would happily have shredded her to pieces if it meant getting a look at the jacket's label.

"Little early for sunglasses, isn't it?" snapped Marion, peering at the tortoiseshell arm, trying to work out the brand. Her mouth opened and shut, no bigger than a Venus fly trap's. Calypso too seemed to be fixated on Marion's threadlike greenish lips, and any minute now, if Ino didn't say something quickly, her daughter would blurt out exactly what was on her child's mind.

"C-conjunctivitis," stammered Ino, throwing her daughter a warning look and then almost laughing with relief as Marion stopped dead. Ino shrugged apologetically. "You know how it is."

"Actually, I don't!" said Marion, stepping back in alarm, lips a spiky leaf line. Ino could almost feel a fly squirming within that tightly closed orifice. She could hardly contain her glee, for if there was something guaranteed to horrify *all* mothers without exception, it was the merest whiff of a contagious infection – especially as there was now a two-day stay-at-home rule in place. What mother would willingly sign up for that? Marion held out her hand, wagging the fingers individually until Celia reluctantly took hold of them. She blinked rapidly. "Well, I won't keep you."

Ino straightened the collar of Calypso's dress, keeping the good side of her face in profile. "Oh, Marion?"

"Yes?"

"What was it you were going to say about Dormer Cottage?" Ino hated herself for it, but curiosity had got the better of her.

She felt Marion brush past, leaving the smell of mothballs and second-hand clothes in her wake. Ino knew she bought all her designer gear on eBay, including children's birthday gifts which she passed off as new.

"Oh, it's nothing; nothing that can't wait – at least till we can chat properly." Marion eyed Calypso closely, as if for any sign of her mother's infection. "Celia is looking forward to crafts today. Celia loves her art classes. She especially likes cutting out shapes." She tilted her head. "Do you like cutting out shapes?"

Calypso tilted hers, subconsciously mimicking the older woman. If Ino didn't do something quickly, who knew where her daughter might go with this? But Calypso, enjoying the attention, was just getting started. She shook the fringe out of her eyes.

"'Despacito,'" articulated Calypso beautifully, breathlessly. "I want to undre… what's the Spanish word, Mummy?" She turned brightly, very pleased with the adults' response. "Mummy is going to—"

"Be late," finished Ino quickly, placing her hands on Calypso's shoulders and orientating her in the direction of the school building. "We really must…"

Other mothers passed them on the pavement. Most of them wore a uniform of Victoria plimsolls, chinos and Breton jumpers.

Ino prodded Calypso forward. "Catch you later," she mouthed to no one in particular, striding ahead.

"I meant to say I saw your husband!" trilled Marion over her shoulder.

Ino almost hesitated, feeling the words bore into her back.

"In the pub. *Again*. He certainly has a fondness for Ye Olde Inne, doesn't he? Never mind the drink! Ho ho. I wonder why he doesn't go to The White Nag? Surely it must be closer to you? I always said there should be a pub in Drayton. Fancy you finding a house in the only village without a pub! I mean, how many times has it been this week? I said to my husband, 'You'd think he didn't have a home to go to!' Clever man like that. As drunk as a lord, he was, and flirting something wicked! He's still an attractive man, that much is clear, even if... well, it's a wonder you let him out at all since that last time..."

2

Rafael
Barcelona
April 2017

Padre Rafael blew out the altar candles and then, lifting up the hem of his cassock, made his way down the aisle of the Church of Sant Vicenç. His pace quickened until he was almost running. Incense always made him sneeze, as did musty brocade cushions. His nostrils would automatically twitch when little old ladies sank onto padded benches, and as the first dust motes somersaulted through the air, he would close his eyes, anticipating that first tickle at the back of his throat. His arms ached. He had just spent an hour holding a none-too-clean porcelain baby Jesus nestled on a faded silk pillow. Even holding it at arm's length, he inwardly shuddered every time a parishioner kissed the tiny toes. It didn't help that it was the very same baby Jesus his grandmother had made him kiss as a boy. The linen napkin upon which the ugly little fellow lolled was now yellow with age, spit and God only knew what else, but it too was the same. He had been alarmed by the practice then and he was alarmed by the practice now, but no amount of argument could persuade his superiors to dispense with the custom. And the only difference between then and now was that, as a boy, Padre Rafael had been incapable of disguising the distaste he felt for what he considered to be nothing short of a pagan invention. As he'd got older, this kitsch pantomime had merely fanned the naughty and irreverent side to his character. He suppressed a giggle. He was becoming increasingly, in his humble opinion, like the unbelieving priest in Unamuno's classic tale *San Manuel Bueno, Mártir*. Though in his case he was neither *bueno* nor, he suspected, all that much loved.

Emerging onto the square, Padre Rafael breathed in the congested air of Sarrià as though he'd been stuck down a catacomb for a month. He threw back his head to look at the cloudless azure sky, squinting in the sunlight. It was spring but already a gentle warmth was nudging them towards the hot days of summer. Ah, it was good to be alive on days like this. And there was nothing like pain and pleasure, yin and yang – *contrast* – to increase his sense of enjoyment. Monday mornings were always arduous with early *misa*, confessions, and the celebration of a saint's day, and this being Spain, there was *always* a saint's day.

He stood on the steps, surveying his clerical fiefdom with some pleasure. He pulled out a packet of cigarettes and slowly smoked an old-fashioned Du Maurier, savouring every inhalation, blowing out smoke rings because he still could. It seemed to him that the pigeons strutting up and down the sandy arena kept time with the church bells clamouring from their neoclassical tower. *And yes, like San Manuel Bueno*, thought Padre Rafael, *I can keep the illusion going – I can pretend to my parishioners that I believe. After all, it's a good story, and one easy enough to believe in.* He thought of the baby Jesus now safely ensconced on a top shelf in the sacristy. *Well, easy enough.* After all, what else could he do? And, as a reward for holding that porcelain artefact until his arms ached, he would treat himself. Yes, he would; this very minute. *Ahora mismo.*

He stubbed out his cigarette with the heel of his expensive Loewe shoe, pulled out his aviator sunglasses and crossed the road. The purple-and-gold canopy with its huge 'MA' initials, which stood for Monte Alegre (pronounced as one word), was as much part of this Sarrià barrio as the church itself. A family-owned business – *their* family-owned business – since 1784, the pastry shop was managed by his cousin Emil. From time to time they toyed with the idea of updating its name to Pan Salto or something more suggestive of bread and the estate from where it had once come, but they never came up with anything catchy enough to warrant the change. Padre Rafael placed a confident hand on the doorknob and entered, just as he had been doing once a week for over thirty-five years.

Generally, the conversation varied little from discussing the European markets, the fight for Catalan independence, and, of course, football. Just recently, the last two had become intrinsically linked. Earlier in the season, UEFA had fined FC Barcelona for waving Catalan Estelada flags and shouting, "*Independència!*" at each half. The dream of being an independent nation burned ardently in the breasts of most Catalans. Independence had last been enjoyed in the eighteenth century, at roughly the time the Monte Alegres had first started baking bread. Despite the reprimand, Barcelona were doing well. Sunday had given their La Liga title aspiration a huge boost with a three-two defeat against the bastards Madrid. Lionel Messi scored a brace in a thrilling last-gasp winner and his five hundredth goal for Barça.

Yes, there was much to discuss, but first things first. With a practised eye, Padre Rafael scanned the refrigerated display units. On the shelves above stacks of Marie biscuit tins were photos from Emil's travels, including the years he had spent in South America. Among unopened packets of powdered chocolate were monolithic replica statues from Easter Island, miniature Peruvian dolls fashioned from brightly coloured alpaca wool, and a paperweight of Iguazu (showing the falls from the Brazilian side). As if the Moai themselves stood sentinel, family photos were protected by a bric-a-brac wall of paper cups and straws and tiny plastic spoons for eating ice cream. At some charity event (Rafael couldn't remember where or what) an artist had sketched Emil and himself in polo gear. Rafael looked closely. Even allowing for artistic licence, they exuded stellar good looks in immaculate white jeans, linen shirts and suede jackets, the collars turned up just so. But never mind the collars! How much hair they'd – well, *he'd* – had! Automatically, he patted the top of his head. He didn't give his looks a second thought any more – well, not in comparison to the way he used to – but just occasionally, when he saw these pictures... And here too was one of Emil's wife. Rafael reached up to pull down the old-fashioned frame. The velvet edge was still intact, although the hue was not as rich as it had once been and the silver was entirely black. He had forgotten how beautiful she was, and how young. But then, they'd *all* been young. How lovely and how innocent. No, perhaps never that.

A hand brushed his shoulder, and the picture was taken from him to be turned face down among the cake boxes and ribbons.

Padre Rafael cleared his throat. "Emil, *cosí meu*," he greeted in Catalan. *Emil, my coz.*

Emil made a little bow of acknowledgement. "Padre Pio," he said in his friendly, mocking way.

"But we weren't particularly *pio* then, were we?" Rafael nodded to the photos.

Emil was deadpan. "Just kids."

"*Pero qué guay!*" sighed Padre Rafael. "I sometimes forget. I forget what lookers we were."

"I don't! I'm reminded of it on a daily basis! Time was when the girls came to this bakery because... well, frankly, because it was me behind the counter. Then they sent their young daughters. Now the young daughters are grown up and have never heard of us!"

Emil ducked behind the counter to grab an apron. He tied it deftly round his middle, his movements as elegant and effortless as they had always been. For a moment Rafael had a vision of his cousin leaping, with the same grace with which he accomplished all things, onto his pony. And then another image, unbidden and unwanted, came to him of them both riding out as casually and gallantly as medieval princes to do battle. In his mind's eye, the sun was behind them and they, in their white jeans and white gloves, stark against tanned skin, were young and strong and fearless.

"Now that *is* sad," said Padre Rafael with feeling. "That is very sad."

"*Así es… y tu?* How's everything with you?"

"Not so bad, not so bad. And all the better for Sunday's victory! What a game! That Messi, *qué hombre verdad*! He was unstoppable!" Rafael bent to look at the delicious *brazo de gitano* (which translated literally as 'gypsy's arm'); a dessert he was especially fond of. Today (although he always thought it), the whipped cream looked particularly fresh and white against the caramelised sponge.

Emil leaned against the counter, happily recalling what had been nothing short of a gargantuan game. "And he's supposed to be on the decline! In fact, the *only* way he could be stopped was by fouling him."

"Yes, I know – Ramos was shown a red card for his trouble. And with only twelve minutes of stoppage time remaining."

"Mmm… but the title is still under Real's control because they have a game in hand. Barça has five left to play. If only he weren't an Argentine…"

"Agreed!"

There was a companionable silence.

"The *Tia* still talking about her son?" said Emil, changing the subject. Rafael needed to be coaxed into reaching a decision about what he was going to have, but talking about football wasn't helping. "The one who everyone knows isn't in the Canaries but in prison?"

"You know I can't say." Padre Rafael blew out his cheeks.

The *brazo* always reminded him of Sunday lunch at their grandmother's – the only day of the week they were permitted a 'proper' dessert. The driver, dispatched to this very pastry shop, would return with the prized delicacies. If Emil and Rafa were playing polo, however, dessert had to wait until they returned in the evening. Which wasn't at all the same thing. Of course, in time the *brazo* had come to represent so much more. It wasn't necessarily the rose-tinted memory of lazy Sundays (because truth be told, Sundays could also be incredibly boring), but the fact that a whole way of life had disappeared with them. Those were the days when families walked home after church balancing their cakes and pastries wrapped up in tissue paper tied with bright coloured string. There was such a delicious sense of anticipation when those parcels were brought out, be it by a gloved maid (as in their household) or a tired worker who'd saved up a week's wages in order to afford this luxury. Now it would seem that, with American coffee shops everywhere, it was Sunday every day. There was no holding back. No discipline, no self-control. *That's it!* He had an idea for his sermon. He would talk about self-indulgence.

Emil, brandishing a knife, hovered by the cakes, but he knew better than to hurry his cousin. It was all part of their little ritual. "No, of course not," he agreed hastily. "Sorry. The usual, then?"

"Mmm… just deciding…" The *brazo* or an *enseymada?* Which? He felt horribly pressurised. "And what about Iñaki?" he asked, playing for time. A judge had sentenced the King's brother-in-law (whom Rafael and Emil knew well) to six years' imprisonment for money laundering.

"Ho ho," said Emil, setting down the knife. "*That* was a surprise! And to think we used to play handball with the guy."

"A lot. Little thieves are hanged but great ones escape…"

"What was that?"

Rafael smiled. "Nothing. I *should* have a *bocadillo con queso* on a durum wheat roll…"

Emil returned the smile. "I suppose cheese *would* be marginally better for you than cream…"

"Then it would be advisable?"

"It would."

"*Or* I could have the *jamón* with a good *pa de pagès*. Pity it's not Salto's." Rafael mentioned the family estate; its full name being

Salto al Cielo ('Jump to the Sky'). "Do you remember the bread from the *forn*? I've never tasted anything that compares. Not ever, and certainly not since."

Emil did remember. One day he would forgo chemistry for a natural process. And when that time came, he would recreate the kind of light yet crusty white bread they had eaten as children. Which actually *tasted* of something. It wouldn't come from the village, either, but would be baked in the huge ovens at Salto, made from their own wheat, ground in their own mills.

Rafael pursed his lips. "Such a difficult decision."

"Life is full of—"

"Quite so, *cosí*, quite so."

But still Emil waited for the final go-ahead to slice into the freshly baked roulade. And that nod would come, as sure as eggs were eggs. It suited Emil to be patient. He rocked on his heels, his gaze drifting to the scene behind his cousin's head. The street outside had burst into life since earlier in the day: a cacophony of sound with the usual bustle of scooters, taxis and buses as hungry Catalans hurried about their business during their lunch break. The habitual gossips of the neighbourhood met outside his shop after purchasing their baguettes of bread, schoolchildren dawdled behind them in their old-fashioned smocks, and the dwindling gaggle of priests from Sant Vicenç flocked together like the pigeons on the pavement beside them, their cassocks billowing in a sudden gust of wind.

"I think, I think," said Padre Rafael, "that it will have to be the *brazo* after all."

"A wise choice." Emil took a doily from under the counter, holding it in the flat of his hand as gingerly as though he were examining a horse's hoof, as he had so often done in the past. He held a knife in the other, having plunged it into boiling water first so that the slice would come away cleanly. He hated when bits of yellowing cream began to congeal on the plate. "Say when."

Padre Rafael gave a bashful shrug.

"*Com això?*" The knife hovered. "Like this? What, *more*? You should be ashamed of yourself!"

"'Should', my friend, is a powerful word."

"I'd have thought 'shame' was. *Bueno pues*, this once." It was *always* 'this once'. Using a silver spatula that had once belonged to their grandmother, Emil slid the dessert into a box. The half-frozen rich *nata* (whipped cream with sugar) remained beautifully upright. Emil waved a fork in his cousin's direction.

"Oh, no need to bother with that," said Padre Rafael. His mouth was already watering, and it took all his willpower (and a few mea culpas) to restrain himself from grabbing the box and stuffing his face with cake right there and then.

"No?"

"I'm going to eat it straight away."

"I'll leave it open, then." Emil handed over the confectionery as though it were frankincense and turned to clean the cake knife. "So," he added as casually as he could, turning away. "Any news from England?"

Padre Rafael paused, relishing this first delicious mouthful, cream forming a moustache around his lips. His mouth twitched. "From England? Or from our English cousin?"

"*Your* English cousin," corrected Emil. He liked to be very clear on that score.

"*Bueno, my* English cousin," agreed Padre Rafael.

"We have you in common," persisted Emil, "but we are not related."

"No, all right." Padre Rafael took another mouthful. He would have preferred to sit on the bench in front of his church, the birds strutting at his feet while he devoured his patisserie in silence, but it seemed churlish to leave. Besides, Emil would be able to see him clearly from across the square, and how silly would that be? Both of them alone on opposite sides of the square? Padre Rafael savoured the sticky caramel, the cold cream, the blessed sweetness that transported him directly to childhood. Leaving his dessert for a moment, he picked up a copy of *La Vanguardia* from one of the tables. Surely reading the paper wasn't too antisocial? A small compromise? Tucking it under his arm, dessert in hand, he was about to settle at one of the tables when he realised that Emil had followed him outside. Which wasn't what he'd intended. "Mmm…" he said thoughtfully, taking another bite.

"Yes?" Emil could not disguise the eagerness in his voice.

Rafael pushed aside *La Vanguardia* and watched as Emil refolded it carefully, marvelling at the attention to detail, the patience in the small movements. His cousin had far more patience than he did. He was also a far better man. He frowned; it was an uncomfortable reminder. He turned back to his dessert. "What I was going to say," he said, after finishing the cake and wiping the last tragic morsels of sugar from his mouth as though it were the Last Supper, "was that I'm not sure that I was being entirely correct. I mean, in assuming that we are not at all related."

"What do you mean?" said Emil sharply.

"What I mean is," said Padre Rafael impishly, as much to chase away the previous emotion as for the enjoyment that would come from the next, "that while it is certainly true that I am both your cousin and Ino's…"

Emil frowned. "Go on. What are you implying?"

Rafael feigned surprise. "*Implying?* I'm not implying anything. I merely *suggest* that if there *is* a connection, it will be very distant."

"Connection? What do you mean, distant? Why should there be any connection?" said Emil testily. "What connection could there possibly be? What *I* think, dear cousin, is that the sugar has gone to your head." He whisked away the pastry box and, fishing out a cloth from his apron, began vigorously wiping the table. "Have you considered testing for diabetes? At your age—"

"Which is also yours, just for the record." Rafael stabbed a finger inches from Emil's chest. "I think, if I'm not very much mistaken, that you are actually the elder by a month. But okay. I'll leave it. Besides, what does it matter? Ino is happily married to her English Archie, *verdad*? You could be brother and sister for all—"

"*Pro!*" said Emil sharply in Catalan.

Padre Rafael put up his hands in mock horror. "*Bueno, bueno,* I'll stop! I should be on my way. You'll be wanting to get on yourself..." He got up from his chair, his eyes sweeping the tiny shop behind them. "I can see you are busy. Thanks for the *brazo*." He settled his sash around his waist and, turning his face to the strong sunlight, stepped onto the pavement.

"You haven't pai—" Emil called after him, as he did every time, but his words were swallowed up by the sudden clamour of a group of teenage girls entering the shop, chattering and texting at the same time. One of the girls removed ridiculous oversized sunglasses from atop an elaborate updo, flashing nails like he'd only seen in pictures of Chinese mandarins. What was this barrio coming to? The girl in question flicked her hair.

"No, there's no credit even if I know your parents," Emil said grumpily before she'd had time to ask. "No credit at all," he added loudly to the empty space vacated by his cousin. "*Ninguno*. And you never answered my question!"

But if Padre Rafael heard him – if he ever heard him – he pretended otherwise, shutting out Emil and his reduced world just as he crossed over to his ever-expanding one. On a daily basis he was confronted with the trials and tribulations of his parishioners: the unfaithful, the unjust, the liars, the miscreants, and the truly good and honourable – all desirous of absolution in their hour of need. And he was happy to give it; after all, it cost him nothing. Padre Rafael narrowly avoided being hit by a scooter, and then by a bus following in its wake. The driver swore, but Padre Rafael only laughed out loud – how seriously drivers took their lives! He, on the other hand, took very little seriously and cared even less about the little he did. As a result, he knew he was a good priest, and a tireless one, because no one person mattered so much as to affect his *bien estar* – his equilibrium. He prided himself on the fact that not even his bishop knew what was really in his heart. Pride, probably, which was another sin – a venial sin. *For my thoughts are not your thoughts, nor are your ways my ways... For as the heavens are higher than the earth, so are my ways higher than your ways and my thoughts than yours...*

Another scooter weaved past him, and just in time Padre Rafael hopped out of its way. No, he conceded, 'Your thoughts are not my thoughts' just as he would never understand his religion, nor entirely believe in it either. Just as he knew his cousin would never believe that he was as unfeeling as he made out. He wondered, too, and not for the first time, how it would have been if things had turned out differently; if Emil's wife and his child had lived. If he hadn't made that absurd promise.

3

Veronica
Geneva
April 2017

Disappointment can do ugly things to a person, thought Veronica. All that hope shoehorned into small dollops of expectancy sticking like gum to the heel of a soul and stretched to the limits of its resistance. In time, though, even its seemingly endless elasticity wore thin. And then one day the hope was all gone; had slipped silently away.

Sitting in her office in Geneva, in the formidable yet pretty blue of the International Telecommunication Union, Veronica drummed manicured nails on her nearly empty Perspex desk. Her agency might be the oldest intergovernmental bureau in the world, but the building in which it was housed was one of the most modern. Her image was reflected several times over, and not just within her minimalist office with its glass and metal surfaces, but outwards to the surrounding mirrored buildings of the United Nations. It would seem that every structure of the complex was designed to reproduce the changing blue-greys of the sky to refract light and enhance its ethereal quality. But today, even to her usually sanguine mind through which ambition and survival coursed in a tsunami of relentless drive, her Botoxed visage, line-free and inter-filled with the latest, safest FDA-approved hyaluronic acid, revealed the tramlines of regret.

Veronica swung herself off her swivel chair, began an inconsequential text, called through to her secretary for a coffee – skinny macchiato, extra soy on the side – and resumed the futile quest for inspiration. She fondled the triple-strand pearl necklace at her throat, smoothed her body-hugging Alaïa skirt, shook back a head of expensive colour. What was the matter with her? Regret should be the least of it! She was at the top of her game and, as the most senior-ranked woman at ITU, was shortly to give a speech; her first as chief of strategic planning. She had thought to kick-start the programme on the incorporation of a gender and parity policy. Then, yet again, she might speak more generally on a subject that was genuinely close to her heart: the need for connectivity for all. Or then again, a little of both? The former topic might be the right approach, especially with the male representatives who were not yet on board with the panel party pledge. They were the ones that needed convincing, while women of all ages needed to be informed of what was in their capability, digitally speaking. Veronica pulled in her stomach. A few pounds gained over the weekend after too much Montrachet – as delicious as it was – made her uncomfortable. The Spanx all-in-one created a smooth line but she could feel an extra inch of tummy folding over her knicker band. She would have to get back to a gym routine.

A discreet knock on the see-through door alerted her to the arrival of her secretary. Leila was an immaculately turned-out Algerian-born Frenchwoman whose haughty veneer embalmed an even chillier interior. She balanced a small tray on one hand upon which a steaming cup of coffee nestled between those cinnamon-flavoured Dutch *stroopwafels* Veronica found difficult to resist. Here at ITU – *especially* here – the selection of food and beverages crossed continents and was enticingly eclectic. Leila waited, impassive in her perfectly tailored black dress and Prada slingbacks. The tapping of her iPad reminded Veronica that she was there for a briefing. Today of all days, however, Veronica felt a million miles away while the immediacy of her presence was being demanded at every turn.

For a moment, Veronica's habitual poise wavered. Was it nostalgia? It was not a sentiment with which she was overly familiar. But if so, for what exactly? Why did her mind keep wandering when she was usually so focused? Why did she feel so… so *hollow*? Leila coughed, but Veronica could tell she was becoming impatient. She too was an ambitious woman whose days as a secretary were merely one rung on Jacob's ladder. After all, wasn't that what Veronica's particular policy at the ITU was all about? The empowerment of women in a hitherto male-orientated industry? Oval, fire-engine-red fingernails punched out the detail as, bent over her work, Leila's thick hair swung loose. Veronica realised with a shock that she knew almost nothing about the woman who had worked alongside her for nearly five years. But then, she seldom wanted to be burdened with life histories. Especially not her own.

Leila raised hazelnut-brown eyes. *Et?* she all but snapped in French. Veronica gave a figurative jolt. *And* indeed. They would issue a press release shortly – a summation of Veronica's work to date and ongoing commitment to encouraging a greater representation of women delegates; the need to bridge the gender digital divide. Equal mobile telepathy and encouraging women into assuming technical positions within these organisations were paramount.

"You could begin by saying something about yourself? I mean, something personal?" The French accent was charming but, coming from Leila, it sounded more like a command.

Veronica blinked steel-grey eyes, expressionless. "Oh? *Tu crois?*" *You've got to be joking!*

"*Bon…*" came with the perquisite shrug; the kind Veronica used to find offensive and now took to deploying herself on occasion. "Men like the story of the defenceless leettle woman."

Veronica felt herself stiffen.

"Made good," added Leila by way of mitigation.

"I think my record speaks for itself." Veronica's tone was tart. Another shrug. "As you like."

Veronica did like. There was, of course, her official profile – the one available on her Wikipedia page – that cited her fluency in Russian, German and French. Nowhere, however, did it mention that Croatian was actually her mother tongue; nor that she had been born in Schumacher, Ontario to refugees from Vis (or, more precisely, Tito and his partisans). Rather, it highlighted the fact that (cliché aside) communication had been the bedrock of her rise through the ranks. She was often quoted as saying that it was her stint as a humble translator (wherein she had been the conduit for other people's ideas) that had given her a different voice, but one that was no less influential or omnipotent.

There was no need to elaborate. The sensation of being cosily tucked up in her silent, vacuum-packed booth, adrenaline coursing through her body as she anticipated the flash of the red buzzer (the go-ahead to begin), was hers and hers alone. No need to share the additional thrill of seeing the delegates duck, dive and turn as they reached for headphones and fiddled with earpieces and dials, tuning in to one of the six official languages of the UN. Veronica took a last sip of coffee before handing the cup back to Leila. No, thank you – that kind of 'sharing' was not for her. But what she would talk about was the agenda set out as far back as 2003 to chart a road map by which information was available to all, to inspire an equal story to—

"I'll be ready by ten," she instructed.

"*C'est bon*." Leila snapped shut her iPad and smoothed down the skirt of her dress, hesitating as she straightened. "*Encore une chose*. Your..." Her eyes at least attempted to disguise the word to come. "Your *daughter* is calling on line one."

4

Emil
Barcelona
April 2017

Unsettled by his cousin's visit, Emil went into the tiny kitchen, separated from the rest of the *pastelaria* by an old-fashioned bead curtain, to prepare himself a lunch of *pan tomcat* and *jamón serrano*. He did this by breaking a *barra* of bread in half and grating both sides rigorously with an overripe tomato. He discarded the skin along with the rest of the fruit, drizzled olive oil over the bread and, even though there was no one to see, ground sea salt over the whole thing with an exaggerated flourish. "*Así es*," he said to himself aloud. "*Perfecto!*" He even kissed his fingers before wiping his hands on a dishcloth. He sliced a couple of diaphanously thin strips from the joint of ham that hung above the savoury goods counter, folding these carefully over the bread. He then took his 'sandwich' to the window, pushing open the shutters as far as they would go so that the copper hinges scraped the painted concrete wall on either side. Catalan flags (the official La Senyera), together with La Estelada (the unofficial one UEFA had banned from being shown at football games), were draped over balconies. He looked again. The latter (really La Senyera, but with the addition of a white star) had come to represent the independence movement and, in this barrio at least, outnumbered the others.

Emil bit into the bread – his own bread – and almost groaned with pleasure. Admittedly, there was competition out there, but their home-baked fare, cooked to exactly the same spec as it had been when the business first began all those hundreds of years ago, was still the best in all of Catalonia. For a moment he thought of the oak- and beech-burning stoves that had once burned so ardently at Salto. Hanging on his taste buds was the aroma of natural woods and the sun-drenched pine nuts they used in their traditional *coca*. But it was this savoury repast that he found particularly irresistible. To his mind there was nothing more satisfying than this home-made snack of tomato bread and ham, but it was a combination that, latterly, had even crept into politics. Only that morning Emil had read an Instagram message that read '*ME NIEGO A COMER EL PA AMB TOMAQUET SIN JAMON.*' Which, roughly translated, meant 'I cannot' or, more precisely, 'I refuse to eat tomato bread without ham.' The analogy was clear. One could not exist without the other: Catalonia without Spain was not a dish. The rumblings about Catalan separatism which had seemed unthreatening even a few weeks before had taken a more serious bent with the President of the Generalitat calling for its own referendum (which the Spanish government was calling illegal) and threatening to declare an independent state within the month. What would the older generation have thought about that? A generation of Catalans who grew up under the Franco regime, whose creed it was that separatism was a tumour to be excised at any cost? It was happening again. The very same rhetoric was being used now as then. Part of Emil rejoiced at his compatriot's rebellious stance, while the other half (and the stronger) acknowledged that '*pa amb tomàquet*' was nothing without its '*jamón*'.

Waiting for his coffee to cool, Emil lit a cigarette. He waved away smoke from his face, channelling it towards the fresh air. Momentarily, he closed his eyes, inhaling the sharp Turkish tobacco, feeling the familiar hit and rush of, if not exactly well-being, then certainly *better* being. He wasn't so perturbed. Politics were for the young, the impetuous, the hot-headed (for the sake of his internal argument, he ignored the fact that the Catalan Premier Carles Puigdemont was a good decade older than he). The current agitation was initiated, in his opinion, by the anti-establishment anti-monarchists among them, and was less to do with genuine anti-Spanish feeling – after all, Catalans had all the attributes of nationhood already: a parliament, a President, a flag (actually, flags plural – as far as Emil could make out, there were now three), a police force, tax revenues, and above all a language – than general Brexit fever. What more did they really want? Well, let them expend their energy somehow. From the window he could see small, laughing figures standing on the flat roof of Sant Vicenç as they attached La Estelada to the belfry. That would get his cousin going. Ah well, as young boys he and Rafael had done far worse.

Emil positioned an ashtray on the ledge. The siesta hour was upon them and the Plaça de Sarrià was notably quieter than it had been half an hour earlier. He loved the early morning as the barrio – *his* barrio now – came to life. He rejoiced in the first sighting of street cleaners, the sound of bartenders dragging out tables to place on the pavements, the jingle of cutlery, the hiss of coffee machines pumping out steam, the unlocking of parasols, the grinding as canopies were slowly wound in as if to announce to the world, *We are here, we're open for business, we are here! Estem aquí!* But he enjoyed the siesta hour even more, when the world scurried like salamanders into the shade, retreating from the world into the shadows. Emil exhaled smoke and inhaled the heavy, tangy smell that heralded the end of spring. He looked once more across to the church. He knew what *he* would like to be doing in an ideal world, but he wondered, as he did most days at this hour, what preoccupied Rafael as a man of the cloth.

Emil stubbed out his cigarette, took a swig of coffee and closed his eyes for his own short siesta. Occasionally, on days like today, or simply because Rafael had been looking at pictures of his travels, his mind wandered to those places – places that had touched him; places where he'd been happy even when he thought it impossible afterwards. And because he could never bear to think too long or too much about polo and his cousin, he thought instead and often of Valparaíso and the climb up to Neruda's house, La Sebastiana. He visualised the rainbow-coloured houses crammed all higgledy-piggledy, jutting out of the hillside spreading from the port above and beyond, along narrow, steep hairpin turns. And if the technicolour of the houses was amusing, much more so was Neruda's place with its tree house feel, teetering as it did so high above the other neighbouring dwellings. With commanding views of the Pacific, the visitor gasped twice: once at the vista of the vast ocean beneath, and then again at the sight of La Sebastiana itself, with an exterior painted a brilliant cobalt blue with large patchwork-like clouds.

It was a strange place, that house, with the presence of the great poet so keenly felt in every room; the scholarly approach to a cultured life sitting within a bon viveur's natural inclination for fun. And then the surprise: Neruda's wife's few possessions among the Russian plates, the mosaics and majolica. In a cupboard in their bedroom Emil remembered the almost-shock of seeing not the presence of a woman, but the evidence of tiny silk shoes and a dressing gown made in Paris. He thought of the many books of poetry open at just the right page. *I like for you to be still*, is what Neruda had written there. *It is as though you are absent and you hear me from far away and my voice does not touch you...*

Emil finished the last dregs of his coffee and went back into the shop, strangely comforted by the memory. And so it was that, even then, even now, with all the distance between them, he felt her presence; knew that he was heard; that one day she would listen...

Archie

Cedar Avenue

*I am full of optimism. I did not anticipate the work being so interesting or tiring! I am at the hospital for twenty-four-hour stretches – no different from my days as a junior doctor or even a registrar, but now there is a purpose: our **shared** purpose. I await your arrival eagerly. There! I am not ashamed to write it. I want to share all of this with you; let you see it through my eyes; let us experience it together.*

*There's no need to be apprehensive – there really isn't. We'll be together, but apart from that, the climate is not so very different from the one you already know. This is a vibrant city, a sophisticated one, and at the same time simple. The people here love their hockey, their smoked meat, bagels, maple syrup and poutine. I enclose a map of the Underground. You'll see that you won't have to go outside if you don't want to. I have colleagues who don't even have a winter coat. You can traverse the city centre – its completely underground subway system runs on rubber tyres, not steel wheels – without ever putting your head above the parapet, so to speak. Imagine that! **All** underground. Une vie interieure; an inner life.*

But ours is going to sing...

5

Veronica
Geneva
April 2017

Veronica watched the approaching topaz silk of Leila's shirtwaister with trepidation. For a moment she was distracted – she was pretty certain that the striking garment heading towards her down the quiet corridor was straight off the catwalk; part of the Dior spring/summer collection. Veronica did a double take, surprised that she'd missed that particular gem. Then again, maybe, just maybe, it was because Leila had held it back. That was the likelier explanation. Veronica often sent her secretary to the Milan trunk shows to pick out items before they hit the shops. Recently, however, she had found dresses appearing on Leila's slender frame long before they did on her own. Clearly, the time had come for Veronica to attend those viewings herself.

She was brought back to the present by Leila's mumbled Arabic; harsh, guttural tones rising from that bony chest to ricochet off the stone surfaces of the office furniture. Apparently, there'd been another missed call from Ino. Or so Veronica gathered. Leila was on another line, one hand covering the mouthpiece but from time to time holding it away from her and *at* Veronica, by which Veronica was given to understand that Ino had again tried calling. Leila, for her part, seemed extremely put out at having to pass on a message (even those of condolence were only grudgingly transmitted) of any kind. Perhaps now was the time to remind her that she worked for Veronica, not the other way round. Those particular lines had become rather blurred of late. Switching to French, Leila was now muttering about boundaries from *her* side of the fence. This was not her job – her *bulot*. It was also of note that Leila never referred to Ino by her given name, but called her '*fille*', which was somehow neutral and clean. Veronica was still taking in the shirtwaister, having dismissed the call completely. *Fille?* Which could also mean just 'girl'. She was ever hopeful. The look on Leila's face somehow suggested otherwise.

"What *fille?*"

Leila stared her down, as she always did when Ino called. "*Bien, la tienne.*" (No formal *votre* for her!) *Why, yours, of course.*

It was at times like these that Veronica blessed the duality of language. Because if 'daughter' was '*fille*' then '*petite fille*', which meant 'granddaughter', could also mean just that: 'little girl'. She looked away first, hiding her displeasure. Leila made an ululating sound, blowing air through her lips before sliding through the glass doors on this season's Manolos.

Aftershocks rippled through Veronica's entire body. She dealt with stressful situations all the time, had worked in inhospitable locations all over the world, and yet nothing filled her with more dread than that one little word. A little word that was capable of sending her mind into free fall. How was it possible that such a biological attachment could be applied to *her* when she'd tried to expunge the whole notion of motherhood? As she often did when taken out of her comfort zone or area of control, Veronica tried to visualise this distasteful news actually being delivered. Steadying her breathing, she closed her eyes, imagining illusory phone lines as a transparent fibre-optic (no thicker than the diameter of a human hair) wrapping itself around every one of her internal organs to communicate digital signals of distress. No electromagnetic interference at all, but a waveguide conveying the sound of Ino's voice. Veronica was a successful woman by anyone's standard, and yet photo crystals rippled through her now, carrying an ever-higher power, an ever-higher potency of dread. Her eyes sprang open. *Daughter!* Da-dah... ping! There it was: a series of rapid incoming messages as violent and staccato-like as gunfire. And yet, ironically, the very medium that was her bread and butter was the one dragging her in now. Suffocating her.

Veronica knew what the phone call would be about. A complaint about Archie, no doubt – Ino's husband, Veronica's son-in-law, the father of... Veronica suppressed a spasm. If 'daughter' was an anathema to her vocabulary, much more so was the word 'grandchild'. She set her shoulders, her disenchantment mounting. If only Ino could be quiet, live quietly! She wasn't asking her to be happy, just content, *contained*. Veronica ran a finger through her stiff but clean coiffed hair. Good heavens, had she had half the opportunities Ino had had, half the advantages or connections at Ino's age, had she the *husband*, there'd have been no stopping her! Veronica had succeeded in a man's world when all she'd ever really wanted was... well, a man. A man like Archie.

Veronica may have been guilty of many things but cowardice was not one of them, and her inner self did not flinch at the admission. But neither was her secret yearning so well camouflaged. When they'd first met (she had, after all, met Archie first), each had recognised something vital in the other. What was it? Ruthlessness? A survival instinct? A mixture of both? They both possessed the same drive and singular ambition. Both lacked compassion, discharging the tenets of their separate professions with awesome ruthlessness. And, honesty being (sometimes) the best policy, Veronica had to admit that she'd been disappointed when he'd chosen Ino over her. For the time they'd dated, Veronica had felt energised; young again. Really young. She hugged herself. For all his naivety (he was as unsophisticated as she had become worldly), there was an obvious maleness to him that she found devastatingly attractive. There was no disguising his virility, unlike... unlike Ino's father. But that was a rabbit hole she wasn't going down now. She consoled herself that her present irritation had nothing to do with that. It was simply that she deplored waste and it seemed to her that Ino was wasting everything: the education Veronica had struggled to give her and, more importantly, Archie.

A blurry image floated before her eyes. While she could recall every inch of Archie's face, she was finding it difficult, if not downright impossible, to conjure up any clear picture of Ino's. She shut her eyes; opened them again. Nope. Nothing. *Rien de tout*. It wasn't going to happen. Her own face, on the other hand, reflected in the huge glass window in front of her, came into focus, ever bright and clear and beautiful. Delighted with what she could see, and immensely buoyed as a result, she threw back her head, noting with satisfaction that her neck was still smooth and unlined. She touched the small bones of the clavicle. What on earth could the kid want now? Not *another* miscarriage, surely? Too much of that nonsense and Archie really would walk. A cold hand of fear clamped itself on her stomach, twisting her gut. For a moment she couldn't breathe. He must never be allowed to do that. Slowly, her head tilted to one side to admire the outline of her lovely cheekbones. She kissed the image. *Just remember, Veronica, chérie, just remember, there isn't a man you've not been able to get, if you set your mind to it.* And 'it' had surely arrived.

Archie

Cedar Avenue

The apartment is tiny... but it doesn't matter. We will fill its space from wall to wall with lightness and warmth... and talking of warmth... I wish! It's colder than Moscow, though not as cold as Manitoba – if that's any consolation.

I don't have time to relax much, but you will, and the city does its best to make the inclement weather bearable. At the Old Port, there's an Igloofest which is an outdoor rave/concert. There are two stages, an ice slide, drinks and games. People wear snow gear including ski goggles but I've realised it's not so much a fashion statement as a preventative measure. I'd like to see you in a onesie! Impressed I know the term, huh? My Canadian nurse is keeping me up to speed.

I refuse to wear thermals. With you here I won't need any... ha ha.

6

Ino
Winchester
April 2017

Ino let herself into the house – the pretty seventeenth-century thatched cottage tucked away at the end of the narrow country lane that virtually made up the village of Drayton. The earworm element of the Latin pop music with its swing rhythm and flamenco-style melody had burrowed deep; was still pulsating uncomfortably through her head even if it did recall happier times. Her hands were shaking – in fact, her whole body was shaking as though she'd caught a chill. She closed the door behind her, leaning against the solid oak for support. She loved her daughter, but the aspect of motherhood with which she struggled was the other mothers, or rather, mothers like Marion. Actually, if she were honest, it wasn't even Marion, although she did manage to get under Ino's skin. Ino knew perfectly well that were she happier in herself, minor irritants – irritating *people* – wouldn't matter so much. Her face began to throb. She touched her cheek, feeling pinpricks of pain fan under her fingertips. She closed her eyes, breathed in slowly, exhaled a couple of times.

She was exhausted – the effort of having to pretend in public that her home life was normal or even just okay was eating away at her. Ino's stomach somersaulted. *Okay? Normal?* Who was she fooling? Had she *ever* known normal? Her upbringing had been unconventional to put it mildly, but she'd known no different and she'd felt loved at times by different people. That was enough. But her married life was something else entirely. She knew there was something wrong with her marriage. Really wrong. Even if you took out the violence... *Even?* echoed her conscience. *Even?* Well, yes, even if you took that out, weren't married couples supposed to have *sex*? Okay, maybe not every day, but occasionally, on high days and holidays? Even in the early days of their marriage, even on their honeymoon, Archie had shown little to no interest in her – especially not physically. She sometimes wondered how Calypso had been conceived at all. Now, Archie was mostly too drunk to do anything other than go to bed when he got home, and bed definitely did not include Ino. But maybe that was how it was with most couples. Some couples, anyway. She had no way of telling, of finding out. She didn't have the kind of relationship with any girlfriend that warranted a heart-to-heart. She had always been reserved on that front; too proud to admit there was anything wrong. She couldn't even talk to her mother.

Waves of physical pain made her nauseous. Probably the thought of her mother, she thought grimly! All thought of sex, at any rate, was obliterated in their wake. When she felt strong enough, she opened her eyes, slowly surveying the debris of the kitchen. The aftermath of breakfast was bad enough. It was funny, she thought, how appealing a table could look newly laid, but how completely unappealing it became after food had been consumed. Calypso's breakfast bowl was exactly where she'd left it, pushed to one side as she'd slid from her chair. Chemically coloured cornflakes floated in rapidly souring milk, with the spoon balancing precariously on the edge. There was sugar everywhere, except in the bowl where it should have been, while jam and grains of coffee had found their way into the butter dish. Ino had forgotten Calypso's reading book which, having been used as a coaster, was stuck to the underside of a cold mug of tea. Archie must have come in after they'd left. She could tell exactly what her husband had had for his breakfast, where he'd prepared it, and the exact spot where it had been consumed. He ate everything on the hoof, standing by the door as if poised for flight. Which, of course, he always was. The remains of the meal that he'd thrown at her, along with the broken plates, lay on the floor by the bin.

Ino moved gingerly forward to crouch by the sink and dig out a dustpan and brush. But the act of bending down sent the blood pounding to her head and she felt dizzy. Time was when she would have tied up her hair, pulled out the old Marigolds and got stuck in. But that was then – when she'd still believed that every carefully chosen object, every plate and spoon, every book and cushion assembled with love could be enough. She had polished, cleaned and gathered up laundry; she had painted floors and ceilings; she had made all the curtains including these new kitchen ones, completed and hung only the day before. In the early days of their marriage, when Archie said they couldn't afford to have curtains made, undaunted she had promptly bought a second-hand sewing machine and taught herself to sew. Pregnant with Calypso, she remembered laying the fabric down on this very floor, manoeuvring her large belly and it, happily absorbed in her task.

Sinking back down at the table, Ino pushed aside a jug of wild flowers – blue mascari (there was a word for Calypso!), cyclamen and narcissus whose delicious scent permeated the kitchen. There were also purple wallflowers, vibrant against their grey-green foliage, and white Japanese anemones. Anemones were her favourite flowers, and she loved that they grew tall and wild against the thatch and picket fence. Once, just seeing these delicate white flowers with their yellow centres would have made her smile. Later, she would have delighted in rearranging them with sprigs of lavender just so, to place on the table at dinner time. Now there didn't seem much point in arranging anything. She might just as well have left them uncut in the garden.

Tentatively, Ino felt her cheek. Her lip, at least, had stopped bleeding. Would that her thoughts were as easy to rearrange!

She felt tears prick her eyes. She wanted to be far, far away from here. Perhaps that was why, earlier, the words *'ahora mismo'* had sprung so readily to mind – words of yearning from and for that one lost summer in Spain. And about as far away from her current situation as it was possible to be. Ino wiped her nose on the back of her hand. She couldn't be bothered to find a tissue. It was so very quiet except for the ringing in her ears, a sharp whistle that competed with her deafening thoughts. If only there was someone she could talk to… and there was so much Ino wanted to say! Once again she made a mental inventory of the mothers of the other children in Calypso's class. The irony was that, while she knew they looked upon her seemingly idyllic lifestyle with envy (her lovely home, good-looking doctor husband and healthy little girl), it was she who envied them. They were all normal, ordinary wives and mothers made extraordinary by dint of the fact that they were beloved. None, she imagined, felt compelled to spend any time or effort hiding a sad and sordid secret.

As a last resort, there was always Veronica, although if their most recent conversation was anything to go by, Ino couldn't count on her mother being exactly sympathetic. Ino had tangibly felt the ice-cold resentment, the intense disapproval on the other end of the phone, from the other side of the world. When she had asked her mother where she was, Veronica had snapped, "Kinshasa", as though Ino was being overly intrusive. Furthermore, as Veronica informed her, she was catching a flight shortly, so Ino would need to keep it "snappy". Ino could visualise her mother lighting a cigarette with perfect, manicured hands and brushing a lock of burnished gold hair out of her eyes, her face tightening as it always did when she spoke of, let alone to, her daughter. There was the familiar intake of breath as she inhaled tobacco. "You have to make this work, Ino," her mother had said in that clipped Canadian accent she imagined sounded so very aristocratic and English, and yet to strangers sounded just plainly North American and working class. "It's a marriage and it's for life. There's no turning back and there's no opting out. For life." For emphasis, and in French, she added, "*Pour toute la vie.*" Veronica had begun speaking to Ino in that language even though, as far as Ino could make out, it was never her mother tongue. It was an unfortunate use of the word '*vie*', thought Ino, having just lost one. Her mother enunciated these last words very carefully. "Archie is a wonderful man. The kind of man you could only dream of. *En fait...* That you should be so lucky. Beats me what he ever saw..."

And so, Ino had resolved to try harder. Not because her mother had told her to, but because by now she felt so confused, could see all her dreams and aspirations turning to dust, that she clung to this last objective. It made things simple when everything around her seemed to be falling apart. Besides, how difficult could it be to make things even more perfect? She would remove all stress from Archie's life so that he was happy with her. And if she did, surely he in turn would drink less as home became the wonderful haven it was meant to be? He wouldn't feel compelled to stop off at The Antler or The Three Cups, or indeed any pub. And he would delight, if not in her, then in Calypso. She would make things perfect, inside the home and out.

Last night, Ino had reminded herself of this as she'd put Calypso to bed, carefully folding away the blue eiderdown: the one with the pink bunny rabbits racing round a clump of daisies. And she thought of it now as, still seated, she began to push the sticky sugar grains along the table with the edge of the cereal box, and to stack the dirty plates. She peeled Calypso's homework away from the teacup and replaced the lid on the jam jar. Last night she had been cautiously optimistic, almost happy as she double-checked the scrubbed pine table with the pretty Luneville china they'd been given as a wedding present, her eye drifting to the cream Aga. If Archie was half as hungry as he always claimed he was, then surely the sight, let alone the smell, of boeuf bourguignon and new potatoes sprinkled with fresh parsley would be welcome?

The dish had taken a couple of attempts to get right but had turned out well in the end. An hour or two later, when it was growing late, the meat, though well and truly tenderised (though not yet pulverised to a purée), was still delicious. Grabbing a cardigan, she had ventured into the lane but there was no other soul about; not even, in the distance, the lights from a passing car. Standing on the dampening grass, the house, with its thatched-framed windows, wisteria and clambering rose, was utterly charming and convivial.

She had stood a moment longer, transfixed by the play of fluorescent light bouncing off the kitchen surfaces. One moment the setting sun made the rocker in the corner shine treacle-gold and bright; the next it was plunged into darkness. An apt metaphor for her marriage, she thought wryly. She turned to go into the house just as the polished antique dresser was bathed in shimmering iridescence. She took a final mental snapshot. What could possibly be displeasing with all of this? An hour or two later, when it was a little darker, the picture viewed from outside was still enchanting. She decided not to draw the blinds. Surely Archie would find it heart-warming?

Evidently not. When Archie eventually pushed open the kitchen door and stood swaying on the threshold, blinking uncomprehendingly, it was not in anything like the happy if silent appreciation Ino had dared to imagine. On the contrary, his entire being registered displeasure, while his tongue darted round his mouth, seeking the last vestiges of alcohol. He stank of sweat and curry in his crumpled, grubby suit. Ino turned to the Aga, tears of frustration, disappointment and anger coursing down her cheeks.

"*This?*" he had said, as if she'd offered him a rancid sandwich. "I don't want *this*!" And then there was the blow, broken china and glass as he swept his arm across the table and across her face.

Ino's mobile pinged, drawing her reluctantly back to the present. She eased herself into a standing position, feeling along the table for support to reach for her phone.

'Be more active' appeared on the display.

7

Emil
Barcelona
April 2017

The hour after siesta time was officially over was always quiet. As with all things, Emil knew it was just a question of patience. He had become practised in recognising the signs; used to knowing that the exquisite evening skies of Rapa Nui, for example, with their subtle metallic colours, could be transformed into a raging storm come morning, their serenity shattered by violent winds. With no feeling of dread, but merely of certainty, like the islanders he would quietly assemble provisions, dismantle awnings. Now he had scarcely placed his dishes in the sink when the tinkle of the door sounded. An elderly woman, though younger than his grandmother would have been, stood by the counter, eyeing up the trays of individually wrapped chocolate bonbons.

"Give me a dozen," she commanded in a thin warble. It was the kind of voice that insisted on singing every response at Mass, no matter how much out of tune.

He glanced at her. She was typical of the local older clientele: expensively though not fashionably dressed; mauve perm; diamond-and-pearl earrings in lobes that had stretched downwards over the years. He looked again. They were nothing like the distorted ears he'd seen on some of the statues of Tongariki.

She peered at Emil as he was peering at her. "The streets are filling up," she said. "Young people chanting, wrapped in the flag."

Emil took down a clear acetate box from the shelf behind him and began carefully filling it with a glassine liner sheet. He then inserted a gold card divider and tiny paper cups. The woman's false teeth were clicking. "Which one?" He couldn't imagine that this old dear would support La Estelada. It might be fast becoming the only flag being flown in their barrio, but he wondered if she would remember (she was almost old enough!) that the addition to the plain Catalan La Senyera of chevron and white star was inspired by the stars on the Puerto Rican and Cuban flags, countries who had gained independence from Spain.

As it happened, she meant neither. Her ears dangled in astonishment. "Why, La Rojigualda! The *Spanish* one, of course – *és clar*," she added for emphasis, in Catalan. "We're sick of all this Catalan nationalism! People are tired of being excluded; tired of feeling that if you don't vote to be separate, you're not a true Catalan. *I'm* a Catalan," she said, wrapping her hands across her brocade-clad stomach. An enormous amethyst set in heavy gold protruded painfully above an arthritic knuckle. "But I'm Spanish first. And I'm being brainwashed on top of everything else!"

"Brainwashed?!" Emil echoed. It was his turn to be astonished.

"Yes," she said. "Brainwashed into having to speak Catalan all the time."

"But don't you want to?" Emil paused in his selection of the bonbons. "After so many years of not being allowed to?" He meant her generation – the generation that had grown up speaking Catalan but not necessarily able to read or write it very well, as Franco had banned it from being taught in schools. It was his friends' children who, in a backlash to that time, were now being taught predominantly in Catalan.

"I do. But language is being used as a political tool when we should all be allowed to speak in whichever language we choose, when we choose. Not because *he* says so."

"He?"

"The Catalan President – Puigdemont."

"Ah."

"What an imbecile! What a fool! The man has no idea. He's not thought anything through. Independence! What nonsense! This has nothing to do with independence. What we need is dialogue and, more importantly, money." She made a karate-chop gesture to indicate that there were enough chocolates in the box, so Emil carefully covered them with tissue before replacing the lid. He didn't dare do otherwise.

"You're Rafael," she said.

This was also something he had grown accustomed to. "His cousin."

"Ah." The woman raised disappointed, watery eyes. "*Dios mío.* What on earth happened to you?"

8

Ino
Winchester
April 2017

Ino sniffed loudly, switching her phone to silent. The pedantic tick-tock of the grandfather clock reverberating from the hall seemed to grow ever more penetrating and draw attention to the emptiness of her morning. In between chimes, the silence of the house fell about her like a heavy, suffocating down coat; the kind that is welcome at first but grows increasingly hot and sweaty as the body acclimatises. Small cobwebs furred up the tops of the kitchen blinds, a fly lumbered unceremoniously along the top windowpane, while shafts of sunlight created a keyboard pattern along one end of the counter.

Not for the first time did Ino wonder how it had all gone wrong. She supposed, as with most things, it had been a gradual process – Archie's drinking ever on the increase and in equal measure to his late returns. To begin with, she had been so busy and delighted with Calypso that she hadn't noticed her husband's prolonged absences or the fact that he was returning home later and later. She had become used to his irregular comings and goings, to him finally wending his way home (she was sure the entire village could hear the revved engine as he careered down the lane), stuttering some excuse about work – a sort of apology, she supposed – then stumbling upstairs. Swaying as he grappled with his clothes, he would say he wasn't hungry before falling not into bed necessarily, but somewhere on his way *to* bed where he'd be asleep within minutes. She was reminded on those occasions of Tolstoy's servants who, in similar mode, would totter to the floor when exhaustion got the better of them. It was Tolstoy's wife Sofia who insisted they sleep in proper beds. She didn't dwell on the fact that the Tolstoy marriage had been an unhappy one.

What she *did* recall now however – what she would never, ever forget – was the night Archie had hit her for the first time. That was when all hope that things would work out had been killed off in one fell swoop. Feeling sorry for herself, Ino wiped her nose again. Why do this now? Why go over it? And yet here it came: that memory, fizzing and mocking, snaking its way through her thoughts. A single moment when she knew that everything would change, that there would be no going back – the moment when she finally understood the kind of man she had married.

As with the night before, Ino had taken extra care over their supper. It would seem that most of their altercations took place over meals. *Over*, she thought ruefully, *not at*. Or maybe it was to do with her inability to manage expectations, or at the very least manage then *reasonably*; the fact that she was always hoping for something more. They'd not slept together since Calypso was conceived (even that was a one-off), but Ino was determined to feel positive; romantic, even.

There had been a farmers' market in town earlier in the day and she had taken the opportunity to buy the French cheeses and clotted cream she knew Archie loved. Later she had prepped the vegetables for a coq au vin and peeled the apples she and Calypso had picked in the orchard for the crumble. By early evening everything was slow-cooking in the Aga, and so she'd had plenty of time to bathe and change. She'd put on bootcut jeans and a white silk shirt. She played a Christina Aguilera favourite of his ('Beautiful'), opened a bottle of red (in those days he downed Amarone, a hefty red from the valley of many cellars, by the gallon) and awaited his return. It was an eagerness, however, that quickly dissipated as early evening became late evening and then night.

By the time Ino heard the sound of tyres ricocheting off gravel, the crumble had the consistency of baby food and the chicken seemed to have completely evaporated into the sauce. Words from the song not only brought her down but sent her spiralling upwards as she fought to stay calm, her mood alternating between hope and fury. But as Archie continued to sit in his car – a delaying tactic being, she imagined, an attempt to sober up – her nerves spiked. She watched aghast from the window as, satisfied that he'd managed to lock his precious Porsche, he urinated on the grass. Babbling indistinctly, he turned unsteadily to the house. Well, 'turning' implied an act of will – what he did was fall headlong. He lay prone on the freshly mown lawn, shavings of grass sprinkling his expensive white piqué shirt, looking up at the sky. And yes, for a brief moment she marvelled that he could take such pleasure in the small things; that nothing, least of all concern for others, could mar his enjoyment. Until, of course, she realised that his eyes were closed, the uneven rumble of his snores vibrating along the pebbled path. She knew she should just ignore him and go to bed, but a stronger urge, a desire for some response in the wake of her unhappiness, drove her outside. Standing over him, she poked him with her toe; she had to resist an overwhelming temptation to kick him in the groin.

"Ah!" he had growled, waking suddenly so that she shrieked, and shrieked again when, as he grabbed her ankle, she concertinaed to the ground.

For a moment, lying beside him (*Be careful what you wish for!*), she marvelled for the umpteenth time at his complete lack of respect for anything to do with her; disregard for her time being the least of it. Each new shock shouldn't have come as a surprise any more, and yet she was always caught off guard. *Quite literally*, she thought wryly. But what she hadn't understood about herself before (but did so now, guiltily, uncomfortably, fatefully) was that, in taking more time than usual over their supper, in dressing up and putting on music, she was also playing out a fantasy and one that ended happily, if only in her mind. She didn't wonder any more whether or not his displeasure was justified, whether or not she had provoked him, but what she did question was her ability to handle him. She pondered that, if she'd been a different kind of person, the kind that could have tousled with him on the grass, not minding that her own white shirt was now grass-stained and torn, when she'd voiced her annoyance and he had punched her, she could have punched him back.

After that, there was a pattern. When he'd been "a naughty boy", as he put it, feigning a Scottish accent (later, she found out why he did that), and put a finger to his mouth in a page-three pose she found disgusting, he would bring her yellow flowers – not quite sober, but not as drunk either as he'd been during the assault. And for a while he would come home on time (well, on time-*ish*), and would ask her, if not about her day, then whether she needed anything for the house or for Calypso. She would push away the increasing doubt and sense of despair, enjoying, if she were completely honest, the shift in power to the dynamic of their relationship. For a short time, she would gain the moral high ground, the upper hand and a sense of authority. Most dangerous of all, she would continue to hope.

Later, when hope began to flatline and the rekindled doubt set in, all she could wonder was how Archie, an eminent neurophysiologist at Southampton General seconded from McGill University, could sink so low. And it was only much later still that she questioned her own role in staying silent. By *not* speaking out, wouldn't she be equally culpable if he crashed his car and caused an accident? A fatal accident? At first, she attributed his heavy drinking and erratic behaviour to stress. Of course it was stress. Naturally, he was stressed! She had only to read the tabloids to understand how stretched the NHS was, while the plight of junior doctors was the stuff of endless articles, radio programmes and TV shows. Archie wasn't a junior doctor any more but a young professor. She knew that the patient cases for which he was directly responsible fluctuated between the truly medically challenging and the mundane. He would tear his hair out – figuratively speaking (although later she wished he really would) – at the endless people who traipsed through his door, faking blindness in order to claim benefits or a bus pass.

When he hit her a second time and she lost the baby, she understood that it was because he hadn't wanted children, *any* child, and she had felt ashamed – ashamed that she could have been so selfish. Why had she imagined that he would change? She had left the General Hospital alone and driven directly to Richmond, to a friend's house. It was early on a Sunday morning, and sitting in her car in front of the two-up-two-down Victorian conversion, she had felt ridiculous and very, very sorry for herself. After the surge of adrenaline that had propelled her to leave in the first place, the crushing reality that her friend wasn't home hit hard. It had never occurred to her that Mary, who'd been at Oxford with her, wouldn't be there. With her friend's absence, Ino's courage failed her entirely. She sat crying, frustrated and desperate. When her sobs subsided, she remained in the car, absent-mindedly fingering the odd pen, the tiny hollow that had once held a cigarette lighter, the Farley's Rusks embedded in the gear shaft. How *did* biscuit crumbs always manage to spread like that? She rummaged in the boot of the car for something to read – anything. She'd forgotten her Kindle, but there was nothing there at all except, of course, the car's user manual. But she would wait. Perhaps Mary was on her way home from a late night out somewhere.

The likelihood of Mary returning home soon began to diminish with every passing hour. Desperation had motivated Ino to flee without even finding out who was looking after Calypso. Now, she had no idea what to do. She could, of course, have walked into the high street; she could have had some lunch in a bistro or gone to the cinema while she waited. But she had come directly from the hospital and no longer had the energy to think about anything. By mid afternoon, tired and hungry, she decided to drive home.

Secretly, she still hoped for a great sea change, an act of contrition, a new beginning. It wasn't too late, Ino told herself. She could still forgive him. Maybe. If only he would acknowledge the pain he had inflicted; was *continuing* to inflict on her. But not only was no apology forthcoming, there was no reference to her recent hospital admission either. Then again, Archie appeared not to have registered her absence – surprise, if anything, showing on his face. "Oh, it's you," was all he said when she bumped into him on the first-floor landing. She, on the other hand, was alarmed to find the house silent, open and in darkness. She called for her daughter, her voice rising in panic. Calypso was still in bed, still in her cot. As far as Ino could make out, she'd never left it. Her nappy was so saturated that bits of plastic and cotton wool had come apart and were sticking to her legs. Someone – Ino could only presume it was Archie – had given her a newspaper to play with. And eat. This was shredded. The sheets and Calypso's lips were stained with black ink.

The reality check of seeing her daughter in such a state was sobering. Even though Calypso hadn't seemed unduly distressed, how could Ino have left her? Her mind numbed at the idea. What might have happened had she stayed away much longer, or had Archie gone off to work? Ino clutched her daughter to her, smothering her face and neck in kisses till she squealed. They both giggled when Ino made a face at Calypso's smelly nappy. This time, Ino didn't rush her daughter's bath as she usually did, counting the minutes until Calypso was in bed and she could have a glass of wine. This time, she savoured the menial tasks: soaping her hair, sponging down her chubby little body, as carefully and gently as though she were anointing it with precious oils. She made up stories as she blew bubbles off her hands. Dressing her in her prettiest clothes, Ino settled the clean, sweet-smelling Calypso on a blanket in the kitchen, surrounding her with her favourite cuddly bears and current favourite toy: a plastic boxlike frame through which different objects were posted. Calypso never bothered sorting the shapes, finding it far more amusing to hammer the same ones into the same hole. *A bit like her mother*, thought Ino wryly. *Stubborn persistence in the face of clear resistance.* From time to time, Ino patted Calypso's damp curls, breathing in the camomile smell of her, the unblemished folds of skin around her plump little neck, and delighting in the clear whites of her chocolatey-brown eyes. Feeling weak, Ino had made herself a cup of tea. The face that she glimpsed in the shiny silver surface of the kettle was as white as the bread she was buttering.

Ino boxed the memories. Going over past grievances was no way to garner strength. And just how to garner strength was something she had yet to learn.

9

Emil
Barcelona
April 2017

After the old woman had left the *pastelaria*, taking her comments with her, Emil reached up to the top shelf, the shelf with the stored polo photographs, to fish out the book he was currently reading. The *vieja's* observation hadn't pricked his ego. Not exactly. Besides, she hadn't told him anything he didn't know. Both he *and* Rafael (time hadn't completely ignored his handsome cousin either!) had aged. He knew that. But sometimes, just sometimes, he felt a moment of unsurpassable longing for the carefree days of their youth. Looking back on it now, he viewed it as a transitory time of belonging.

Recently, Emil had sought to recapture those feelings by rereading the biographies of famous men, seeking to relive their wanderlust and drive. The story of Simón Bolívar's rise to fame had always inspired him. It was one that he practically knew by heart. Ever since he was small, Emil had been captivated by this hero, initially because he recognised something of Simón's lackadaisical student days in himself: the boy who was happier in the field, on a horse, anywhere but in the schoolroom. Like Bolívar, Emil had also been orphaned as a child and brought up by relatives. When he was older, Emil skipped to the sections describing the endless battles and skirmishes that accounted for most of the soldier's life. It was only when Emil was older still that he understood the disappointment that comes when dreams turn to dust. He was moved when reading that the 'Liberator of South America' had become disillusioned with the very independence movement he'd created. And then came the time when, also displaced, Emil embarked on an epic journey of his own. Retracing Bolívar's footsteps, he hoped to find some essence of the man as he crossed continents, zigzagging from country to country.

Flicking through the well-thumbed pages, the drone from the refrigerator, the clicking of the bead curtain in a whisper of breeze, and the sounds from the street all faded as Emil's thoughts turned inward. Unpicking his own tangled narrative, though, was not as easy as reflecting on a life well ordered through the biographer's lens. But truth to tell, there was only one beginning; indeed, one truth. As the past with all its hopes and dreams swirled round his head, he necessarily thought about *her*. And in thinking about her, he had also to think about polo, and of course about Sol...

When they were young, Emil and Rafael were often mistaken for twins – it was a fact of life they had both become accustomed to. Sometimes it played to their advantage and amused them, rarely it annoyed them (until later in life), but most of the time they didn't give it a moment's thought. It was almost unconscious, the way they spoke, dressed, quite simply *were* as one. But on that afternoon their similarity was particularly pronounced (and they knew it) as they lolled together on canvas deckchairs, watching the game in progress. Identically dressed in white polo jeans and with the name of their team, Los Salto Duendes, emblazoned across their backs, they sat in the same pose, their right leather-shod riding boots crossed over their left. At times, and today was no exception, they could only be distinguished by the numbers on their shirts.

Now, as they watched intently, La Bamba (whom the cousins supported) were a goal behind Los Borrachos. Emil's gloves lay on his stomach; Rafael fiddled with the strap of his knee guard, a polo mallet draped across him as though it were a lance.

"*Dale, dale!*" he yelled hoarsely to Grant, the American and the only player who hadn't scored. Blood streamed from a cut on his pony's mouth and its flaring nostrils were crimson. "*Ay carajo!*" he shouted in frustration. "That couldn't have been an easier shot!"

Emil sat up as Grant and the pro, Nacho, cantered past to change ponies. "Two goals each!"

The bell sounded, the umpire threw the ball into the fray, and with a slashing of sticks they were off.

"What's he doing *now*?"

Rafael smirked. "Doing what any *thinking* Argie should be doing with outstanding bills to pay. He's finally put the ball in front of his patron."

A companionable silence ensued, punctuated only by the tapping of willow root on hardwood mallets as they followed the game. Hooves thundered past, kicking dust into their faces. There was a roar from the crowd as Emerson, the Scandinavian patron who hadn't come near the ball in the previous chukkas, now pushed it between the posts.

"Well, someone's going to be relieved," said Rafael. "Nacho should be rehired for the next season after that goal. Are they Emerson's own horses? I don't recognise the mare." He nodded in the direction of the number four, who had moved the ball to the boards. Successfully defending the goal, he hadn't, however, managed to take it forward.

"His own," said Emil. "I think he's saving the best till last."

"He always does. But it's a risky business. I mean, to wait till penalty and then…" Rafael didn't have to complete the sentence. They understood each other perfectly.

It was a beautiful afternoon in July. The bright green fields, expensively maintained to this exacting degree, were in stark contrast to the dry backdrop of the Montseny. From the hills came the sharp click of cicadas through the cloud of desert heat that hung above them. Ponies tethered to iron rails nudged each other, twitching, irritated by the flies buzzing round their noses. Against this was the robust clink of glasses from the clubhouse where players mingled with patrons, and further away, the excited chatter of women enthralled by the sight of so many Hispanic men in tight white jeans and jewel-coloured shirts. But the cousins were oblivious to the fascination their presence generated. For Rafael and Emil, all that mattered was polo and horses and more polo. Anything else was on the periphery of their existence; a distraction to be instantly dismissed. As always, the only blip on their otherwise perfect horizon was the performance of a favourite mare.

Now Rafael leapt to his feet, his polo stick tumbling to the ground. "*Has visto?* Did you see that?" he raged.

"Yes, yes, Rafa," said Emil calmly. "*Pero siéntate por favor. No pasa nada.* Sit down, please. It's not worth getting upset about. It's not our game."

"No, but it affects who we meet in the semis!" exclaimed Rafael. "It impacts – if we get the same *hijo de puta*!"

Emil laid a hand on his cousin's shoulder to lower him back into his chair. "Shh! *Primo*, keep your voice down! You know your language—"

"Is what?" said Rafael, turning aggressively.

"I was going to say offensive."

"*Ay!*" Rafael punched his fist, shaking off his cousin's hand.

"Wouldn't it be better to keep your... energy for the game? *Ay que sí?*"

"No!" Rafael shrugged. "Okay. Yeah, yes."

Emil patted him. "Good. Check out number one. Could be a Cambiaso in the making."

"*All* sponsors are Cambiasos in the making."

"*Rafa!*"

"Okay. *Vale.* But just look at his team. They really do play nicely. I'm not envious, not really."

"These Argies, I know. It's in their blood. They start early. Look at the kids." Emil gestured to the surrounding area, where small children, the offspring of professional players, ran about the grass, practising their ball skills using tiny foot mallets. "But that's *all* they do, you know that. It's their life. We have other things."

"I don't," said Rafael sombrely.

Emil shot him a look. "You mean our *pastelaria* business doesn't interest you?"

"Over my dead body!" Rafael exclaimed passionately. "I'd rather die than be involved with that."

"Actually, so would I," conceded Emil. He buttoned a glove and began to play with his mallet, hitting the ball from a sitting position. His eyes crinkled in the bright sunshine as his attention was drawn once again to the game.

"No, it's polo for me," said Rafael, following the umpire through narrowed eyes.

"And me," said Emil.

They fell silent, their dark heads turning right and left as they watched the galloping riders. There was a rumble of hooves as the players passed within a hair's breadth of them, their ponies snorting, pumped up and foaming with sweat. The 'twins' leaned forward.

"They really do work well together, don't they?" said Rafael, rising once more out of his seat in admiration.

Emil didn't bother to restrain his cousin this time. Tiring quickly of the game, he called to his groom. It was time, anyway. Despite the heat, the Argentine wore his habitual black felt hat, and on his employer's nod he led out two beautiful, fresh young ponies.

"And we do too. Come on. Look," said Rafael, motioning to them. "Let's stick-and-ball to warm up."

Emil checked himself, took a deep breath and stretched. "*Suerte hermano,*" he said, clasping his cousin in a shallow embrace. "Good luck, bro."

"*Y vos,*" Rafael replied, using the South American polite and formal case. "*Vamos Los Duendes!*"

When it was their turn, the game was fast and brutal. The one thing the Monte Alegre cousins (known familiarly as 'the MAs') excelled at was the seamless way in which they interacted. It was more than teamwork. It was almost telepathic, so it was said, the manner in which they anticipated the other's every move, covering, backing up and calling. Brought up as brothers, they had taken their first steps together at Salto al Cielo and learned to ride horses before they could straddle a bicycle. It was this acrobatic performance that made them formidable players. If nonchalant elegance was their natural state off the pitch, on it they were ferocious and febrile. Between them they had already broken sixteen bones. They were used to playing with an arm not only in plaster but strapped to the body, stitches and concussion notwithstanding, and they rarely had the patience for physio. Being so ferociously competitive, they seldom lost a game, and if they did lose, they would relive every moment again and again in the days to come.

True to form, Rafael played a spectacular offensive game, scoring from impossible positions. Emil's had been solid and defensive, preventing the unstoppable Argentines from equalising. When the bell went, they cantered off together, feeling exceedingly smug. But when they jumped from their sweating ponies in unison, it was with such effortless grace that they lost all arrogance. Their grooms promptly sprang into action, untacking the horses, then sponging them down. Laughing, shaking their heads like the very horses they had ridden, the cousins grabbed their own bottles of water, saturating their heads before drinking thirstily, their shirts now clinging to their virile young bodies. But while Emil was completely content, on a high from the synergy of riding man and beast in brilliant sunshine and on a campo he loved, Rafael was instantly dissatisfied. He watched the opposing pivot canter past – an Argentine pro – with distaste.

"Boy, he knows the women are watching, doesn't he?" said Emil, noting his cousin's change of mood.

"Well, I wouldn't mind having a go."

"What, at playing number three's position?"

"Yeah, why not? I think I could do that."

"I'm sure you *could*, but…" A disturbing thought crossed Emil's mind. "You don't mean that seriously, do you?"

Rafael gave his head a final shake, like a dog after a swim in the river, droplets of water landing on Emil. "Why not?"

Despite the heat, Emil felt himself instantly cool. "But what about us?"

"What about us?" echoed Rafael. Unpeeling his gloves and grabbing a towel from round the neck of his groom, he began patting his face dry.

"We… we've just always played together." Emil had never imagined a time when he wouldn't play behind his cousin at number one.

"*Lo sé*. I know. We'll still play *together*." Rafael slapped his cousin on the back. "Just different positions. *Tranquilo*, it was just a thought – I mean, I'd move to three and you could—"

"And the Argie?" interrupted Emil. "Where would he be?"

"I don't know."

"*Ves?* See? It wouldn't be the same."

"No, you're right," Rafael agreed. "It wouldn't; it would be different."

"Well, I don't want it to be different." It was Emil's turn to sulk. He combed back his hair with his fingers. "I'm going for a smoke."

Rafael shrugged. "Please yourself."

As Emil made to leave, a pretty girl in a short pink dress with sleek, shoulder-length blonde hair motioned to them. Sunglasses were perched on the top of her head like a crown. Her tanned skin glowed, and immaculately painted toenails peeped from gold Grecian-style sandals.

"Ah, *hola*, Sol," said Rafael indifferently. Despite her name and golden appearance, she was the least sunny girl he knew.

"*Hola*, MAs," she said, smiling to reveal slightly buck teeth. Rafael usually didn't hold this against her, but today he scowled.

There was something vaguely *cloying* about her. "Now, which one of you is going to buy me a glass of cava?"

Rafael looked away. It wasn't going to be him. By contrast, Emil's heart began to thump, counteracting the tension in his groin. Was it his imagination or was her attention really fixed on Rafael? Didn't her gaze linger just that bit longer on him? Emil pushed a collection of small stones together with his boot, not daring to look at her, and felt almost relief when a familiar voice said, "Actually, neither of them, *hijita*."

"*Abuela!*" exclaimed Emil, so enthusiastically that the elegant woman making her way along the edge of the field stopped short in surprise. She looked behind her, as if wondering that her arrival could arouse such a reaction. Hiding her amusement, she stroked the nose of Rafael's pony, which was still being held by the groom as she passed.

"*Condesa.*" Sol approached the older woman, brushing her cheek with hers, and in turn giving the horse a pat.

The older woman touched the younger girl's cheek, mouthing a greeting. But when she spoke to her grandson, hers was more a demand than a question. "Rafael?"

"*Sí, hola,*" said Emil's cousin, with less enthusiasm.

Abuela, in her seventies, was still a beautiful woman. Her ash-blonde hair framed a tanned face and her slender form was dressed in white capri pants and a green-and-pink Pucci top. There were pearls at her neck, wrists and ears. When she smiled, as she was doing now, her teeth were as even, white and expensive as her jewellery. "*Ay qué lindo!*" she said soothingly to one of the ponies. "What a stunner! From the Villapadierna stud, I imagine. Or even yours?"

Sol shook her head.

"You were right first time," said Rafael. "We had its mother too."

"Ah yes, I remember." Abuela continued to coo and whisper sweet nothings, the horse's head in both of her tanned, capable hands. "I'm sorry, Sol," she said casually at last, giving the pony a final pat and nodding to the groom. "I need the boys for something this afternoon."

"What? Both of us?" countered Rafael quickly.

Emil shot him an agitated look. Was that a wink? Had Rafael just *winked* at Sol?

Seemingly unperturbed, Abuela turned her face to the sun, closing her eyes. "Ah, how good that is. It's always so much warmer here than at Salto."

"Abuela?" Emil coaxed her gently.

Abuela opened her eyes and waved vaguely in their direction, pearls clinking at her wrist. "Well, I suppose I don't need you *both*. I just thought it would be good if..." She had switched to English, which didn't surprise the twins as everyone spoke two if not three languages at polo, and Catalans alternated easily anyway between Spanish and their own language. What did surprise them, however – in fact, it rendered them virtually speechless – was the interruption made by a young girl who now appeared at her side.

"I don't need a *babysitter*! *Coño!* I mean, how old do you think I am?"

There was a stunned hush, as much at the use of the expletive as at the fact that it had come from the skinny, dark-haired little person who had stomped towards them. The twins blinked. The girl was a child all right, but there was no denying her gypsy-like beauty. Rafael confessed later to thinking she was Argentinian; the daughter of one of their grooms. She could certainly swear like one. With her sleek ponytail and extreme slenderness, she reminded them of their Arab ponies. And if this girl was an Arab, Sol, with her cool blonde looks, was a palomino. The twins were momentarily silenced, absorbing the contrast the two girls made: one so seemingly at ease despite still being a child; the other clearly disgruntled in spite of being older and more sophisticated. Sol noted only Ino's Chanel ballerina flats. Even in her rarefied world, she wondered at the kind of mother who bought her child such expensive shoes. She wished hers did.

"Why, Ino," said Abuela mildly, turning to the girl. "Of course you don't, but surely it would be more fun to have someone show you around? As I explained earlier, I have meetings this afternoon."

"Ino?" interrupted Rafael. "Not Ina? Is it short for something?"

"No, it's Ino," said Ino. She exaggerated the 'O'. Then made a face.

Rafael's eyes glinted in amusement. He admired friskiness of any kind. "Ino-Bambino," he said tauntingly, rolling the words together. "That's more like it."

Ino pursed her lips, mouthing a "Whatever", which only broadened his smile.

"Well, as reluctant as I am to leave such delightful company…" he let his words linger, "I'm afraid I too have a meeting." The look Emil shot him was rewarding, as was the fun in riling this new cousin. "As much as I'd like to, *por su puesto.*" Rafael flashed a charming smile. "*Encantado.*" He clicked his heels and bent over Ino's hand, his lips the requisite inch from her skin. The flash in her eyes reminded him of his witchiest horse. He studied her thoughtfully. She'd grow up to be an interesting woman, of that he was certain. He dropped her hand before deftly taking his grandmother's. "Abuela." Again, his lips brushed air as he bowed before moving on to Sol. Only this time, he kept hold of Sol's hand. Pulling her with him, he bent towards Emil. "Have fun with the bambino; she's all yours."

"*Bam—*" spluttered Ino, but Abuela shook her head.

"*Calma,*" she said, her hands pumping air, accordion-fashion. "Calm! If you react to everything that boy says you'll be in a constant state. Don't pay him any attention."

"I don't," said Ino, glowering.

And in a flash, just as Emil realised what was happening, Sol and Rafael scampered towards the clubhouse, their laughter floating after them.

"What? Wait… *joder*! Sol, I—" protested Emil.

"Looks like you lost the girl," said the girl.

Abuela held up her hands in mock despair. "*Què podem fer?* What can you do?" Then, turning to Ino, she said in English, "I'm sorry, that was actually your *real* cousin, your blood cousin. This," she motioned to a scowling Emil, "is Emil Leon y Monte Alegre, your cousin's cousin."

Archie

Cedar Avenue

Today I dealt with a child who'd stuck out her tongue to lick snow off a railing... and got stuck. No need to tell you that saliva also freezes, sticking to metal like superglue, and that those wonderful textured taste buds – so useful for appreciating chocolate eclairs – only grip the metal with more incredible strength.
    Pretty dumb, huh? Go figure...

10

Ino
Winchester
April 2017

Ino swept up the last pieces of china, wrapping them in newspaper before carrying them out to the recycling bin. *Out of sight and out of mind*, she told herself firmly. She walked slowly back along the narrow brick path that ran parallel to the low thatched barn; so low, in fact, that she could use the edge for support. The barn wasn't attached to the house, and the estate agent had lauded its potential. "An office," Archie had said aloud, while Ino had thought, *A playroom*. From this end of the garden, the lawns swept uninterrupted towards open fields. In a vague way, the view reminded her of Salto, her Spanish grandmother's estate. There was a pond surrounded by high yew hedges, and on the other side of that, a kitchen garden. Apple trees, and even a mulberry tree had Ino decided that this was the place where she wanted her children to grow up. Now she wasn't so sure.

The sound of crunching gravel alerted her to the fact that she was not alone, and she fumbled automatically for her glasses. Ridiculously, her hands were still shaky. She took a deep breath, staring down at them, willing them to be still. She could do this, of course she could. Hadn't she countless times before? Maybe her mother was right after all. It *was* up to her. She had a duty – it was her *deber* – to make things work. She would start again; she would try harder. *Just once, just once more*, she promised herself. From somewhere she heard the gruff low-pitched notes of a wood pigeon.

And then what? said that taunting small voice of reason. *If he hits you again, what? You'll tidy the house again? That's just insulting. Come on! You're an intelligent woman. You're more than that! You don't have to put up with this – you have a choice.*

I know, I know, I know, the wood pigeon seemed to eco in response. Not the childhood refrain *Take two spoons, Peggy*, but *I know, I know, I know.*

Her head felt clammy; her body slick with perspiration. *Okay, if he hits me again, I'll leave. But I'll give it just one more go.*

And then what? You will *leave, will you?* The voice was relentless. *You will what? I can't hear you!*

I will leave. Thank you. Happy now?

No!

Why not? Isn't that what you wanted to hear?

Not entirely. Why wait? It will be worse next time. It is always worse. Each time the violence is that bit worse. Look at yourself! Have you seen your face? You were beautiful once.

The wood pigeon was cooing. *Why wait? Why wait?*

I don't know, I don't know, I don't know—

"You really are miles away," said a raspy voice. "You aren't a writer, are you? A musician? Ah, that's it – you are, aren't you? You're collecting sounds for a cinema score."

Ino almost split her lip in the relief of seeing that it was her neighbour. She was surprised that she hadn't heard the dull putt-putt of his mobility scooter. "What? Oh, hello, Michael. Good heavens, no. No, of course I'm not!"

But Michael seemed to have formed an impression of her that he liked, and was sticking to it. He pushed his scooter forward so that he was wedged between the hedge and the barn. His upturned face was alive and eager, just as the rest of his body, which was wasting from the effects of motor neurone disease, was not. She couldn't say she knew him well; she had only met him a couple of times since she and Archie had moved in. Michael's wife worked at the local council and he was on his own during the day. Ino often saw him scootering up and down the lane but he had never visited before.

She turned away from him so that he couldn't see the bruised side of her face. She snapped a rogue twig from the shoulder-level thatched roof. "What did you mean by 'collecting sounds'?"

"You tell me…"

Ino smiled. "I'm really not a musician. I can't play a note. I was simply putting out the rubbish."

"Really?"

"Really."

"Ah well." Michael seemed to accept this, but there was no masking his disappointment. "I was so sure…" He sighed, then visibly brightened, remembering what it was he had wanted to tell her. "I listened to a programme on the radio this morning," he said. "Apparently, cinema composers have changed. You – all right, not you," he corrected when Ino shook her head, "*they* have moved on from the orchestral era and the enormity of sound, say, of a James Horner or a Hans Zimmer."

"Oh?" Ino wasn't exactly sure how interested she was in any of this, but his voice, though laboured in places, was soothing in its very monotony.

Michael blinked by way of agreement. "Yes," he said slowly. "There's a new wave of composers who have backgrounds in rock and folk. They collect sounds. They have sound *libraries*."

"Sounds fascinating," she murmured.

"Oh, it is! What they do is amazing. Mica Levi, who composed the music for that biopic of Jackie O., for example, didn't even see the film beforehand. Relied on her library. She has a band called Good Sad Happy Bad."

Ino had never heard of the composer; nor had she seen the film. But he was lonely and so was she. She let him talk. Although he could no longer walk and his upper body was compromised, his eyes remained alert and observant.

"I was just passing," he added. "It's Ino, isn't it? Not short for anything?"

Ino, cariño. The way he had said it that first time – a pun spun off the tip of the tongue, more to amuse himself than anything, but then later it was his special name for her. 'Ino' and 'love', '*my* love', rolled into one. Where was all this coming from? This whisper from the past; from Salto…

"Yes," said Ino. "Not I-N-A." She stressed the 'A'. "People always think—"

"That it should have a feminine ending?" finished Michael. "Yes, I know. The *Odyssey*?"

Ino shrugged. "I doubt it. My mother called me 'kid' while she came up with a proper name. Then I was 'bambino', but I don't think she realised that I was actually a girl until I was older."

"And did she? Ever come up with one?"

"No."

"So the nickname stuck?"

Ino nodded.

"She of the beautiful ankles." It was a statement. Michael wasn't trying to flirt. Nor was she. If she were, she'd have held out her leg.

Ino was used to provoking a certain reaction when she gave her name. Those who didn't know their Greek mythology – especially Latins – assumed it was misspelled, and those who did were always shocked that anyone would name their child after such a tragic character. Ino was the white goddess sometimes known as 'Queen of the Sea'. Which was fanciful: she was better known for murdering her offspring.

Michael's eyes narrowed. He looked especially thoughtful when he enquired if she was enjoying her new home. The *house*, yes, she wanted to say; it was just everything else that was the problem.

"I haven't seen you for a while," he said. "Guess you're busy with the children."

"Child," corrected Ino. "Just the one. A daughter, Calypso."

"*Calypso?*" Now his surprise was unrestrained.

Ino smiled apologetically. "I know, I know, but it's not what you think. *I* called my daughter after the character in Mary Wesley's novel, The Camomile Lawn."

Michael's eyes darted. She supposed he'd have shaken his head if he could have. "Don't know it. Why?"

"Why?" Ino echoed.

"Yes – why that one? What's so compelling about that Calypso?"

Ino was taken aback. She'd never been asked the question before. "Unrequited love has always struck me as singularly sad. And romantic."

"Is that what this *Camomile Lawn* is, then? My Lordy, women do like a good weep, don't they?"

Ino's expression was sheepish. "I guess. I never thought of it that way. *The Camomile Lawn* is a wonderful story, though. It was later televised."

Again, Michael blinked his ignorance, so Ino rattled on.

"It's a family saga set during the Second World War," she said, her whole being warming as she remembered how much she'd enjoyed it. "There's this couple; she – Calypso, that is – marries Hector for his money, to begin with. He never thinks she loves him and she doesn't think he loves her, until years later their son sees a wood from the air that his father had planted, and he sees that it spells out his mother's name: Calypso. So, contrary to what he had always thought, his parents had really adored each other…" Ino's voice tailed off. "I don't know why. I just always found the story so… so poignant."

Michael touched his handbrake, preparing to move. "Another tragic heroine, then."

"No! Yes, in a way. The book was full of hope and a chance to make things right, to make things work. A second time."

"Is that what you're hoping for?" His eyes bored into her.

Ino was flustered all at once. It wasn't a conversation she was ready for. "It's just a novel…" Except that, of course, it wasn't. As a story about cousins and a house by the sea, it resonated; was evocative of Salto and the Monte Alegres.

"Mmm… you may have lost me there." Michael broke into her train of thought. "I think the *Odyssey*'s a lot more straightforward."

Ino made a vague gesture to the cottage, suddenly self-conscious of her chatter. "Would you like to come in? Have a coffee?"

"Are you sure?" Michael had released his handbrake at 'would'. "Are you sure you can spare the time, with the baby and all? I often hear a baby crying when I pass this end of the lane. When I'm on my constitutional. The carer sends me out. Says I get under her feet." He smiled, and Ino couldn't even begin to imagine what it must be like having to adapt to such a disability.

"Actually, Calypso is six – seven soon. Not a baby any longer. And she's at school."

Michael frowned. "No, agreed, not a baby. Odd, that. I could have sworn I heard a baby crying coming from this direction."

"Must be someone else's," said Ino.

"Must be."

There was an awkward silence soon filled by the sound of Michael's contraption negotiating the narrow paths as he followed Ino.

"Have me own mug," he said, whipping out a plastic contraption from underneath his seat. "But I'll just stay outside. You can bring out the coffee. Not sure I'd get in the house without a ramp, and I'm far too heavy to push otherwise. Once I'm wedged in, it's hard to move me. Not easily, anyway."

"Then find a spot. I'll be back in a moment." They were facing the kitchen side of the house, and now she gesticulated to the patio area identifiable by its dwarf hedge shaded by a sprawling pergola. A rectangular garden table and cushioned chairs peeked invitingly above clumps of primulas and stone pots stuffed with auriculas. There was a wide enough stretch through which he could manoeuvre the scooter. "Are you sure you can manage?"

"Yup," said Michael, inclining his head with a stab at gallantry. "Shout if you need a hand," he added out of habit. He couldn't have come to the aid of a fly.

Ino was surprised by how cheerful she felt at the prospect of a chat over coffee. These days, she and Archie rarely had people to the house; they seldom met people anywhere, for that matter. In the early days of their marriage, Archie had invited the odd work colleague for drinks or dinner, but over time that too had dwindled. His hours, let alone his behaviour, had become too unpredictable. Already, her memory of the evening's violence, if not forgotten, was slipping away. In fact, set against the reality of having someone visit, it was becoming downright surreal.

Ino flew into action, putting the kettle to boil on the Aga, whipping open the dishwasher, and virtually hurling the breakfast dishes onto the crockery trays and stacking the evening's pots and pans. She wiped down the table, emptying the sugar bowl and all its crumbs and grains into the rubbish, and set a tray with her prettiest plates. She opened a tin of home-made biscuits and emptied milk (thank goodness she'd remembered to buy milk!) into a pink-and-green jug. By the time she had finished, the kettle was singing, the coffee brewing, and, though breathless, she felt altogether brighter. She smiled to herself as she carried the tray out to the garden. Michael had driven across the lawn, leaving a neat trail through the dew-drenched grass. It was exactly the kind of thing to infuriate Archie. Ino set the tray on the wrought-iron table under the pergola swathed in clumps of wisteria. A delicious scent of lilac mingled with that of a clambering honeysuckle, and branches from a weeping willow brushed tall meadow grasses. She was inordinately happy to see this stranger – anyone, quite frankly, that wasn't connected with the police station or Calypso's school.

"Archie's a lucky man," said Michael quietly when she'd poured coffee into his special mug with its attached straw. His fingers seemed to have gone numb again, so she gently placed his hand around a biscuit and held it steady. For a moment, bending close, she was aware of his gaze on her face, but if he wondered at the cause of the bruising, he didn't comment.

"Kind of you to say so," said Ino. She couldn't bring herself to lie by adding, as her girlfriends would have done, that she was the lucky one.

"You're not from around here, are you?" he said when he'd slurped his coffee. "Sorry about that," he added, but she made a dismissive gesture.

"You're forgetting I have a six-year-old." She flushed. "Oh, I didn't mean—"

But Michael was unperturbed, blinking happily and appearing to stare at some distant point. "Wait till you hear my coughing!"

Ino nibbled a biscuit, but the sharpness hurt her lip so she set it down, tucking it behind her cup. "And in answer to your question, not originally. My father was Spanish – no, it's okay," she added quickly, seeing his look of concern. "I never knew him. He died when I was a baby. My mother is Canadian – I really grew up there."

"Blimey. I've not moved out of Hampshire! Lived in this same village for forty years."

Ino remembered Marion's comment about her house. "Then you've seen a lot of people come and go."

"Some. Though not many have left. Most have stayed. It's that kind of place."

Ino dabbed her face with a napkin and tried to keep her tone casual. "And… this house? Did you know the people who lived here before us? I know it had been empty for a while."

Michael hesitated. "Not well, but yes. I met them – a couple. Young mother like yourself."

"Oh, that's lovely," said Ino with relief. She wasn't sure why, but for some reason she'd been afraid of what he might say. She had picked up on a negative vibe from the way Marion had spoken. But then, that was Marion all over.

Michael's eyes widened and he almost choked. "Depends

which way you look at it," he said, and began coughing almost at once, biscuit crumbs carpeting his shirt front.

"Are you all right?" Ino asked in alarm. She had no idea what to do if he couldn't breathe or something went wrong. There was a number on a sticker on the side of the scooter.

"I'm fine," said Michael, hardly above a whisper, just as she was about to tap the number into her mobile. "No need to call Agrippina."

Ino smiled. "Is that what you call her? Now look who's talking about names!"

"Touché." Michael smiled. "Seems as though we have something in common after all. I like my classical mythology. Beautiful and domineering, is my Agrippina. Yes, the name fits." After a while, when he had recovered himself, he said, "Did you know she had a double canine in her upper jaw?"

"Who? Your carer?"

"Agrippina."

"I know she is thought to have poisoned Claudius."

"Ah, very good. A closet classicist, along with being a musician. I knew it!"

"I'm not a musician," said Ino, shaking her head. "I told you. Some education, that's all."

"Canada?"

Ino nodded. She relaxed too now, knowing that Michael wasn't about to expire on her. The ease with which they conversed was immensely comforting; birdsong and the occasional humming bee underscoring the steady pulse of his voice. Maybe there was something in this talk of a sound library after all. A *memory* library would be even better. For those emotions recollected in tranquillity. Or the other way round: tranquillity to be recollected in moments of turmoil. "Yes, but I came to university here." She wanted to say Oxford, but somehow that didn't seem appropriate. She wanted to say she'd run for her life one summer and never looked back, but this relative stranger with his own problems didn't need to hear hers, although he did seem to expect more. "I met Archie, my husband," she said, encouraged by the warmth in Michael's eyes, "when I was doing postgrad in my home town."

"Which was?"

"Montreal. Archie was on sabbatical at the Children's Hospital there."

"Ah…" said Michael. "Love at first sight, was it?"

"Not exactly." Ino leaned back in her chair. "Actually, my mother met him first. It may well have been for her."

Michael's eyebrow twitched. "Has it raised?" he asked. "It's becoming a case of the mind wanting and the flesh resisting. I never know how responsive I'm being! I want my eyebrow to rise sardonically without having to say, 'Wow!' to emphasise a point."

"It has," said Ino kindly. "It absolutely has."

"Phew."

"But it wasn't like that." Except, actually, it was. That was exactly how it was. She made a fluttering gesture with her hands by way of explanation. "I was studying at McGill University, and although my mom – *mother* – was living there at the time, I was in halls of residence. She travels a lot, which is why it seemed sensible that I should live in halls of residence."

"Go on," said Michael. "This is interesting."

Ino shrugged. "It really isn't. Veronica – I call my mother Veronica – invited me to dinner because she said a family friend was visiting."

"And this 'family friend' became your husband?"

Ino nodded. "Yes, that was Archie."

"Is he actually from Southampton? I mean, I presume he works there now."

Ino nodded. "Yes, he's a neurophysiologist at the General. He applied to work there so that he could sail in his free time." Not that he appeared to have much of that (at least none that he wanted to share with her), and she'd never seen him anywhere near a boat.

"Yes, a lot of chaps like the water."

"Did you? I mean..." Ino stopped herself.

Michael looked set for another coughing fit, and Ino half-rose in her chair. "It's okay." His eyes fluttered. "It's like this, I'm afraid. I come with a bit of a health warning..." There was a pause as he caught his breath. "Yes, I did. Loved it. Best thing in the world, being out on the water like that."

Ino smiled. "I had – *have* – a cousin," she corrected herself, "who thought the same: he enjoyed sailing almost as much as polo. Funny, I've not thought about him in ages." She took another sip of coffee, feeling light-headed from too much caffeine. It felt even stranger talking about Rafael in English to a stranger.

"Oh well, I've never played polo. Not too keen on horses, myself. Mother's or father's side?"

"I'm sorry? Oh, father's. He's a priest now. I mean, the cousin is."

"A *priest*!" Michael managed a whistle of sorts. "Gets better and better."

Ino made an expressive gesture with her hands. She thought of Rafael and his penchant for linen shirts in ice-cream colours, soft-as-butter leather shoes, velvety suede jackets, and cashmere. Lots and lots of cashmere, purchased, according to the season, in just the right colour and weight. He was even more fastidious than Veronica, if that were possible. "It was a surprise to us all. He'd always been... well, such a playboy, and probably the least religious person you'd ever meet. And when I knew him, he was always the one getting into trouble." *Trouble! Ha! That was a bit of an understatement.*

"Something must have happened to change him so."

A small, heavy silence wedged itself between them.

"Do you believe in epiphanies?" ventured Ino after a while.

"Me? Hell, no! Not religious at all." He gave her a challenging look as if to say, *Would this make sense if I was?*

Ino reached for the cafetière. "More?"

Michael blinked twice to indicate a negative.

Ino set the coffee back on the tray and met his thoughtful gaze straight on. "We got diverted. We were talking about the lovely couple? The previous owners? I suppose it's because I'm living here now that I'm curious about them."

For a moment Michael returned her look; then, emitting a kind of snort, he began pressing various knobs and dials. The chair too seemed to come to life with a low humming sound, inflating like a hovercraft. "On reflection," he said, pressing his mug into a side pocket, "I think maybe it's better we continue this another time. Really must be going. Any moment now, Agrippina will come looking, and you don't want that. Trust me."

"Oh," said Ino, disappointed. "I was so enjoying our chat."

"So was I, but keep them wanting more, isn't that the trick?"

"I think I'd always want more. I enjoy chatting to you," said Ino warmly. "That's quite a contraption," she added, rising to her feet. "Something between a go-kart and a bike."

"Go-kart, eh?" said Michael. "I'll have you know this is a top-of-the-range all-terrain scooter, and the only one of its kind. It should be, for almost eight grand! And I've called her *Copenhagen*."

"Expecting a Waterloo?" said Ino. The words were out of her mouth before she could stop herself.

"That day will come," said Michael without a touch of self-pity. "That day will come."

"And how fast can she go?" said Ino, eager to make up for her insensitivity.

"Up to twenty-one kilometres. You've clearly not seen me in action!"

"Actually, I have. Occasionally, on the lane."

Michael's eyes narrowed. "Well, look out! On a good day I'm Emerson Fittipaldi. Thing with this is that it has no rollback function even when completely stationary. Well, you've seen that, haven't you?"

"Yes indeed. *Copenhagen*'s a fine beast."

Michael tapped the metal arm. "Couldn't do without her."

"Look, I hope you'll pop in again," said Ino kindly.

They began to move slowly, Ino beside Michael, her hand resting gently on the back of his chair. There was a slight breeze; lilac branches carelessly strewing blossom onto the path. The day was warming up.

"Ta very much. I'd like that, but I've stopped far too long now. And tell your husband to come to the parish meeting once in a while – haven't met him yet. I like to put a face to newcomers."

Haven't met him yet... For a moment Ino's mind went blank and she couldn't speak. *So, all those evenings when he said he was going to parish meetings...?*

"Ino? There you go again – collecting sounds. I knew it!"

Ino was collecting sounds all right, and memories from a catalogue of stored misdemeanours. With one recollection in particular bubbling to the surface. *Of course* Archie had never gone to a meeting! How naive could she be? Had she ever really believed he'd volunteer for something as mundane as a parish meeting? Naturally, he'd been going to the pub. She had even caught him out once, when he was supposed to be somewhere else. Stopped at traffic lights on her way to collect Calypso from a play date, she'd idly watched a young mother with a pushchair and dog in tow negotiate a busy crossing. But they had melted away as her attention wandered to the pub's bay window, which was at eye level with her driver's window. A blond man in a pinstriped suit was playing pinball. She'd been fascinated. There was something incongruous about the scene: the suit, the game, the time of day, but most of all the expression of complete concentration on the man's face. It was only when he reached up mechanically for the pint perched on top of the gaming machine that she recognised Archie.

"Ino? Queen of the Sea?"

Ino blinked. Michael's voice could actually be coming from the *bottom* of the sea, it sounded that far away. "Yes, I'll tell him," she muttered.

"You all right, lass?" He coughed. "Frowning now," he said.

Ino barely glanced at him, and failed to register his stab at humour.

"You've turned a funny colour." And when she didn't reply, he accelerated. "Or, better still, you could come on your own. From what I understand, I think half the village would prefer it if you came alone anyway."

Ino didn't dare ask him to elaborate; nor what he meant by 'half the village'. Marion, she wouldn't be surprised to hear.

"Thanks for the coffee."

She nodded, muttering the usual platitudes; something along the lines of "Any time" and "Hope to see you soon." There was a whirring sound as he reversed around the barn. Or was the whirring in her head? She went back to the patio to gather up the mug and plates, feeling sick with suspicion; the optimism she had experienced chatting with Michael quickly evaporating in the wake of his disclosure. Archie often blamed his tardiness on parish council meetings. But if she thought about it carefully, had he actually *said* he'd *been* at a parish council meeting? Or had she just assumed he had? He was so often waylaid at the hospital that perhaps it was just that. Maybe he wasn't lying and there had been a misunderstanding. Whatever the explanation, Ino wasn't sure she cared enough any more to find out.

She went into the house and shivered. Out of the sun, it felt suddenly cold and so very quiet.

Archie

Cedar Avenue

Things are not the way I expected. The weather, for one thing, is so much colder. It was exciting at first but now it's just tedious. So many months of darkness, of grey. No hint whatsoever that there will ever be a spring. I'm told there isn't one; that one day to the next it's full-on summer. Impossible to imagine now, with temperatures plummeting all over again. Just when I thought the worst was over. The houses are well insulated but life is lived indoors. In winter, that is. Most of the shopping and entertainment are linked by underground malls, as are the university, Metro and office buildings. You'd like that part, like I told you.

Why don't you answer? I feel I'm repeating myself; that I have to in order to get a response. Or maybe I'm just forgetting what I've already written. There's no sense of continuity; no sequence. No cause and effect. I lose track of time.

You'd almost never have to go outside and get those dainty feet of yours slushy. You could probably pass a month without breathing any fresh air if you tried hard enough. And believe you me, sometimes you don't want to. The cold is so biting it tears into your skin and eyes, and before you know it, even your tears have frozen.

I've been so busy at the hospital I have no life out of hours. Other than the one I imagine us to have... the one we might have had. Oh, why don't you come?

Just leave – I promise...

11

Veronica
Geneva
April 2017

There was a knock at the door, but without waiting for Veronica to answer, Leila burst into the room. Hot on her heels, and virtually tripping over his own mules, was the Persian-born, Chinese-educated Indian who headed the VIP team of make-up artists (artistes, *p-l-e-a-s-e*) and personal shoppers, compliments of Gucci. Sometimes Veronica found Chaand amusing. His campness was highly exaggerated, as was his overloud New York accent (courtesy of the American School in Hong Kong) and experience in working private jets, but today his flouncing gestures and shrill "Nurse!" every time he saw what he perceived to be a designer calamity set her teeth on edge. The sound of chairs being scraped forward didn't help either; nor did the clattering of aluminium boxes as cables and extension leads spilled onto the marble floor.

"What I *really* want, Ms V.," Chaand was saying now as he lowered her firmly into a chair, "is to go into comedy. Stand-up comedy."

Veronica's eyebrows, despite the Botox, managed half an arc, as if to say, *Of course, what else?*

He threw up his hands. "I know, I know. But I tell you one thing. All this…" He executed a neat half-pirouette while his fingers traced a circle in the air. "Just material."

I'll say, thought Veronica. Part of her hovered above his conversation, submitting to the distraction of being pulled and prodded, turned this way and that. She opened and closed her eyes on demand, bent forwards, now back.

"Is that *Marni*?" Chaand swooped on an asymmetric necklace nestling on a velvet cushion. To Veronica it looked like a collection of plastic dinosaur teeth. "Oh my *God*! This retails at fifteen thousand *dollars* US! You just *have* to have it!"

"You think?" Veronica was sceptical.

"Absolutely!"

"Don't be absurd," interrupted Leila. "It looks terrible."

Veronica shot her PA a grateful look. It wasn't often that she valued the woman's candidness. Chaand's expression was indignant.

"*Totalement*," said Leila firmly in French.

"Well, obviously I'm not going to make her buy something she doesn't like," he said petulantly. "And if you don't trust me…" His eyes filled with tears.

"Of course I trust you," said Veronica, craving a cigarette now more than ever. If it weren't for her imminent speech, she'd nip out to the terrace, but there wasn't time. She'd even consider a quick vape. Would Leila…? A surreptitious glance in the woman's direction, all slick black Theory ankle-skimming front-tie shift of it, was enough to tell her that Veronica would be pushing her luck. She said a prayer invoking patience to stem the rising *im*patience she was experiencing in their company. Failing that, there was always the rosary. Mantra, mindfulness, call it what you will, a quick prayer often did the trick of calming her right down.

The Marni necklace landed with a velvet thud on her lap.

"I *really* want you to wear it," whispered Chaand when Leila's back was turned.

Oh, blessed be Joseph and all the saints… These people were supposed to *remove* stress from her life, not add to it.

Twenty minutes later, Chaand was still sulking, despite the fact that he'd managed to coax Veronica into a boxy Prada shirt dress. It wasn't a look that she usually embraced, but she felt suitably edgy and perhaps it was just the kind of image she should be projecting after all. Her nails were being lacquered 'Moroccan Tangerine', with Leila periodically making those ululating clicks Veronica found unnerving. She said another Hail Mary and turned once more to the vast windows, her back to Chaand. She fingered the tiny silver cross that was virtually invisible underneath her heavier necklace.

She often marvelled that she had managed to keep her faith – any faith at all. Her lips moved silently in prayer. She knew that this unknown fact about her (let alone the presence of the rosary she carried in her handbag) would come as a surprise to many of her colleagues. Actually, everything about her past would astonish her colleagues. It did her. Even as her lips ran through the prayer, her mind cast itself off the grid lines of the surrounding buildings to lurch down the tramlines of memory.

Yes, who indeed would have thought that it was religion that had saved her, albeit not in any conventional sense? Veronica had been liberated from the drudgery of her existence all right. She, not God, had illuminated a shining path not to the shedding of material things, but to their acquisition. In fact, her life outside work was dedicated to the glorification of the brands that spilled from her cupboards. Sometimes of an evening, she would potter in her dressing room (or *rooms* – she'd had to take over another guest room to accommodate her many clothes), positively salivating over the beautiful tweeds and silks and fur. She worshipped the semi-precious stones that she'd purchased when she started out; the more expensive Cartier gems as her career took off. No, no altar candles could replace the delicious smell of Hermès leather. There was no ecstasy, no long night of the soul greater than seeing a coveted bespoke handbag emerge from layers of tissue paper and out of a box exquisite in its own right. No incense could dispel the stench of poverty quite like the aroma of luxury, of privilege, and forever-and-ever-amen expunge the mineral stench that was Schumacher, Ontario—

"Jump!"

Veronica was suitably startled.

"Oh, not *you*!" tinkled Leila, her heels trip-trapping across the marble floor as she directed Gucci dressers into the hall and catering staff away from the beautiful dresses hanging from portable clothes rails, texting all the while. Her thumbs bobbed up and down in much the way Veronica had played the children's game... how did it go? *Fly away, Peter! Fly away, Paul! Come back, Peter! Come back, Paul!* Where exactly was her mind today? It kept wandering off through caverns measureless to man... down to a sunless ice rink...

"Jump!" the voice commanded. "Higher! *Higher!*" Her trainer's voice cut through the silence, as crisp and scratchy as the sound of her blades lacerating the ice. "I said *higher*! Double Axel! Let's go!"

Drajica had spiked herself once already. Blood pooled around her left ankle and cold air rushed up her leg through the hole in her tights.

"Again!" The voice reverberated round the rink.

"So tired." With a start, she realised that not only had she spoken aloud, but that the pathetic, whimpering voice was hers too.

"What was that!" It wasn't a question but a statement of incredulity and disgust.

"I'm cold," she sniffed, feeling sorry for herself. Her cheeks stung, and she alternated between feeling hot and clammy and clammy and cold. Her lips were chapped; her tongue flicked over the rough skin. Her limbs still ached from hiking through the snow from her shack to the McIntyre Rink. It was a rink that still relied on natural ice. She glanced up at the large, round face of the clock set above them in the centre of the arena. It was 4.15am, and the wind whistling straight off the lakes and through the tin mines splayed her like so many icy tentacles.

"We are never tired and we are never cold, Drajica. Again."

Drajica took a deep breath. At that moment she hated skating as much as she hated her trainer, Dom Selebj, a Croatian-speaking first-generation Canadian like herself. In fact, she hated everything about this godforsaken mining village that wasn't even sixty years old. But she especially hated (and didn't thank) its founder, who had gifted McIntyre miners thirteen dollars' worth of coupons per month to allow them and their families use of the facility. At the opening ceremony she had heard the great Mr Bickell pronounce, "The pick-and-shovel man must know that he is every bit as welcome here as the highest mine executive." Noble words, but they had done nothing to dispel the shame of knowing that she had sprung from the former. But the reminder that she was a miner's brat was enough to reinvigorate her with new energy.

"Camel spin."

Drajica set her shoulders, preparing to wind up. Preparation for the rotation which so many found counterintuitive – left hand outstretched, back flat, body parallel to the ice – came easily. She stepped forward, her inner core facing her outside skating leg (when gravity should make it do otherwise), and pushed into the entrance. Seamlessly, she turned ninety degrees on one foot, then the other, before rising up, arching but still holding on to one leg. Then she held out her arms as though holding an imaginary basket; expanded them wider as though dropping it. Triumphant, she skated away from the boards, her hair coming loose from its long plait. If there was a moment that made the pain and training worthwhile, that refuelled the compulsion to keep going, it was this: this gliding backwards at speed before turning into the next jump.

Out of her peripheral vision she spied row upon row of empty seats. Well, one day this rink and others far more famous would be crowded with spectators who were there for her and her alone.

She raised her head to the second-floor balcony, to the criss-cross of metal, a giant cobweb raked across the roof. Focusing on it, reaching for it, she skimmed the clean patch of ice and leapt. Legs and arms tightly coiled, she spun and spun before landing neatly, spiking the ground with her toe and coming to a perfect stop.

There was a slow clap. Elated, adrenaline pumping through her, she once again looked up to the balcony. Her trainer, too, had turned in surprise. Mr Bickell himself stood in the director's box. He was a small, portly man in a heavy navy overcoat. An astrakhan cap sat jauntily on thick white curls. He puffed on a cigar, the rich, exotic aroma curling through the air.

"Who's the kid, Don?"

Dom shuffled across the narrow, carpeted plank in his too-big galoshes to shake hands with the rink's owner, the wealthiest man in Schumacher. Mr Bickell always got it wrong and called him Don. Drajica stood still, trying to control her ragged breathing, glad she had worn her velvet skating dress with the Mary Stewart neckline, but very unhappy that her stockings were stained. She crossed her feet, hoping to hide her bloody ankle.

"What you doing here, Mr Bickell? At this hour?"

"Heading for early morning Mass is what, but as I'm early, figured I'd check on my little project on the way. See that it's being used." Bickell made an expansive gesture to the huge rink. "Ice plant next year, I reckon."

"Ah, that'd be fantastic, Mr Bickell, sir, it really would."

"Well," Bickell raised a jovial eyebrow, "can't have the other mining towns outdoing us on sports facilities, now, can we? Have to get more men shooting pucks, though."

"You like sport that much?"

Dom Selebj and Mr Bickell looked at each other in surprise, then down at Drajica. She flushed. Adrenaline pumping through her body from jumping was nothing compared to what her heart was doing now. But here was a chance to be noticed! With his fur hat and thick gloves, Mr Bickell was the most affluent-looking man she'd ever seen. He was someone whose attention she needed to attract.

"Apologies, Mr Bickell." From the viewing gallery, Dom made shooing gestures to the ice below, which Drajica ignored.

Mr Bickell, for his part, didn't seem so put out. On the contrary. "No need, Don," he said. "Miss…?"

Drajica approached the balcony, looking up, making her eyes wide and innocent. She blinked slowly a couple of times. While she gave the impression of doziness, her mind was whirring. She thought of the pictures left by former tenants pinned to the boarding-house walls; pages ripped from out-of-date fashion magazines. In fact, so out of date and fashion they were of the recently deceased film star Veronica Lake. But in those crumpled pictures the actress was still young and easily identifiable by her trademark curtain of yellow-blonde hair. "Veronica," she said firmly, imitating Lake's peek-a-boo stance. Drajica had been told once that hers was a look to drive a man wild. No one had specified his age. She added, "Harris" for good measure.

Dom's eyebrows shot to his receding hairline, but to his credit, he stayed silent. She didn't care. Veronica Harris sounded a whole lot better than Drajica Herak. She was fast realising that 'Drajica' wasn't going to get her anyplace (not soon enough, anyway), and Drajica – *Veronica* – was in a hurry. But if Mr Bickell picked up on anything untoward, he pretended not to notice. Drajica liked the way her new name sounded.

"Well, Miss Harris," he said, drawing on his cigar and smiling. "No, I don't like sport so much, but we organise sports and the miners think less about meetings and unionising, or about bars. You catch my drift?"

Not in her experience, thought Drajica. Not at all. The men she knew *only* thought about bars.

Mr Bickell unbuttoned his overcoat before extricating the fob of his pocket watch. It was secured at one end by a cigar cutter. "From my own mine," he said proudly, flashing the timepiece in front of them as if daring them to calculate its worth. It was shiny and smooth, mirroring the lower half of his face. Drajica nodded hungrily, following his movements. He emanated cleanliness (which was very close to godliness, as she very well knew), good food and wine. She could virtually picture the soft sheets he slept in, in the kind of house that was so overheated the men could walk about in shirtsleeves. She was overcome with a visceral need to escape her own house. She held his gaze; those grey eyes as cold and clear as cut glass. Her skin had the same translucent lustre as the ice.

"You a Catholic, miss?" said Mr Bickell.

Drajica blinked. Was she? She'd been raised one – the majority of Croatian immigrants were Catholic, and on Sundays they traipsed together in their brightly embroidered shirts and shawls to St Jakub on First Avenue. But even there she had wanted to shrink from the foreignness of them all. She was mortified by the plump women in their ethnic costumes; the ruddy-faced farmers; the thin, wiry miners, hard-working and stoical. She hated their suffering, their air of self-sacrifice, their fatalistic blanket of community that, even before they opened their mouths, set them apart. "I…" She swallowed. Dom's look could have cut a hole in the ice the Cree would have been proud of. She threw back her head. "Yes, I am, sir."

Mr Bickell puffed air through his lips and began humming. "Then grab your coat, honey; you can come with me."

What Drajica hadn't been prepared for was how much she had loved that first Mass with Tom Bickell. She soon discovered that entering any building, even a church, with a man like Bickell was an experience like no other. It gave her kudos. It gave her the security she craved. Let the women gossip; let them smirk all they liked – Drajica felt safe for the first time in her life. She felt like someone, not just the dirt-poor kid from the mines having to skate early because she couldn't afford the membership fee; having to rely on the good humour of a trainer like Dom. But it wasn't just being there with a man like Bickell, coming in from the freezing cold and being instantly warmed. She was soothed from the tips of her toes to her bleeding ankle to every tiny hair follicle on her head. The priest, intoning in English rather than the Serbo-Croat she switched off from, spoke to her as though she were the only person in the place; his words giving her succour and solace. The prayers wrapped round her mind, embracing her whole being to give her purpose and intent.

Bickell handed her a hymnal, which she accepted gratefully, greedily, as though it were a passport to freedom, which it sort of was. If she could be accepted here… Drajica watched carefully, noting the pages turned, miming the responses. With their eyes closed, women in smart fur hats and elegant fur boots rattled off prayers they'd learned by rote before they could read. She looked at the solid men in their astrakhan caps, knowing that, once outside, a mere flick in their direction would signal the arrival of a fleet of large, heated cars ready to ferry them and their families to spacious clapboard houses far removed from the smells of boiling cabbage and turnip. Here the incense was exotic and expensive, not the sickly, cheap, cloying stuff that was no different from the toilet water women in her community sprinkled on themselves before they went out of an evening. Here was a new world; an accessible world if only she played her hand right. Again, she was so desperate to become part of it she felt dizzy. Gone was the pain in her ankle. She glanced at the page in front of her, memorising a line at a time so that if she caught someone's eye, they'd think she too knew her catechism. She sank to her knees just as Mr Bickell did, rising just a fraction later so that he would appreciate her piety. She looked at the pretty walls – painted, though she did not know it at the time, to represent the Sistine Chapel.

Mr Bickell put a hand on hers to lead her back down the aisle. When later at coffee he introduced her as his niece, she didn't contradict him.

Drajica pulled off her apron, jamming it behind the cash register. From the moment she'd arrived at work that morning she'd felt jittery. She'd taken orders quickly, not lingering to chat as she usually did, her attention swivelling once again to the clock above the sink. She'd counted the minutes until she could officially leave, and now that the moment was upon her, she couldn't be ready fast enough. One hand holding her coat, the other felt for the Indian pouch of dollar coins she'd been saving for months. Holding on to the clothes stand, she shoved her feet into the fur-lined boots Nada from the community coffee shop had lent her. They were a couple of sizes too big and she'd stuffed newspaper in the toes to make them fit better. That wasn't the only issue. One of the zips was broken and the soles were so worn they left a trail of rubber as she walked. But the fur lining and trim were real and the leather soft, and Drajica felt as glamorous as any of the mining executive wives. She was certainly a darn sight prettier, with hair colour that didn't originate in a peroxide bottle and a figure not compressed by a Playtex girdle.

The muffled sound of a church bell chimed the hour as she left. Above waist-level ruched curtains, the windowpanes steamed up behind her as if she too were dissipating into the ether. Drajica made her way down the snow-banked main street. A snow plough hadn't been down it in weeks and the only way through the Porcupines had been on snowshoes. Snow caked her lashes, frost clung to her cheeks. The tips of her fingers were already frozen in her sodden woollen mittens. But unlike at that morning's 4am practice, she didn't mind at all. The cold air hit her lungs, capable, it felt, of reaching every internal organ. She walked on, trying not to let her thighs touch, her scratchy tights irritating her skin.

And all the time she walked, she prayed, going over and over the Apostles' Creed so that next time she recited it in company, she would be word-perfect. The words were soothing: *I believe in God, the Father Almighty, Creator of Heaven and earth...* Never had she been so oblivious to the cold; to the difficulty of walking through virgin snow. Never had she enjoyed the quiet more; the deafening silence of grey snow clouds doing their utmost to confuse sky with the land's horizon. For a while there was only the scrunch of newspaper as her big toe rubbed against it to break the silence. Looking up, she spied a common redpoll, its pink breast outlined against the branch of a birch tree.

When she reached him, the Commissioner for Oaths Stephen Plank (or Stjepan Plosker as he was originally) was chest-high in folders, books and miscellaneous paperwork. Several ashtrays brimming with cigarette butts played leapfrog amidst index cards. Given the significance of the occasion, Drajica felt he might at least have cleared his desk. Nor did he seem too troubled (unlike Dom) by the fact that she was relinquishing her citizenship. *Their* citizenship. He hardly looked up.

"Yeah?" he said in English, not Serbian. A cigarette dangled from the corner of his mouth and ash had collected on his tie. His sleeves were held in place by clips. Just as well, she thought, as otherwise they too would have been stained by tobacco and ink. He seemed unmoved by the significance of the appointment, but not by her physical attributes. There was a glimmer of appreciation for her bright hair and glowing skin, but he was too busy to allow this to distract him for long.

Drajica spoke clearly – the first step to drawing a line between then and now. Stephen Plank didn't hesitate; seek to dissuade her as she'd half-expected he might. He called for his secretary, who appeared to pop out of a small cupboard. She dropped a lemon-coloured document bound in pretty green ribbon on top of the various bundles already open in front of him. Three paragraphs later (*I absolutely and entirely renounce and relinquish and abandon the use of my former name of Drajica Marija Herak and assume and determine to take and use from the date hereof the name and surname of Veronica Harris... And I make this solemn declaration conscientiously believing the same to be true and by virtue of the Ontario Evidence Act*), she was reborn. She stammered her thanks, emotion almost getting the better of her. But once outside in the snow again, she pulled off her hat, throwing her arms wide and, in the last spontaneous gesture she would ever make, gave a yelp. Some janitor's transistor radio was purring Elton John's 'Goodbye, Yellow Brick Road' with a gentleness more suggestive of Miami, white pianos and bell-bottoms than decrepit boots and snow blizzards.

Veronica made a little skip, halfway between a ballet frappé and a skater's figure of eight. Inside she was singing, opera-singer loud. *Goodbye, yellow brick road...* And somehow, somehow, very soon she would also say goodbye forever to Bruce Avenue, South Porcupine, Northern Ontario.

12

Emil
Barcelona
May 2017

There was a commotion outside. In recent days the rumble of discontent that had gathered momentum over the past months had grown into barely contained anger. The regional government had set a date for a referendum. Catalonia, and not Madrid, would determine its fate. It was also a given that this resolution should be peaceful and democratic. But right here in front of Emil's bakery, and under the banner of Catalan separatists, all manner of '-ists' vented their spleens. Emil stood smoking a cigarette under his own banner – the 'MA' canopy – watching as members from the (historically neutral, now hysterically pro) LGBTQ community shouted their support for the Catalan President. Emil wondered vaguely what percentage of polo players might fall into that category. Probably higher than he imagined. But though he was making light of the demonstration (it was in his nature not to take anything too seriously), even he could feel the growing tension of the people.

Surrounded by members of the clergy, Emil's cousin had also emerged into the sun. From across the Plaça de Sarrià, and across a sea of bobbing heads and banners, they acknowledged each other with a slight incline of the head. While probably sympathetic to each other's cause, the various groups could not have contrasted more extremely, but then Emil and Rafael were also light years away from their former selves. There was something tragicomical about their current situation, which was so far removed from their polo-playing days that Emil had to refrain from laughing out loud. Their entire year had once revolved around polo as they moved around the world from Deauville to Palm Beach to Palermo, chasing chukkas. Rafael's robes billowed around his ankles and Emil inwardly shook his head in disbelief. Then, the only billowing skirts skimming calves had been those belonging to the young beauties who stumbled onto the field to tread in the divots. There really was something hilarious and demented about it all… And yet… and yet… in a way, only the name of the cause was different; the single-minded purpose and passion behind it wasn't so very different.

When a placard with sharp, polished edges caught him on the temple, Emil decided it was time for a drink. Wincing in discomfort rather than actual pain, he had time to observe what looked like preschool kids shouting slogans of "LGBTI!" and "Yes Scotland!" together. He got the Scottish thing (Catalans were drumming up support from *any* country with a secession movement), but what did the 'I' stand for? He'd only just wrapped his head round the 'LGBTQ' bit. And for a moment, as he went into his bakery to fetch a beer, he thought not about people with sexual identity issues or preferences, but about the wider issue behind which they united in solidarity.

He remembered the plastic stand-up globe Abuela had given him as a small boy. He knew that then there were ninety-five sovereign nations; now, at the last count, there were 195. On that map the USSR still existed and Macau belonged to Portugal. He hit the beer bottle on the side of the counter to flip off its cap. This desire for change and independence was nothing new – boundaries were relocated all the time and redrawn; *renamed* if they were lucky. If they weren't, they disappeared altogether. But he wasn't about to share these reflections with this increasingly volatile bunch.

Emil took a swig of beer, saluting the spot where he imagined Rafael to be. His cousin had quickly become engulfed by the crowds swarming through the police barricade. This kind of thing was anathema to Emil. At the age of these youngsters, he and Rafael would no more have thought of joining a demonstration than they would have thought of riding a badly broken pony. But then, not many suffered from their particular kind of obsession. And obsession it was. From the moment Emil could trail a foot mallet behind him, he had felt the fire in his belly and known that he would do anything to play. An addict on crack cocaine couldn't have hankered more for a fix than he had for just one more chukka at the end of a season. The savagery, the risk-taking, the adrenaline rush suited the wildness in both him and his cousin. It was in their blood. The fact that participating in this ancient game demanded a special kind of courage only added to the feeling that they were chosen warriors surging forward to do battle. Even now he accepted that nothing would ever replace the thrill of galloping at over thirty-five miles an hour along pitches the size of ten football fields, knowing that at any moment he could die. Contemptuous of danger! Pah! They defied it, they taunted it, laughing in its face. Yet here they were now – one a baker, the other a priest. The one dealt with hysterical schoolgirls across an ice-cream counter when once they had screamed at him from the stands, while the other had traded a glitzy international crowd of bored beautiful people looking to be distracted for... well, maybe there were similarities after all.

And this youth that was all around him today – this *divino tesoro*; divine treasure? Well, it was absurd all right, and it was divine, and it was only now that Emil understood. Now that he was no longer young. Having loved and lost. He thought again about the first time they'd met. He took another swig, feeling mellow, ignoring the shouts, the bangs on his window, the police when they arrived. He lit another cigarette, warmed by the memory. And the filth that had come out of that angelic mouth! Where she'd picked up those expletives in the short time she'd been in Spain, he could only guess. What in his opinion was far worse was the fact that the kid couldn't even ride! Nor did she like horses! Up until then he could honestly say he'd never met a person who couldn't or didn't. And all the while, Rafael was away with *his* girl… But then, that was par for the course.

Emil downed the rest of his beer, raised an arm in a vague gesture of support. It was time to set out the cakes and pastries for the *merienda* hour. Someone from this rabble was bound to be hungry sooner or later. If nothing else, this demo might be good for business, although he doubted it would appreciate the diversity of the bread on offer. This was a generation used to industrial sandwich bread and frozen fare that could be instantly warmed. It was also quite tasteless.

By association, his thoughts turned to the coveted Golden Crumb Award and how one day he would win this accolade for a bread that had weight, a crumb that was both moist and just a little bit rubbery, and a crust that was crisp and clean. He thought that although he had left an enormous carbon footprint in traversing the globe, one day he would redress the balance. Using stoneground flour from Salto he would create a product that was both sustainable and delicious. The rural world (never mind the political) might be vanishing, but under his watch its tradition of bread making would not. It was simply a question of *paciencia*; a great deal of patience…

Archie

Cedar Avenue

You say I don't read poetry. Well, I do. D. H. Lawrence for a cold evening to an even colder lover.

> When we get out of the glass bottles of our ego,
> and when we escape like squirrels turning in the
> cages of our personality
> and get into the forests again,
> we shall shiver with cold and fright
> but things will happen to us
> so that we don't know ourselves.
>
> Cool, unlying life will rush in,
> and passion will make our bodies taut with power,
> we shall stamp our feet with new power
> and old things will fall down,
> we shall laugh, and institutions will curl up like
> burnt paper.

13

Veronica
Montreal
No Date

She noticed him immediately. Handing her dripping umbrella to the doorman and sidestepping both, she ran a practised eye down the length of the Palm Court. It was early for cocktails. Ensconced in deep velvet-upholstered chairs, couples drank tea from Herend china, the muffled sound of voices punctuated only by the tinkle of silver cutlery. Waiters in black, white-gloved and balletic in movement, glided from table to table, twirling doily-lined cake stands crammed with dainty finger sandwiches and tiny pastel-coloured iced cakes. With the requisite harp playing in the background, plushness and wealth oozed from the buttermilk combination of ivory and pale gold. Sofas the width of a small train compartment separated hotel guests from the rest of the tea drinkers, and on her right a mahogany bar slid sleekly beneath row upon row of glass shelving. At the very end, a short flight of stairs, flanked on either side by huge indoor palms, led up to mirrored double doors and a more secluded seating area. Painted ferns in the softest sage green formed a border along the ceiling, arching towards the centre.

Veronica groaned inwardly at this inviting tableau. Her feet were wet through, though miraculously, her hair had managed to stay sleek. She patted it carefully, just to make sure that there were no lingering frizz-inducing droplets. Like some Caesar looking down disparagingly on the hoi polloi, and elevated by dint of sitting (or rather sprawling) on a high-backed stool, the man at the bar was the only drinker. Tumbler halfway to his lips, he paused, appraising her candidly as their eyes met.

She felt a lurch of desire – so unfamiliar as to be almost unrecognisable. Afterwards when she tried to analyse her reaction, she couldn't even say what it was that had attracted her to him in the first place. It certainly wasn't his grooming. This man's shirt tails were untucked, the top buttons undone, his tie curling, eel-like on the counter, and his jacket tossed on the seat beside him displayed a vibrant silk lining – a wanton splodge of colour against the neutral shade of the salon's decor. He would have looked like a bum but for the obvious quality of his beautifully cut clothes. Veronica noted appreciatively that these were no Renfrew concessions or 'Armani for Saks' purchases, but the real thing. 'Milano' was stamped in silver thread on the inside of the jacket's collar. 'Modern tech hub meets European-inspired charm' were the words used to describe the Ritz-Carlton at 1228 Sherbrooke Street West. They summed up Archie Agnew perfectly.

Her nostrils flared as they only did when she was sexually aroused. She adjusted the comforting bulk of her brand-new Fendi Zucchino under her arm (she'd smirked when she first purchased the handbag, thinking the sales assistant had mispronounced 'zucchini') and unwound the very long satin tie of her Dolce & Gabbana leopard-print blouse. The faint smell of new kid leather, the heavy aroma of Mexican tuberose, and the even headier perfume of an unlimited trust fund propelled her forward. She walked slowly towards him as though he were the only person in the room; as though she were undressing for him alone.

One leg acted as a propeller as he too swivelled towards her.

14

Ino
Winchester
May 2017

The fact that Archie was home at a decent hour altered Ino's mood, though whether it was for the better, she hadn't quite decided. From the kitchen window, she observed him alight from his car without the usual prevarication. The bonus was that it didn't look as if he'd stopped at the pub on the way home either. She hastily set the table, shifted the vegetables to the heating oven, and untied her apron. Pulling on her fringe to cover the bruised side of her face, she took a deep breath before going outside to check on Calypso, who was happily playing on the lawn with Oreo. The male rabbit had a pink bow tied round his tail and Calypso had redecorated his hutch with pink cut-out hearts. Ino had bought the pet a new water dish in the shape of a carrot. She could hear Calypso humming to herself. Ino stopped herself from doing the same. On the face of it, this was a happy domestic scene. And from where she was standing, Archie looked like any other forty-something middle-class British male. His suit, though crumpled from the drive home, was a pinstriped bespoke Savile Row. His tie (undone and halfway round his neck) was silk, and his brogues too were bespoke. But he wore good clothes out of necessity and not because he was at all vain. His blond hair was ruffled, framing a lightly tanned, handsome face.

Archie, ignoring Ino, went directly to Calypso, flopping down on the grass beside her with no heed for his beautiful suit. This was something that had once appealed about him: this complete disregard for clothes and an unfussy approach to dress. It was in complete contrast to her Spanish family's obsession with appearance, opulence and almost baroque excess. In fact, everything about Archie's uncaring attitude was refreshing. It had amused her at first that all he ever wore was his suit – weekends included. "Charming and eccentric," Veronica had called it, virtually drooling as she described her son-in-law. Ino now thought it something else entirely. But at the time it was indeed, if not alluring, then different. Ino was always amazed that her cousin Rafael and his cousin Emil could spend so much time with their tailors, or shopping for riding boots and polo gear, or getting ready to go to a nightclub. Archie was into his suit faster than it took her to step into the shower. He dressed to attract women to other men, he used to say when she teased him about his weekend get-up. Ino had loved that about him. It was becoming just about the only thing she still did.

But now, observing Archie's genuine delight in Calypso, Ino's eyes filled with tears. As she went back into the house, she felt a stab of self-pity and a deep nostalgia for what should have been. It was answering Michael's questions earlier that had triggered these feelings, she reasoned. She knew perfectly well that she couldn't change anything, and yet she couldn't help her thoughts turning inwards. Not that, as she had told Michael, it had been love at first sight, nor anything remotely like it, but she felt an enormous sadness for herself; for the utterly hopeful and innocent girl she had once been. Michael's earlier visit and his questions about Archie had made her marvel all the more at how things had changed between them – drink notwithstanding. Or had they? Had she just been oblivious to his drinking? Not thought it significant?

Mashing the potatoes, sprinkling salt and pepper and adding butter and milk, part of her wondered what she was doing even preparing a meal for Archie given what he'd done with the one the night before. What he'd done to *her*. But there was Calypso, she told herself. She must endeavour to keep things as normal as possible for Calypso. Draining boiling water from the various pans, feeling steam curling her hair, she stood back from the hot Aga. Water splashed onto the floor and she bent down to mop it up, noticing a cobweb tremble in the space between the skirting board and the dishwasher. Rising, perspiring gently, she remembered how annoyed the maid had been when Ino dripped all over Veronica's floor. Back then, dissolving snow had been the cause of her ire. Ino hesitated, pan in hand, ambivalent still about the first time she met Archie, the memory of which, when it surfaced, was neither consoling nor kind.

If tonight was warm, by contrast, the night she'd met Archie had been one of the coldest on record. In fact, she would never forget the cold in Montreal that year. She had taken a bus from her university digs downtown to visit her mother, who lived uptown in the affluent suburb of Westmount. Veronica was on secondment to ICAO, the International Civil Aviation Organisation; a branch of the United Nations. Ino had decided on a postgraduate degree at McGill in the vague hope that she might see something more of Veronica. If Ino was hoping for any sort of intimacy on her mother's part, however, she was quickly rebuffed. Veronica made it very clear that she had a new 'boy' friend and that, given their mutual work commitments, he was her priority. Surely the man was retired? Ino had made the mistake of commenting, because when she eventually met him, she would have called him more of an 'old man' friend herself. But it seemed that the relationship with the 'friend' might be on the wane, because when Ino asked after Ken, Veronica said he was in Vancouver. Ino's spirits had soared on hearing the news; delighted, childishly so, at the prospect of seeing Veronica on her own.

In her mother's honour, Ino wore a new khaki cashmere jumper that she knew suited her dark colouring. She hoped, too, that Veronica would approve of her slightly less formal look – she wore jeans these days. McGill wasn't the place for her Barcelona couture dresses; compliments of Abuela. She had pulled her hair out of its habitual ponytail – still a little on the collegiate side, according to her roommate (*That's okay; I'm a student again*, thought Ino) – grabbing the bottle of Rioja she had bought earlier to take with her.

It was already snowing as she headed out the door, but so far public transport was still operating as normal. By the time the bus dropped Ino in front of Cantor's the bakery on the corner of Sherbrooke and Grosvenor, thick wet flakes were falling heavily. Her casual updo was definitely an up-down, and pinpricks of ice stung her cheeks with painful precision. Every pore tingled, while her hands and feet felt numb. She hoped she wouldn't get frostbite. She wriggled her toes to keep the blood circulating, cursing her vanity at having chosen suede boots and a chic coat over more practical attire. She clutched the bottle of wine for support and, head bent, trudged up the increasingly steep incline to her mother's building. By the time she pressed the intercom buzzer she was panting and apprehensive.

"Come up!" barked Josie over the intercom, in a tone that was about as welcoming as a Viet Cong guerrilla surprised in a tunnel. Financial success had led Veronica to dispense with South American illegals and, in their place, employ domestic staff of Asian extraction.

Ino's spirits, which had begun to sink at that point, did a further dive as she took the private elevator up to the penthouse flat. By the time the lift doors opened onto the vast, square marble-and-glass hallway, she felt about four feet high and like a child once again. And, like a child, she stood helplessly looking around. The intimidating entrance hall was entirely lined with pink marble, giving it the feel of a beautiful, giant cube. Salto was grand but Ino had loved it. The castle, despite its vaulted ceilings, turrets and sweeping staircases, always felt welcoming. This place (which could have been mistaken for the lobby of an upmarket undertaker's) emanated an entirely different feel. Then, just as Ino was beginning to think that she had got the wrong floor, and/or that she should leave, Josie appeared, wizard-like, through the wall.

"Oh, coming in," she said, her narrow eyes disappearing beneath dyed purple eyebrows. With jet-black hair cut in a 1920s-style bob, Josie looked uncannily like the Billy Kwan character in *The Year of Living Dangerously*.

Ino's mind went off on a tangent. Linda Hunt was the first actor to win an Oscar for portraying a character of the opposite sex. Ino peered at her mother's domestic more closely. Could she actually be a man? Ino shivered, and with every passing second wished she'd stayed home. Hovering awkwardly, balancing on one foot, she tried to kick the ridges of snow from her heel.

Josie's smile faded as her glance trickled downwards. "Eww... so wet!" she screeched. "I bring towel."

"Oh, no, that's okay," said Ino. "It's so warm in here, I'll soon dry off." And it was warm: already she regretted wearing cashmere. She could feel her skin, which only a moment before had been tingling with cold, now prickly with heat. She stood inelegantly, legs akimbo. The hems of her jeans were soaked through and water streamed down her back.

"I bring towel," repeated Josie.

"Fine," said Ino quickly, not daring to contradict.

Josie's rubber-soled shoes once again disappeared soundlessly through the wall. This time, but only because she was looking for it, Ino could make out the faint outline of a door frame, and for a moment she caught a glimpse of a second, even larger entrance hall. *Like a Pyramid*, she thought wryly; *this must be the vestibule to the vestibule*. She had a flash of more marble (had Veronica's builder sold her a job lot?), gilt furniture and oversized bowls of orchids. This part was familiar only in as much as it could have been the decor of any number of beautiful rooms to be found in glossy magazines on home furnishing. But Ino couldn't have found her way to the master bedroom or beyond. She had no idea where the kitchen was; nor which of the many closed doors led to the drawing room. From the time she was fifteen, she'd never had her own bedroom in any of Veronica's homes. Still hanging on to her bottle of wine, Ino shifted her weight, hoping that Josie would hurry. She stood in a veritable puddle of melting snow, trying to mop it up as best she could with her feet. She was still wondering what to do when another invisible door slid open and with it came the tinkling sound of crystal and popping champagne corks and her mother's distinct low laughter.

"Oh, hello," said an unmistakably English voice as a good-looking blond man emerged, smiling.

Self-conscious and bedraggled, Ino muttered a kind of greeting in return. She was aware of powerful shoulders, a crisp white shirt, a general impression that made her uncomfortable. And now one eyebrow was raised, his face twisting with critical appraisal. Not in response to her, Ino realised, but to her mother's chatter that followed him from the room…

Calypso's chatter now stalled that memory and Ino resumed the task of placing plates in the warming oven before going over to the window from where she had a clear view of her daughter. Archie was now lying on the ground on his stomach, absent-mindedly plucking handfuls of grass and blowing the odd dandelion head. He looked like an overgrown toddler, or maybe a beached seal. In answer to Calypso's insistent questioning, he would roll from side to side and then, without moving his lower body at all, lurch at her unexpectedly. Calypso skipped around him, squealing with delight as she ducked under his arms. It irked Ino that Archie had become the very embodiment of fun (albeit drunken fun), while she had become the killjoy. She saw him crouching now, head tucked under himself as though he were praying to Mecca.

Calypso took a few tentative steps, daring herself to be caught. "What are you doing, Daddy?" Ino heard her say.

And then, when she'd prodded him a couple of times, he rose to his knees. "Shh!" he said in a loud whisper. "I'm an oyster."

Yup, he'd been drinking… It was bewildering how he could appear sober when he wasn't, and vice versa. Ino was becoming slack at recognising the signs. Unamused, she collected ivory-handled knives (knives that had to be washed by hand – Archie wouldn't eat from anything else) and laid the table. They were interesting first impressions; the opinions formed in those initial seconds of meeting.

Archie was tall, well built and well dressed. On the face of it, he should have set her pulse racing (except that he was blond and she generally preferred dark-haired men), but an overriding arrogance stopped him from being completely attractive. To her, at any rate. Her cousins were handsome creatures but an inherent humility gave them *duende*, or charm. They would make the plainest girl in the room feel the most beautiful; the most beautiful fall in love. Ino was certain that this wasn't the case with Archie. There was no one more important to him than himself; no work more meaningful than his own. At the time, though, she'd taken a casual remark to mean interest. And, sad to say, that had been enough.

"Good heavens!" he'd said, looking at her feet. "Is all that water coming from you?"

"Yes," said Ino, wishing a tsunami would wash her away.

"Who is it?" called her mother from the room behind him.

"I don't know!" the man called back, while insolently looking Ino up and down. She felt herself flush. "Some girl – probably a Jehovah's Witness."

"Yeah, they're a plague! How'd she get in? Must have been Josie. Tell her to skedaddle."

"You heard the lady."

The man tossed the comment in the same way that Josie, appearing a moment later, flung a towel over Ino's head and shoulders. Ino was momentarily hidden beneath folds of lavender-scented extra-thick terrycloth.

"Dry hair!" Josie's yap was muffled.

The towel was warm, soothing against Ino's neck, and seemed to possess extraordinary properties. Her hair was dry in no time. Distracted by the clean, enveloping whiteness, she smelled only the delicious, expensive scent of whatever washing powder Josie used. She'd have loved to keep the towel. She'd have loved to stay hidden forever, or at least until she could escape out the door.

"Hey, wait a minute…" The man's foot was a doorstop to Josie taking another step. "The kid needs to go. This isn't an excuse to dawdle!"

"Hair wet!" spat Josie in the kind of voice that made Ino wonder if she had a sushi knife tucked up her sleeve.

"What's going on?" Veronica's voice travelled through the wall, tight with impatience. "It doesn't take *that* long to fetch ice!"

"Just coming!" the man said to the wall, rattling his tumbler. "Be with you in a tick. Let her dry her hair, then," he said ungallantly. "Then adios."

Josie glowered; eyes narrow slits of loathing. "*You* adios," she muttered.

"What was that?" The man frowned, his whole countenance suddenly belligerent.

"Hello, Veronica," called Ino, taking a step forward. "It's only me."

"Boots!" yelled Josie, blocking her way. "Remove boots!"

"Oh, sure," said Ino, and then remembered she was wearing mismatched pop socks; one with a hole in the big toe.

"You're not…?" the man began without the faintest hint of embarrassment.

"Yes," said Ino.

"Really?" He looked doubtful.

"Yes, really," repeated Ino.

"You're not like your mo… Veronica."

"That's what they always say."

"Mmm…" For a moment he seemed so preoccupied by his own thoughts that she wondered if he'd forgotten she was even there. "I'm Archie," he said eventually. He shifted the glass to the other hand and held out his right.

"I'm Ino."

"Not Ina?"

"No."

Archie appraised her for a moment. "Catch you in a mo, Ino," he said.

Yeah. Ho ho, thought Ino.

"Arch, Josie can get the ice, for God's sake." Veronica was becoming tetchier by the second.

"It's okay. Just coming." And he disappeared through another segment of the marble wall. These conjuring acts were becoming tedious.

Josie hovered at Ino's feet, crouching on all fours. Every time Ino so much as breathed, she began a frantic swiping action.

"You don't have to do that," said Ino as the cloth swatted her ankles.

"Eek!" squawked Josie. "Look what you do!" There were more swipes before she made a neat acrobatic jump backwards, landing on her feet like a cat.

"Through here?" said Ino, taking a deep breath and motioning vaguely to the expanse of wall.

Josie shooed her away. "Oh, so much work," she muttered.

Ino padded determinedly towards the wall. Touching the stone tentatively, she was genuinely astonished when a door actually sprang open. She turned gleefully to Josie, but the maid was already on her hands and knees, applying some kind of wax to the floor.

Following the direction of voices, Ino padded down the corridor and entered the living room. There was an immediate hush followed by an "Oh, darling" of disappointment. Ino hoped it was in response to the wine she clumsily placed on a small side table rather than to her appearance. She was sweating gently. She felt completely disadvantaged in her damp clothes, frizzy hair, and make-up that felt as though it had slid halfway down her face. Her mother, on the other hand, was as beautiful and immaculate as ever. Her streaked blonde hair was sleek and expertly coiffed. She clearly hadn't trekked up Grosvenor in the snow recently. Her grey eyes were accentuated by the duck egg colour of the velvet sofa upon which she was draped wearing a silk kaftan that clung to her magnificent figure. Ino was reminded of the picture of Princess Margaret sprawled on a white sofa while on holiday in Mustique. Here, at least, it felt like the Caribbean with the central heating on sky-high.

Having taken a deep breath, Ino now exhaled slowly, looking around her with genuine pleasure. Wherever her mother lived, she recreated a drawing room in exactly the same aqua blues, with pale Persian rugs on polished honey-coloured floors. Large silver bowls of creamy roses were displayed on the baby grand piano, while mirrored furniture and large floor-to-ceiling mirrors emphasised a feeling of light and space.

"So," said Veronica, looking at Archie with adoring eyes as he came back into the room with their drinks refreshed. "You've met the infant."

"Not such an infant," said Archie, appraising Ino, but, on noting Veronica's scowl, he amended this quickly. "Not that she could be your daughter, anyway. I mean, you're far too young!"

Veronica laughed in a tinkly, pleased way. "Then meet Archie, Ino, all the way from England."

"Hello, Archie all the way from England." It sounded cringey even to her ears, and Ino wished, as she had done ever since ringing the doorbell, that she was back in her hall of residence.

"And is she in school?" asked Archie, ignoring Ino and directing the question to her mother.

Veronica tapped the edge of her glass, a brightly polished nail as translucent as the crystal, and made a face, but it was Ino who replied.

"As in the North American definition or the Anglo-Saxon?"

Archie's face lit up briefly. It became animated once more after a glug of wine. There was an awkward silence. Ino could almost feel her mother balk at having to say that her daughter was actually at university – and not even as a fresher, but as a postgrad student at that.

"I'd say both," said Veronica after a while, and she and Archie laughed as if at some private joke.

Ino was perched on the edge of a tiny boudoir chair, feeling as though she were back in kindergarten, let alone school. Her feet were tucked under her. Her legs were cramping, and she longed to stretch out and wriggle her bare toes on the beautiful, shimmering rug. The metallic tones of platinum and taupe combined with the palest buttermilk and sea green gave the textural design a glamorous edge. But then, everything in the room was glamorous, effortlessly so, including her mother. Ino tried rearranging herself in a similar pose but only succeeded in wedging her knees uncomfortably on either side of the low chair. Nothing was going to compare favourably to the elegance of her mother reclining on velvet.

Only Archie sitting on the sofa beside Veronica spoiled the gorgeousness of the picture. In his stocking feet, like Ino, and clutching his wine glass as though it were a baby's mug, he suddenly appeared comical and completely harmless. He was also younger than he'd seemed on first appearance – much younger than her mother, at any rate. She wondered whether Veronica had asked him if he knew that Leonard Cohen was from Montreal. It was practically the first thing she asked anyone. Ino suppressed a giggle.

"And why are you in Montreal?" Emboldened, she fixed him with a stare, just as Josie, gliding into the room, handed her a glass of champagne. Or rather, thrust it in front of her face. Everyone seemed to be drinking their own tipple: Archie red wine, Veronica vodka and Ino champagne, for which she was exceedingly grateful.

"Archie's a doctor," said Veronica, answering for him and in such reverential tones that Ino glanced at her sharply. "A very clever doctor too."

"Yes," agreed Archie. "To both charges."

Having thought him harmless, Ino liked him rather less with that remark. She took several sips of the deliciously cold vintage rosé (Veronica bought only the best) until she could feel the chill dissipate. In the buoyancy of the moment she even felt a tepid warmth emanating from her mother. "What kind of doctor? PhD or medical?"

"Both," said Archie.

"See?" said Veronica, suddenly swinging her legs off the sofa, downing her drink in one, and patting his arm. "Told you!"

"And you?" asked Archie, making no effort to move and watching Veronica.

Ino's mother frowned. "Dinner," she said, clapping her hands as though summoning a bevy of slaves, and annoyed at the attention being diverted away from her. "Can't tolerate cold food."

Later, even Ino wondered how it was that she had gone from disliking a man as intensely as she had Archie at first sight, to marrying him within six weeks of their introduction. Maybe it was because, despite his arrogance, he also seemed rudderless; genuinely homesick for England. It was a sentiment she misinterpreted as vulnerability. And while she was already 'home' in theory, she did miss aspects of the UK and so could empathise. She had completed her first degree there, after all, and initially they were able to talk about Oxford – she'd been at Christ Church, he at Oriel, albeit at different times. Through his eyes she began to revisit her own university days. She also began to think about the future. She hadn't thought beyond completing her own studies, while his time in Canada was a means to returning 'home'. The whole notion of 'home' had become a complicated one for Ino, but Archie had such a clear idea of his that he made it seem an enviable, worthy goal. The vision he presented for the future – the vision he intended to return to – became a captivating ideal that she might also share.

He would complete his internship at McGill and then return to Southampton. He would live in a cottage by the sea, he would work in the neurophysio department (he was a specialist focusing on that tiny part of the brain behind the eyes), and he – *they* – could build a life together.

For all his eccentricity, Archie appeared to be a good man, his ambitions altruistic and sound. He was ten years older than Ino, already established in a career. He appeared stable. Most importantly, he was the complete antithesis of her Spanish family and almost autistic in his lack of empathy. His anaemic logic, his lack of passion was what appealed the most; that and the fact that her mother loved him. Whatever the reasons – reasons she subsequently spent time re-evaluating – she accepted his proposal. Except that, when she thought about it, hadn't it been more of a *proposition* than a proposal? A theoretical proposition that went along the lines of "What would you say to…?" Perhaps it was simply to get far away from Montreal, knowing instinctively that the place wasn't quite big enough for mother and daughter.

Actually, she wasn't being completely honest. All those reasons were true in part, but the main one was that, by saying yes, she would draw a line over the past. By saying yes, she would make it impossible to go back. By saying yes, she would torture herself with loneliness.

Absorbed in her memories, Ino jumped when Archie appeared at the kitchen window. He didn't appear as drunk as he had earlier.

"Lovely evening," he said cheerfully. "Come on out, why don't you?"

Ino wiped her hands slowly on her apron. While she had no desire to spend one minute in his company, she did want to enjoy their daughter. It was rare that she could just enjoy being with her rather than doing things for her. Why not? It was a lovely evening and they were having fun. Ino wanted some of that light-heartedness too. She followed him out into the garden.

"Daddy!" cried Calypso in delight at seeing her parents approach her together. "Come back! I was 'plaining to you about Oreo's new hutch."

"I see, I see," he said, hunkering down again and kissing the top of her head. "My, he's grown. He's grown even in the time since I went to fetch Mummy!"

"Oreo is a she," corrected Calypso testily. "I've told you."

"Ah, yes, I forgot. Okay. *She* has grown, then."

"No, she hasn't," said Calypso.

"Oh, I think she has."

"No, she hasn't." There were tears in her eyes.

"You don't want her to grow?"

Calypso shook her head vehemently. "She won't be cute and little."

Archie looked perplexed as he stroked the rabbit's neck. "But she'll be loved, won't she?"

"Not if she grows up."

"Oh, Caly, Calypso," said Archie, reaching over to pull her to him. He began fondling her head, then sniffing her hair.

"It's okay," said Ino, interrupting; she hated when Archie did that. "Oreo still looks the same," she said reassuringly. "Oreo looks exactly the same. Supper's almost ready," she added.

"Not that hungry," replied Archie, his attention once more diverted to Calypso's head.

"Oh. O-kaay," said Ino tightly. She could feel irritation course through her veins; feel her cheeks grow hot with annoyance. But then, it was her own fault. What did she think would happen? She turned to go back to the house, but Archie, in a surprisingly agile move, jumped to his feet.

"Let's walk around the garden," he suggested.

"What? *Now?*" Archie rarely noticed the garden except to make sure that the lawn was seeded at the right time of the year, and that, when mowed, the stripes were exactly uniform.

"Yes, now – the food can wait."

She hesitated, her heart beginning to thud. He was right – food in an Aga could always wait – but he sounded suspiciously normal, and that made her wary. "All right," she said carefully.

"Just all right?" His tone was menacing.

"That would be... nice," she corrected quickly.

It was a lovely evening. A gentle breeze fanned the scent of lilac. The mulberry bush by Calypso's tree house was in bloom ahead of its full lush fruit. The fields all around them were green and fresh. Honeysuckle and rose clambered over the pink-washed summer house, completing the altogether idyllic scene. And yet, in his presence she was fearful; the mild throbbing along her collarbone and her cut lip reminders of the brutality of which he was capable.

"Come," he said, taking her hand.

Ino's fingers were limp in his. She could smell the antiseptic smell of his shirts – no thanks to her; they were laundered externally and delivered back beautifully packaged. She wasn't sure why, but she'd always been susceptible to laundry smells. Closing her eyes for a moment, it took her back to those early days in Montreal. The snow, the warmth, the plushness of her mother's apartment, the cosiness of his. And hope untarnished by what came later.

"The hedges are looking good," he said, motioning to the crisp yew rectangles.

"Aren't they?" She could have wept with gratitude. If their gardener had been around, she would have kissed him.

They advanced through a rockery of alpine flowers, over a wooden bridge to the orchard beyond.

He frowned. "But the apple trees..."

"The apple trees?" she echoed. "What about them?" She tried to keep the alarm from her voice even as she sensed the change in his, which had developed a menacing stealth. Ino followed his line of vision. The orchard was her favourite part of the garden. Espaliered pear trees covered the walls on the side that formed a boundary with the walled garden. Elsewhere there were cherry and plum trees, with the apple trees forming a boundary on the north side. Ample shade was provided by so much foliage, and it was a lovely place to sit with a cup of coffee.

"The crab apples have to go." His words fell heavily through the static air.

Her heart began to pound. *Say nothing!* warned a voice, but the more insistent the warning, the more painful became her heart's hammering. She withdrew her hand. "But I love that one," she said defiantly. At that moment nothing seemed more important than preserving her trees.

Archie, making binoculars out of his fingers, trained them on the orchard, pointing directly towards the setting sun. He stuck out his chin just as defiantly. "They're diseased. They have to go."

She felt giddy with a sudden fury equal to his own. "No."

Ino wasn't sure whether or not he'd heard her. He was looking at the house; then at the lawn sweeping up towards it. In the early evening it was beautiful, but not to Archie. That much was soon apparent. He was blinking furiously, his glacial blue eyes frozen behind palpitating lids.

"What the *hell*?"

Her whole body felt tense now; her shoulders and arms stiff. A pulse beating in her stomach was replicated in her heart. Anger gave way all too quickly to familiar anxiety. "W-what?"

"Those marks on the grass." Archie's hands were raised as though ready to wring her neck, the fingers sprawled, clawlike, the veins protruding from the skin. If she was shaking inwardly, he was shaking visibly, standing like a bear on hind legs, ready to claim his victim. She envisioned him as a cartoon with a balloon rising out of his head. The buzzing in hers was such that at first his words seemed muffled. "What. Are. Those. *Scars*?" He appeared to be speaking very slowly, modulating every sound.

"Scars?" repeated Ino. She followed his line of vision. "Oh, *those*! They're Michael's," she giggled nervously. "I mean, his chair's! Obviously."

Archie's mouth had begun to twitch, and his breathing was suddenly uneven. "There's nothing *obvious* here. Michael?"

"Yes, Michael. You know."

"No, I don't know." His lips formed a thin line. "Who the *hell* is Michael?"

"Why, Mich—"

Archie took a step towards her, gripping her forearm, and now Ino began to tremble. Her stomach heaved. She closed her eyes, anticipating the first blow. She took a step back, but to her astonishment, Archie dropped her arm.

"Don't take this the wrong way. And I'm asking you very nicely." He smiled at his own restraint, as though commending his immense self-control in trying circumstances. "I'll ask you just once. Are you having an affair?"

Ino was incredulous. "Am I… What?" she said disbelievingly. "Having an *affair*? With *Michael*?"

"Oh, so there *is* someone?" Archie's quiet tone had risen to a scream. "Not Michael, but someone?" He began pacing on the grass, walking in circles, stomping off, then coming back, shaking his finger in her face.

"No!" shouted Ino, forgetting all resolve to be calm herself. "No, of course not!" In spite of herself, tears of frustration pricked her eyes.

Archie glared as though her reaction were an admission of guilt. "You think I'm stupid, don't you? You think I don't know how you are. You think you can *trick* me?"

Ino was shaking her head. "Of course not!" She gulped air. "Don't be ridiculous! Just *listen*!"

"Listen? To what, more lies? You couldn't tell the truth even if you wanted to. You're just like your mother!"

"My *mother*?" Ino knew this was no way to argue; she knew she should appeal to his logic, to his common sense, to anything other than this emotional balderdash, but she could only respond viscerally. She was so tired of it all. She *wanted* to strike back.

"What's there to hear? The evidence is there, plain as day." His face was apoplectic.

"What 'evidence'?"

"Are you saying there *aren't* lines on the grass? Well, are you?"

"No!"

Archie gave an unpleasant little laugh. "Oh, you are crazy! Can you really stand there and say there aren't any lines? Can you? *Can you?*"

"Oh, please!"

"So, you won't answer? You refuse to answer?"

"I don't believe this," she muttered.

Again, that cruel little laugh. It was at times like this that she thought he really was insane. Archie grabbed her by the scruff of her neck, forcing her to face the lawn and see the offending tracks. "Are there or are there not marks?"

"Yes, but—"

"Yes! Exactly. So, you're a liar too – contradicting yourself."

"This is ridiculous!" screamed Ino, as much to be heard as to vent her feelings. "The lines are Michael's: his chair – his wheelchair!"

Archie looked at her, calm now, as if to say, *See what I have to put up with?* "Oh, so now he's disabled."

"He *is*!"

Archie shook his head. "Look, you bitch," he said hoarsely. "I see so-called 'disabled' people all the time! In fact, most of the pathetic people I see every single day claim to be disabled and not one of them is! You think you can pull that one on me, you slag?!"

"Mummy, Daddy!" called Calypso. "Why are you shouting?"

"Stop it!" hissed Ino. "Stop it now! Keep it together! Do *not* do this in front of your child!"

"Why? You don't want her to know the truth about her mother?" shouted Archie.

"Mummy!" called Calypso. "Why are you being mean to Daddy?"

Archie smiled triumphantly. "You see? There's nothing more to say. Guilty. Guilty slag. I always knew it. I knew it the first time I saw you in your tights, waving your legs at me provocatively. Your mother did her best, but really…" Yet again he shook his head as if there was nothing to be done with a case such as hers.

Ino, astounded, fought back tears, unable to speak.

"I want you to know that if I catch you with that… that *Michael*, if I see his fucking tracks on *my* grass again, I will divorce you."

Archie

Cedar Avenue

*I know congratulations are in order but you know how I can't bring myself to felicitate you for something that should be **my** happiness. How could you have been so cruel? To think that you could be here, I could be there, that we could be in this together. Not suffering apart as you are, as I am, and separated by so many seas and oceans. I don't even remember why we quarrelled. Do you? **Can** you?*

I came to you – I told you I was ready; that I could move on. That it was time. But you had done that already, hadn't you? In the very short time we were apart, you had moved on. And now this. Part of me thinks it serves you right; part of me delights that this is happening. I mean, why should it be easy for you? Why should you know joy when I am in torment? Can you answer that honestly? But then I think of you, and your suffering is mine. And if I do, it is quadrupled, multiplied a thousand times, and I want only to take care of you. And from a professional point of view, I want to be tender, to administer, to love…

15

Rafael
Barcelona
May 2017

Padre Rafael stood behind the elaborately carved pulpit to deliver his Ascension Day sermon. There was the usual rustle of tissues and the flick of fans from the old ladies in the front pews, then the gap left vacant between them and the younger families, and finally the intermittently seated youths who comprised the rest. When Padre Rafael was a boy the men wore chinos, button-down shirts and loafers (without socks) to church; their sons were small replicas, their hair combed back with cologne. Women and little girls donned their prettiest dresses and were shod in ballet flats. Today it was virtually impossible to distinguish between the genders. The young were in hoodies and platform trainers, looking as if they'd stepped out from a *Pokémon* cartoon.

En cima, it would have been heartening had these heads been bowed in contemplation, but Padre Rafael knew better. Few were paying him much attention, and he knew exactly what the glint of blue light coming from under a carefully positioned hymn book represented. Still, he supposed he should be grateful that any young person had turned up at all – holy days and days of obligation were observances of the past.

Padre Rafael looked at his prepared script: four pages of neatly typed print. He had already decided that he would stay away from politics – his church looked like a gigantic birthday present as it was. La Estelada fluttered from anything that it could be tied to, and that particular tide would take everything in its wake no matter what *he* said. He could appeal for calm, for logic, for perspective, for patience and for *time*, but it wouldn't do any good. He could, more importantly, begin by stating that this day marked an earlier Christian festival around 68 AD (or CE as the books were now calling it). He could say that ten days before Pentecost (which, incidentally, meant 'fifty' in Greek), Ascension Day marked the fortieth day of Easter when Jesus took his disciples to the Mount of Olives and – whoosh! – ascended into heaven. He had also been going to talk about the parable of Nathan but, when he reread it, had remembered that he had never fully understood it, and if *he* didn't, he could be pretty certain his dozy congregation wouldn't either.

He folded away his notes and, ignoring the older ladies, focused his attention on the youths at the back of the church. "There is shocking proof," he said in his no-nonsense '*dale, dale*' polo voice, "that we are all naturally good. And by 'shocking', I mean literally, as in the use of MRI scans and electric shock treatment. Sartre's position, that man can just as easily bend towards evil as he can good, is turned on its head by a recent study coming from England."

To his amusement, there was a rustle from the back benches. *That's woken 'em up*, he thought, pleased.

"Since long before the Mount of Olives," he continued, wishing he could light a cigarette and have a proper discussion, "philosophers have asked the question: why do people usually choose to do the right thing? I say 'usually' because I know the smart ones at the back will argue that history – recent history alone – attests to just the opposite. But scientists in England claim to have found an answer. An answer that lies in the physical world, not the spiritual one." He paused, leaning into the lectern. "Scientists using magnetic resonance imaging and electric shock observed volunteers' brains as they made their decisions. They recorded a region of the brain called the striatum being activated. You see, when we make decisions, a network of brain regions calculates how valuable our options are – ill-gotten gains evoke weaker responses in this network. In other words, at a physical level at least, decency is found to be more satisfying than deception."

Padre Rafael paused, noting the effect of his words: young people had stopped fidgeting, and the spark of light from mobile phones and iPads on the right side of the church had extinguished completely.

"Their findings would explain how it is that most people would rather *not* profit from harming others. Findings suggest that the brain internalises the moral judgements of others, simulating how much others might blame us for potential wrongdoing even when we know our actions are anonymous."

Padre Rafael puffed out his cheeks as if blowing imaginary smoke rings. "The desire to do good is underpinned by an ontological argument that we should all try and conduct daily. Which brings me on to what I call 'Selfism.'"

He made a face, as though preening himself in front of his mobile. There was a titter. He held up a hand to silence the slightly hysterical giggles that had begun with the girls in the penultimate pew.

"'And what exactly is Selfism?' I hear you ask. 'Is it even a word?' Not sure, but it should be! I'm using it, anyway." Padre Rafael smiled, fixing his tawny eyes on one of the young matrons. To his amazement, she coloured prettily. The subsequent rush of pleasure this afforded him made him guiltily aware not only that pride was a venial sin, but that this lapse on his part demonstrated precisely the very thing he was trying to get across! "Selfism," he rushed on, "is the complete obsession with self. The taking of selfies being the least of it! The excruciating and quite frankly boring minutiae of daily life are then made public. Does all this bring a sense of fulfilment? Of happiness? Of course it doesn't, because happiness is now contingent on how many 'likes' a post generates. But this has to stop. *Pro!*" he said in Catalan. "Enough! Are we so weak that we need constant affirmation as to our existence? Because that is what it is. Constant affirmation.

"We don't need a thousand likes to know this! We exist while our brain functions. We exist, and we will continue to do so long after our breakfast preferences have been tweeted or Snapchatted or TikToked or whatever new communication is invented to allow us to *not* communicate. We know that we exist," he repeated, casting his gaze around the congregation and noting with satisfaction (pride again!) that the young were captivated, "because our brain tells us so. But we know more than this. We know that we, as humans, have an inherent desire to do good. And by 'good' I mean not 'the good I would but the evil that I would not, that I do', but 'good' pure and simple. I'm not talking about what we may have *intended* to do and somehow it all goes wrong; I'm talking about the *impulse* to act well. We know that generosity and altruism are governed by a specific region of the brain, and that it works better and more naturally in some than in others. So, do not be dormant, my young friends! It is not enough to exist only in the mind's eye of another. I am not asking you to believe in dogma, not in Jesus's literal ascension, but I am asking you to have faith. We must all have faith."

Padre Rafael's voice dropped to a stage whisper. Had he blasphemed? He may well have. The horrified faces of the aged women in front of him gave him the impression that he had. Perhaps he shouldn't have said 'literal ascension', but come on! It was a bit much to ask people to believe *au pied de la lettre*, and yet that was what he must do, of course. It was what was demanded of him.

He closed his eyes, crossed himself, and hoped that the dowagers were distracted by his contrite face and act of piety. "We must work on our existing faith," he said in his most convincing voice. "And make it stronger. My brothers and sisters, believe – just believe…"

"Well," said the beautiful woman as he stood in the sunshine, mulling over the impact of his sermon. "That was quite something."

"Too much?"

"Let's hope not."

He was silent because he could have said so much more, but then if he had, he might have talked himself out of a job. In terms of a reaction, he really didn't care.

"You don't recognise me, do you?"

Padre Rafael blinked. The woman could have been any one of the sporty groupies who hung around the polo club when he used to play there. She was of a certain age, and impeccably dressed in a sky-blue shift dress with a matching cashmere cardigan draped casually over her shoulders. Her tanned wrists sported gold bangles that jangled as they moved first to her hair, then to the jewellery at her throat. Her nails were freshly polished. She exuded discreet wealth. Now that he thought about it, her Spanish, though fluent, was slightly accented. Her blonde elegance reminded him of Abuela.

"I…" He shrugged apologetically.

"*Soy* Verónica."

And as she said her name, in the Spanish way, Rafael couldn't hide his surprise. *Of course!*

"De Monte Alegre," she added unnecessarily.

"I know who you are." He inclined his head over her proffered hand. "Señora." His lips settled on the air a good two inches above her skin, though he then kissed her cheek, and this time his lips touched her cheek.

"It has been a long time," she said.

They examined each other dispassionately, but both taking pleasure in what they saw.

"Wait for me," said Padre Rafael. Out of habit, he allowed his hand to linger in hers. "I will just finish here." He motioned to the thinning line of parishioners queuing to shake his hand. "And then we can talk."

Verónica de Monte Alegre nodded, also moving towards the sun, tilting her face to feel its strong rays, enjoying the balmy weather.

"So," said Padre Rafael when he'd blessed the last OAP, cooed over the last child, and agreed with so-and-so's mother that her son should study harder. "What brings you to Barcelona after so many years?"

"Why, you, Padre." Verónica de Monte Alegre smiled. "You do."

Afterwards, Padre Rafael would always think of Verónica as that creation of Flaubert's in '*Un Coeur Simple*'. But he would regard her with rather less compassion than that writer had in observing, '*Elle avait eu, comme une autre, son histoire d'amour.*' He found it hard to believe that Verónica de Monte Alegre's heart was ever simple; nor that she had ever experienced a true love story. Sitting with her as he was doing now, he felt it prudent to discover what the *vipera* wanted before inflicting any more pain on his cousin Emil by announcing her visit. In the Calle Petritxol, the most famous of famous streets of the Barrio Gótico, Padre Rafael also marvelled at how well he could mix pleasure with pain. He dipped fat, crispy churros into a steaming bowl of thick hot chocolate while his aunt by marriage, Verónica Harris de Monte Alegre, sipped green tea.

But then, of course, she must have done, he reflected as he bit into his churro and contrasted the merits of it versus their home-made version. She must have had an *histoire* once. Well, he knew she had, because Ino was the product of, if not love, then what? An experiment? An unsuccessful one on Santiago's part, that much was known. The detail was all Verónica's. As he diverted her attention, Rafael observed those extraordinary grey eyes, wondering at how easily she must have captivated his uncle, that lover of beautiful things, Santiago – the uncle who had taught him to play polo. A career diplomat, Santiago had met this woman when they were both working at the United Nations in New York. She had been his interpreter, and after a whirlwind romance they had married (or so she had said); then she had fallen pregnant and been widowed all in the space of a year. The fact that no one had ever met that offspring until Ino appeared in her two-tone Chanel slingbacks did not seem to have ever troubled Verónica. He cast a surreptitious glance over the rim of his chocolate. Or had it?

Rafael had to admit that he was curious. He would decide later whether or not he would even mention this encounter to Emil. Emil would want to know every detail while pretending otherwise. When he wasn't devouring his snack, eyes half on the sensual pleasure of the repast, Rafael found himself staring, looking for traces of his cousin in her mother. There was the same intonation of accent, but otherwise they were chalk and cheese; the one as dark as the other was fair. In much the same way Rafael had once compared Sol to Ino, he did so now with this woman and what he remembered of her daughter.

He took a final mouthful of thick chocolate – more a mousse than a beverage – and sat back in his chair. His belly, at least, was full. So, what could the enigmatic Aunt Verónica possibly want with him? It was never going to be a case of *Aunt Julia and the Scriptwriter*, that was certain, and he doubted it was to catch up on old times. The opportunity for that might have been at Abuela's funeral, but neither Verónica nor Ino had attended. He couldn't actually remember ever having had a proper conversation with Verónica, and it was years since he'd last seen Ino. The two women weren't on speaking terms, he seemed to recall. No, not 'seemed'; they weren't.

"I was delighted to hear you'd become a priest," Verónica was saying.

Padre Rafael almost choked on his last churro. It wasn't a compliment people generally paid him. In his youth he was known for his distinctly *un*priestly ways. "Do you mind if I smoke?" he asked for good measure, leaning his head on the wall behind him.

"Isn't smoking banned in Spain? Since 2011?" The grey eyes were steely.

Padre Rafael hesitated. As much as he would enjoy blowing smoke into this woman's face, his innate good manners dictated that he wait. "In enclosed spaces, yes." He flicked a gaze round the tiny restaurant.

"Not terraces?"

Padre Rafael shrugged.

Verónica's lips puckered. "A matter of interpretation, then?"

"A matter of *degree*. But of course, if you object…"

"No." She waved an impatient hand. "Go ahead."

Even with permission to do so, Rafael hesitated, rolling the tip of the cigarette between his fingers before tapping it on the tabletop to loosen the tobacco. "Delighted?" He referred to her earlier comment. "I'm surprised to hear you say that."

Verónica appraised him coolly, her manicured hands clasped round her teacup. An enormous diamond flashed on her left hand. On her right was a three-band Cartier Russian wedding band, and not from the pedestrian range either. Each ring consisted of a row of coloured diamonds: pink, yellow and white. It was a ring that retailed at upwards of forty thousand euros. In another lifetime, knowing this was the kind of trivia he and his girlfriends might have discussed. "Why? I'm a Catholic like you."

How little you know me, thought Padre Rafael. "Practising?"

"I was at church, wasn't I?"

Padre Rafael said nothing.

"Oh," laughed Verónica; a high-pitched, girly laugh that belied her… what? Fifty-five years?

He realised with a start that if he was ten years older than Ino, then this woman must only be some ten years older than himself. Was she flirting? No; he suspected flirtation wasn't something Verónica engaged in. He lit his cigarette at last, enjoying the first drag. He'd have preferred to be smoking alone.

"That was childish, wasn't it?" she continued. "I'm supposing you don't know much about English Catholics, then?"

Padre Rafael drew deeply on his cigarette, blowing a stream

of smoke out of the side of his mouth. He wanted to say that he knew even less about Canadian ones, but thought better of it. "Not a great deal. I did read that book once: *Helbeck of Bannisdale. Una agonía.*" He shuddered. "A veritable agony."

Verónica really laughed this time. She had beautiful teeth he couldn't help admiring. And no fillings. Any mercury ones must have been replaced. Yes, she was flirting, he was certain of it. "And by the redoubtable Mrs Humphry Ward, no less. I expected you to say *Brideshead Revisited.*"

"I read that too, or maybe I watched the television series, I don't remember. I have to say, Sebastian and his teddy bear…" He attempted his most engaging smile.

"Aloysius."

Padre Rafael smiled again, looking her straight in the eye this time. "*Aloysius – ay qué nombre!*"

"It's the Latinisation of 'Lewis', dear Padre, but I expect you know that. And there is, of course, the saint…"

So now he was 'dear Padre'. God forbid that she started on religious matters! He'd been surprised to learn she was a Catholic. He didn't recall her being particularly devout, but then when she'd known him, he hadn't been either. And look where that had got him.

"Yes, well, anyway. The boy and his bear always troubled me. We don't have this custom. You know, to take a teddy bear around with you – especially to Oxford." He rolled the 'R' in 'Oxford' in what he hoped was an amusing manner.

"That was rather the point."

An edge had crept into her voice, and to avoid further analysis of the sacred and profane memories of Waugh's Charles Ryder, Padre Rafael redoubled his efforts.

"You know, for a Spaniard, the pronunciation of these 'H's, Helbeck…" He pronounced it: "'Jellbeck' and 'Jumph-freee.'"

Verónica tossed her mane of golden hair. "Yes, yes," she said impatiently. "Not so easy, I know. But tell me: could you identify with Helbeck?"

Ay, this woman! Why the obsession with this character – this Helbeck? It wasn't as if the book was on anyone's general reading list! It was even most probably out of print. "He's certainly a complex character: the would-be Jesuit—"

"Marvellous, isn't he – the Jesuit, I mean? You're right, exactly."

Padre Rafael grimaced. "No, I don't mean that pest! I mean Alan Helbeck himself." San Manuel give him strength... She wanted to talk about the book? He'd give her the book! "Wouldn't Alan have become a priest if he hadn't that crumbling estate of his to worry about?"

"Well, yes, of course. He's a very devout man, courageous and principled."

Rafael raised his eyebrows. *Anyone out there? God, even? Are you listening?* She really was serious! "Principled? Mmm... in some ways, perhaps. Maybe the book is a little... how do you say... dated?" Which was an understatement! The book had merits, but it was a nineteenth-century novel and, if he remembered correctly, the Alan character was such a fanatic that he cut his sister off from the rest of the family when she married out of the faith. The book's themes centred on exactly the kind of religious fundamentalism Rafael abhorred.

"So, you *don't* identify with him?"

"Not at all," said Rafael. "I mean, how could I? Helbeck falls in love with a woman of completely opposing religious beliefs. This has not been my experience."

"Then you are lucky."

"It's not luck." Padre Rafael smiled. "It's circumstance. Spain is predominantly Catholic. Or at least it was when I was growing up. I know statistics today point to another story. But whether practising or not, Spaniards still identify as Catholic. Well, you've seen for yourself. But I have never believed in senseless self-sacrifice. Especially when it's in the name of Catholicism."

"No?"

"No," said Rafael firmly. He finished his cigarette and motioned to the waiter to clear the plates and replace the chocolate with coffee. He'd left self-sacrifice to others. And paid the price for it.

"But Helbeck shows how it is possible to practise one's religion intensely *within* a relationship," insisted Verónica.

Padre Rafael considered his aunt thoughtfully. "Correct me if I'm wrong, dear *Tia*," he said. "But doesn't Alan's fiancée commit suicide? Precisely because they are *unable* to reconcile their religious differences?"

Verónica frowned. "Yes, but—"

"No buts." Rafael held up a hand authoritatively. Women had always liked his hands; the backs less tanned than the wrists from wearing riding gloves for so many years. His fingers were straight too, unlike his cousin Emil's, who had broken most of them at one time or other. "Now, Verónica." He omitted the '*Tia*' this time. "You didn't come all this way to talk about religious differences in English novels, did you?" He was used to debating matters with colleagues and students of theology. It seemed pointless arguing with someone whose knowledge of religion seemed to have been gleaned through fiction. Unless, of course, the greatest fiction was being called into question. Somehow, he didn't believe Verónica capable of that.

Verónica moved an expensive bag – Chanel, if he wasn't mistaken – from the seat beside her and placed it on her lap. She opened a flap and pulled out lip gloss. He watched her slender, tanned fingers trace her lips. She really was a very beautiful woman. She snapped the bag shut – all eight thousand euros' worth of it – before depositing it once again on the chair beside her. "Actually, I did," she said, turning those clear, crystal-like eyes on him. Beautiful and clear and utterly devoid of feeling. "It's not very complicated," she said. "I've come to ask a favour."

Which wasn't at all what he'd thought she was going to say.

"All the way from Canada?" This time he was unable to hide his surprise. He lit another cigarette and put it to his lips, sucking smoke gently. "You could have emailed?"

"I'm living in Geneva now. Yes, I know. Second tour of duty. Different job." She waited for the words to impact but he wasn't about to give her the pleasure. He noticed a twitch of annoyance and took unpriestly delight in remaining silent. "I thought it was important," she explained impatiently. "Besides, I travel a lot. It's no big deal."

"*Estoy para servirle*," he said formally, though only he knew the level of sarcasm levied. He took steady breaths, holding the smoke in his lungs.

"I want you to speak to Ino."

"*Perdón?*" he said, exhaling so quickly that he began coughing as though this were his first time smoking a cigarette. Still spluttering, he then bumped the waiter's arm just as the poor man was setting an espresso in front of him. A thick, creamy line snaked along the white tablecloth.

Much to Verónica's annoyance, the waiter, grabbing a couple of napkins from another table, began ineffectively mopping up the spillage and making more of a mess in the process. In exasperation, she snatched the napkins from him, shooing him away.

"I'd like to speak to Ino too," said Padre Rafael. Verónica was still fussing with the tableware, piling the plates to one side (his included) and folding back the cloth. He couldn't help thinking that she'd make an excellent sacristan. He made his voice super agreeable. "One day," he said, because he was quite certain that Ino would not be wanting to speak to *him* any time soon.

The expression 'gritted teeth' was invented for Verónica. "Not 'one day,'" she said acidly. "Now. I need you to talk to her about…" But then she hesitated. Rafael had never known her to be anything but confident. Perhaps the woman was capable of feeling after all. But he wasn't going to make it easy for her.

"About?"

Still Verónica was reticent.

O-kaay, thought Padre Rafael, if it was going to be this protracted then maybe he should consider a little ice cream?

Although, he really was quite full... A bevy of women flashing past the window caught his eye. They were energetic and long-limbed, with the fresh, dewy skin the young never appreciate at the time. He sighed with feeling.

"About her marriage."

What *was* Verónica on about now? Padre Rafael was enjoying his cigarette, enjoying being in the very coffee shop he and Emil used to visit with Abuela for *merienda*, and now this! "Come again?"

"Her marriage." Verónica's mouth was a thin, intractable line.

"I see." So it was marriage guidance she was after. Which had never really been his thing. He was frequently called upon to intervene in all kinds of issues, but seldom that. The older generation was pathetically stoical, putting up with all kinds of nonsense, while the younger one wasn't in a rush to marry at all. In his opinion, it was the latter category that had a healthier attitude towards relationships. The young women he encountered didn't put up with anything much for very long. He wondered idly if the recipe for churros had changed. He would have to ask Emil. His had been ever so slightly sweeter than—

"I don't think you do."

Rafael fingered another unlit cigarette, rolling it in the palm of his hand. He inclined his head ever so slightly. "You're right," he agreed. "I don't. If this were the nineteenth century, I'd have to wonder if, like Helbeck, she hadn't fallen in love with an atheist? But it's not so..."

Verónica tapped the table with her lacquered nails. "This is no time for jokes. That would almost be easier. No, she married a Catholic."

"Ah..." He was beginning to get the measure of this woman: strange and familiar *a la vez*. But he would never have had her down as a fanatic. "And I suppose she married that most precious of things: an *English* Catholic?" He couldn't keep the sarcasm out of his voice, but Verónica seemed not to notice.

She nodded. "Thankfully, we're not talking about a mixed marriage."

Padre Rafael's eyebrows shot up at the term 'mixed'.

"But she's not a good wife," she said scathingly. "She's not a good Catholic." The beautiful eyes had shifted to anthracite. A vein pulsed at her temple. Her entire body was tense.

Rafael added another sachet of sugar to what remained of his tiny cup of coffee. He couldn't be bothered to order another. "You seem very concerned."

"I am! I *am* concerned!" Her voice rose shrilly. "What mother wouldn't be, seeing her throw it all away?!"

Padre Rafael stopped rolling his cigarette, downed the coffee (more of a burnt glaze than a drink) and sat up straight. The chair, too, seemed like a leftover from his childhood; hard and wooden. "Throw away what exactly? I'm afraid I really haven't kept up with Ino. I have no idea about her spiritual life, or indeed any aspect of her life. Besides, don't you think it's a little late to be interfering?"

"*Interfering?*" Verónica's eyes were piercing. Padre Rafael felt skewered between two steely pinpricks. "You're a *priest*! If you had any sense, you'd be worried too, if one of your flock had gone astray!"

"*Ay, Tía* Verónica," he began, thinking that by calling her 'auntie' he might appease her. "But that's just it: she's *not* one of my flock. I don't even know her! Not properly, that is. Surely it's her husband who should be concerned? Assuming there is anything to be concerned about? She has a little child, yes?"

Verónica's body was as toned as an athlete's, but her slender figure was less attractive up close when he could see the veins so close to the surface of her skin. "Yes! And going the way of the mother."

For a moment they stared at each other. He was the first to break the silence. "She has been baptised?" He didn't know what else to say in his capacity as a priest or otherwise. He felt uneasy discussing anyone's marriage, let alone his cousin's.

"No – yes. Yes, of course."

"*Bueno pues.*"

"There's no '*bueno*' in this. None at all."

"No?"

"No! You don't understand. Archie is a wonderful, wonderful man." Verónica's face suddenly lit up, softening it. Padre Rafael saw a hint of the attraction it might hold were she to care enough about anyone other than herself. Angry tears hung on her lashes. "He's so clever. He went to Oxford."

Padre Rafael frowned. "And Ino also, *verdad*?" He knew she had.

Verónica considered him as if he were demented. "She read *modern languages*. Archie is a *doctor*." She said it with utter reverence.

"With all due respect, *Tia*, so is Ino. I think she's actually a *real* doctor – medical doctors hold a courtesy title—"

"Don't be clever. Archie does proper work."

To his surprise, she reached for his hand. For a moment he thought she was looking for yet another napkin.

"He practises…?"

"He's a neurophysiologist. Professor of."

"Ah, I see." And he did. *She's in love with him herself.*

"I knew you'd understand."

Padre Rafael extracted his hand, wondering how on earth his aunt had reached that conclusion.

"She's threatening to leave him," she finished dramatically.

"Then… she must have her reasons." Padre Rafael was suddenly weary and ready to go back… he would have said 'home', except that his residence near the church was never that.

"What?" Verónica hit the table emphatically. "No! She darn well doesn't! How can she? She can't leave him!"

Rafael shrugged. "Why not? If she doesn't love him?"

"Padre Rafael, I am shocked! Shocked to the core! How can you say such a thing? You're a *priest*!"

Padre Rafael was shocked too, but by her outburst. So much anger beneath that cool exterior! He looked beyond her to the other clientele: a young couple talked quietly, their heads bent close; another sat in silence, stoicism oozing from every gesture in view of the husband's deafness. A child played a computer game on a tablet while directing the occasional well-aimed kick under the table at his sibling. An old man looked with cataracted eyes at nothing at all.

Rafael met Verónica's frustrated gaze. "Yes, of course I'm a priest." *For my sins…* "But I'm also a man, dealing with real people." *Not fictitious characters out of some obscure Victorian novel!* "Look, I don't know anything about this… this Archie. I last saw Ino when she was… what, nineteen, twenty? A long time ago, anyway." It *was* a long time ago, but how could he forget that awful, awful meeting in Oxford? Padre Rafael's English was generally perfect but he allowed a 'jes' to slip out while staring into the middle distance.

"Padre Rafael!" Verónica's sharp reprimand brought him back to the present.

"I can say, and I will say," said Padre Rafael, "that she must be sure of what she is doing. That she must know herself and know her heart, and above all trust in…" He thought of his earlier sermon; the one this aunt of his had heard. "And trust in an innate resolve to do good." He waved the waiter over. "After all, what else can any of us do?"

Verónica slammed the table again, only this time his coffee cup jumped from its saucer. He was beginning to think that if there was anyone needing help, it was Verónica.

"That's simply not good enough!" she said angrily. "Not good enough at all! That's the advice you give? You, a priest?! I shall take it up with your… *bishop*."

"You take it up with whomever you like," said Padre Rafael mildly. "It won't change the fact that, from what you're telling me, Ino is unhappy. She must be. The fact that she is thinking of leaving her husband when she has a young child means that she must be suffering—"

"*Suffering?*" Verónica sputtered. "*Suffering?*" she repeated, her tone rising. "You've got to be joking! She doesn't know the meaning. Whatever sentiment she claims, it's not enough. She hasn't suffered enough! Besides which, she will not destroy *my* life! I will not allow it."

Her life? Surely, she must mean Ino's? Why was Verónica so fixated on this Archie anyway? Was it because her short time with Santiago had been, well, short? It couldn't be because this Archie was such a catch. Didn't Verónica remember that the Monte Alegres were grandees of Spain? That… actually, he couldn't be bothered finding out what motivated this woman. Nothing he'd heard so far warranted his intervention. Padre Rafael considered Verónica with blatant distaste. Who had said, 'Great minds discuss ideas; average minds discuss events; small minds discuss people'? Verónica had started off well enough, but he would never give her credit for being intelligent.

"Roosevelt," he said, thinking aloud.

"I beg your pardon?" said Verónica, suitably nonplussed.

"Eleanor Roosevelt. Sorry, I was thinking of something else." He made a swirling gesture, as though unwinding a ball of string. "I mean, while you were talking."

"Clearly." Verónica's tone was glacial.

"Look, it's not meant to be a competition," said Padre Rafael in his most conciliatory, silky tone. It was time to end this drivel. "The ability to suffer, I mean. Besides, no one knows what goes on in another person's marriage. Anyway," he tried changing tack, "you're her mother; surely there's room for compassion? Surely she must need you now as never before? Why don't you try and find out what really is in her heart?" *Although*, thought Padre Rafael, *I have a pretty good idea I know the answer to that…*

Verónica snatched the bill from the waitress's hand. Padre Rafael let her take it. "I don't know what kind of priest you are, Padre," she said aggressively. "Ino is a trollop. She is married to as near a perfect man as you could hope to find. Apart from the fact that, as you well know, for a Catholic there is no question of divorce—"

"Well… an annulment might be possible."

"Out of the question."

"In that case, I don't know what I can do. Have they tried marriage guidance? It can be very effect—"

"So, you refuse to help?" Verónica's voice rose wildly.

"I haven't *refused*, dear Verónica," said Rafael testily. He'd had enough of this melodramatic woman, beautiful as she undoubtedly was. "I just don't think we should meddle. Ino is an adult. If it's a priest you want, there are others closer to home, so to speak. What about her own parish priest?"

Veronica's fury seemed to melt just as quickly as it had been incited. "No," she said quietly.

It was Padre Rafael's turn to be astounded. "*No?*"

"She can't go to him."

"Why ever not? I would have thought this is precisely the moment *to* go to him; the time for speaking to someone she trusts."

Again, Verónica shook her expensive head of hair. "If she's to see anyone, they must be from outside Archie's community. That's why I thought of you. I don't want anyone to know. It… it would look so bad… it might affect his career opportunities. Actually, there are a million reasons why not." She draped her cashmere cardigan over her shoulders and pulled her handbag towards her. "Look, it's very simple," she said. "She's not leaving. She is not throwing everything away that I've worked for. She is not going to ruin *my* life."

There – she'd said it twice now. Padre Rafael shot her a strange look, and what he saw in Verónica's face chilled him to the bone. She was definitely in love with her son-in-law, and keeping Ino married to him was the only way Verónica could keep him in the family; keep him close. Perhaps she really did believe in all this church etiquette; really didn't want a divorce in the family. But one thing was clear to Rafael. Archie didn't want the mother. He was pretty certain he didn't want the daughter either. But really – *her* life? *Poor, poor Ino*, he thought. *Pobrecita*. And if he hadn't before, he certainly understood now.

"John, chapter eight, verse seven," he muttered.

"I'm sorry?"

"Oh, you know it?" He was genuinely surprised a second time. But then he revised his impression. Of course she did: surely other priests besides him had quoted the verse to her, no doubt with her in mind.

"*May he who is without sin...*"

"That's the one."

"Well, I don't know what you mean," she said haughtily.

"Don't you." It wasn't a question.

He glanced at the bill. Twenty-five *euros* for a few coffees? It was daylight robbery! It was a wonder he ever had a decent espresso with what it cost to have one *por la calle*. He wasn't often depressed by his encounters with parishioners, but he was deflated as he got to his feet now. He went through the motions of taking Verónica's hand (he couldn't bring himself to kiss her cheek), of making a vague sign of the cross that ended in a damp little wave, and then hurrying away just as quickly as was polite, turning into the nearest busy cobbled street. For once he welcomed the crowds bustling with gypsies, tourists and buskers.

Had Padre Rafael been a religious man, he would have made his way to Maria del Mar, nestling right there in the heart of the Old Town. Built in the fourteenth century, it was the only remaining church constructed in pure Catalan Gothic style. He might even have knelt at the window of the ascension, this being Ascension Day after all. But Padre Rafael was not a religious man, and nurtured the heart – or rather, stomach – of a true Catalan. And it came to him that what he needed to wash away all vestiges of the distasteful meeting were a few tapas. Not right away, obviously, as the chocolate cream still rested a little heavily, but in a *futuro próximo* – a short (very short) while. He would take the Metro to Sarrià – a hop, skip and a jump from Plaça de Catalunya – and stop by Emil's. He might also have an horchata – that summer drink made from the chufa nut which was utterly refreshing and appropriate for this time of year. It was a drink that reminded him of polo… Ah, back when a *partido* of polo would have done the trick. That and… yes, well, that too. But that was then and now was now.

He thought again about Verónica. Perhaps he should admire rather than distrust her rigidity. Would that he could be as dogmatic with his parishioners! Maybe he hadn't been quite as priestlike as he ought to have been. Maybe she was right. Perhaps his bishop would be disappointed at his reluctance to lend support. He stopped to buy a Metro ticket. He would go and see Emil. He'd try and be kinder to his cousin, too. He did feel guilty about goading him about Ino. He would discuss the matter with him. And he would absolutely not think about Sol, or Ino, or Oxford, or any of what followed after.

Archie

Cedar Avenue

Just tell me what you want? How can I help you if you don't know? If you need help, get it!

You say you don't like yourself? Then tell me: how am I to like you? How is anyone? That's got to be the first step.

My work isn't in that field. I know nothing about it. Why are you asking me, anyway? You wanted something else, didn't you? You wanted him. Well, he's yours... make the most of it.

Of course I remember the cottage – I'm not that callous.

16

Emil
Barcelona
June 2017

Emil unwound the canopy that shaded the small tables closest to the shop window. It was already thirty degrees Celsius and the heat continued to rise through the pavement; unrelenting, merciless dry heat that reminded him of Argentina. But he was used to it and hardly broke a sweat despite lugging out the chairs and the small cactus plants used as decoration. The horchata machine churned quietly in the background. It was a drink he'd never found anywhere else in the world. Made well, it should have a rich *turrón* (or nougat) colour, and the consistency of single cream, with ice crystals hanging around the edges. If he wasn't careful, he'd never sit on a horse again, let alone mount it, and certainly if he continued to drink the stuff at the rate he was currently doing. He thought briefly of a time when he had struggled to put weight on, not take it off.

A couple of girls in the uniform of the nearby Sacred Heart collapsed breathlessly onto the chairs he'd just brought out. He knew them from frequent visits to the *pastelaria* and he fancied he might have slept with one of their mothers. But he couldn't be certain. He and Rafael had had their fair share of girlfriends, and between them…

"Is that you?" said the pretty blonde in Catalan. She had

sunglasses perched on the top of her head in the way Sol used to. In fact, this girl reminded him of Sol in an unsettling way. Her pleated skirt was far too short, barely grazing the tops of her tanned thighs, and white knee-high socks only accentuated their slenderness. What was more unsettling was the fact that if she was flirting, it was probably illegal.

"Is that me where?"

The blonde jerked her head in the direction of the shop. Even with his back to the shelves, Emil knew she meant the polo picture.

"Shouldn't you be in school?" he said, wiping down the table.

"It's too hot."

"Too hot for school, eh?"

"So, is it? You? On the horse?" The more beautiful (but quieter) brunette motioned to a photo visible through the open door on the glass shelf.

"No, that's my cousin," lied Emil.

"You mean the priest?" the blonde said in genuine astonishment.

Emil smiled inwardly. "Yes, the priest."

"Wow – he was *guay*..." She had switched to Spanish, and Emil realised that the brunette probably didn't speak Catalan.

"He sort of still is, for an old guy," said the brunette.

"So why on earth did he become a priest if he looked like that?"

Emil smiled outwardly this time. Ah, *juventud, juventud...* youth! At this moment he was glad he was as old as he was. How ridiculously simple everything was when you were these girls' age. "Well, that's a very long story," he said dismissively. "What can I get you both before you go back to school?"

"Horchata. Two. But we're not going back," said Blondie. "*She* doesn't have to, anyway." She flicked her hair in the direction of her friend.

"No?"

"She's an exchange student," said Blondie.

"Oh? From where?"

"Oxford," said Blondie, answering for the other girl. "By way of New York."

Halfway to pouring the horchata, Emil paused, a memory thin as a tapeworm wrapping itself round his gut. "Oxford itself?" he said, hoping he sounded polite but not too curious.

"Not the university," said the brunette, and it was only then that Emil picked up on a slight accent. Otherwise, her Spanish was flawless. He could see that she was also a little older than Blondie; more assured. She met his gaze steadily. "And not Oxford itself, but a village outside it called Kirtlington. Actually, you might be interested to know, they have a polo club."

After the girls had left, Emil busied himself preparing for the *merienda* hour. Clearing counter surfaces to make room, he set about filling little brioches with *jamón serrano* and walnut bread with slices of Manchego and quince. And all the while, he held the memory of Kirtlington close. Like a cigarette waiting to be smoked after a long ride, he drew it out, savouring the moment. When he had finished his tasks, a *tinto* and tobacco in hand, he sat at a table outside on the pavement, oblivious to the passing crowds. The girls' visit had conjured up all manner of emotion, not least the joy, the uncomplicated confidence of being young with the world at his feet. And if he thought back to that day, and that day alone, he remembered what it was to fall in love, to be in control of his destiny, and to feel truly happy for the first time in his life.

Emil had forgotten that he'd agreed to spend a morning sightseeing. *Any* time wandering around a city was too long in his view, but because Rafael liked old colleges, they had agreed on a compromise: the Kirtlington Tournament (spread over five days) for a morning's tour of a few Oxford colleges – *one*, if Emil had his way. They had managed to get through the entire week without a further word being said about sightseeing but Emil was premature in thinking Rafael had forgotten. Bright and early on the morning of the last match Emil found himself traipsing behind his cousin, wishing he was anywhere but in Oxford. His mind was focused solely on the game, given that this time there was a real prospect of beating the Argies. There would be no game fixing; not in Oxfordshire, not this time. But it wasn't just the university they would be visiting. As Rafael reminded Emil, his cousin Ino was a student there.

"Do you think we look conspicuous?" Emil hissed as they crossed the morbidly silent quad, their riding boots clattering on the cobblestones.

Rafael examined his map. He had asked the 'scout' for directions and the man had helpfully planted a large 'X' to indicate Ino's rooms, only it covered up everything else as well. Rafael held up the map, comparing it to the building in front of them. Her rooms appeared to look onto the quad itself.

"Where is everyone anyway?"

"Asleep, I guess. They're students."

"The place is creepy," said Emil, sulking.

"Creepy?" echoed Rafael, genuinely surprised. "Not romantic?"

"*Pues no.*"

"Really? I find it fascinating." Rafael fished out a visitor's pamphlet he'd been handed on entering and was soon absorbed in its contents. "Did you know that Christ Church was founded in the sixteenth century? On the site of an older monastery, and *that* monastery dates back to an earlier settlement from around the ninth. *Jolines*... Listen to this! During the English Civil War, King Charles – *primero*, that is – lived at Christ Church and held his parliament in the Great Hall. Just there." He grasped Emil's shoulders, orientating him in the right direction. "Look, that's Tom Tower, designed by Christopher Wren."

"Who?"

Rafael made an exasperated face. "Architect? Doesn't ring a bell?" The attempt at a pun was lost on Emil. "Designed St Paul's Cathedral. Come on, *primo*, aren't you a *little* bit interested?"

Emil flicked a glance in the direction of a building whose mellow yellow stone arches, turreted walls and blue-faced clock weren't so far off their own at Salto, albeit on a slightly grander scale. In fact, its casement windows, now that he looked again, were exactly like those at Salto. "I am, actually."

Rafael's expression was jubilant. "In that case, we could—"

"In polo," interjected Emil. "The reason we came, remember? Sightseeing wasn't on the agenda! At least not for me."

"There you're wrong," said Rafael mildly. "You agreed to it back when we were discussing this whole trip. Now, going back to here. Christ Church has produced thirteen Prime Ministers, bishops—"

"Oh my God! Enough with the bishops!"

"*Oye*, Emil, enough with *you*! We're here; we might as well look around."

"No, I want to do what you said we would. *Hola qué tal*, hello and goodbye, and finish. I want to get to the *campos*."

"Well, if it's *meadows* you're after, why didn't you say so? It says here that the college is bounded by two rivers: the Cherwell and the Isis. There might even be time for 'punting.'"

"That's it."

"What? What's the matter?"

"*Me voy*. I'm going. I'm tired and I want to go back."

Rafael rolled up the pamphlet and tucked it into his jeans pocket. "You don't want to know about punting?"

Emil glared.

Rafael ignored him. "Ah... and the principal of Christ Church is always a dean."

"*Qué es eso?*"

"A kind of priest. In their church."

"*Fenomenal*. Really interesting."

Rafael stopped walking. Emil was wiping invisible specks of dirt from his pristine jeans and taking his time about it.

"Why the sarcasm?"

"What sarcasm?" Emil feigned innocence.

"You know exactly what I mean. You're being... *qué sé yo* – I don't know. Annoying. Like you don't want to be here."

"I don't."

"Not even to see our cousin?"

"*Your* cousin."

"But you liked her."

"Liked?" Emil shook his head. "You know something? You are amazing. Simply amazing."

"Thank you."

"It's not a compliment. *Liked?*" Emil repeated, his voice rising. "Are you forgetting the time you dumped her on me, and then went off with *my* girlfriend? No, you're right. 'Amazing' doesn't begin to do you justice."

Rafael considered his cousin, sucking his teeth. "First," he said calmly, "I didn't 'dump' you in anything. That was Abuela."

Emil made a face. "Yeah, maybe, but you didn't stick around to help, did you?"

"I don't mean *then*. I mean now. Abuela wanted us to, as they say here, 'pop in.'"

There was a brittle silence. Emil ran a hand through his hair. "This isn't 'popping'. This is a whole *visita*. I've done my time. I spent an entire afternoon—"

"*Jolines!*" cut in Rafael, frowning now. "You still think about that? That was *years* ago. *Hermano*, I recommend you learn not to dwell on things. Besides, Ino's no longer such a kid. She's a student here, isn't she?"

Emil didn't care what she was; didn't want to spend two minutes in her company. All he wanted was to get back to the polo. Besides which, Rafael was beginning to irritate the hell out of him. "Yeah, yeah, blah blah." He thought of something else. "How do you know she'll even *want* to see us? Will she even know who we are? I mean, it's been years, as you say."

Rafael stopped short, genuinely shocked. Of everything that had been said, that was the most outrageous. He spread his arms wide as though embracing the whole college. "*Por faaavooor! Pleeease!* We're the MAs, aren't we?"

Emil couldn't disagree. "True," he sighed, giving in at last. Rafael was clearly not going to be dissuaded.

"What?" Rafael took a deep breath. "Why the long face?"

Emil sniffed. "I just *knew* there'd be some religious element to this visit."

"What do you mean?" said Rafael, genuinely affronted.

"Sometimes, I don't know what you enjoy more: hanging around churches, or polo." There! Emil had finally voiced something that had been niggling him for a while.

"You can't be serious?"

Emil kicked a loose stone. "Look, it's just that we could still be in bed! Aren't you exhausted? I know I am. And surely Sol will want to know where to meet up. Sol—"

Rafael patted Emil's arm, finishing the sentence. "…can wait. It's far too early to call her. She loves her sleep, as you know – oops, sorry, you don't."

Emil bit back a retort. An "Ouch" was all Rafael got in response. They still had a game to play, and if they allowed things to escalate, if they weren't friends by the time it started, they'd lose. It was as simple as that.

Rafael seemed to be thinking the same, because suddenly he slung a conciliatory arm round his cousin. "Look, we'll be quick. I promise. Hello and goodbye, like I said. Nothing more, like *you* say." He forced a smile. "There might even be time for some stick and ball. *Vale?*"

Emil visibly brightened. "Okay. Forty minutes, tops. You agree?"

"*Está bien.*"

Emil's eyes narrowed. "And no leaving, not even for a smoke. I'm not babysitting again. Besides, I need time to *mentalizarme* before the game."

"Relax, *primo*," said Rafael. "We're going to win today. I feel it in my bones."

"Huh. The only thing I feel is—"

"I think this is it," said Rafael smoothly. They'd come through an arched passageway before emerging onto an inner quad. He checked the map. An oak door marked the entrance to Ino's staircase. "We're here!" he called up, taking the stairs two at a time, throwing an impatient "*Apúrate!*" to his cousin.

"I'm hurrying," muttered Emil.

They were still squabbling moments later when, in answer to Rafael's loud thumping, a female voice called a friendly, "It's open! Give the door a push."

They found Ino sitting on a high stone window seat. In the morning light there was something medieval about her blue nightshirt – the azurite colour associated with ancient manuscripts – and the way her hair tumbled down her back. She resembled one of the effigies they'd seen earlier. On the other hand, the coffee mug she nursed between elegant fingers was distinctly modern.

"Oh!" she said with a wide, warm smile. "It's the Hardy Boys!"

"The who?" said Emil when he'd recovered from the shock of seeing the gawky kid of memory replaced by this beautiful, welcoming young woman. Their eyes met, and he felt an electric impulse of instant attraction. To his gratification, she coloured.

But while he was still wondering as to the most casual way to greet her, Rafael had swooped down to coolly peck her cheek. Emil suppressed a violent urge to knock his cousin down (he imagined him as a skittle in a bowling alley) and slip his own hand behind Ino's neck and touch that long hair. He shot Rafael a malevolent look. How on earth did his cousin know about these… these 'Hardy Boys'? He wasn't kissing her hand, which was something.

Emil elbowed his cousin out of the way, bending to Ino's smooth, tanned face. He felt the fleeting softness of her skin against his lips, coupled with an equally fleeting sense of guilt. For beautiful she was. Out of loyalty to Sol, he reasoned that perhaps Ino was fractionally less polished – it really was only fractionally. Emil could tell that his cousin was not immune either, and watched in amazement as Rafael offered to make their coffee, pulled up a chair, and said of course they would wait while Ino put on some clothes. Emil, for his part, would have been happy to see her in less.

"What are you doing?" Emil hissed when Ino left the room.

"Whaddya mean?"

"You know *exactly* what I mean."

"Of course, you aren't *really* the Hardy Boys," chirped Ino, coming back into the room. She had pulled on a pair of jeans and a white shirt. Effortlessly elegant with her hair tied in a ponytail and tanned feet revealing red-polished toenails. Around her neck on a long gold chain, Emil noticed the family signet ring – her family's, that is; the Cabeza de Vacas'. Emil was once again reminded of the blood relationship between his cousin and Ino. In the past he might have felt a twinge of jealousy at their close connection, but at this moment he couldn't have been happier that she was Rafael's cousin, not his.

"Ah, no?" said Emil. "Then *cuéntame*." Tell *me*, not us. Ha! Take that, Rafa.

He was rewarded with the full brilliance of Ino's smile. "No, you really aren't at all alike, Emil," she said, touching his arm and fixing her attention on him. Only him! Her fingers barely brushed him, but even so, his skin tingled. "The Hardy Boys are American fictional characters – the twin sons of a well-known detective. Like Nancy Drew – sorry, another North American invention; also a detective's offspring – they go about solving crimes. I grew up reading about them. I loved them."

I loved them… The words echoed round his head. She was prepared to love *them*!

"Then that's us," said Rafael, carrying in a tray of mugs he'd had to wash up, and a Spanish *cafetera*. Emil was amazed Rafael even knew how to heat water. There weren't too many modern appliances at Salto. They certainly didn't have such a thing as an electric kettle. But he was happy to note that any finesse ended there: he'd clearly lobbed the biscuits onto a plate, as some were still stuck together.

"Except one is blond, the other dark."

"Oh," said Emil, scratching his chin. "Not us."

Ino laughed again, a lovely light sound, unlike Sol's nervous titter. Emil leaned against the fireplace, feeling warmth and well-being flood through him. Rafael came to stand beside him, trying to nudge him out of the way. "Shall I light a fire?" he said, stamping on Emil's boots, but Emil stood firm. He wasn't going to be pushed out of the way again. Not for Rafael. Not to make room for a girl they both liked. But then again, Ino was out of bounds to Rafael, and Rafael had Sol. The thought cheered Emil up no end. He thrust his hands in his jeans pockets; a pose designed to be casually cool.

"It's a little chilly," added Rafael, who clearly had no intention of moving. As they both jostled for position, Rafael's elbows dug into Emil's ribs.

"You aren't *really* cold, are you?" She was laughing again.

Emil blinked. This girl's laughter was contagious. It made him feel happy and light-hearted, and it certainly made a change from Sol, who, despite her name, was anything but sunny.

"I mean, it's June. If you think *this* is cold," her eyes were wide, "you should see what it's like in December!"

Emil was thinking that he didn't care what time of year it was. Or what she was saying. She could talk all day if she wanted to.

"Old buildings are always cold," piped up Rafael.

Emil mouthed, "Genius", and wished his cousin would shove off and look at some more churches. "Like the *castillo*," he offered, and could have kicked himself. Except that her rooms *were* like Salto. The books, the faded rugs, the wood furniture, even the casement windows fragmenting the golden light reminded him of home.

"Yes, like Salto…" Ino's voice drifted. "So, what brings you to Oxford?" Her eyes swept over their polo gear. "I mean, apart from the obvious. You two are always so immaculate, though I can never tell if you've finished playing or are just about to."

"About to," they said in unison.

"Kirtlington," said Rafael. "Later on. Charity match. The 3pm game."

"With the Prince of Wales," blurted Emil, and this time Rafael didn't have to knee him in the ribs; he'd have done it himself. How gauche did he sound? He glanced at Ino surreptitiously, but happily, she didn't seem to mind.

"How exciting!" she said, clapping her hands. "How thrilling! I don't know a girl here who wouldn't kill to watch that game!"

"Then why don't you come?" Emil said quickly.

Rafael took that moment to pat his back pocket, feeling for his mobile. "Ah, Emil, *primo*, I think Abuela wants you to call."

"Oh, I don't think she wants *me*," said Emil, his eyes never leaving Ino's face.

"Oh, I think she does," said Rafael silkily.

"No, I don't think so."

They glared at each other.

"Do you want *me* to talk to her?" Ino offered.

"*No!*"

Ino poured small cups of coffee from the *cafetera*, passing them round. "Well, I'd love to come," she said, taking a biscuit. "If you can wait while I change. Again."

There was a small silence while the two men considered the delectable, waiflike creature. Emil cleared his throat. Once again, he was distracted by the thought of her undressing. He nodded.

"Yes, *de acuerdo*," said Rafael.

"Oh, brilliant!" said Ino in childlike delight. "Abuela sent me a dress only last week. I didn't think I'd have a chance to wear it so soon!" She set down her coffee, but helped herself to another two biscuits, which she sandwiched together. "Do you want to have a look around the college? While I change?"

It was now or never, thought Emil. His heart was thudding. "I think Rafa would love to," he said quickly. "He's fascinated by history. Especially churches."

Ino's green eyes locked onto his for a moment before swivelling to their cousin. "I didn't know this about you, Raf. Why, how wonderful. There might even be a tour—"

"Which he would *love*—"

"No, he would not," said Rafael shortly. "I mean, yes, sure. Another time, absolutely, but not today. Actually, we just stopped by to say a big hello and pass on *un abrazo* from Abuela."

Ino looked from one to the other. "And one back." She had begun scooping up her hair, and Emil watched her slender arms as they reached above her head. "I can change superfast," she was saying. "Stay there. I'll be two minutes." And before they had time to answer, she skipped out of the living room and into the bedroom.

"Have you thought of who will mind her?" hissed Emil. "I mean, when we're playing?"

"That's no longer a problem, is it? She's not a child!" said Rafael, amused.

"That's *exactly* the problem. What's going to happen when the Argies see her in the stands? They'll be like bees to a honeypot, never mind the grooms!"

Rafael touched his forehead with his hand, letting the fingers splay. "My God, you're right! We can't allow it." He sprang to Ino's bedroom door. "Ah, Ino-Bambino," he called through the closed door. "On second thoughts – about today, don't you have homework or something?"

"*Homework?*"

The door sprang open, and Rafael, who had been leaning against it, almost fell against his cousin. Emil cursed.

"Is this okay?" Ino's hands fluttered to her sides, touching the fabric. She wore a poppy-red sleeveless linen shift that skimmed her knees, accentuating her long, tanned legs. On her feet were flat gold sandals. She had diamond studs in her ears, and carried a nude-coloured Prada bag. She exuded privilege, youth and beauty. She also looked very Spanish. Emil revised an earlier observation. She was *more* polished than Sol. He was unable to speak. She was simply the most beautiful girl – no, correction: *woman* – he had ever seen. And she was certainly unlike any student he'd ever known.

"Not bad, little cousin," said Rafael, raising her hand to his lips and actually kissing it!

Emil bumped into him as he held the door open. "Stop it! Just stop it!"

Rafael frowned. "Stop what? What am I doing?"

"You're flirting! Well, don't!"

Rafael ignored him and, entirely for Ino's benefit, slapped his cousin on the back. "Come on!" he said. "Let's kill 'em and let's win today! Let's kill those bastards. *Arriba Los Duendes!*"

Afterwards, Emil was amazed that they had indeed won. Perhaps it was because the Prince was playing and the match was rigged after all, or maybe it was because Rafael had played in position three. Whatever the reason, it certainly wasn't thanks to him. Normally, Emil was completely oblivious to the crowds. They were usually one large blur out of his line of vision; out of the ball's periphery. But today his attention had been constantly diverted to the girl in red, so clearly visible from where he sat on his horse. She was a bright, flashing beacon, vibrant against the white-painted stands, while every stray player and his dog made some excuse to go and sit beside her. Emil was only thankful not to be riding Ceniza, the mad, witchy pony who leapt every time she saw the letter 'H' painted on the grass, as though it were a jump. The colour red produced a similar effect. '*Ceniza*' meant 'ashes' in Spanish; something Emil was almost reduced to each time he rode her. Only now the horse was not his undoing.

Jumping from his pony and throwing the reins to his startled groom (Emil normally walked his horses to the stables and waited to chat about the game with the other players), he ran slap into Sol coming out of the hospitality tent. At any other time, just the sight of her – straight blonde hair, demure baby-blue shirt dress – would have set his heart racing. But not any more. In fact, he was shocked at how quickly lust had become, if not disgust, then certainly indifference. They exchanged quick pleasantries; she: "*Pero cuidado, E.!* Watch where you're going!" and he: "Sorry, sorry. Yes, yes, great game. Prince was on good form – played well." He brushed past her, ignoring her protests as she arched away from the too-full glass of champagne grabbed from a waiter which Emil thrust unceremoniously into her hand. Anything, really, to keep her occupied. Mentally punching the air and thanking Providence for Sol's arrival, he tacked his way to the clubhouse.

As anticipated, Ino was surrounded by players, her ponytail flicking from side to side as she tried to answer their questions as politely as possible. She looked up gratefully as Emil advanced. He wanted to kiss her. Instead, he bent down, pulling her to her feet. He heard the name 'Monte Alegre' ping-ponged among the players, accompanied by the tiresome jokes that always followed.

"Hey! We were talking," said Piggy Duarte, one of the Mexican players.

"*You* were talking," said another, and Piggy laughed. "Your little cousin wanted to know what '*Los Salto Duendes*' meant."

This was addressed to Emil. Emil kept his face neutral. He could pretty much guess what was coming. "Oh? And what did you say?"

"I said it meant 'goblins.'" Duarte smirked. "From Salto."

Emil smiled inwardly. The man was completely transparent. "Perhaps 'sprites' would be a better interpretation," he offered, enjoying himself.

"Or '*marica*'?" Piggy's expression was antagonistic in the extreme. Though physically fit, he was one of the ugliest men Emil had ever encountered. Unusually for a Mexican, he had bright red hair with a blanket of freckles that covered his face and neck. Calling him 'Piggy' was actually a kindness.

Ino turned her innocent face to Emil. "What does '*marica*' mean?" she asked.

There was a collective guffaw. The women these men were used to weren't generally so innocent.

"Fairy, darlin'!" said Duarte, taking a swig of beer and plonking his feet on the chair in front of him. "And I don't mean the twinkly kind."

"Yeah, you do!" someone called out.

"Really?" Ino's eyes were wide.

"No."

"So, you'd go with—"

"Conversation's over," said Emil gruffly. Placing a firm hand on her back, he guided Ino away.

Duarte looked at his pals and made a face.

"Emil!" Ino giggled over her shoulder, looking at the men. "I can take care of myself, you know."

"She can take care of herself, Emil!" Duarte called after him.

Emil flicked a finger. Still guiding her by the shoulders, he led Ino away from the clubhouse, away from the stables, and purposefully in the opposite direction from where he knew Rafael and Sol to be. Passing another hospitality tent, he grabbed a couple of glasses of champagne from one of the waitresses dressed in riding boots, tiny shorts and blazer. Rafael called it "the slutty/preppy look". It was a look designed to set even a 'fairy's' pulse racing, Emil thought wryly. Ordinarily, he would have been very happy to hang out with any one of them while deciding which description fit best. Under the shade of a giant plane tree, he stopped to hand Ino her glass, clinking its rim with his. He wanted to touch more than that.

"*Salud*," he said. He watched her take a sip, noticing pleasure spread across her face, and grinned. "I was a bit fierce, *disculpa*."

"No, I liked it," she said candidly. "I liked that you cared."

He felt a muscle tighten in his groin. "I just wanted to talk to you," he said. He leaned in close, smelling her fresh scent, her hair and… something else less fragrant. "Damn," he said, recoiling. "I'm sorry; I'm all sweaty from the game."

Ino took a step closer; so close that her breath fanned his face.

Her eyes never left his face. "Not to me," she said, and his heart began thumping all over again. He wondered that she didn't jump back from that alone.

"Ino." He took the glass from her hand.

"I don't mind a bit," she continued, taking a step back, which made him think she was nervous. Which was surprising. But then, he was beginning to realise that she was more innocent than her acquired poise would suggest. Maybe he'd misread the chemistry between them. Maybe—

"I'm so glad we came," she was saying now. "So, so glad! And I'm so glad you rescued me just now. I thought my Spanish was okay, but I couldn't keep up with the Argentines."

"That's because they don't speak Spanish! And the accent – *horrororoso!*" Hearing a catch in her voice and mistaking it for more nerves, Emil tried to keep the tone light, rolling his 'R's and making a face.

It had the desired effect when Ino burst out laughing. "You really don't like them, do you?" she said, touching his arm.

"I don't like cheaters." The chemistry was back. He was instantly distracted by the hand on his sleeve. Even tanned, her skin was much lighter than his. Could he kiss her now? Or was it too soon? He was more nervous of her reaction than he'd ever been riding Ceniza before the letter 'H'.

"Ah."

"But we are not going to talk about them," said Emil firmly. He balanced his glass on the top rail of the fence and leaned back beside it. He would be patient. "Tell me about you, Ino," he said, crossing his arms in front of him. Into his head popped the image of her from earlier in the day. She was undoubtedly beautiful sitting on her window seat, but there was something else he hadn't been able to identify. Was it unhappiness and other-worldliness that set her apart? Or was it loneliness? "*Te gusta estar aquí?*" *Do you like it here?* For it was unimaginable to him (and, he assumed, to Rafael) to be happy anywhere but Salto. He really didn't know a thing about Ino, now that he thought about it. What was she even doing here? Wasn't her mother Canadian?

"Happy enough," Ino replied lightly. "It's funny: no one ever asks me that. It's never a consideration."

"Perhaps it's a modern thing," agreed Emil quickly. "I mean, to bother about being content. It's become the obsession of late, whereas when we were small, as long as we were clothed and fed…"

Ino tossed back her head, looking at the field in front of them, watching the riders canter by as the umpires galloped ahead of them. To Emil's relief, he could see that Rafael, in his new number three position, had been sequestered for this match as well. She was looking at him earnestly. The sunlight bouncing off the leaves framed her face, making her eyes seem even greener.

"You're a long way from home, that's all," he finished lamely. He wanted to know about her, but inadvertently he had taken the conversation to a more serious level. Not his intention at all.

"Not really. Oxford feels as good a home as any. Besides which, I've never been *fijo*, as it were. I'm used to moving around. I mean, you've met Veronica…"

Emil raised an eyebrow. Yes, he had met Veronica. There were mothers – or so he imagined – and then there was Veronica.

"She was never really into the whole mothering thing."

Emil blinked rapidly, and Ino looked stricken.

"Oh, I'm sorry – I'm so, so sorry! I wasn't thinking. I mean, at least I *have* a mother…" Her hand flew to her mouth. "Oh my God, that's even worse!"

Emil smiled gently and stood close, taking her hand away from her mouth. "Shh! It's okay. I don't remember mine at all – Rafael says he does his, but I don't believe him. He's even competitive about that! He just says it to have something more."

"Did they… do they…?"

"Know what happened?" finished Emil. He hesitated. His parents' death and that of his aunt and uncle wasn't something he wanted to talk about. It wasn't something he ever talked about with Rafael, or with Abuela for that matter. "No. Two couples went out on a sailing trip in the Costa Brava and two couples came not back."

"Such a tragedy." Tears glistened in her eyes.

He shrugged. "They shouldn't have gone out. The weather was bad; there were warnings. I really don't remember them, Ino."

"Abuela inherited a bunch of orphans."

"Except you aren't one."

"Might as well be one," she muttered.

Emil finished his champagne. "I know."

"But see, that's where we're different. You and Rafael, you've always had Salto."

Emil looked towards the polo fields. "I'm not sure that we 'have' Salto, as you put it, but yes, it's always there in the background. Unmovable, immutable. But it's also an insatiable beast; it needs feeding and constant attention."

Ino's eyes were puzzled.

"It's not all sunshine and wisteria at the *castillo*," continued Emil, adjusting the chain round her neck which had become twisted, the clasp closer to the front. His fingers lingered as long as they dared. "It can be a burden too. Neither Rafa nor I want the business; we hate everything to do with cakes and bread and damn *pastelarias*!"

Ino laughed. Emil was on a roll.

"So, it's you who has the advantage," he said softly; his turn to be so close that his face almost touched hers. "You can be free; you *are* free. You should enjoy that."

"I do."

"But not too much!" he teased, only partly sincere. He didn't want this girl to have any freedom at all! He wished they would return to the light tone of their earlier banter, but Ino met his gaze with all seriousness. He was beginning to understand how different she was from the girls he'd grown up with – Sol in particular. Ino thought about things; really thought about them. They seemed to have enough in common. The lack of influencing parents for one, and the omnipresence of Abuela for another.

"Yes, but you know that whatever happens, you can go back there," she was saying now. "It's unchanging. There's huge comfort in that. You have a home." She sighed. "I suppose we always want what we don't have, don't we?"

The only thing, the only *person* Emil wanted at this moment was her. The attraction he felt towards her had been as sudden as it was powerful. "But it's the same for you! You of all people can go to Salto whenever you like." He touched the ring on her chain. "You know that. After all…"

"After all what?"

Emil hesitated. He wasn't in the mood to explain the family's genealogy, some of which she must know anyway. Technically, Emil was an MA in name only. His mother had been Rafael's biological aunt, but she was not Ino's. Ino's father's brother-in-law (*her* uncle by marriage) had been married to Ino's biological aunt. What Emil and Ino shared was Rafael as a first cousin. Therefore, Emil and Ino were not related by blood. When Emil's parents died, Abuela had thought it easier to adopt him as her grandson and for him to assume the Monte Alegre name. They were extended family, after all. Their parents (before they died in that ill-fated boating accident) had not only been related to one another, but best friends. "You too are an MA," he said carefully. He didn't follow it up by adding, More MA than I am. What he did say then – in an unguarded moment; in such a low voice that, when he went over it all later in his head, he was pretty certain she hadn't heard – was "And it's yours…"

Ino laughed. "No, that's you and Rafael – the Hardy Boys, remember? No one else fits the bill quite like you two do. You know," she added, eyes shining, "I still remember how kind you were to me when I was little."

"Pah! It was nothing," said Emil, but he was warmed all the same. And a little uneasy. She obviously remembered things differently. He hadn't been all that happy babysitting. Nor did he want to be reminded of the age difference between them.

"Oh, but it was! I had just arrived, and my bravado was just a cover-up for how alone and alien I felt. And you – why, you had to give up an entire afternoon to look after me when I know you really didn't want to."

"Bravado, huh?" Emil, reaching behind her, took another swig of champagne. "I think extreme bolshiness, more like."

"You're right," she agreed sheepishly. "I *was* a bit of a brat. I did have fun, though. I still remember it. Well, I remember the bruises."

"Ha! Where were the...?" He cleared his voice. "Do you really?"

Ino nodded. She did remember. All of it. She remembered how strange she'd felt during that first visit to Spain, packed off to spend the summer with an Abuela she had never met, and all because her mother had a new boyfriend and didn't want her getting under her feet. Jet-lagged, confused, not knowing the language – it had all been so bewildering! Furthermore, her cousin Rafael had been as big a disappointment as she clearly was to him. But Emil had been sweet. "You weren't very happy at first. In fact, you were horrified."

Emil downed his drink. "Your language..."

"Oh, that." She had the grace to blush.

"Yes, that, and the fact..." Should he say?

"Yes?"

"Well, that you couldn't ride." He touched her arm lightly.

"Right."

He too remembered how an afternoon that had prevented him from seeing Sol had turned out to be quite amusing after all. Ino hadn't a clue about polo or ponies or anything at all to do with horses, but he had found that he had an aptitude for teaching. Well, perhaps 'aptitude' was an exaggeration. If neither rider nor horse responded by the count of three, a whack on the rump made even the doziest nag move. If the rider wasn't thrown in the process, that is.

"And now?" Ino said coquettishly.

"Now what?" he asked softly.

"Still horrified?"

Emil brushed back his hair. Now. The moment was now. He looked at her moist lips; the pulse at her throat. She was so close to him; her hip almost touching his. He pulled her to him, his hands encircling her waist. "No," he said hoarsely. "Not horrified at all." His lips brushed her cheek; stayed there. "I think I've been waiting a long time for this," he said.

"For what exactly?" she whispered, but she leaned into him, small against him, trusting.

He could resist no longer, desire clouding everything but his need for her. His arms wrapped round her, hungry for her in a way that he had never been for any other woman. She laughed, crushed, breathless, reaching up, and he, bending down, found her mouth with his.

Archie

Cedar Avenue

I have tickets; the flights are booked. Just think of the warmth, the sand under our feet, no hospital rounds, no alarms, just balmy, balmy water and a skyline that looks like something out of Avatar. *I am excited. There, I've said it. The idea of a week together. I am giddy with the thought of it. I can't wait to get my hands on that delicious, delectable body of yours! I have a hard-on just thinking about the last time. You don't like when I 'talk dirty', as you call it – I can't help it. You do this. You do this to me.*
    Come.

17

Ino
Winchester
June 2017

Ino arrived at the schoolyard just as the bell rang. Children erupted from classrooms all over the building – a collective energy sprung from an afternoon of lessons – to begin impromptu ball games. Teachers and monitors positioned themselves to sign out the pupils. Several boys used their school jumpers as whips to thwack each other's legs, and others, having dumped their bags, were playing a game called 'It Build Up', weaving through the huddled groups of chatting mummies. Calypso's 'gang' among the children was the loudest. Wanda, the Polish mother, was weeping. Candy, the American, looked red-faced with fury, while the two fashionistas were more concerned about the fact that they were wearing similar coats. It was true that the garments, though differently cut, were the same colour. But their Prada bags and shoes were actually identical. They eyed each other critically like gauchos, knives drawn, circling round a campfire. Ino made herself small, hoping to go unnoticed, but Marion whirled as she walked past.

"Hey, hey," said Marion, eyes even more protruding than usual. Her black hair combed straight back from an alabaster face was more Morticia Addams than Margot Fonteyn.

"Oh, hi," said Ino, doing her best to disguise a lack of enthusiasm.

"You've not heard, have you?" said Marion, crossing her arms across a thin chest.

"Heard what?"

"Well," said Marion, taking a big breath. "Well," she said again. "You'll never guess what's happened."

"Oh," said Ino ingenuously. "You mean in Spain? A bit of a nightmare, I gather. Things are moving quickly but I'm not really in touch any more with—"

"*Spain?* No, not Spain!" Marion punctuated the word as she redirected a tennis ball that had come her way. "Nothing to do with *politics.*" She spat the word. "It's to do with *Wanda.*" She waited for her words to register, and when Ino merely blinked, carried on regardless. "Well, you know how Wanda is always late?" She leaned in close. "For once, she was actually on time; maybe even a little early. Anyway, Candy was sitting in her car, waiting. They had a little chat, and Wanda told Candy that she'd been at a really boozy lunch. So Candy went off to tell the headmaster. *He* said Wanda mustn't be allowed to drive, and in fact went and got Andrew himself from his classroom and made him sit in the staffroom. So now everyone's wondering who should offer to drive her."

There was a silence, and Ino realised that she was actually expected to take all of this seriously. Make a comment. "Surely that should be Candy, seeing as she's so concerned," she said wearily.

Marion took a step back. "Aren't *you*?"

"Just because Wanda was at a 'boozy' lunch doesn't mean *she* was drinking."

Marion rolled her eyes. "Oh, come on – it's *Wanda* we're talking about."

"Maybe. Sounds a bit underhand, though, the way Candy went about it. Going to the headmaster like that? She's supposed to be a friend, isn't she? A quiet word might have been… better."

Marion snapped open her handbag – another eBay designer knock-off. For once she was so distracted by imparting gossip that she barely registered Ino's clothes. "Don't think there was time for that. Candy felt she had to stop Wanda leaving. Or rather, driving, to be more exact."

Ino herself was distracted by the playing children as she scanned the group of younger ones for any sign of Calypso. A small boy whizzed past on a scooter, catching Marion's ankle. She squealed, leaping into the air as though she'd been shot.

"All I'm saying," said Ino, once Marion had stopped rubbing her leg and sending hate stares to the poor child in question, "is that there are other ways." She was surprised at herself for speaking out. Generally, she was non-committal. It wasn't that she would agree with other people simply to keep the peace, but she hated confrontation of any kind. There was something about the way the women were ganging up on Wanda that made Ino want to contradict them just for the hell of it. And because it was Marion egging them on.

"Candy was being *responsible*," said Marion equally firmly, her lips a thin red line. "And talking of responses, your alarm has gone off again – was still going off when I left Twyford."

Ino felt thin pricks of frustration needle their way through her stomach. "Oh, excellent," she breathed.

"*What* did you say?" Marion shot her a curious look.

"I was just wondering how it went off when it's not even set!"

Marion appraised her coolly. The lines from nose to mouth appeared suddenly pronounced; deep gouges on either side of her face. In the bright light she looked old. But then, Ino thought, Marion might be thinking the same about her. "Shouldn't it be? You won't be insured if the alarm isn't on."

"Yes, I know," said Ino thinly. "I mean, it's just for a moment while I pick up." She could have kicked herself. Why explain?

"It only takes a moment to rob a house," said Marion primly. "I should know. We deal with break-ins all the time, but people like you make it all the easier."

"Then people like me had better run," said Ino through clenched teeth.

"Think you'd better," agreed Marion smugly. "It's going like the clappers. Half the village can hear it!"

Ino spotted Calypso playing an exuberant game of pit-pat, her plaits flying this way and that as she ran to swat the ball with her hands. Ino caught her as she lunged forward. She was breathless, and loose tendrils hung round her face. She looked very pretty and very cross.

"I'm playing!" protested Calypso.

"I know, but we've got to hurry!"

"*Why* do we? Why do you always say we have to hurry?!" said Calypso, turning back to her game.

"Because this time we really have to – the alarm has gone off at home."

"It's always going off!" Calypso suddenly thought of something. "Does that mean someone is trying to hurt Oreo?"

"No, of course not, darling."

"Did you even *feed* Oreo?" asked Calypso suspiciously.

Had she? Ino's head began to throb. "What? Yes, yes."

"*When* did you feed her?"

"Mmm?"

"When '*xactly* did you feed her?"

Good question. She must have done… After she'd put out the rubbish in the morning? Or was that the other day? The broken-plate day when she'd been careful to wrap up the china pieces in newspaper so that Calypso, who noticed everything, wouldn't. Ino couldn't remember. The days recently had begun to merge into one another. "We've got to get back quickly," she said sharply, panic making her tetchy. "The alarm is going off and apparently the village is almost as cross as you are."

Unamused, Calypso contemplated her mother. "Yes, but, Mummy, this is 'portant."

Ino scooped up her daughter's book bag from where Calypso had thrown it on the ground, together with her blazer and boater. "All the more reason to get home quickly," she said, and then added feebly, "so that you can check on Oreo."

"So you *didn't* feed her" said Calypso accusingly, her voice beginning to warble.

"Oh, Calypso," said Ino helplessly.

"'Oh, Calypso,'" mimicked Calypso. "That's what you always say when you haven't done something."

"Oh, joy – how much better can today get? Don't answer that, Calypso!"

A police car was parked in the lane outside Dormer Cottage. Its open window was in line with the wrought-iron gate that led to the front door. It was such a pretty facade, with the two oversized cypress trees that brushed the second-floor bedroom windows; small casement panes that amassed their scale-like leaves along the bottom when the wind blew hard. To the right of them, an uneven stone path wound through a herbaceous border to a wooden portico. To the left, a wooden postbox was nailed halfway up the flint-and-stone wall. Beneath this was an oak bench, presumably built to assist in the reading of correspondence. The heavy medieval door with its brass studs and enormous lion knocker was imposing, and no one except the postman ever used the entrance. Visitors preferred to skirt the house and enter from the drive, past the box hedges, magnolia tree and row of stone mushrooms with their unsteady tops.

Ino ignored the car and the policeman standing sentinel under the porch and pulled into the drive. Some of her neighbours were huddled together, talking in hushed tones and gesticulating to what they didn't realise was simply a decoy. The genuine alarm was mounted on the wall at the rear. Ino mouthed a "Sorry!", pulling briskly on the handbrake. Calypso, already straining in her car seat, shot forward with a squeal. Her little arms embraced Ino's headrest, catching her hair. Ino reached behind her to pull her long hair free. At the last moment she remembered to pop on her sunglasses. Taking this as a sign to move, Calypso unhooked her seat belt and had hopped out of the car before Ino had a chance to caution her. She ran towards her rabbit's hutch just as Michael emerged from the front lawn.

"Oh dear," said Ino sheepishly, hurrying past him. The alarm really was deafening.

Michael pressed the controls, moving his chair forward. His hands were swollen with large purple patches where the community nurse had recently taken blood. "Actually, I was passing anyway – heard that baby crying again, and then the alarm went off."

Ino inclined her head. "Baby?" she echoed, but the wailing siren coupled with Michael's whirring scooter distracted her. "Let me just deal with this alarm business and then we can have a cup of tea, if you have time."

Michael smiled. His hair looked thinner, his skin pastier, and there were heavy pouches under his eyes. "Yup – I have time."

"Make your way to the garden, if you like. I'll see you there."

Ino unlocked the back door. The whole of the westward-facing first floor and second-storey bedrooms looked onto the drive, orchard and lawns. This end of the village attracted only occasional hikers (and Michael), but Ino sometimes felt exposed with people being able to see in. As Michael's contraption struggled to gain purchase on the uneven ground, though, for once she was grateful that the garden was clearly visible from the house. She prised open the dusty cupboard under the stairs where the alarm was housed. Cobwebs shrouded tins of dried boot polish, elastic bands, spare light bulbs (that almost certainly had blown), plastic shopping bags – a general graveyard to detritus shoved onto the shelves in the hope that it all might simply disappear. Keys to who knew what hung from butcher's hooks. She peered at the control panel. By the look of things, the alarm hadn't been activated after all, but she tapped the code to switch off the sound.

"You *didn't* feed Oreo!" yelled Calypso from the lawn.

Ino closed the cupboard door and went back to the kitchen window. Her daughter was a tiny ball of fury, her small fists bundled by her sides.

"You stay with Michael," said Ino sternly. "And don't shout!"

"No," shouted Calypso, planting her bottom firmly onto the grass. "I need to look after Oreo."

Ino felt herself flush at her daughter's defiance, but Michael, reversing slowly, manoeuvred himself beside Calypso on the lawn.

"Of course you do," he said smoothly. "Let me help. Do we need to take Orfeo some water?"

"Actually, it's Oreo," said Ino. "Like the biscuit."

"Ah," said Michael. "You've broken with the Greek theme."

"I don't know what that means," said Calypso crossly. "And Oreo is a girl." She sat legs akimbo, her school socks round her ankles, pulling up tufts of grass by the roots (just as her father had done the day before, but rather more emphatically) and dropping them on her lap.

"My mistake," Michael said quickly.

Unimpressed, Calypso eyed him suspiciously. Leaning back on her elbows, she began pushing the scooter wheels with her feet.

"*Copenhagen* won't budge," he said benignly, catching Ino's alarmed expression from the window. "Oh, sorry," said Michael. "You've not met, have you?"

Calypso stopped short. "Is... *Copenhagen*... your pet?"

Michael glanced at Ino. "Not exactly, but I rely on her just as much. There's a pouch at the back of the scooter. Take a look. You'll see that I've brought hi... *her* some carrots, and there are some chocolate brownies for you. But maybe you don't like chocolate brownies?"

"I do," Calypso muttered at length.

"What was that?" said Michael. "My hand, you understand, should be at my ear."

"I do, actually," shouted Calypso in a tone that was just on the edge of being rude, but she had stopped leaning back and was now sitting cross-legged and attentive.

Michael turned the whole scooter so that he was facing her head-on. "Well, isn't that lucky?" he said. "Otherwise, I'd be eating them all myself." He looked at Calypso. "And this is where I'd normally wink," he added, "but I don't think it's quite worked."

"No, it hasn't," agreed Calypso bluntly.

"Ah, well. Can't have everything. Look, let's get away from your mother. I sense her watching us. Show me where you keep Oreo and let's feed her some of those carrots, shall we?"

Their voices faded as they progressed leisurely across the lawn, Michael pausing now and then to demonstrate *Copenhagen*'s impressive array of gears. Calypso was completely fascinated, but Ino winced as she appeared to be reinforcing the fresh tramlines made by the chair. Her acrobatic daughter hung off the handlebar as though it were some sort of trapeze: feet above the ground; knees at ninety degrees to the ground. Which was bad enough, but as the chair moved forward, she lowered her legs, dragging her feet through the grass as though treading in the divots. *Divots?* There it was again: that reference to the past. The thought of what Archie's reaction might be when he saw them, however, was enough to bring her smartly to the present. Ino nodded curtly to the dispersing crowd of curious neighbours as she sidled into the kitchen. The air was static and thick; a few buzzing wasps spinning away from the thatch to circle the upper windows. It felt as though time itself stood still. For a moment.

There was a crunch of gravel. "You've a nest," said a policewoman, breaking the silence and pointing to the chimney and then to the balcony that ran off Ino's bedroom. The woman's head and shoulders filled the space framed by thatch and casement, and she had to duck to avoid her hat catching on chicken wire.

"I was just coming to find you," said Ino hastily. *Though not any time soon...* She'd actually hoped that if she dawdled long enough the police would go away. Which she thought they had. Certainly the man at the front had driven off.

"Jane Leeming, by the way. I'm your PCSO."

Ino looked blank.

"Police community support officer? You'll have to get that

sorted." Jane Leeming's head jerked in the direction of the wasps. "Excuse me," she mouthed as her two-unit radios began whirring and the various buckles and zips squeaked as she turned to talk into her chest.

Just like on *The Bill*, thought Ino with satisfaction. She was always relieved when people she imagined doing certain jobs actually did them. But she was mistaken if she thought that Jane Leeming would be preoccupied enough to leave her alone.

"I'll do that," said Ino quickly. She was dying for the loo and to make that cup of tea.

But Jane Leeming's entire body turned around slowly. Her gaze took in the orchard and box hedges; Calypso's tree house with its matching thatched roof. Ino could tell she was making a mental inventory and doing the math. "Nice place, this," she said. "Mind if I take a look?"

She wasn't asking for permission. Ino had barely breathed, "Go right ahead" when Jane Leeming was suddenly standing by the door jamb, eyes flicking round the kitchen with undisguised curiosity.

"Best show me the alarm panel first, yeah?"

"Sure."

"And the front door is…?"

Ino nodded in the direction of the hall. Jane Leeming had to stoop. In the kitchen she could just about fit between the rafters, but the hall ceiling was even lower. There was something rather comical in the way she now cocked her head.

"The key?"

For a second time Ino ducked into the hot cubbyhole of a cupboard under the stairs, inhaling the airless, musty sedge smell. She held out a foot-long iron key. Jane Leeming was perched on the low windowsill by the stocky, bolted oak door. The hall was always dark and echoey thanks to the overhanging thatch and the cypress trees. Though a cottage, the interior had always seemed more in keeping with that of a manor house, albeit on a miniature scale. Its oak floors, inglenook fireplaces and flagstones had something of Salto about them. The places Ino loved best were always those that called to mind the Spanish castle, not the modern, metallic contours of her mother's homes. Later, Ino had experimented with three different paint colours and material for the curtains in an attempt to make the entrance more welcoming. In the end she had settled for a hideously expensive French fabric in autumnal colours of melon, burnt orange and sage green. On the wall opposite the casement window hung a Napoleon III Empire mirror, but the glass in this was too cloudy with too many black smudges to add much brilliance. The pretty painted table had a marble top, and the rug, though thick underfoot, seemed to disappear on the dark wood floor. Individually the pieces were pretty enough but the overall effect was still cold.

"Like something out of *Horrible Histories*."

That bad, then… "Which is why we never use it. We tend to use the back door. The key, as you see, is totally impractical to carry around." Ino was beginning to think that everything in the house was impractical. It was only the garden that generated any sense of calm. "Shall we…?"

"Yes!" Jane Leeming, squeezing herself along the narrow corridor, ducking to avoid the oak beams, couldn't get to the kitchen fast enough. "Old houses are so uncomfortable, aren't they?"

Ino couldn't have agreed more. "What I don't understand," she said instead, "is that the alarm wasn't switched on."

"These things happen," said Jane Leeming, rubbing her neck. "Could be any number of issues: faulty electrics; a mouse might have chewed through a cable. Who knows?" Her eyes slid sideways as if to say, *Or all of the above*. "Have it checked out, though. You need to notify the alarm company, and it might be worth having a keyholder who can come in if you aren't able to. That way, the disturbance is down to a minimum."

"Yes, of course." Ino made a contrite face. She'd had this advice many times over. She added an "Okay", by which she meant that officer was free to go.

Jane Leeming appeared far from ready to go anywhere. She had removed her hat, which was touching the top of the beams anyway, and was leaning comfortably against the dresser. Every time she shifted her weight, the little coffee cups that hung from hooks along the top shelf, rattled precariously. A cork noticeboard with its random tacked pictures drawn by Calypso and newspaper cuttings citing the various accolades awarded to Archie caught her attention. "Hubby?" She nose-dived onto the noticeboard.

Ino said nothing. She felt a sudden tension. She'd seen too many police series not to know that an indifferent question always led somewhere unexpected.

"Ah, same name." Jane Leeming flicked a look upwards. "Must be hubby." She paced slowly round the kitchen, looking out of the window under the eaves towards the garden. Then with her back to Ino she said casually, "It's not the first time."

"Oh, I know," stammered Ino, surprised by the disarming tone. "The alarm's always going off—"

Jane Leeming stopped her pacing and began fondling her radio. She had wispy hair – the kind Victorian novelists described as 'flaxen' – and a pink complexion. She was pretty in a big, wholesome sort of way. "Oh, I don't mean that. We get a number of landline calls from here."

"From *here*?" Ino couldn't hide her surprise. "From Dormer Cottage?"

The woman nodded. "Sometimes they're aborted but a patrol comes out just the same – more than we'd like. You're going to have to sort the alarm."

"I know, I know," said Ino, somewhat perturbed now herself.

"We've had a couple of 999s too." Jane Leeming fished out her mobile, her carpenter's thumb swiping the screen. For a moment Ino wondered about those kind of thumbs – were they a sort of deformity? "More than a couple by the look of things."

Ino's mind scrambled. "Must have been Calypso, my daughter," she decided at last in relief. "You know what children are like."

Jane Leeming glanced at her phone, once again texting rapidly. Her radio unit gurgled, and to Ino's relief she seemed ready to leave at last. With her hand flat against the door, she paused. "Everything okay here, is it?"

Ino flushed. "Of course, why wouldn't it be?"

Jane Leeming shrugged. "Lovely house and kid, successful hubby, beautiful wife. Seen it all before."

Ino's stomach clenched, but her tone was cool. "Seen what exactly?"

Jane Leeming hesitated before pushing the back door open wide so that it scraped against the flint wall. Ino winced. Her cheek was beginning to throb too. Jane Leeming noticed Ino's reaction, but she didn't embarrass her by lingering on her face; her gaze travelled, rather, to the neatly mowed lawn, the orchards, the expensive pots of hybrid flowers. Hand still on the door handle, she turned back to Ino.

"No one can stop this but you, you know," she said. Her tone softened before adding kindly, "There's a lot of support out there."

"Thank you," said Ino firmly. "But we're fine."

Again, Jane Leeming hesitated. She scratched behind her ear; replaced her cap, smoothing its Sillitoe tartan band. "Okay. As long as you are. I don't care about hubby. But you – you have a kid." Her fingers drummed the door handle. "I don't have to tell you—"

But Ino had had enough. "No, you don't."

Jane Leeming nodded, resigned. "Make sure you get the alarm serviced. You don't always want to be crying wolf."

Ino made a pot of tea, mixed up some squash for Calypso and took a tray out to the garden, not forgetting to first pop on her sunglasses. She felt nauseous again. The strain of creating a kind of normalcy and hiding her shameful secret was often too much to bear. Despite her best efforts, Jane Leeming had guessed the truth. It was a kind of relief, and yet again it made Ino afraid. Because once one crack appeared, would another appear, and then another, until her whole facade crumbled completely? Michael patiently nursed Oreo on his lap while Calypso gave the rabbit's hutch a clean. There was a cloth on the grass with the required paraphernalia neatly laid out: Dettol, sponges, a bowl and lots of pink ribbon.

"Honestly, Calypso," said Ino, setting the tray down on the garden table and opening the umbrella, less to protect them from the afternoon sun than to make use of the space beneath. "I'm sure Michael doesn't want Oreo on his lap!"

"Oh, he doesn't mind," said Calypso chirpily. "He can't feel a thing. He says I could stick a pin in him and he wouldn't feel it!"

"Well, I wouldn't try, and I'm sure it's not true anyway," said Ino sternly.

"Actually, it is," said Michael placidly. "He… sorry," he corrected as Calypso glared at him, "*she's* a good little thing. As long as *she* doesn't, you know, do anything, I'll be fine."

"See?!" said Calypso, happy again and taking a bite out of another brownie.

"How many is that?" asked Ino suspiciously.

Michael was silent.

"It's the last one, Mummy," replied Calypso truthfully.

"Isn't it lucky, then, that I just happen to have some biscuits?"

Calypso looked fit to burst, but the sight of her happily skipping round them both, fussing over Oreo and Michael as Ino poured tea, cheered Ino no end. Never far away, she kept coming back to check on Oreo and make sure that she didn't fall, as Michael couldn't have been able to catch her if she had. From time to time, she gave Michael things to 'watch', tucking various items into the pockets of his chair. Ino knew that her daughter already thought of Michael as just a bigger version of her pet rabbit.

"Luckily, the chair is huge," said Michael, amused. "But I never thought it would be put to this kind of use." Operating one of the gears, he moved it fractionally closer to Ino. "Everything okay?" he asked when Calypso briefly disappeared to the loo.

"Yes, of course," said Ino brightly.

"No, not 'of course,'" he contradicted sternly. "You could take off those glasses, for starters."

Ino shook her head. "But it would spoil the look. I'm channelling *Vogue*'s Anna Wintour."

"Never heard of her."

"She's... oh, never mind. Not important." Ino poured herself another cup of tea, trying to make herself comfortable by curling up in her garden chair. The wicker prodded her in all the wrong places, but even so, she felt tension seep away. She wouldn't let the fact that Archie was jealous of Michael mar his visit; she wouldn't deny the poor man a few moments of diversion in what she knew were increasingly dull days as his faculties decreased. And if she forgot about Archie entirely – which she intended to do, if only for an hour longer – the scene was idyllic. Her gaze swept over the grounds. Neat green lawns were framed on all sides by a border of poppy, cow parsley and dog rose. The gorgeous wild flowers appeared to be held in check by an invisible fence as they strained to encroach on the jewel-like brilliance. Sprawled over the pergola, jasmine and may cast a delicious scent.

"You wouldn't do me a favour?" said Michael after they'd been sitting in convivial silence for a while.

Ino felt increasingly mellow and, as the lovely afternoon wore on, the upset caused by Archie's drinking seemed to fade in view of Michael's degenerative illness. "Of course." She smiled.

"You wouldn't wipe my nose?" he said. "Oh, don't be alarmed," he added, catching her expression. "I don't mean blow it! It just tickles."

"It must be the *glicina*," she said, gesturing to the pergola.

"Come again?"

"*Glicina*," she repeated, and then, when he continued to stare at her incomprehensibly, she realised that she'd spoken in Spanish. "I meant... what's it called? Wisteria."

Michael appeared thoughtful as their eyes met and hers shied away. As well his might, she didn't wonder. *Where* was all this

Spanish suddenly coming from? She'd not thought of any of it in years. '*Glicina*', which always sounded to her mind like 'glycerine'.

"I keep forgetting you're half Spanish" said Michael amiably. "Yes, just there, you've got it."

Ino patted the bridge of his nose and tucked the tissue into his breast pocket.

"Thanks. I mean, you certainly look it with your long dark hair. And what are they, green or brown, your eyes? Of course, if you took off your sunglasses…"

"Nice try," replied Ino, settling back down. "Changing the subject, can you really hear the alarm from all the way down your end?"

"Yes, I can. And the baby."

"But I don't have one, I think I said. Just Calypso."

"I know."

"I wonder whose it is, then. Do we know anyone in the village who's had a child recently?"

"Nope," said Michael. "I wish I could shake my head. Maybe I should get some placards."

"As in Shakespeare's *A Midsummer Night's Dream*: this is 'wall'; this is 'moonshine'…"

"Yup, that's the one."

Ino smiled. "You're funny."

"Not as funny as I used to be," said Michael.

"There's a row of cottages up by the post office," said Ino after a while. Without really understanding why, she was bothered by the fact that he mentioned a baby most times they met. "Going back to the crying baby you keep hearing and where it might come from. Everyone says there are lots of children in the village, but I've not met any. Not of Calypso's age, at any rate. She'd love it if there were."

Michael looked across the fields. "They don't really mix in, do they, that lot?"

"No, it's a shame. I've tried. When we open the garden, we always have a bouncy castle and other entertainment for the kids, but no one from the council estate ever comes. And it's not that they don't know about it: there are posters all over the village advertising the event. Perhaps they're resentful. What they perceive…" She flushed.

Michael was silent.

"What?" said Ino, trying to second-guess him. She wasn't sure if he was quiet because he couldn't or because he wouldn't communicate.

"I don't think it's that," he said with some effort. He suddenly looked tired; the folds under his eyes creased.

"What do you mean?"

"I don't think it's anything to do with having or not. Hazarding a guess, I'd say it's because it's this place: Dormer Cottage."

Ino felt a flare of indignation. "Oh?" Her fingers dug into clenched palms. "Why? Because… because as you've implied, Archie isn't… popular?"

"No, that's not the reason."

Ino's heart lurched. She had been feeling uplifted talking to him and trying to forget all the unpleasantness of the past few days, but now that familiar dread took hold of her again. "Then what is?" she asked in a small voice; her heart thumping. "What is it about Dormer Cottage?"

Michael tried to clear his throat, coughed, swallowed. When he managed to speak at last his voice was raspy and Ino had to strain to hear him. "You really don't know? The estate agent never said?"

Ino shook her head. "I… we knew it had been vacant for a while but we assumed it was because it's not to everyone's taste – horses for courses and all. There's the expense of rethatching, the fire risk, the low ceilings…" Her voice drifted. Come to think of it, she couldn't remember what the estate agent had said exactly, she had been so enchanted by that first viewing. She had gone alone; Archie had been too busy at work. She had parked the car down the lane, closer to the church, and walked the remaining few yards to the house, which was just visible through topiary hedges. The sun breaking through a gap between the cypress trees made the flagstone path shimmer. Maybe it was because the cypress trees reminded her of Spain. Whatever the reason, everything on that spring day had seemed fresh and new and hopeful.

"Shouldn't be for me to say, but it's no secret," said Michael. "I used to wonder if everything was all right up here – you hear things, you know. And you being here on your own most of the time with a young child – I mean, it has been noted. It's a small village and your husband doesn't seem to spend much time at home, does he?"

"Tell me about the house," said Ino stonily. "What don't I know? More importantly, what *should* I?"

An odd chortling sound came from the depths of the wheelchair. "Don't worry," he reassured her. "Just internal waterworks."

"Phew," said Calypso, coming up quietly behind him. "Mummy doesn't like nappies and things."

"Calypso!" said Ino, mortified.

"Is that so?"

Calypso nodded. "Mummy said the time—"

"Yes, thank you, darling."

"It's true," insisted Calypso, enjoying the sudden attention and racking her brains to remember more. "'Member when—"

Ino contemplated her daughter, who was breathless and giddy with excitement. She was undeniably adorable in her gingham dress, one sock on, one sock off, hair tied up in matching ribbons. She was also a rogue missile ready to launch. As Calypso brushed past, Ino caught hold of her. Calypso tried to wriggle free, but Ino held her firmly between her knees, one arm across her shoulders. "Why don't you finish combing Oreo?" she said into her hair.

"Oreo doesn't need her hair combed. I've been done that." Calypso twisted and turned to face Ino, taking her face in both hands in a gesture Ino loved and that was designed to melt away any misgivings she might be nursing. Danger, too, seemed to have been averted. "Mummy?"

"Yes?"

"Do you think Oreo needs a new hutch?"

"No."

"Why not?" Calypso was now pushing back against Ino, digging her heels into the grass, looking up at the sky. "Mummy?"

"I said no. Calypso, that's enough now."

Calypso trampolined to her feet. "I was only going to ask if that was a red kite? I think I saw one."

"There you go," said Michael. "My, you're a clever thing. I tell you what, Calypso. Would you fetch me some water from the kitchen? Do you think you could do that? You'll probably have to push a chair to the counter. Do you think you can manage?"

Calypso nodded vigorously, while Ino was doubtful.

Michael's gaze slid back to her. "She'll be fine," he said.

Calypso was soon out of earshot, heading away from them down the narrow stone path, Michael's water bottle clasped firmly in both hands.

"Tell me quickly about the house before Calypso returns," said Ino. "What were you going to say?"

"It's not a happy tale," said Michael slowly.

Grey clouds as diaphanous as jellyfish wriggled across the sky. "Go on," she said, shivering inwardly.

"Do you really want to know?"

"I do," she said harshly.

"Okay then, okay. Well, what happened was... a young couple moved down from Scotland..." He paused.

"I'm listening!" Ino's tone was sharp but Michael seemed not to notice.

He continued calmly. "Perth, I think it was. No, Edinburgh. Anyway, she was a lovely lass, that Catherine: big girl – not fat, just big-boned, as my wife used to say. Lovely complexion, lovely musical voice – a really bonny lass. She married a fellow Scot. Had been engaged to another man, it was rumoured, but he went abroad before the wedding and didn't return. This fellow's mate felt sorry for her, courted her, and hey presto, wasn't long before they married."

Ino, unable to see how this was relevant, began to relax. Michael's tone was so soothing, so respectful that she felt an intense yearning for the kind of relationship she'd once imagined for herself; an aching nostalgia for the innocent girl who'd dreamed it. "And were they happy?" Again she was reminded of her girlhood; remembered what it was like to have all her life ahead of her. What it was like to be drunk on the sensation of simply being young, once, during that summer in Spain.

"At the beginning, yes. I think so." Michael shot her a look. "I can't believe you didn't know this."

Ino shook her head. She really was only half-listening. She would hear him out and then pop in the salmon steaks she had ready for supper. All she had to do was spread the sauce and quick-fry the samphire, but that was a last-minute thing and could wait. There were fresh raspberries and clotted cream for dessert. She felt a surge of optimism. Everything would be all right. It would, it *had* to be. And it would be, as long as she kept everything together, perfect and ordered.

"Anyway, Catherine had a baby, and after the baby a touch of… well, that depression that affects women – pre… pre… prenatal—"

"*Post*natal, I think you mean," said Ino, amused, although she guessed that some women might feel depressed *before* a child was born. His delivery really was painful. At least he hadn't said post-coital! It was beginning to sound like the usual story of divorce; sad but not uncommon. It could so easily be hers… Her mind drifted back to what she could make for dessert if they didn't have raspberries. Maybe pears with ginger? There was certainly a surfeit in the orchard. When Michael left, she would get Calypso to go and pick some. She could easily reach some of the low-hanging fruit. It would keep her occupied for a while.

Michael gurgled and, after a pause, said, "Aye, that's the one: postnatal depression. So, her husband sent her home to Scotland to spend time with her family. Thought a change of scenery would do her good."

There was mint in her little 'oriental' square of chilli and coriander plants. Ino could make a watermelon and feta salad as a side. It would balance... Michael was watching her. Her sunglasses hopefully disguised the fact that she really was miles away.

"And... did it?" she said when the pause was protracted enough to make her realise he expected some kind of response.

Michael paused. "There was certainly a change," he said.

"Oh, that's... a relief."

"But it wasn't for the good."

They were both silent. Ino wondered vaguely why it was she could never get basil to grow. Or not for long, at any rate. When Michael continued, his voice was so low that it took Ino a moment to realise that he was actually speaking. Had she missed something important? She had to lean forward to hear him.

"Catherine came back unexpectedly one day with her new baby. He was a bonny bairn like his mother: blond, pink-cheeked, bursting with health. Or as his mother was before the baby. Alexander is what they christened him, though his father referred to him as Alec. Catherine wasn't right, though. I mean, physically she had recovered just fine, but mentally... well, anyone could see she wasn't herself. Her sunniness had gone entirely. She was withdrawn, pale and so strange."

Ino thought back to Calypso's birth. Archie had been present – just – disappearing for a week afterwards. He had said he was just 'popping out' to pick up some nappies and never returned to the hospital. He hadn't been there to collect them from the hospital either, so the matron in charge had called her a taxi. So suffused with happiness at the tiny, sweet-smelling bundle in her arms, Ino hadn't thought to question any of it. The fact that Veronica – travelling in Azerbaijan at the time, and despite her role in global telecommunications – was also uncontactable struck Ino as ironic. At the time, she wouldn't allow anything to mar her happiness. She could still remember the weight of Calypso against her breast; the little mouth; the twisting, kitten-like gestures of the newborn. Ino had experienced moments of bewilderment, disappointment and occasional rage at Archie's indifference but she had never felt depressed. "So... what happened?" She had lost track of the story.

Now it was Michael's turn to look at Ino strangely.

Ino brushed a crumb from his arm and endeavoured to try harder. "Sorry, I mean, I don't quite understand. What does this woman, this Catherine, have – what do *they* have – to do with my... with Dormer Cottage?"

"Well, it wasn't called Dormer then," said Michael carefully. "I expect the estate agent thought it prudent to change the name. That was a good thing, what with the press poking around and the Book of Face or whatever it's called."

"Facebook," said Ino.

"That's it."

A faint, vague connection was being made in the fog scooting across Ino's mind to protect her psyche. "So... I'm guessing this... this Catherine lived here? At Dormer?"

Michael did a double blink, which Ino took to be agreement. "You have to understand she wasn't well."

"Catherine? I do, I do. Is that it: the connection? That another sad woman lived here?"

The words hung in the still air. Michael continued to look at Ino oddly, and Ino met his look, unflinching, but inside she was horrified. She hadn't really said that, had she? She could not *believe* that she'd been so rude; nor admitted to any unhappiness herself.

"I sincerely hope that's the only connection," said Michael mildly.

"I'm sorry, that came out badly," said Ino quickly, continuing to feel mortified. "What happened? Did they move back to Scotland?"

Out of the corner of her eye she caught sight of Calypso lumbering towards them from the far end of the garden. She carried a flask of water as carefully as though she were competing in an egg-and-spoon race.

But then his next words jarred her. "If I could, I would frown, you understand, and if I could weep, I'd be doing that too."

"Oh dear," said Ino.

"It was 'Oh dear,'" said Michael gruffly. "You see, Catherine came home one day, cooked her husband his evening meal and then shot him – shot him dead. She then went upstairs and shot the baby too."

"God," said Ino, sitting up abruptly and knocking over her cup in the process. "God."

"Aye. Don't think *He* was around much on that day, do you?"

Ino felt sick. She wished she could remember everything he'd said instead of sliding off into her own daydreams. She could hardly ask him to repeat it all either. "Does anyone know why?"

"If I could shrug… Something like that is too big, isn't it, to ever understand why? Who knows what was going on in the poor lass's head? Some say she was on some sort of medication when she was living down south, but when she went up to Scotland, when she went home, well, some doctor – actually, the very same beau that jilted her – turned up again in Edinburgh and persuaded her that she wasn't depressed, that she was quite well, that she didn't need it. Others say that she'd never got over that first love, and that when she met him again… Whatever the reason, she stopped taking her medication and went completely doolally."

"Doolally, indeed," said Ino quietly as something sank in her like a stone; made her legs start to shake uncontrollably. And suddenly, any pretence seemed contrived. She removed her sunglasses with trembling fingers, then hugged herself tightly. "That doctor, that… beau of hers…?"

Michael's expression was impassive. Her eyes were green, he decided. And her face was battered. No amount of make-up was going to disguise that. "Why, that was your husband, lass," he said. "I'm sorry. I thought you must have known. Why else would you have moved here?"

18

Emil
Barcelona
June 2017

Emil, preparing to smoke his first cigarette of the day, was neither ready nor willing to engage in conversation. He had his happy little routine. Half asleep (though showered), he arrived at the *pastelaria*. The near pitch dark suited him perfectly. He'd never been one to leap out of bed, and even now he struggled to take stock of his surroundings, acclimatising slowly to what his life had become. Over the years, there had been glimpses; windows into the life he might have had. At times he saw himself in the courting couple buying rolls for a romantic picnic, then cake for their first child's baptism, snacks for *merienda* and a growing brood, and then, as those people too grew older, the same couple accompanying a grandchild. All were snapshots of what he'd imagined belonging to him. The turn, the fork in the road, the sliding door, whatever you wanted to call it, had been so sudden, so staggeringly abrupt that even now Emil wondered if any of it had really happened. But one thing was certain: cigarette in hand, he was not ready, not ever, for shitchat (his word) before his first cup of coffee.

With an unlit cigarette dangling from the corner of his mouth, Emil felt his way in the dark pastry shop. He often thought he'd do pretty well if he were ever to lose his sight – at least, in this place; he knew it like the back of his hand. Still in the dark, he unhooked the plastic hood that covered the cold meat section, switched on the coffee machine (he always emptied the coffee beans into the container the night before, ready to flick on a switch), and with a satisfying pat felt the warmth belting from the ovens, knowing that the loaves would be ready for breakfast. Once, he had dreamed of reviving not only the *forn* at Salto, but its mills too, grinding flour from plentiful fields of its own wheat. But over the years, that dream too had slipped onto the shelves of what might have been.

Only when he was ready to pour himself a coffee did he unlock the front door. The air was always cool at 3.30am, welcome and faithful in the brief hours before the merciless, punishing heat rose from the pavements to wreak its damage. Emil loved the shape of the early dawn: the church dome etched blearily against an ever-lightening sky; the flagpole still and unwavering. Most of all, he loved the quiet. A quiet that always reminded him of Rapa Nui and a remoteness to which he returned in his head, again and again. Except that this morning it wasn't quiet. The usual background drone from the baking drum was fragmented by unmistakable sobs coming from... He pushed a table with his foot, and took a quick drag on his cigarette before hunkering down to peer underneath.

"What the...?"

Stretching out his arm, he pulled a girl to her feet. She was crying – well, he would be too, dressed like that. She wore the tiniest white shorts and an even skimpier top, exposing a tanned midriff. There were smudges of mascara on her cheeks and shiny nose. Despite her obvious distress, Emil recognised the Oxford exchange student (by way of New York) from the other day.

"Here." He pushed her into a chair. "I'll get you some water." He didn't wait for a reply but, taking another couple of quick puffs, left his cigarette smouldering in an ashtray before ducking back into the shop.

She was still sniffing when he returned with a bottle of Salto Spring, two cups of espresso, and a couple of *Bocado de Damas* fresh from the oven. She was hugging her knees, her face hidden. When she eventually managed a few words, they were incomprehensible.

Emil shook his head. "You can tell me when you've had this," he said, more to give himself a chance to down his own coffee than out of genuine concern. Although when he stole a sideways glance, noting her tousled hair and grubby shoes, he felt a pang of something alarmingly akin to pity. This girl seemed younger than she had the other day, and far less knowing.

With a final sniff she wiped her nose on the back of her hand, ignoring the tissues from the little tin box that seemed indigenous to Spanish coffee shops. He slid the plate of *Bocado de Damas* towards her. He pretended not to notice when she snatched one and began nibbling the edge in a mouse-like fashion, as though too much might make her sick or fat. Was she anorexic? No, she didn't seem to be. When she had finished, he made a wiping motion. Sugar glistened on her top lip.

"Those were delicious," she said, pushing the empty plate away.

"*Hechos en casa*," he said in Spanish. "Well, not strictly true. *Baked* in house, to be more precise."

She was listening. Just. He took a swig of coffee. *Keep things neutral. Keep her engaged. Keep her talking...*

"Do you know what *Bocado de Damas* means?"

She shook her head, then nodded. "A mouth... something of ladies?"

"Yes, sort of," said Emil, leisurely inhaling on his tobacco. Cup in hand, he stretched out his legs, sitting comfortably. This was more like it. Having to smoke quickly always gave him indigestion. "'Bite-size for a lady', I suppose, might be the closest translation. You see, they were favoured by high-society ladies because they were small, and the rippling spiral effect with sugar made them sweet and delicious."

She smiled wanly.

And still he rambled on. "They're pretty, aren't they? I first came across them in Chile and I've wanted to reproduce them here ever since. And of course, they're no longer just popular among the ladies, but they're ideal for snacking. Children love them... I mean, not that you..." He let his voice trail, and then rushed on in case she'd taken offence. "Time was when everything – flour, wheat, pastry, *todo* – it all came from the *castillo*. But today..." He made an apologetic shrug.

"The *castil-lo*?" She pronounced it with a foreign accent, which was surprising as he'd thought her Spanish pretty fluent when they'd chatted the other day.

Emil finished his coffee and lit another cigarette, blowing smoke out of the corner of his mouth, away from her direction. "Ah yes, I always forget people don't know our history..."

"Why? Is it complicated?" She sat forward, elbows on the table, head in her hands. She was like a child, he thought: temporarily forgetting her distress in being distracted.

"Yes and no. It's by no means unique. A lot of large country houses didn't survive the Civil War; nor more recently the isolation, the number of staff required to keep them going. It's all a bit antiquated." He smiled apologetically. "Salto survives – just." Barely. Not at all. But he wasn't going to say that. Emil motioned to the logo on the little canopy above their heads. "It's the place where I grew up. Once upon a time, the bakery there supplied the whole village."

"And now?" She was watching him, wide-eyed, and he felt stupidly flattered by her interest. It was almost a relief, being able to explain how it was to a complete stranger. *How it is*, he corrected himself mentally. *How it is*.

"Well, it began as a sideline; a kind of hobby." *It sure as hell was never intended to be* our *sideline*, he might have added. "But the ovens and flour mill haven't been in use for a long time. We bake all pre-prepared goods here." He drew a line with his cigarette to the shop behind them. "The other is finished."

"That's a shame."

"It is." He shrugged. "*Los tiempos cambian*. Times change."

She was looking at his cigarette.

"Do you smoke?"

She nodded. "Just a puff."

"You know, you shouldn't get hooked," he said lamely, handing her his half-smoked cigarette.

She hesitated only briefly, then held it clumsily between two fingers, inhaling delicately. She began spluttering at once, more tears spurting from her eyes.

"Mmm... not sure that you do smoke, *niña*." He took the cigarette from her.

She shook her head. "It's..."

"What is it?" he asked kindly then. He was awake now. He'd had his coffee. He could afford to be kind. "What's a nice kid like you doing... well, hiding under one of my tables, for starters? At..." he looked across the square at the clock tower of St Vicenç, "4am?"

She smiled through her tears. "Oh, just stuff."

"Stuff?" He raised an eyebrow. "What, homesick stuff?"

She shook her head.

He leaned back, cigarette alight, enjoying the cool air. It wouldn't be long before the sun was high in the sky and the neighbourhood burst into life. "Please don't tell me a boy is making you unhappy? Or..." It just occurred to him that he might be out of step with the current generation. "A... girl?" His turn to mumble. But he'd said it. He was quite pleased with himself. Wait until he recounted all this to Rafael!

There was a moment's silence. But then, to his relief, the girl burst out laughing. "You should see your face!" she said. "You can't imagine anything worse, can you?!"

"No – well, actually..." He could. Lots.

She shook her head. Long dark strands falling over her shoulders reminded him of... "It's just different here, that's all." Her shoulders folded in. "Sometimes I just hate being this age." Her eyes filled again. "I just want to be older..."

"Older?!"

"Yeah... like you. I mean, you're kind of done, now, aren't you? I envy that."

Emil had been leaning back, his chair tipping against the table behind him, his foot wedged on the frame. Now he brought it forward with a thump. "Now *I* want to cry!" he said. He wouldn't tell Rafael that part.

"Oh, I don't mean—" she stuttered.

"It's okay, I know what you mean." He inhaled deeply on his cigarette before letting it rest on the edge of the ashtray. "But please don't wish your time away. It'll pass quick enough, believe me."

"Has it for you?"

"Well, I hope I'm not entirely done living." He smiled, amused by her solemnity. "Some parts have gone quickly; others not so much. You should travel."

"I am travelling!"

"Okay, but more. Further afield."

"Depends on one's point of departure, doesn't it? This place is far enough from my home town."

"True, but is it different enough?"

"Again, depends on what you're used to." The girl finally took dainty sips of her espresso, which by now must be tepid. She didn't seem to mind.

"The point is to get away," insisted Emil. "Sure, this is different to home, but it's still relatively safe; it's *recognisable*. You need adventure; you need to know yourself."

"Like you did? You got away?"

"Yes. Yes, I did." Emil stretched. And what wouldn't he give to be back on Easter Island now, walking towards the Moai at Tongariki? Or setting off along the coast from Hanga Roa with a glimpse of the white-eyed statue towards Te Peu? He'd never known such peace; such welcome solitude. The place had saved him; saved his sanity.

"So where shall I go?"

"Mmm? Go? Why, everywhere! I'd start with South America. You're learning the language. So, use it."

"I just… I don't know. I want to be taken seriously."

He tried not to stare too long at her orange-painted fingernails, silver shoes and belly piercing. "Then do something seriously."

"Like what?"

"That, *mi niña*, only you can decide…"

19

Ino
Winchester
June 2017

After Michael had gone, Ino remained seated under the pergola for some time. She made placatory sounds in Calypso's direction while her daughter finished decorating Oreo's hutch with stickers and flowers. Ordinarily, Ino would have been irate – Calypso had merrily lopped off the heads of Ino's prettiest roses to make garlands for the rabbit – but she was too preoccupied with Michael's news to take much notice. Her mind was in turmoil. She was as shocked by the revelation that it was Archie who had been Catherine's doctor as by the terrible event itself. She wanted answers right away. She wanted to ring Archie at once and ask him why he'd never told her about the house's history.

Instead, she sat immobile, watching as the sun began to set across the sweet-smelling camomile lawn. Fine cobwebs glistened for a moment before being cast into shadow, and from where she sat, her house, her Dormer Cottage, was perfect with its neatly sprung thatch and honeysuckle trellis. She found it almost impossible to equate her beautiful cottage with a tragedy of such magnitude. But it was a Pandora's box, thought Ino, whose lid should have remained forever sealed. Where to go with all this information? With all these thoughts? This confusion? Her head buzzed with questions. Why? Why would Archie even *want* to live here, knowing that such a terrible thing had happened? Was his drinking somehow related to the tragedy? Michael had said that the doctor in Scotland who had treated Catherine was also the man who had jilted her. Was Catherine the reason Archie didn't really appear to love Ino? Because he was still in love with Catherine and felt guilty that she had died?

Ino closed her eyes. Her right eyelid twitched, as it did more frequently these days, even without the recent trauma to her face. She needed answers. She needed to understand. Only then might she be more sympathetic towards Archie. Only then might she ever forgive him.

Archie

Cedar Avenue

I've met an amazing woman. Ha, that should get you going – what's good for the goose, hey? But – and it does pain me to be honest – it's not like that, although she'd be up for it, no contest. She's about fourteen years older than me, so keep your hair on. Don't relax yet, though – I know you – because she's by far the sexiest woman I've met in years. And yes, I could screw her. I want to. She wants it. I'd start an affair if I had the time, and she's always travelling so it would be a train wreck and I don't need that. I don't want a casual thing. You've ruined that side of things for me – you have. I blame you.

But getting back to her – she's a sophisticated, intelligent woman with a cruel sense of humour and an animal ambition second only to my own. She's nothing like you – nothing to remind me of you.

Nothing.

20

Rafael
Barcelona
June 2017

Padre Rafael was grateful to be alone in the sacristy while he put away the chalice and communion cups. He wiped the paten with embroidered cloths and folded his vestments, knowing that the little Maltese nun in charge of housekeeping would certainly redo (and redo perfectly) what he had only performed in such a cursory fashion. He reattached his dog collar and blew out the candles. He cast a glance at the piscina, made sure that the storage cabinet housing the parish records was locked and grabbed a packet of cigarettes from his coat pocket. He was unsettled, and would have admitted it freely had anyone cared to ask. It took a lot to unsettle Padre Rafael, but Veronica's visit had done more than that. It had disturbed his usual calm and, like a geologist sifting sand through a pan looking for gold, his memories had been tossed carelessly to the surface.

Only, Padre Rafael's memories were far from golden; at least not the ones he turned over now. He genuflected in front of the altar, dipped the fingers of his right hand in the font, and crossed himself while fingering a loose cigarette with the other hand. No amount of *postre* the evening before could wipe away the taste of Veronica's visit, and he could only thank Providence that she had not attended the morning's early Mass. For once, too, he was grateful that Emil appeared to be indisposed. As yet, the awnings were still rolled firmly tight and the *pastelaria* was in darkness. Padre Rafael needed to think. He needed time and he needed to be alone. He sure as hell didn't need to see his cousin's tortured face; his stoical figure hunched over the *turrón* and angels' hair while they both religiously danced around a subject that had been haunting them for over a decade.

But where to go? He was far too well known in this barrio of Sarrià, either by current parishioners who did attend Mass, or by inhabitants who didn't but knew him from his frequent walks around the neighbourhood, or by an older generation who remembered his parents (and the fate that befell them) and, more to the point, could recall his own story. He could but wouldn't go to the polo club – that really would be macabre – and he had absolutely no desire to bump into a well-meaning fellow priest.

He inhaled as he walked with no particular destination in mind. He passed nursery-age children on their way home for lunch, maids sent out to buy bread (Sarrià was the kind of barrio where most residences employed domestic help), businessmen on their way downtown. He passed the ancient Pedralbes Monastery at the foot of the steep incline that began the first ascent away from the city. As was the case with the houses near his church, he passed buildings swathed in either La Senyera or La Estelada or both. Some flew the flag of the EU as well.

Tia Verónica… He couldn't get her out of his mind, and it wasn't just the surprise of her (robust) religious stance. Were they so very different, he and she, in the end? He had taunted her with the Roosevelt quote but actually – and here he hardly dared credit her with a modicum of intelligence – she *had* been talking about ideas. In relation to Ino, it was true, but they were ideas, nonetheless. Religion in both their cases had served to staunch a pretty healthy river of guilt. He was paying, and he would continue to pay, for what had happened, for what he alone had set in motion. His actions; no one else's.

But Verónica? What was she hiding from? What was she guilty of? Her visit was certainly a cry for something. Or someone. That had seemed genuine enough. He was beginning to understand something else, too. It was Verónica who was sending him on this hike God only knew where. Had it all really begun with her? He supposed in a way it had. And then, as his steps took him further away, the scent of syringa and nostalgia enveloping him at every turn, he knew that there was only one place where he could go now.

21

Emil
Barcelona
July 2017

"I've got something for you."

Emil knew, before looking up, that the voice was coming from under the table. He sighed. His early morning routine was being completely destroyed and yet, having won the girl's trust, he wasn't sure how to say that she really couldn't keep turning up like this. It was the one time of day he had always enjoyed. To himself. Without even looking, he reached down a hand to winkle her out. Like a cork, Gemma popped up fresh as a daisy. Gone were the doll-sized clothes and in their place were jeans and a normal T-shirt. Her long hair was scooped up in a scruffy bun and she clutched a folder. She was also wrapped in not one but two versions of La Estelada: the one that boasted a white star on a red chevron (for independence); the other on a blue (independence coupled with republican ideals).

"Do you know what time it is?" he said grumpily.

Gemma motioned to the clock tower. "Yeah, and so does the whole barrio." She eyed his dishevelled appearance. "Aren't we having *Bocado de Damas*?"

"So, it's table *and* breakfast."

"Well, duh." Her eyes were sparkling, veritably dancing.

He did an about-turn, ducking back into the shop, emerging seconds later. "You're early. Not even the first batch is ready."

"But never too early for a ciggy, huh?"

Emil raised an eyebrow. He had an uncanny feeling that she was getting the upper (if not better) hand. "I thought I told you smoking was bad for you."

"You did. You're the one who needs the smoke."

"You know me better than I thought. But not that well." He touched the flags. He touched his heart. "Put those away. Independence is what you carry here."

Reluctantly, she unwound the banners from around her neck. She seemed disappointed. "I thought you'd be with them."

Emil grimaced. "In spirit, perhaps, but I'm too old for such antics."

"Old?!" Gemma's eyes were wide. "There are people *much* older than you out there!"

"That's reassuring." Emil lit a cigarette, and for a moment was distracted by a huge, diaphanous spider's web that hung precariously from a corner of the brick wall and sprawled to the side of the shop's canopy. Invisible in broad daylight, in this hesitant dawn it shimmered strong yet vulnerable, delicate and fragile. *Like this girl*, he thought. *Like Ino.*

She seemed to be waiting for more.

"Then I'm just lazy," he added with a smile.

"No, you're not! I don't believe it."

"Look, Gemma, my walking down the Ramblas isn't going to change anything. I know it's exciting having this… this common purpose. You're young; you feel a sense of camaraderie with the next man or woman. But the fact is that no one, least of all Puigdemont, has really thought through what this so-called 'independence' means. Like Brexit in England. Independence for Scotland. No one actually knows. In the meantime, I have a business to run." He took a deep drag, exhaling through the side of his mouth. He balanced his cigarette on the edge of the ashtray, crossing his legs and leaning back. "I know you've got something there. I know you're hiding something. What is it?"

Gemma ducked under the table. "I've been thinking..." she began, emerging breathless, an artist's sketch pad tucked under her arm.

"Uh-oh."

"You said to do something; you said—"

Emil tapped the cigarette. "I say all kinds of things – most you can ignore."

Gemma rolled her eyes. "Whatever." Sucking her teeth in disapproval, she brushed ash from the table and opened her sketchbook to the centrefold pages. In the dim light, Emil couldn't quite register what was on them. "Voilà!" she said proudly. She was flushed; triumphant.

Squinting, Emil moved closer. "Can I...?" He took the book with both hands, moving back to the shop, where he flicked on the lights.

"It's a new logo," she said, following him.

"I can see." His tone was stiff.

She was at his shoulder, tracing the image with her fingertip (bitten nails, he noted). Gone was the gold outline of a castle against a bright blue background – and not any old blue, but *Oxford* blue, Ino had informed him once – and in its place was a simple bunch of wheat within a circle. The stems were held in place by intertwining letters: M and A. Well, at least those hadn't been lost to creativity. The colours appeared to consist of only two – ecru and a dull gold – but on closer inspection the background showed itself to have flecks of apricot, orange and white. It was well drawn, he'd give her that; as unsettling as it was sophisticated.

"I can tell you've spent some time on this," Emil said carefully.

Taking his comment as approval, Gemma spun away from him, going into the shop to bring out coffee. "The blue has to go," she said excitedly, reaching for the fringe of the canopy that just skimmed her head. "It's no different from all the other places you see in La Barceloneta or the port. It's tired; too fuddy-duddy. I mean, once, maybe..." Her eyes flicked sideways to the framed polo pictures. "But if this is who you are now, then you have to move on."

Emil closed the sketchbook with a thud. He wasn't sure if he could fully explain the feeling of panic that had crept over him. One thing he did realise, though, was that if the *pastelaria* was antiquated (and seeing the mock-up and hearing this girl's marketing jargon made him realise that it just might be), it was because he hadn't wanted to change a thing, not really. He frowned. But why not? Wasn't it time? And then he realised something else. His sense of panic was due, rightly or wrongly, to the belief that if he changed, even if he took tiny steps to effect change, it would mean that he was ready to move on. And if he was ready to move on, it would mean removing those photos from the top shelves behind the biscuit tins. It would mean it was the beginning of the process of letting go completely; of forgetting. "What if I don't want to?"

Gemma's face disintegrated. "I'm sorry?"

"Cute pictures, I grant you."

"Ouch," she said in a wavering voice, and immediately he felt regretful, but still, you had to be cruel to be kind. She snatched back her scrapbook. After a moment's pause, she turned. "What's the matter with you? Should I have waited for you to have your smoke?"

"It might have helped." He marvelled at her maturity, but he couldn't soften now. "Nothing's the matter. I like opening up by myself."

"Opening up, sure, but not *to* anyone."

Emil shrugged. "You need to stop hanging round here. You need to make friends—"

Gemma's eyes filled with tears. "I thought we *were* friends."

Emil ran a hand through his hair. This was precisely the kind of thing - the kind of conversation - he'd hoped to avoid. "Yes - no! Look, I'm too old to be a friend; the kind you need. You're talented, Gemma, and you're a sweet kid, but you've got to stop coming around here. I have work to do. Real work. Quite frankly you're becoming a distraction. I'm not sure that you're putting in the hours at school that you should be either. Look, I'm sorry if I'm blunt, but you'll thank me in the long run. I don't want to see you any more in the morning."

Archie

Cedar Avenue

You're not coming. You didn't come. You won't be coming, will you?
   I never want to see you again.
   What the fuck am I to do with the tickets?

22

Ino
Winchester
July 2017

Ino could hide her misery no longer. Tears coursed down her cheeks and she emitted pathetic sniffles as she did the washing-up. Calypso's small person had pushed a chair and climbed up to sit beside her on the counter. Ino had tried (ineffectively) to ask Archie about the woman Catherine and the terrible murder that had taken place in their home. Their *home*. Not another random house in the village, but right here. Surely if he knew anything, anything at all, he had a duty to tell her? He would *want* to tell her? Out of consideration? Kindness? Was it so unreasonable to want to know? Apparently, it was. Archie had called her a gossiping bitch and stormed off to the pub.

"Why does Daddy hate you?" Calypso asked now with that honest, blank child's expression that never failed to pierce Ino's heart.

"Hate?" Ino wiped her nose with the back of her Marigold. "No, no, no, darling, he doesn't hate me," she said, although even to her ears she sounded unconvincing.

"Then why is he so mean?"

Ino closed her eyes. Why? Her daughter was right. Why? Because he had probably never really loved her. *Couldn't* love her after what had happened with Catherine. Ino knew she was leaping to conclusions, only speculating, but somehow it was an explanation. She didn't want to believe that Archie was just a selfish monster and a drunk. "I don't know," she said softly.

"Yes, you do," insisted Calypso. "You do."

Ino took a deep breath. "I don't think Daddy's very well," she said, daring to meet her daughter's look head-on. "I think he has a drinking illness that makes him so unwell that he lashes out. You know, like when Oreo scratched you once? She was in pain, but it wasn't because she didn't love you, was it? And you didn't stop loving her."

"No, but that's different," said Calypso, scooping out soap suds and blowing a bubble in Ino's direction.

"Why? Why is it different?"

"Because," said Calypso, pricking the bubbles, "afterwards Oreo went back to loving me, but Daddy never goes back to loving you."

Out of the mouths of babes... Ino was beginning to think Calypso was right in more ways than one. She bit her lip. "But he always loves *you*," she said, peeling off her rubber gloves and lifting Calypso from the counter.

That bit, at least, was true. It wasn't that Ino doubted that Archie loved his daughter; it was that she doubted he felt anything for *her*. For a moment she held Calypso tightly. Calypso tolerated her mother's embrace for a minute longer before wriggling free. Ino couldn't remember the last time Archie had touched her (unless it was to hit her), let alone embrace her. She wondered if he had ever really loved her, even at the beginning. For her part, she realised now that she had mistaken loneliness for love; mild attention for commitment. And now, that tiny, shored-up store of fragile love, so carefully nurtured, was being gradually whittled away. Or not so gradually. At alarming speed. Soon, if she wasn't careful, there would be nothing left at all. Calypso spilled a tin of crayons onto the kitchen floor and, lying prone, began colouring on a large sheet of black paper. Ino, leaning against the kitchen counter, watched her daughter make teardrop-shaped splodges. They looked like overlarge raindrops. Or snowflakes.

Snow... Ino had always associated Archie with snow, ice and cold. As Calypso coloured, throwing her entire body into the endeavour, Ino's thoughts slipped far away. Was it ever fun with Archie? Why had she thought he was even interested in her? Any closeness between them, never mind harmony, seemed unthinkable now, but surely there must have been some spark once?

There certainly hadn't been the first time they'd met. If there was a spark to be felt, it wasn't for Ino but for her mother. Even now, Ino remembered her surprise when Archie had got in touch a week or so after that initial uncomfortable meeting at her mother's apartment. The snowstorm that had gripped the city the week before had blown over, but despite the city's best efforts, six-foot snow banks made tunnels of the roads. Montreal was beautiful, airbrushed in swathes of thick white snow, and quiet, so quiet, as a result. To be on the safe side, he suggested meeting for a drink (not dinner, she noted, relieved) downtown so that she could always walk home to her university digs should the weather take another turn for the worse. There was a new, cool bar called Le Lab on Rachel Street. Ino had heard of it. With nothing better to do, but not exactly excited either, she agreed.

"Does the name of the place appeal to the scientist in you?" she asked him when a heavily tattooed waitress had seated them at a small table in a corner by the fire. The place was kitted out like an English pub, with lots of oak and smoky mirrors. Ino could feel the snow melting through her hair, but this time she had worn her thick winter coat and proper snow boots.

"No, but they mix their own home-made spirits and liquors, and that does," said Archie. He was already a couple of drinks ahead of her, and barely acknowledged her arrival.

Ino attributed this coolness (not 'cool' in an on-trend kind of way, but a coolness devoid of passion) to his profession. And after the excess of her Spanish relations, his restraint was the most attractive thing about him, although it soon became clear that it wasn't something he could exercise in all areas. He drank heavily, talked to other people, and didn't seem all that interested in her. He could be silent for long periods, staring openly at other women in the restaurant. Perversely, Ino didn't mind. Again, used to her cousin's old-world chivalry, she only found this disdain – if it could be called that – all the more challenging. But she wasn't used to her looks being ignored. In Spain they had been openly acknowledged and appreciated, and Ino had become accustomed to generating some sort of response in the opposite sex.

"You find her attractive?" she said at length, fascinated rather than offended by his obvious attraction to someone else. Archie had spent a good fifteen minutes staring at a blonde woman in a cobalt-blue blouse.

"I like blondes," he said. "Redheads at a push. She's absolutely my type."

"Oh," said Ino. That last had taken her aback. The 'boys' – her cousin Rafael and Emil – had never hidden their obvious attraction to her. "Then in that case, you probably find my mother—"

"Your mother is amazing," he interrupted.

"Then perhaps you should be having a drink with Veronica."

Archie had looked at her then, as if noticing her for the first time. He'd laughed, but Ino had sipped her cocktail, confused.

"So, what do you feel?" asked Archie, ordering yet another glass of red wine and tucking into a plate of chips. He'd almost finished the plate before offering her any. He wiped a crumb in an absent-minded sort of way from the front of his shirt.

"About?"

"English or Canadian?"

"Neither." Ino crossed her legs under the table. She decided the best way to deal with this odd man was to simply answer his questions directly.

Archie was now comfortably installed, his arms stretched over the back of his chair and sitting at right angles so as to better see the other drinkers. "Then what? You sound English."

"English-*ish*, I'm told. I went to university in England."

"Oh yes, that's right, Oxford. And you're here because…?" His eyes flicked past her to the crowds gathering at the bar. It was snowing heavily again, and people began to come in off the streets to warm up. Every question he asked seemed forced, as though he couldn't care less about the answer. He was staring again at the blonde in the blue blouse.

"I wanted to join a circus, drugs cartel, prostitution ring. In that order." She waited for a reaction.

"Is that right?" he said mildly.

"No." She waited for him to register, and when he didn't her eyes narrowed. Was the man for real? Why was she even sitting here? She had better things to do! Except the truth of it was that she didn't, and despite his staggering rudeness, he was distracting because of it. "Needed a change," she muttered, wondering if he even heard her.

Amazingly, this seemed to resonate, for he knocked back his glass of wine in one and tapped the rim to indicate that he wanted another. "Fuckin' right. I know that feeling."

She took a breath, making an effort. "So, you're going to stay? In Montreal, I mean?"

Archie passed a hand over his face. "Hell, no. Means to an end. I'm headed home in the autumn – you guys call it fall."

"Not I," said Ino primly. She took another sip. This man was as acerbic as her drink. "Tell me about your work," she said. Either that or she would get up and go. She would give it ten seconds. *One, two…*

Archie stretched out a leg so that it was outside the perimeter of the table. Perfectly placed for any poor punter to trip over. Once or twice other customers stepped over him on their way to the cloakroom or the bar, but Archie appeared not to care. *Three…* She could see the pale skin peeping from beneath his pinstriped trouser leg. There was something so weird and eccentric about him. *Four, five…*

"Oh, you don't want to hear about that. *I* wouldn't want to."

Ino let a nervous laugh escape. Archie looked surprised but not displeased.

"You don't love it?"

"Nope."

"So why do it?"

"We all do things we don't love, don't we?"

Ino looked around the bar at the geometric tiles and exposed brick wall. Ornate mirrors refracted the light and, with it, Archie's face. *Six...* "Yes," she said in the direction of his reflection. "I suppose we do."

"Look, you're young," said Archie. "When you get to my age, the job's a means to an end. Nothing altruistic at all. I know Ver… your mother likes to tout me as some sort of miracle worker."

Ino tried to meet his eyes, but it was impossible. He was looking everywhere but in her direction. "Are you?"

"Of course not."

Over by the counter, the bartenders seemed to have gone into a frenzy, juggling and spinning. Archie's next drink – the drink after the bottle of wine, that is – was lit tequila; the flames engulfing the alcohol and served in a teapot.

"Good heavens!" The atmosphere in the bar had become charged. The lights had dimmed; the burgundy colours of the different alcohols reflected off the mirrors, the marble counters and the gilt beer pumps. Through half-closed eyes, Ino could imagine herself back at Salto. Outside, thick ropes of snow caked the iron window frames until there was only the smallest glint from the road. Inside, the warmth and noise were all-embracing. And suddenly that was exactly what Ino wanted: to be erased; subsumed by someone else's story.

"Have something else," urged Archie. "In fact, I insist. I'm choosing." He winked at the tattooed waitress.

"I don't usually drink on a school night," said Ino.

"What are you?" said Archie in disgust. "Twelve?" And he looked at her, his eyes widening in a louche sort of way.

Seven... Ino bit her lip. "Okay," she agreed. "You choose."

"I have," said Archie. "And it's here."

The waitress placed what Ino could only describe as a concoction; a wizard's brew; a cauldron – a huge jug, anyway. The drink was topped with an orchid and a retro 1950s postcard of a girl in a bathing suit.

"But that's too much!" protested Ino. "I can't drink all of that!"

"It's called Sex on la Beach," the waitress announced helpfully in an unmistakable French-Canadian accent.

When she'd gone, Ino took a tentative sip. The liquid slid directly to her veins, hitting her stomach, torpedoing her thoughts. "Is that what you'd like?" she said boldly.

Archie didn't miss a beat, but he didn't look at her. He was looking, if she remembered correctly, back at the blonde. "Always," he said.

Eight... "Did my mother suggest this?" Ino asked, suddenly suspicious.

Archie shrugged, not at all embarrassed. "Maybe."

"God!" said Ino, taking a sip. "I might have known."

"She said you were lonely."

"What, and this would cheer me up?"

"Does me," said Archie, distinctly slurring his words.

Nine... "I'm not lonely," said Ino. "I like to be alone."

"So do I."

Ten.

And look where that admission had got her! Ino hardly slept that night, tormenting herself with 'what ifs'. Half-expecting Archie to reappear at any moment, she waited, listening for the crunch of gravel, the key fumble, and the inevitable cursing as he stumbled up the stairs. But after he'd stormed off to the pub, he didn't come home. Had she known for certain that he *wouldn't* be coming back, she would have enjoyed the solitude. She would have locked the back door just as the PCSO Jane Leeming said she should. But after putting Calypso to bed, and even after a relaxing bath, she still couldn't concentrate on the new Henry Neild book she'd been saving for just such an evening. A couple of times, as if doubting the luck of being so completely alone, she checked on Calypso, who was fast asleep in the position she always adopted: starfish on her back, her whole being completely surrendered to sleep. She need not have – this child was not waking up.

She made herself tea and toast for a late supper and went downstairs in her dressing gown, padding through the empty rooms. How peaceful it was without Archie, and, although the default tension she was so used to kept her body rigid, she knew that, for one evening at least, he wouldn't be bothering her. She opened the back door for a final glance at the garden, its topiary illuminated by the full moon. The crickets were out in force; the air was balmy and still, save for that crying baby somewhere down the lane. Clearly the parents had trouble getting it to sleep and were walking with it even at this late hour. Calypso had been a good little sleeper and Ino had never resorted to driving round at odd hours with a baby in the back, desperately trying to get her to nod off.

And if the neighbour's baby couldn't sleep, neither could Ino. She couldn't stop thinking about what Michael had told her about Dormer Cottage – well before it was called Dormer Cottage. She couldn't stop thinking about the woman called Catherine, or the murders that had taken place in her home. Her *home*! Ugh! Ino shuddered. It was such a terrible, terrible thought, such a terrible thing to have happened, and right here. She wondered where exactly it had happened. Had death been instantaneous? Had they suffered? How long, she wondered, did it take for a heart to stop beating?

She shook herself mentally. She must stop thinking this way. But how could she *not* have known? How could Archie have kept such a thing from her? She'd never have moved in had she known. And to think that Archie was somehow involved! It changed everything she felt about the house, and it certainly changed what she thought about Archie. Or did it? It was exactly in his nature to keep something as enormous as this to himself! If only he would talk to her, if only to reassure her that he wasn't responsible; that he didn't feel responsible. Did he? Was that why he drank so much? She almost hoped that was the reason why he had become so erratic, so... unmanageable, because that would somehow give shape to this: to his drinking. If they could pin the blame on that, then surely they could get help together?

The following morning, after dropping Calypso off at school, Ino went straight on to park at the Discovery Centre in Jewry Street. Even though she had hardly slept, she felt exhilarated at being proactive for once in her married life, and, after buying a coffee in the cafeteria area, settled in a corner with her laptop. She could have worked at home, but the quiet, punctuated by the sound of that crying baby, was getting on her nerves. She would ask Michael if he'd found out who it belonged to the next time she saw him.

The library – it had been renamed the Discovery Centre only a short time before – was full of regulars. The old woman with a cane who was always first in no matter how early Ino got there, and who managed to bag the daily papers, reading every single line, poring over them and guarding them zealously. No one else ever got a look-in, and by the time she gave them up it was time to leave anyway. The Discovery Centre was located alongside a homeless shelter, and so it also got its fair share of drunks and jobless. And then there was the dribs and drabs of lonely mothers like herself with toddlers trailing behind them.

But on this morning, Ino felt she was on a mission – a mission of discovery of her own – and the feeling was empowering. She flipped open her MacBook Air, read a few emails and then began googling. At first there was nothing – at least, not regarding a crime related to postnatal depression. There was a catalogue of bloodthirsty murders, the reading of which made Ino's blood run cold. There was one in a neighbouring village where a disgruntled handyman had returned to kill a family of five. She felt dizzy and sick. 'No one wanted to buy Sleepy Hollow in the wake of the horrific crimes committed there,' said the *Daily Echo*. Funny, that. 'The house was eventually demolished.' Should that have happened to Dormer Cottage? No wonder its name had been changed from the original! What did a house have to go through for it to be condemned? Did three deaths not compare to the five at Rosebriar?

Ino got up to order some ginger tea – ginger was supposed to be an anti-emetic, she seemed to remember from her pregnancy with Calypso. She nursed her cup, letting the liquid cool, and went back to surfing the net. It wasn't long before she found the entry she was looking for. She took another few sips, almost delaying the moment when she would finally know the truth. She shut her eyes, heart pounding. *Okay. Now.* And there it was.

> *A mother with postnatal depression is thought to have killed her husband, her child and then herself in what has been described as the most horrific crime in the history of the small village of Drayton. Catherine Parish, 35, suffered a fit of psychotic postnatal depression before shooting her husband Harry Parish, also 35, and their six-week-old baby, Hamish. The attack happened just a few days before the family was due to go on holiday in Scotland. Catherine was said to have shot herself in a deliberate act of suicide. Sources have confirmed that she was suffering from postnatal depression following the birth of her baby. The eminent pathologist Sir James Freed arrived in Winchester on Thursday. The horrific scene was discovered by Mrs Wright, the Parish family's housekeeper, when she came to work on Wednesday morning. She became alarmed on discovering the front door wide open. At first, she suspected foul play. Police officers who attended the scene were overcome with grief as the family was known to them.*

They and Mrs Wright have been offered counselling by local authorities.

"We are all shocked by this terrible crime," said one local resident who wishes to remain anonymous.

Postnatal depression affects one in every ten new mothers in the UK according to the NHS, though other studies have shown the figure to be one in seven. Cases of postpartum psychosis are much rarer, affecting one woman in every 1,000 who give birth, according to the Royal College of Psychiatrists

Ino swallowed back her tears. This story didn't make her feel queasy in the same way the last one had; it just made her incredibly sad. What a terrible thing to have happened. And even more terrible was the fact that it had taken place in her home; in her idyllic cottage. Which begged the question as to why the estate agent at the time had kept silent. Hadn't he a duty, a legal requirement, even, to disclose what had occurred there? Or maybe he'd just assumed that Archie knew. Which, of course, he had. Only too well. Ino shivered. But now *she* knew, and was glad that she did. Michael had been right, of course. But how many more secrets were there lurking in the background, waiting to be uncovered? How much more was Archie hiding? Or, if not exactly hiding, then choosing not to reveal?

On the other hand, Ino too was keeping secrets. She felt her face; the bruise that had spread across her cheekbone. She was amazed it wasn't broken. *Without fear of judgement.* How comforting those words sounded! That was how it should be. It was time that she too spoke out. After all, if she couldn't, then what was to be gleaned from stories like the one she'd just read? She was an intelligent woman. Why was she allowing a man like Archie to treat her in this way? Was this the example she wanted to give Calypso? She shouldn't even blame Archie. She and she alone was *facilitating* his behaviour. She was allowing it to happen. Every cliché hurled its message: 'in this day and age'; 'feminism'; 'Oxford graduate'. Abuse, the great leveller...

Ino felt instinctively for the signet ring she used to wear on the little finger of her left hand, and then later, when she no longer wanted to have anything more to do with Spain, on a chain around her neck. And then later still, not at all. And suddenly, memory after memory came flooding back. She remembered who she was. Being with Archie all these years, and then the fast and furious months of early motherhood, had made her lose sight of herself; of the girl she once was. She had been blind; lost in a fog of self-pity and inertia. It was then that she thought of her mother. They might not always agree, let alone like each other, but if anyone possessed self-belief, it was Veronica. Ino might try absorbing a little of her single-mindedness. Would Veronica allow a man to treat her in this way? The notion was risible.

Ino sat up, straightening her shoulders, planting her feet firmly on the faux wood floor. With every sip of the hot ginger tea, with every glance at the dreadful article, with every twinge of pain flickering across her face, she felt herself grow stronger, her resolve to act quickened at last. With every recollection. *How* could she have forgotten who she was? She was a Monte Alegre (though perhaps not such a happy one at present) *and* a Cabeza de Vaca. A cow all right.

Ino glanced around the library cafeteria with its abstract tapestry pasted to the concrete wall. She remembered other city walls; other tapestries. Another castle: not in ruins, as was the Bishop's Palace, but one that stood on the brow of a hill overlooking a city, and a village that was... all hers. The recollection was a shock. How could she have relinquished so much? *Forgotten* so much? Why was she not keeping up with the news coming from Spain, and not just Spain, but Barcelona? *Her* Barcelona?

Another quick look encompassed the many newspapers discarded on tables or stacked on the racks by the till. Each and every headline dealt with the question of Catalan independence:

'Catalan Separatists Stage Protests,' said one. 'General Strike Called for Tuesday,' said another. The yellow and gold of La Senyera unfurling across one paper produced a quick stab of nostalgia. Cabeza de Vaca, Monte Alegre, Salto al Cielo… where did Ino and her family fit into that maelstrom? What had it to do with the glass cabinet displaying chocolate brownies and rock buns, or the central island selling greetings cards, knitted toys and stationery sets? How on earth had she ended up here, so far from everything she had once loved? A scab, a jolt of memory was unpicked. Weren't those the very questions she had once asked at Salto?

Everything she had once loved… Ino set down her mug of tea. Not 'once'. Not 'once loved', but still: *still* loved. Because she did. She always had. *To go forward, you must go back.* Who had said that? But she saw it all so clearly now. The past *was* the present, and without understanding the past, without remembering, wasn't she doomed to repeat it?

23

Ino
Barcelona
June 2002

The summer Ino turned fifteen would always stand out in her memory. In retrospect it was the year when everything changed, a rite of passage, and more impactful than realising, when she was very little, that she didn't have a father. Not that she was ever told that she didn't have one; not exactly, in so many words. Instinctively, she had always known that he had either died when she was a baby or never been on the scene in the first place. Either way, it had never seemed appropriate to ask about someone who had clearly impacted her mother's life so little.

And because he was never mentioned, Ino was never curious. Later, at school, she discovered that most of her classmates' parents were divorced anyway; that they were the products of what were then called 'broken' homes. No one referred to the absent parents, and neither did Ino. But the so-called broken home was just one of the many grown-up concerns she dismissed. Her own home was a very robust environment. Her mother wasn't around much, but the infrastructure of their comfortable home was sound. A South American housekeeper was at hand to produce fresh, nutritious food – a daily home-baked loaf of bread, and cake when Ino got home from school – and to ensure that her uniform was periodically laundered.

School was a single-sex girls' institution modelled on the English public-school system. Situated at the top of the steep, one-way Simpson Street, the school was named after a battle in a bay far away and a long time ago – yet another abstract Ino accepted unquestioningly but could neither relate to nor envisage. When Veronica wasn't travelling she did the school run, depositing Ino on her way to the ICAO building where she worked. In the afternoon, Ino took the bus. She would walk down Simpson alone to the corner of Sherbrooke, where she caught the bus to Westmount. The stop was some two blocks away from where they lived on Grosvenor, and Ino walked the remaining distance. The last bit always seemed the longest.

Home was a black-painted Victorian detached house with a porch. Ino had a key which she wore on a chain around her neck. Most times she was too lazy to take it off to unlock the door, choosing instead to stoop down with her neck virtually touching the letter box. The silence of the house never alarmed her. She knew exactly what to do and what to expect. She would take off her shoes, drop her bags in the hall, and pad along to the corridor hung with Eskimo art: black outlines of igloos etched on red tiles, green soapstone carvings of polar bears carrying fish in their mouths, and block prints depicting Inuit people lying on their bellies on the ice. It was only later that Veronica adopted a pastel palette when decorating her homes, doing away with the artefacts acquired in the different countries she had visited. But not seeing the Japanese ceremonial doll preserved in its own glass cage, the fans made out of sandalwood and still smelling of spices and exotic places, the straw Māori masks, the ebony statues from the Côte d'Ivoire, was something Ino would later miss.

In the kitchen, Ino would either cut a slice of the freshly baked bread which was still warm, or the cake (as yet un-iced) left out for her. Her mother called it 'icing', not 'frosting' as the other Canadian mothers did. This was on account of the time Ino had placed a whole package of 'frosted' Pop-Tarts into the freezer. Now

Veronica wanted Ino to be absolutely clear as to what was involved. Ino would make herself a cold chocolate milk – sometimes she popped a straw into the glass to give it a restaurant feel – and take her snack on a tray down to the basement.

From 3pm to 5.30pm, Rosa, the Guatemalan maid with a topknot like Wilma Flintstone's, would open the door to no one. In fact, she hardly looked up when Ino tiptoed in front of the TV screen to curl up in the waiting armchair; the one with the worn arms and the funny old-fashioned antimacassar. The tiptoeing served a twofold purpose. One was that Ino genuinely didn't want to interrupt a show (Rosa was enthralled by the new cable television from the States that Veronica had recently signed up to, and ahead of most of Ino's classmates); the other was that, if she did, Rosa would then mutter something about homework. Apart from the occasional puff-puff from the steam iron, both would soon be transfixed by the then-latest television serials such as *Gulliver's Travels*, *Get Smart* and *Bonanza*. Rosa said these reminded her of the Mexican telenovelas she had seen in well-to-do American households.

Every year, come June, Ino's little family dispersed. Veronica was usually at a conference in some far-flung corner of the world, Rosa returned to her family in Jalapa, and Ino went to a camp at Eagle Mountain in Ontario; a place renowned for its abundant lakes and creeks. The Montreal house was closed up (Ino would be forced to remove the key from around her neck), and the mosquito screens were tightly bolted on the door frames.

Ino loved Ontario. She loved swimming in the streams, picnicking with the camp leaders, and eating crunchy peanut butter sandwiches with clear apple jello (later, at Oxford, she learned to refer to it as 'jam'); a combination she had not eaten since. She enjoyed helping with the young kids. But what she never, ever got used to was having to lather insect repellent on her sticky, hot skin at night. She would lie awake for hours, her legs akimbo to stop her thighs touching, listening to the incessant sound of crickets. Eagle

Mountain was a change from the unwavering routine of city life, and Ino enjoyed meeting new people. Every year, even the intake among the staff changed completely. But the summer Ino turned fifteen, summer camp came abruptly to an end, and she would never forget the day when it did.

One morning, at the start of the vacation, Veronica breezed into Ino's bedroom with an announcement. Things had changed. Apparently. Ino wasn't going to camp that summer, but to Spain.

Ino was nonplussed. 'Things had changed' – what things? And *Spain*? Where was that? Had Veronica blindly stuck a pin on a map? "You're the one who travels, remember?"

"Don't be rude," Veronica had snapped.

Ino tried a different tack. She'd be more than happy to stay home alone, in *Canada*. Besides, what did she have to do with *Spain*? Her mother knew how much she loved summer camp. Was that why she couldn't go that year? Was she being punished? Had her grades been poor?

"Don't be ridiculous."

If Veronica needed more time for work, Ino pleaded, then Ino would be happy to spend *three* months at Eagle Mountain rather than just the two. Hell, she'd set out tomorrow if that's what Veronica wanted.

"Don't swear!"

"'Hell' isn't swearing."

Sighs all round.

"Why, oh, why Spain? Why that random country?"

Veronica had appraised her daughter dispassionately and – when Ino had stopped ranting, had been through every counterargument she could think of, when she was quite spent and red in the face – gone to the mirror. Veronica pressed her lips together, checking her teeth for traces of lipstick, patted an imaginary rogue hair from an immaculate coiffeur, drummed red nails on the painted pine mantelpiece. "Spain is not a random choice, not at all." Ino's father, the man whose image she had never seen, not even as a scrawl on her baptism certificate (in the province of Quebec, baptism certificates stood in lieu of birth certificates), was Spanish, and that's why Ino was going. She was to fly to Barcelona, where she would stay with Abuela.

"Abuela?" Ino's eyes widened in alarm. "What is that?"

"That is Spanish for 'grandmother'. Obviously."

Not so 'obviously', actually, Ino had thought. The father might be dead, but apparently the grandmother was very much alive. And another thing. Ino had gone by her mother's name of Harris, but from now on she was to be known as Ino de Monte Alegre.

"Monte-what?"

"Monte Alegre." Ino remembered that Veronica had had the grace to mumble.

"Which means?"

"Which means… 'Happy Mount.'"

Ino had burst out laughing, no longer angry, no longer able to contain herself. She couldn't wait to tell Rosa! This was *exactly* like one of those telenovelas the housekeeper was always telling Ino about. Abuela just needed to be blind for the story to be complete. But amusing as it was, there were still unanswered questions. Ino wanted answers. At which point Veronica had seemed uncharacteristically uncertain. And all at once, having never been curious before, Ino was – intensely so. She wanted to know how her parents had met and, more importantly, what her father looked like.

Once, when she was much younger, she had found a black-and-cream sepia photograph, a tiny passport-size picture, hidden between the pages of a book. Because she was afraid that she might not find it again, or that somehow it might be lost, she had concentrated very hard to commit the image to memory. For no reason other than pure instinct, she had thought it important. And now, so many years later, she remembered that first impression: the way the rough, thick card had felt between her little girl's fingers. There were two pinpricks, as though the photograph had been torn from a file or passport, while the man himself looked as if he had stepped directly from an El Greco painting.

Ino closed her eyes, summoning up the image as his face swam before her eyes as though she actually had the photograph in front of her. She remembered thinking that even then, when most grown-ups were old to her, he had seemed young. His skin was completely smooth and unblemished. His hair was black, wavy, angled upwards from the faintest widow's peak. His ears were neat, close to the sides of his head. He had a long nose; a trim moustache. He was in uniform. There were epaulettes on the shoulders of his light-coloured jacket. Or maybe it was sun damage that made the jacket appear light, because later Ino would learn that the uniform was in fact brown. Pinned to the collar was a diamond-shaped insignia. Curious as to what this might represent, Ino had used the magnifying glass Veronica kept in the top right-hand drawer of her desk. Under its concave shape, a castle complete with turrets and portcullis expanded within the tiny diamond frame.

Ino was excited. Could that be him? Was that her father? Remembering the image, she raced downstairs to find the book of poetry. Veronica had continued to look shifty, impatient to move on, to go back to work, but Ino insisted. She had found the book; had turned to page eighty, holding her breath, threads of emotion coiling in the pit of her stomach. And there it was.

"Found it!" Her voice, unanswered, had echoed through the house. She removed the precious photograph as though it might disintegrate just by looking at it. Who was this person who had lived and loved and was no more? Certainly, he was not spoken about in their household; nor kept alive through fable or memory. How was it that a person could have walked and breathed and talked (in many languages, apparently) and then vanished as though he'd never existed? Why was that? Why weren't there more photos? Other parents had wedding pictures all over their houses, followed by baptism ones when a child was born. Where were Ino's photographs? Where were Veronica's? Why didn't Veronica tell her about him?

Ino had waved the tiny postage-stamp picture in front of her mother's face, but Veronica, squinting as though doing her best to recall a face long forgotten, had merely shrugged. "Can't really say." When she'd first met Ino's father he'd had a beard; a small goatee. "He'd have been much older than this man. That must have been taken long before I met him."

Ino hated her mother's disinterest; hated her icy demeanour, her casual indifference, her total disregard for her – Ino's – feelings. She was panicked at the prospect of being sent to Europe, to people she had never heard of, and with a brand-new name to boot! And she was supposed to accept it all. She wasn't even allowed to be curious! Was it so unreasonable to want to know how her parents had met?

As if she'd rehearsed this bit, as if she'd known that one day Ino would ask, Veronica had actually seemed relieved. This was a question she *could* answer, albeit sketchily. But when Ino wanted to know where they'd married, Veronica seemed less certain. And as to his death... well, on that point she seemed positively hazy. And then finally, Veronica had shown some emotion: she appeared angry, but whether angry at having been left on her own with a young child or because a great love had been taken from her, Ino couldn't tell. "You'll find the answers," was all Veronica had said. "You'll find the answers to all your questions over there. In Spain, at Salto in Monte Alegre."

"Same name?"

Veronica had smiled a rare smile. "Yes. Same name." She had turned from the mirror, shaking out the foot of her new on-trend wide-legged jeans. She was bored now; the whole exercise in reconstructing a partial memory too tedious for words.

"Why all the mystery?" Ino had demanded; frustrated, upset, needing so much more.

"No mystery," her mother replied in a clipped, dismissive tone.

Ino must understand it was a long time ago. She examined the tiny slither of her Cartier wristwatch. "To be honest, I can't really remember. I never really knew much about him."

"'Him'? You mean, my father!" Ino had shouted. "'Him' – as if he counts for nothing!"

"Well, not *nothing*." Veronica smirked. "You're here, aren't you? And don't shout!"

Still Ino had waited, skewering Veronica to her beautiful reflection. Uncomfortable, Veronica had finally admitted to not knowing him very long.

"Or well, you mean."

In answer to Ino's glare, Veronica had been forced to say more. She had spouted something along the lines of career commitments keeping them apart.

"You mean literally?"

In a nutshell. She'd got pregnant; he'd died shortly after. End of story. Their story, anyway. Ino didn't dare ask if she looked like him; was like him in any way.

And then the dreaded day arrived. Hers was an evening flight, so Ino had hours and hours to try and suppress the alternating round of excitement and apprehension that kept her stomach twisted in knots. By the afternoon a series of deafening, sky-splitting thunderstorms had brought torrential downpours but also relief from the sweltering heat. The branches an arm's length from Ino's bedroom window were heavy with raindrops, the leaves waterlogged. The scent of drenched lilacs wafted through the unscreened panes. Her suitcase was packed, and for the flight itself she had a plastic bag-load of books; mostly Nancy Drew and historical romances by Jean Plaidy. Along with Veronica's cast-offs, she also had a new white skirt and a peasant blouse, the green of which matched her eyes. Or so Rosa said. Her mother commented that she only hoped that Abuela would find her presentable.

Ino remembered the flight in excruciating detail. She hadn't been able to sleep or read much. She'd never been on an airplane before; didn't understand the gadgets, the handset, what buzzers to press and what not to. Most of the time she had felt so awkward and self-conscious that she wanted to hide in the toilet and cry. And she would have done too, if it hadn't meant clambering over the middle-aged man in the seat beside her, and then the young man with smelly feet in the seat beside him.

A brief respite had come when a meal was served, but that was challenging too, with all the little packets in foil and cutlery sealed up in paper bags. Everything – every little detail – was unfamiliar, and Ino was rigid with fear. While her school friends had all wintered in Bermuda, Ino would ski at a place called Smugglers' Notch in Vermont. And because she travelled incessantly for work, the last thing Veronica wanted to do when she got home was fly anywhere with Ino in the holidays. As a result, Ino was untravelled and unworldly. She wished now that she'd paid more attention to accounts of her mother's trips: the journeys to the airport, the missed flights, and especially the stories of the flights themselves. If she had, Ino would know how to plug in her headset, and that she didn't have to pay for a Coke with extra ice.

Horror of all horrors and worst of all, Ino had to change planes in London. The thought alone had kept her in a high state of alertness for the last two hours of the flight. Her eyes were glued to the in-flight entertainment screen, tracking the plane's trajectory, and every time she nodded off, panic soon shook her awake. She had listened attentively to information about the transit lounge, but it was only when she boarded the much smaller aircraft that she was able to relax. After flying on a jumbo jet to London, however, she remembered thinking that half the plane was missing. This time the flight was much shorter, and she must have slept after all, because it seemed as if only moments later it was announced that they were going to *tomar tierra*.

Arriving in the slick marble Barcelona Airport, she followed people she recognised from the plane. The arrivals hall seemed vast and confusing, and arrows indicating various amenities appeared to go nowhere. And then she was holding her breath all over again. How was she going to recognise this… this *Abuela*?

Once more, in the absence of photographs, Veronica had been short on detail. "Don't worry," she had muttered. "She'll find you. She always does."

But what if she didn't? The thought terrified Ino. She had stood clutching her small holdall – Louis Vuitton, as it turned out, though Ino wasn't aware of brand names at the time, but at that moment it seemed like her only link with her mother, and she hugged it even more tightly. Earlier in the week Veronica had insisted she have it, pulling the monogrammed bag from the top shelf of her immaculate walk-in wardrobe. The whole room smelled of her mother's Guerlain scent, the beautiful clothes systematically arranged according to colour – an exotic kaleidoscope of silk and cashmere. There was even a specially designed miniature refrigerator set at the exact temperature to store perfume. Evening shoes in suede, linen and velvet lined an entire wall. Ino was transfixed by the hues and textures; Veronica by her daughter's Converse trainers worn without laces. She emitted a shriek as though she'd seen a moth decimating her wool. Ino was just surprised Veronica had only just noticed them, as she'd been wearing them all year.

"Those?! You can't wear those!" Veronica had turned to her row upon row of footwear as though she were analysing spreadsheets and, in a spurt of generosity, gifted Ino a pair of Chanel ballerina flats.

Conveniently, Ino already had the same size feet as her mother. The fact that they were Chanel meant nothing to her. They were comfortable, they hardly had any heel and they flattered her slender feet.

"Abuela needs to know we're doing well," said Veronica in between exclamations of "Don't touch! Be careful! Did you wash your hands?"

Ino was confused. They *were* doing well, weren't they?

In the end, just as Veronica had said she would, Abuela found Ino. It was just as well because Ino, eyeing up any number of little old ladies dressed in black, gold crosses nesting within folds of fat, had wondered which of these horrors was destined to claim her. These women had white, thinning hair, large bellies, and thick ankles. Over time, gravity and heavy, dangling earrings had elongated their earlobes; holes that began higher up now stretched dangerously close to the bottom of the ear. These women jabbered away in their foreign language, emitting shrieks of joy at the arrival of a loved one, and continued to shriek, cry and laugh once he or she was in their arms, to be covered in noisy, wet kisses. In the merciless light, Ino killed time counting the black hairs sprouting from their weathered chins. Shivering with apprehension, she was grateful for the first time in her life that Veronica was not the demonstrative type. Small children, hair slicked back with cologne, ran about, darting in between the luggage trolleys, clutching hunks of bread and chocolate. Adults munched pastries wrapped in small squares of tissue paper, or chewed sunflower seeds, spitting out the husks directly onto the floor. From time to time the men, in a graceful *ocho atras* tango move, stepped back to make sure the debris didn't soil their shoes. A miasma of smoke hung over everyone. If the men weren't already smoking, cigarettes dangled unlit from their mouths, and Ino watched, fascinated, as they still managed to talk and eat with their cigarettes moving, accordion-fashion, up and down between their lips.

But Abuela was nothing like these people. The woman who touched Ino gently on the shoulder and said, "*Ino, hijita?*" was tall and slender. Beautifully dressed in a white shirt dress, she didn't appear to have smoked a cigarette in her life. Her clear blue eyes were calm – not cold; merely observant. She held Ino close, then, with surprising strength, swung her away from her, making a bridge of their extended arms. Her eyes swept over her, missing nothing, from Ino's loose dark hair to the pretty shoes. In those initial moments, Ino sensed that Abuela was pleased; that she had all the information she needed; that she had understood everything. More importantly, for the first time in her life Ino felt that she was not hiding behind her mother's magnetic personality; that she was recognised and welcomed as a person in her own right.

Abuela tucked Ino's hand into hers, guiding her through the labyrinth of taxi drivers holding up signs for travellers who appeared to have gone adrift between baggage collection and arrivals. From behind a family of Peruvian musicians, a short, stocky man in a grey suit (which, though well cut, seemed to have been made for him when he was an entirely different shape) leapt onto the pavement. To Ino's alarm, a powerful hand clamped down on hers.

Abuela laughed at the tug of war that ensued. *"No te apures!* Don't be alarmed! It's only Edu. He's no one to fear; his family has been employed by ours for *siglos* – generations. He's here to drive and carry. He's a general... how is it in English? Dogsbody?"

Ino nodded uncertainly. She had no idea what Abuela meant. Had never heard the phrase. Veronica had men like Edu in her life too, but Ino had never seen them carry so much as shopping bag. Edu's expression was pained, as if he'd understood the 'only' from the tone of Abuela's voice.

Abuela was oblivious to the offence she might have caused, concentrating instead on crossing the busy car park. She explained that it was "a bit of a drive to Salto" but Ino could catch up on her sleep during the journey.

"Salto?" For no particular reason, Ino had imagined Abuela living in the city itself.

Her grandmother made a vague, non-committal gesture, but didn't elaborate. "Follow me."

Ino executed a kind of leapfrog to keep up with her grandmother's elegant slingbacks, and to avoid her own ankles being biffed by tiny children in control of luggage trolleys they couldn't see over. The air was heavy with smoke and exhaust fumes, and she kept her eyes on the ground; on the pretty tiled pavement. She commented on the design.

Abuela turned abruptly, her heel catching on one of the square sections. "It's a *panot* – a floor tile." Her navy toe pointed. This one is the *Flor de Catalunya*; the Flower of Catalonia."

The car, when they eventually came to it, was a large, high black vehicle with seats smelling of new leather. Edu was suddenly everywhere: unlocking doors, emptying then rearranging the boot, fetching bottles of water for the trip, fussing over Abuela and Ino. Ino did her best to copy her grandmother's neat slide into the car but ended up doing a sort of splits instead. She tugged at her skirt, squirming to gain purchase on the slippery seats. Flustered, she glanced at Abuela to see if she had noticed, but her grandmother, oozing serenity, was looking out of the window. Her face with its high, prominent cheekbones framed by blonde hair bore an uncanny resemblance to Veronica's, but whereas in one the beauty was showy, in the other it was quiet and restrained.

Except that it could also be animated, as it was now. Abuela was saying something about the tiles, the *panots* first laid when Barcelona was known as *Can Fanga* – Mud City. Apparently, proper pavements didn't exist at the time. The council didn't pay for them, so it was up to individuals to sort them out. "You can imagine the result!" Abuela smiled. "Some better than others, but it does mean that five million square metres of the city are now covered by these *panots*."

Ino, racking her brains to think of a clever question, came up with an obvious one. "Were they always designed with a flower?"

Abuela, pleased by Ino's interest, shook her head. "All different – originally, the plan was to have an almond in the centre."

"Or a skull," contributed Edu.

"Yes," agreed Abuela. "Or a skull."

"I'm glad they settled on a flower."

Abuela patted Ino's hand. "So am I. You'll see them when we go to the city, but now we have a bit of a drive; try and rest."

How far exactly *was* 'a bit of a drive', Ino wondered, when after an hour they were still crawling past countless factories and ugly industrial estates? And what exactly was 'Salto'? What did it mean? She had so many questions, but Abuela was no longer in a chatty frame of mind. Ino could wait. She'd find out soon enough, and yet she couldn't help feeling anxious all over again. One moment she was excited; the next, totally unnerved. She even missed Veronica, which was saying something. After what seemed an age, Edu tossed coins into a wide toll basket; the start of the *autopista*, he said. Which was hardly enlightening. The motorway to where?

Within a short time they had picked up speed. Finally, they appeared to have left the city; the surrounding landscape dominated by massive billboards advertising sherry and Coppertone Colorblok. Ino's eyelids drooped, but unease as to where they were going soon forced them open again. The brilliant, harsh sunlight was a further reminder that she was in a foreign country; that she hadn't been dreaming; that she wasn't, in reality, on her way to camp in Ontario.

Ino must have nodded off after all, because the rhythmic sound of the car's indicators woke her. Surely now they had to be nearby? They had left the motorway, veering onto a minor road. Sparse vegetation was interspersed with misshapen boulders, and a gently rolling backdrop of brown hills was shrouded in mist. The temperature was much cooler than in the city. After a while, tarmac became a narrow, dusty track. In the distance, she thought she could see pine trees.

Abuela tapped the window. "They're the King's Pine Forest, planted a long time ago by the Spanish Navy to provide timber for building ships. The planting is a mixture of stone pines and cork oaks. Those are ours – those corks. You'll see lots of them here."

As they climbed and the car hiccupped into gear, Abuela pointed out purple thistles, patches of yellow Spanish oyster, and fennel with its unmistakable lime-green flower heads. Her knowledge of the native fauna was prodigious. Ino glanced at her grandmother in admiration, but when she was told to roll down the window, she was grateful for the air to fan her embarrassment, her anxiety, her desire to cry.

"What do you smell?"

Ino knew nothing whatsoever about plants – she could identify a maple leaf (what Canadian couldn't?!) but that was about it. And as for smells? She mumbled something indistinct. Was it spice, maybe? Like the cookies at Christmas?

Did Ino know camphor?

Ino did not. Ino wished that Abuela would just inform her rather than test her. Now she was saying something about the undergrowth being called *irula* – similar to ragwort. Rag-*what*? Again, Ino shook her head.

"It's a nectar for butterflies, and once upon a time was used as a dye."

"Oh…" Should Ino have known that? Did every Spanish girl? Ino felt clammy. She wished she were back home in her hammock in the garden with a book and a glass of pink lemonade.

"Look!"

Ino followed Abuela's gaze. She tried to be enthusiastic. On the plus side, Abuela's voice was soothing – mesmerising, even – and Ino clung to the resonances of it, trying to shut out all thoughts of home, of camp, of everything that was familiar.

"That's red-and-yellow hibiscus." Abuela tapped the pane with an immaculate polished nail, just like Veronica's. And she was beginning to sound ever so slightly like something out of Veronica's *National Geographic*: interesting but somehow turgid. Abuela's voice continued in its modulated tones. "Sometimes after a scorched summer only it and sea daffodils give any colour to this parched land. See there? Ah yes… Later there will be tamarisk with its frothy pink petals. Later still, ox-eye daisies and bugloss. *Créeme*, you too will be excited when those droplets of colour appear. I can't describe the joy of seeing yellow anemones or darling little periwinkles! At the end of a summer in this desert of ours, you too will pounce on the smallest flower. *Te lo prometo* – I promise…"

Abuela could have promised anything she liked. Ino picked up only on the inference that she would still be in Spain at the end of the summer. She wasn't sure that she wanted to be. It had all been very nice – wrong word; it had been nerve-racking, *terrifying*, different – but now she'd quite like to go home, thank you; *gracias mucho*. This Salto place, for all the hype, had nothing to do with her. Veronica might not be perfect but she was familiar, just as 492 Grosvenor was familiar, Rosa was familiar, the food left for Ino (especially frosted Pop-Tarts) was familiar. She suppressed a strangled sob. This was all… well, just *weird*. All of it. Even Abuela. Ino stole a glance at the beautiful woman beside her who was so unlike the stereotype of a grandmother. She was certainly unlike any Ino had read about in novels. She was no white-haired, dirndl-clad German Oma of the *Heidi* stories. Ino would almost have preferred it if she was. Abuela was much more akin to the White Queen of fairy tales. And together, as in those stories, they seemed to be heading to the Queen's fairy kingdom. As the road wound ever higher, as the nearside smells of opulent buckskin and rich perfume combined with the outdoor aroma of spice and salt-logged sand, Ino was further transfixed and afraid. She stared openly at Abuela as though, as she had done with the tiny photograph of her father, she would later have to rely solely on memory. It took only a few moments to make an inventory of Abuela's skin, her tanned hands, the sparkling emeralds on her fingers, the tinkling string-thin diamond bangles that caught the light every time the sun catapulted into the car from behind the surrounding hills, and the delicate bones protruding from the silk of her white dress.

Dust clogging her throat, Ino closed the window on the thin lines of gold (yellow spiny broom, apparently) twisting a trail through the gorse. There was something missing, though. Some*one* who jarred this controlled landscape. "My father…?" she asked.

Abuela appeared not to hear. "Yes? No, no, don't look at me. You'll miss it."

"Miss it? Miss it…" Ino's voice scuttled under the branch of an echo.

"The first sighting is always the best. Keep your eyes… how do they say in English? Peeled? Yes, peeled. You'll see Salto any minute now…"

"And Salto is?"

"Salto al Cielo, of course!" Abuela vaguely pointed to the sky, the horizon, the middle distance. "All this is Monte Alegre. We are Monte Alegres. But the house… the house… You'll see in a minute. Around this corner, just… there!"

She was right. As the road became even narrower, no wider than the car itself, meandering through cave-like walls fringed with canopies of French lavender, Ino could see towers and a belfry. She caught her breath. From this viewpoint the 'house' across the lake was a fairy castle apparently supported by nothing but cloud; suspended in the mist. It was magical all right, but also vaguely sinister. Then again, perhaps it was only the mist that made the place appear unearthly and completely isolated. She couldn't make out a road or route, or any access to the castle whatsoever.

Abuela smiled. "You see?"

Ino nodded, the snakes of misgiving creeping back. She did see. "And is that a… church?" She wasn't sure what she'd been expecting but it wasn't this. This building – these *buildings*, she corrected herself – were much bigger than a church. They were as wide at least as Montreal's Mary, Queen of the World, where Ino had been baptised.

Ino's mind whirled to another memory; to another one of Veronica's titbits of information casually dangled in her direction. In fact, Veronica had only considered sharing this particular one after Ino had returned from a school outing one day. Ino would always remember the trip for the cold that had assaulted her when they'd emerged from the overheated Metro station of Bonaventure onto the corner of Metcalfe. She was knocked sideways by the wind, gasping as the frigid air expanded, needle-thin, through her lungs. Looking up, the seventy-six-metre-high basilica was etched black against the snow-logged sky. It could have been a frame from Gotham City (she and Rosa were currently watching *Batman* reruns). Inside, paintings depicting the martyrdom of the Jesuit priests tortured to death by the Iroquois made her quake in horror.

"Oh yes, Mary, Queen of the World." Standing before her in the hall, when Ino finally arrived home and Rosa stripped off her wet clothes, Veronica's grey eyes shifted in mild interest from the papers she was marking by the fire. She looked as cosy and relaxed and rugged up as Ino was bedraggled and frigid. "Was it… educational?" It was rare that Veronica asked Ino anything.

"Not especially." Ino was hungry and wanted to go into the basement and watch TV with Rosa like she always did. Veronica was never home this early, if at all, and Ino resented the disruption to her routine. She'd begun tiptoeing away when Veronica stopped her.

"Actually, you know something? You were baptised in the chapel of that cathedral."

Ino's eyes expressed surprise, not the respect Veronica imagined.

"Oh, anyone can be baptised in the chapel," Veronica had said, shrugging it off. And then, as an afterthought, "Your godfather was the Marquess of Pescara. Don't get excited. He vanished virtually the same day. Never heard from him again. He was the delegate to the Spanish mission at the UN; that's why Sant… that's why your father chose him."

Now, so many years later, this place produced a similar sensation of wonder, with its sprawling stone arches and tiled roofs that hugged the side of the mountain and then appeared to fall directly into the water. But there was something else: a dissonant air of unease.

Not to Abuela, though. She was elated. "Well, here we are.

There it is! I can always breathe again when I'm home. I hate the city. That's Salto al Cielo, which literally means 'Jump to Heaven'. Which it is. You'll know this in time. But you're right, *hijita*. The castle has its own *capilla*, which is what you can see. Monte Alegre is the estate: the countryside, the tenant farmers, the bakery—"

"Bakery?"

"Why, yes, of course. A castle was always self-sufficient. It had to be. We never knew who'd be invading, attacking, trying to steal us away. Anyway, the tannery, the stables, the *cortijo* and the school all form part of Monte Alegre. Oh, but I am forgetting, of course – and the *castillo*. The castle. Salto is what we call just the castle now."

Ino was awestruck. She could deal with the bombardment of names for flora and fauna but it was an understatement to say that she was astonished to learn that her father's home was a castle. "Salto. Jump. Did anyone ever want to? You know… into the lake?"

Abuela seemed horrified. "Certainly not! Why would they?"

Ino shivered. It looked gloomy.

Abuela's beautiful blue eyes were feline. As if she could read Ino's mind, she added that Salto was pure heaven – heaven on earth. "You'll see. Your heart will jump too, and you won't want to leave."

Yet her father had. The words stuck in Ino's throat. It wasn't just the physical position of the place that was giving her vertigo; it was also her thoughts.

Abuela, by contrast, seemed energised. "Look alive! We're here."

The car gave a final shuddering lurch. Edu's driving made Ino fear that they were headed for the next world. But no – round the last stomach-in-the-mouth hairpin bend, they emerged onto a flat stretch of land. Ahead, massive stone lion statues flanked a wide wrought-iron gate. As the car nosed into the dusty arc, the gates swung open before a seemingly endless drive lined with cypress trees. Ino rolled down the window. Somehow, without having gone over any bridge, they appeared to have crossed the ravine. The air was warm; the dappled sunlight caressed her cheek. On either side, arid fields were spotted with rocks and a blue-and-purple undergrowth. In the distance, a streak of gold flashed along the skyline.

"Sunflowers," said Abuela.

As they clattered over cobblestones, passing through the castle's portcullis, Ino felt that they too were entering another country; a lost horizon.

On the broad stone steps that fanned outwards from an enormous oak door, a diminutive woman dressed in black waited to greet them. She had sparse white hair and a face criss-crossed with lines. But beneath scraggy brows, her eyes were alert. The eyes were a surprise, as though somehow they had found themselves in the wrong face. Abuela swooped to kiss her cheek. Ino held back.

"This is Nuria, who has been with me since I was a little girl. If there is anything you need, anything at all, Nuria is the person to ask."

There was no sign of an Abuelo, and, as if in answer to the unspoken question, Abuela tucked a strand of Ino's hair behind her ear. She waved a hand to encompass the cool, vaulted hall.

"This is a house of women. But we're no *House of Bernarda Alba*. You know, the Lorca play? The one about the oppressive household of a matriarch and her unmarried daughters? Well, a lot of Lorca plays are about matriarchs and unmarried daughters…"

Ino wasn't familiar with the play, but instinctively she made a connection closer to home. The Iroquois (or People of the Longhouse) also came from a matrilineal society. Proudly, she said so, but Abuela only looked aghast.

"*Ay, hijita*, so much to learn; so much to explain!" She cupped Ino's chin. "Who are you like? Who are you like?"

Nuria emitted a low, guttural sound that made Ino jump. She hadn't expected such a timbre from Nuria's tiny frame.

"Well, according to Nuria, you are exactly like him…"

'Him'? Did Nuria mean Ino's father? From that moment on,

Ino was alert, forensically searching for any trace at all of the man whose very absence was so omnipresent. The sensation that he was all around was so powerful, she wouldn't have been surprised had he erupted through the walls or leapt from an oil painting. Unable to shake the feeling of disquiet, she kept looking over her shoulder as she shadowed Nuria up more swirling stone steps. Each landing had marble floors, walls hung with tapestries and long gilt mirrors. The darkened glass did little to reflect the small segments of light that managed to winkle their way through the casement windows. Nuria's tiny feet were soundless; Ino's hands barely skimmed smooth walnut banisters as they passed floor after floor and still kept climbing. Ino glimpsed large oak chests crowded with photographs, bowls of flowers, silver objects, heavy damask curtains, closed doors. She was itching to examine the pictures, to linger in those mysterious barred rooms, but Nuria chivvied her on. Clutching Ino's bag (which she wouldn't let Ino carry), Nuria finally came to a halt.

"Here?" Ino was breathless.

"*Sí sí.*" Nuria pushed open a door, Ino so close behind her that her nostrils filled with the onion/tomato aroma emanating from Nuria's clothes and skin.

Beyond was an amorphous, airless black cave. For a moment, Ino was disorientated when Nuria, dropping Ino's bag on the floor, plunged into the dark. Within seconds, the room was suffused with light as Nuria pulled back voile curtains; unhooked shutters. Ino gasped. Meadows of wild flowers and gently undulating fields stretched uninterrupted towards the mountain range. From the dizzying height of her turret bedroom, Ino felt as though she could touch the clouds. However, bedrooms here – Ino glanced longingly at the four-poster with its damask cover and inviting, plump linen cushions – were clearly not designed for relaxation.

"*Comer.*" Nuria made a hand-to-mouth gesture which Ino understood to mean 'food'. As the old woman's fingers flexed, the tendons protruded, and the veins turned a mauve colour under the translucent skin. Walking backwards as though paying homage to some Eastern deity, Nuria retreated, performing all the same tasks in reverse and in double-quick time: the shutters were closed, the curtains drawn, the door firmly shut, and then they were racing back down the cantilevered stairs, through the great hall and endless reception rooms, and out onto a vast stone terrace.

If Ino had been breathless before, she was even more so now that they were out in the fresh air. All at once, the fatigue of her long journey caught up with her and she was dizzy, alternating between feeling prickly with heat or shivery with cold.

"*Aquí*." Nuria's head jerked in the direction of a pergola swathed in wisteria. The scent was intoxicating.

"And if you really are like your father," Abuela's voice glided through the foliage, "you'll love this dish. Come, *hijita*. Time just to be…"

Ino's grandmother, framed beneath strands of purple flowers, was a vision. She could easily have been an advertisement for expensive perfume, a piece of jewellery, glasses – anything. Ino blinked. It was all so surreal: the heat of the dusty drive, the strange view from across the craggy ravine, the castle itself, and now this… this *House & Garden* image of a beautiful and serene woman. Even the table was beautifully laid with starched rose-coloured linen, scallop edging, delicate flower-pattern china, silver cutlery, and bowls of *glicina*. Abuela broke off a tiny bud of the fragile flower. She let the petals fall through her fingers.

"Touch! Like silk, no? And they smell… why, the scent is *divino*." That word again. She laughed. "You see? Heaven; *divino*. It's all here. We're self-sufficient – always have been. *Glicina*. I see you wondering… It's the Spanish for wisteria. You like it here already, don't you? I can tell."

Ino didn't contradict her; didn't dare. She sank onto a flowered cotton cushion. Her grandmother's voice was an undulating current; a rhythmic beat punctuated with smiles. Ino succumbed, letting the sounds wash over her; the comfort of the chair; the food displayed before her almost as gifts.

"You try." Nuria's tone was raspy. "Your father's favourite dish."

Abuela's was soothing; more persuasive. "Such a simple peasant food, but oh! Every Catalan loves it. *Pa amb tomàquet*; bread and tomato. The bread must be Salto bread, of course. Yes, I'll show you everything – the mill; everything – but there's time, no? And tomatoes... ah, you anticipate already what I might say: Salto tomatoes too, of course. You taste the sweetness? The freshness is something else! Here the air is so pure." Abuela closed her eyes. "You can breathe here, can't you? How different from the city. Rainwater saturating the earth." Suddenly, Abuela ducked down to scoop up a handful of soil. Taking Ino's hand, she dribbled grains of earth into its palm. Ino tried to pull away, but Abuela was stronger. Her hands held Ino's holding dirt. "Salto – never forget something that is more important than love; than anything you will ever know. Something more powerful. Salto. She closed her eyes for a moment. Then opened them. "We should toast..."

"With Salto wine?"

"*Claro.* Naturally, with Salto wine. Oh, and Manchego. Our Spanish cheese. Here – a slither with *membrillo*; quince. They go together so divinely." Abuela released Ino's hand. "*Divino.*"

And now Ino was laughing. Because surely bits of earth were mingling with the food? But Abuela merely shrugged.

"Salto earth!" they said in unison. "What is it? What is so funny?"

But it was Abuela; it was Abuela herself. She was so different from what Ino had expected. She *looked* so perfect, and yet was quite rugged in her way.

"I thought you'd be old and ugly."

Abuela smiled that wonderful smile – even white teeth; eyes dancing with life and delight. "And you aren't what I expected either. You had to be beautiful – Santiago's child would always be that – but you are so much more: graceful, intelligent, sensitive."

It was Ino's turn to be delighted. And just like that, they were friends. Ino's cheeks were flushed. No one had ever paid her so many compliments. For a moment she forgot that earlier she'd wanted to go home. She bit into her bread, feeling oil drip down her chin. "Oh! I'm sorry!" she said, mortified.

"Don't be silly. Look at me!"

And they both laughed.

They finished with peaches as large as oranges. Had Santiago enjoyed peaches too, Ino wondered? *Santiago.* She found the word 'father' too awkward. It was such a new concept. She preferred to think of him in the abstract. Strong and splendid and alive. Which was what he was here. Death was the unspoken word, the ghost that lingered at every corner. This was more Santiago's place than Abuelo's. Whoever he was.

Abuela rolled her napkin, threading it through a silver napkin ring that bore a coat of arms. She passed an unbranded one to Ino. "Yours is being engraved. You'll have it soon." She rose. The chair scraped against the paving stones. A final dusting of wisteria petals cascaded onto her shoulders, a net of stars decorating her hair.

Ino followed, uncertain.

"We'll start outside."

They began by descending stone steps that led to the meadows and orchards Ino had glimpsed from her bedroom. They crossed streams; passed by a small pavilion.

Abuela shaded her eyes against the sun. "The *castillo* has a complex history. It began life as a Moorish *alcazaba*. You saw the outer walls from the car across the ravine; you can tell by the interval square towers, which are indestructible – well, by almost everything but time. In the twelfth century your *antepasados* – your ancestors – built this church." In front of them was a white stone chapel. Layers of plaster were coming away in large chunks to reveal pink sand and clay underneath. "Another built the bell tower." She traced flower motifs on the white stucco. "And here is Mudejar."

"Come again?"

"Mudejar is a design; a flower pattern created by Moorish craftsmen working in the service of Christians. A little like the *Flor de Catalunya* you saw earlier. Ah, now this was where your father took his first steps…"

Ino learned where Santiago had first ridden a bicycle, a pony… and where, on one unforgettable night, he had gone missing only to be found outside close to where they were standing by the cork trees, lying under the stars, listening to the owls. In fact, he had carved a small whistle from bamboo so he could copy them. Cupping his hands together, he learned to imitate all kinds of birds. But that was later, when he was older.

"You see, we are all made of carbon, Mama," he had told his mother when she'd stretched out on the ground beside him to look up at the constellations to divine what he could see. "So are the stars. I like to think I am looking up at my ancestors."

Abuela smiled then, feeling for Ino's hand and pressing it. "I like to think it too, but it's not conventional Christian thinking, if you know what I mean. But it is *divino*, don't you think, to possess such an original mind? He was only small at the time," she continued. "But you see, he was always coming out with things like that. Thoughtful things. He thought about everything – there was nothing impulsive about him, which was why when he… when you…" For once Abuela appeared lost for words.

"Yes?"

Abuela frowned; a tiny crease in an otherwise smooth forehead. Her signs of ageing were not obvious. "That comes later," she said smartly. "Let's keep with the boy for the moment, for the boy was so sweet… What is it?"

"I just don't understand any of it. I don't know why Ver… my mother never told me about any of this: about you; about my father…"

Abuela squared her shoulders. "She'll have had her reasons. Don't judge her too harshly, *pequeña*. The adult world is a complicated one, as you are discovering. Very complicated."

"And you have been here all this time? You never moved somewhere else?"

Abuela was shocked. Ino realised then that almost nothing shocked Abuela unless it was in relation to her beloved Salto. "No, absolutely not. Where else would I be? I could never be anywhere else."

That night, as Ino lay in bed in her turreted room with its whitewashed walls and pretty grey linen curtains, she mulled over the events of the day. Already Montreal seemed light years away and the long journey far removed from the isolation of this place. Through the open casement she could hear an owl, the clicking of cicadas, an odd cricket. The scent of gardenia lingered on the cool night air. She wriggled her toes beneath crisp linen sheets, pushing her head into a pillow embroidered by Abuela as part of her trousseau so many years before. She had opened wide the shutters. Moonlight cast unfamiliar shadows across the oak floor and the delicate gilt furniture, but she preferred those to tomb-like darkness.

Everything here screamed history, but it was someone else's story she was interrupting. And there were constant, unavoidable reminders of this. Unlike Veronica, who didn't display personal photographs, didn't hint at family of any kind, photos abounded of Santiago. Every stage of Ino's father's young life had been recorded and celebrated. She had seen him at his christening, taking his first steps, his first communion, and then in uniform – a larger copy of the head-and-shoulders picture that hid between the pages of Ino's book. But there were none of his marriage to Veronica, and none of Ino. She didn't mind. She was beginning to understand that things were done differently at Salto, and for whatever reason neither she nor Veronica were part of it. It was as though that later chapter of Santiago's life had never happened at all. And, despite the numerous references to a life lived here, she was still none the wiser as to how her father had ended up so far from home, and why her mother chose to forget him.

It was true that Ino had never been curious before this visit. She had been completely happy in her world of school and reading, but now questions buzzed in her brain, making sleep impossible. Who was Santiago? Who was he really? Had he cared about her at all? An even more depressing thought took hold. Had he known about her? That Veronica was pregnant? It was suddenly important to Ino that, even if it was for a short time, he had claimed her.

She wanted to know so much more. Photographs were not enough – they documented events, commemorated milestones, but they did not convey a person's spirit; nor his character. Here especially, they only told part of the story. Ino also realised with a pang that Santiago wasn't a distant relative she might yet meet during her stay. She wouldn't be seeing him at a later point, as she would a certain Rafael; yet another relation she had never heard of, let alone met. Santiago wouldn't be waiting for her in another part of the castle or the city – this so-called *Can Fanga*. What remained of him – or rather, what had formed him – was to be found here within these walls. Yet Ino doubted she would ever really know him. She hadn't the wealth of memories to draw upon that Abuela did. She couldn't see a blade of grass and recall a conversation; nor pick up an object that would remind her of the touch of his hand, his lips on her head. She would never know the sound of his voice.

The questions didn't stop there. Why did Veronica never come here? But then again, for all Ino knew, perhaps she did, on her way to or from a work engagement. With a start, Ino realised that if she knew little about her father, despite technically living with her mother, she knew even less about Veronica. Veronica never spoke about her childhood and growing up; about anything personal at all. Ino did not know where she had been born or where she had gone to school. And what about these people? Ino's few belongings had been hung neatly in the painted wooden cupboard by Nuria, a woman she had never met until today. Who were they really? Everything Ino had seen of Salto testified to an ordered, controlled life. Why, then, had Abuela never been in touch, never called or written, never come to see *her*? Why had Veronica kept them apart?

It was only as the sun filtered through the open shutters, and to the sound of birdsong, that Ino finally fell asleep.

24

Ino
Salto al Cielo
2002

At first Ino couldn't remember where she was, she was so submerged in a dreamless sleep; so jet-lagged that she struggled even to make sense of the ear-splitting sound of glass against stone that now made her cry out. And then she remembered Nuria as they both hollered at each other as though they'd seen a Salto ghost.

Unannounced, Nuria had marched into the bedroom and, on discovering the open window, slammed the shutters shut, dragging heavy fabric across a resistant curtain pole. "*El sol!*" she screeched, pointing to the sun.

Ino was amazed to learn how afraid of the sun they all were. The sight of Nuria alone was enough to make anyone jump out of their skin. Ino fell back on the pillows, heart thudding.

But Nuria had other ideas. "Up! Up!"

Abuela must have taught her the words. The air was suffocating now that the windows were shut. Ino felt grubby, and there was the sweet smell of perspiration around her. Her head ached; her mouth was dry. Nuria held out a piece of paper. Ino squinted. There was barely enough light to read by. Compromising a little, Nuria opened one of the shutters. "'Countess out—'" read Ino.

Nuria snatched the paper back. Underneath the English,

someone had spelled the words phonetically. "'But you'" (it came out as 'dew') "'dew must dress, then *desayuno*.'" She made an eating motion. "And brum-brum." Another gesture, and then a tap of her watch with arthritic fingers. "Polo! Polo? Jes... yes... *El Conde Rafael y El Conde Emil... polo.*"

Conde? How many counts were there? And what was a count anyway?

Nuria's eyes narrowed. She oozed disapproval.

"Ah," said Ino, bemused. "*Sí*, thank you."

Nuria made no attempt to leave. Her tiny feet in their black espadrilles were firmly planted by the side of Ino's bed. Again there was that nauseating smell of onions about her. Ino was eager to start the day, to explore the castle, which already felt different; less threatening than it had the night before. The place was waking up. There were voices in the garden, the sound of water hoses being pulled about, the scraping of garden furniture being moved. The slow chirp of cicadas. Did they never sleep? She propped herself up on one elbow.

"Up! Up!" said Nuria immediately. This was clearly going to be a mantra in the days to come. "*Y dúchate antes de vestir.*" She dropped a couple of towels on the bed, but Ino didn't need persuading to take a shower. "Like your moder."

"What? What did you say?" Ino swung her legs over the side of the bed, cuddling the towels to her chest. "Like my mother?" Her heart bolted. "*Qué?* You said my mother? Veronica? She was here?"

"Me no know."

"You *do* know!"

Nuria's stare was bland; unresponsive.

"You said my mother," insisted Ino. She heard the hysteria in her voice and was both ashamed and appalled at her lack of restraint.

Nuria looked away, her mouth set in a determined line. "No."

"Yes!" Ino was determined. "I heard you!"

But Nuria merely shrugged, as if to say she had no idea what Ino was talking about. She didn't speak English, remember, and

Ino didn't know Spanish. She jabbed the towels. "*Ducha, ahora ducha.*"

"Got that," muttered Ino, thinking, *Rather have a bath.* She padded into the vast if old-fashioned bathroom – the black-and-white tiled floors were attractive enough, but she had trouble making sense of the taps. 'C' turned out not to mean 'cold'. Ino was fast appreciating Veronica's homemaking skills; the fact that wherever they lived had the most modern appliances, particularly when it came to plumbing. With impeccable attention to detail and an aesthetic eye, her shower rooms were art exhibits in themselves. Here, there didn't appear to be any soap.

"After Civil War." By way of explanation, Nuria passed Ino a bar that appeared to have been made up entirely of odd ends of old paraffin.

Civil War? What civil war? And what had it to do with soap? The only history Ino had been taught at school concerned The Great Beaver Wars and the Iroquois' fight against the Algonquin-speaking tribes. Whenever this Spanish war was, it sounded as though it had taken place a long time ago. Surely the soap couldn't have survived all that time?

Washing away such thoughts, Ino dressed rapidly, putting on a white cotton Diane Von Furstenberg dress Veronica had bought her a few days prior to her departure. Ino had wanted to say that a DVF dress was probably too sophisticated for a fifteen-year-old, but then again she wasn't about to quibble with her mother, who clearly hadn't the foggiest idea what kids of her age wore. Ino wondered if Veronica even remembered her birthday. Plus, she'd seemed genuinely surprised at how few clothes hung in Ino's cupboard.

"How come?" Veronica had lit her tenth cigarette of the hour as ash dropped onto Ino's desk. She waved smoke away from her face, inhaling as though it was her last; sucking in her cheeks with the effort. She was suspicious, as though Ino had been hiding an entire wardrobe under the table.

Er... because you haven't bought me any? But Ino hadn't said that. Instead, she reminded her mother that, as she wore a school uniform most of the time, she really didn't need many home clothes.

Veronica frowned, glancing at her wristwatch in irritation. Running out of time (Veronica was preparing for a meeting), they had run to Holt Renfrew, the nearby department store, to purchase a dress. Now, Ino was pleased they had. She pushed her feet into Veronica's Chanel flats and pulled her hair into a ponytail.

So... Veronica had been here, and often enough for Nuria to have got to know her. Ino skipped down the wide marble staircase to the vaulted hall below. She fancied herself as a modern-day Nancy Drew, determined to ferret out every snippet of information and gather clues wherever she could. With the new day, she was also beginning to feel more positive. The night's rest (such as it was) had removed that horrible sick feeling; the yearning for home that had been with her ever since she'd left Montreal. Homesickness – she understood the word better now, because it really was a physical feeling; a sickness of the soul. But this morning she was brimming with curiosity. The castle itself felt less intimidating and she was determined to find out everything.

Nuria's clucking brought her up short. As much as Ino felt her grandmother's spontaneous affection, it was balanced by the open resentment on the part of this domestic. Ino hesitated at the bottom of the staircase, uncertain where to go. Nuria was behind her, taking the steps one at a time. The marble was slippery. Ino pointed her toe like a ballerina, tracing figures on the flagstones, waiting, impatient, hungry, making her dress billow around her. Apart from the sudden fluttering of a bird's wing, the castle was quiet. Ino watched as the bird soared towards the vaulted ceiling before swooping down again, gathering small insects for a nest that balanced precariously on a beam. Everything on this floor was open to the elements, and the heavy iron bars had been removed from the vast double doors. A cool breeze dragged dry leaves this way and that across the stone flooring until, as though being swept up by an invisible broom, they disintegrated and became dust.

"*Desayuno.* Breakfast?"

Nuria led the way to the dining room, past suits of armour and glass cabinets displaying china ginger jars. Ino winced at the dead birds and mouldy-looking fruit depicted in the oil paintings. The kitchen, Abuela had explained the night before, was strictly the domain of maids; functional, impersonal, and off limits to Ino. The dining room was where the family ate most of their meals, and a place had been set for her there at the long rosewood table. A silver napkin ring with the Monte Alegre coat of arms had been placed by her plate. *Quick work*, thought Ino, remembering Abuela's promise of the evening before to have a napkin ring engraved for her. Bowls of peaches, *pa de pagès* and *jamón serrano* were, with the exception of hot chocolate, a repetition of what she'd been given for supper.

"Ah, I like to see a girl with a healthy appetite." Abuela, sailing into the room, was a vision in white capri pants, a turquoise Pucci top and pearls; her tanned, smooth skin belying her age. "You look lovely, *hijita*," she said, noting Ino's dress and Chanel shoes.

Ino would have loved to have told Veronica right there and then that her sartorial choices had gone down well.

"And much older than your tender years."

Which Ino was less certain was a compliment. She, on the other hand, was utterly sincere when she complimented Abuela on being much younger than hers.

"Well, that's the right way round, now, isn't it?" Abuela was clearly pleased.

Ino, finishing the last dregs of her hot chocolate, wanted to know about the soap.

Abuela, pouring herself a cup of coffee, made a clucking sound. "Nuria didn't give you one of those patchwork soaps, did she? Ah, I can tell by your face that she did!" She spooned three teaspoons of sugar into her cup, hesitating coquettishly over a fourth, and stirred her coffee. "During the Civil War – and before you ask, yes,

I was alive then – we suffered all kinds of hardship; soap, or lack of, being just one of them. Nuria used to go around collecting all the odds and ends and melting them together – trouble is, she still does. She thinks bought soap a luxury. I have to sneak it into the house and use it sparingly. I'll get you some of mine, but remind me. Just make sure she doesn't see it."

"My mother..."

Abuela turned her wide-apart blue eyes. "Yes?"

But Ino had lost her nerve. "My... mother does the same," she finished lamely. Which wasn't really true. Veronica loved good soap, but did use it down to the last sliver.

Abuela raised an eyebrow. "Does she? I had the impression," she glanced at Ino's Chanel shoes, "that she was something more of a spendthrift." She finished her coffee, pushing away the cup. "Come – I want to give you something, and then we must be off. The game starts at three so we have to move *sin pausa, ni prisa,* as we say. And it means 'without pausing, but without hurrying.'"

"We say, 'more haste, less speed.'"

"Which isn't quite the same thing..."

"No." Ino blushed, twisting her napkin into its silver ring as she had seen Abuela do, and got to her feet, eager to make up for her gaucheness.

Abuela's heels tapped across the flagstones as she led the way to the smallest of the great halls (there were four, apparently), past portraits of truly hideous women in unflattering black dresses. Despite the pictures, Ino liked that hall best. There, all decoration and colour stemmed from contrasting textures: soft grey stone and linen-covered walls in taupe and olive green. Two slender black marble columns supported a ceiling made up of diamond-shaped cedar wood. And above each full-length casement window there was a four-leaf clover sculpted into its elegant arch, the underside of which revealed a chequerboard of white and black marble. Latticed panes meshed between apple-wood frames threw off kisses of tiny, shimmering shadows.

Ino emitted an "Oh!" of delight, and rushed to the nearest window to clamber up the three wooden steps to its stone seat. Below, the water lapped gently against the castle walls, cool and clear and calming.

But this was not where Abuela wanted to linger. "Yes, those elaborate window seats were designed for the ladies to sit and sew by the natural light. And don't be fooled by the water."

Cautiously, Ino leaned out of the window. It seemed hard to imagine that such seemingly benign waves could turn traitorous. "Oh?"

Abuela sniffed. "It is beautiful, of course, but also practical: once upon a time, our little lake formed a natural moat; a defensive promontory. We also had a luxury that few other places could boast of: namely, fresh running water. Can you imagine the stench in summer without it?"

Ino shook her head. She couldn't.

"Come." It wasn't a request.

Ino scrambled down from her stone throne. She could have spent all day staring out across the water but, as with beds, here seats of any description were clearly not meant for lounging. It was no coincidence, she was beginning to think, that the *castillo's* chairs seemed medieval too: wooden frames with a seat of worm-eaten leather hammered in place with brass studs. Not a place conducive to curling up in with a good book.

Abuela moved swiftly, saying something about Salto originally being constructed around four small courtyards, and that to begin with, the castle was just a collection of some twenty-five little buildings crammed onto the rocky island. Over time her ancestors – *their* ancestors (Ino felt a small thrill when she said that) – had merged and extended these buildings. "See?" Abuela patted the wall behind her. "Note how these old rooms and outhouses have been connected to each other through a network of internal and external passageways."

Ino nodded, trying to take it all in, to feel the same reverence for the place that Abuela obviously did. But it was too vast, too museum-like. All over again, Ino had a fresh yearning for the cold, for the winter. She had another pang thinking of her own cosy basement and watching TV with Rosa. Enveloped in the embryonic warmth of that cellar, it was just as easy to lose track of time.

Abuela swept past several rooms, all of different sizes and usage, before stopping in an antechamber; a small room with a single arched casement window, a rug, and a beautiful walnut chest. There were dozens of photographs – some black and white – of Santiago and Abuela. There was one of Abuela as a very young woman standing between two men in uniform. Both the men held plumed helmets tucked under an arm; both had sashes round their middles; both wore the exaggerated britches of the day, their chests adorned with medals. But while one was the ugliest man Ino had ever seen, the other was one of the best-looking.

"Our present King's grandfather."

"So good-looking," breathed Ino.

"No, that is my husband. The King is the other man."

Ino giggled.

"Yes, the upturned moustache doesn't help."

The moustache was the least of it, thought Ino. "And your husband? My grandfather – Abuelo?"

"Dead." As if that was the end of the matter, Abuela waved a hand. "Come over here; I want to show you this."

She beckoned Ino to a life-size portrait of a woman in medieval clothes. At first Ino saw only the extraordinary get-up: the flowing white gown, and what appeared to be an entire heraldic banner draped over one shoulder. Up close, she observed that the lady's clothes were actually painted in several different shades, and were not uniformly white at all. The skirt itself was a patterned crimson brocade, while the fluted sleeves were in a contrasting design. The cloak had square black patches depicting ensigns, gold castles, crosses and lions. Despite the archaic costume, the woman was still very lovely. Her dark hair above her perfectly oval face was held in place by a velvet snood. In the unforgiving morning light, her almond-shaped eyes glinted green.

"She's beautiful."

"She is. I think she's you."

Ino's cheeks blazed. "Do you really think that I look like her?"

"I do."

"You are kind."

"Not kind. Accurate. This is the first Countess Monte Alegre y Cabeza de Vaca, grandee of Spain."

"I have no idea what that means."

"Well, you know what 'Monte Alegre' means. 'Cabeza de Vaca' translates as 'Head of a Cow.'"

If Ino hadn't thought it before, this last titbit of family history merely confirmed it. The place and everything to do with it was bonkers. Stark raving mad. Of course, there was another possibility (equally crazy), and that was that she was dreaming and hadn't left Montreal at all. "You are joking."

Abuela turned, owl-like, as though her neck and head were suddenly fused. "Not remotely. You think it's funny?"

"Don't you?" Ino, realising her mistake, stammered an apology. From Abuela's tone, there was nothing to joke about. But seriously? 'Head of a Cow'?

Abuela frowned. "It's your name. A very old and noble one, too. You come from grandees of Spain: explorers, statesmen; a direct line from them to us through this woman. This first Monte Alegre."

Ino looked again at the face of the girl in the painting. She really was very beautiful, with fine, arched eyebrows, high cheekbones, and a faint widow's peak – just like Santiago's. Ino recollected the small passport-size photo. None of the other pictures of her father she had seen here showed that distinct hairline. This woman was proud, majestic. There were jewels on her fingers, in her hair, round her long throat, and despite the heavy symbolism of her costume, there was also a liveliness to her face, and a sense of fun. Which was more than Ino could say at that moment of Abuela. "What is a grandee, Abuela? I'm sorry to interrupt."

Abuela's tone was haughty. "A grandee is a title conferred upon the highest ranks of the nobility."

"Is that you? I mean, are you part of the... nobility?"

"Well, yes, *hijita*, put simply, I am, and so are you."

"Does that mean my mother...?"

They exchanged a look.

Abuela shrugged. A grandee, she continued, was slightly different. "It's in addition to a title you may already have. In fact, it's a title first mentioned in the Middle Ages. The first grandees were a handful of rich and powerful men who had acquired privileges together with their wealth."

"What kind of privileges?"

"Do you really want to know? I know it sounds silly, but one was that they could keep their hats on in the presence of the King."

"Come again?"

"I warned you! By the sixteenth century the number of grandees was limited to twenty-five, but by the eighteenth there were more, and these were divided into three classes. Those who spoke to the King and received his reply with their heads covered; those who addressed him uncovered, but had to put on their hats when he replied; and lastly, those who waited for the King to allow them to cover their heads."

Ino was incredulous. The whole thing sounded fantastical and not remotely relevant to real life. It wasn't even entertaining like *Dawson's Creek* or *Bonanza* or—

"And one more thing," said Abuela. "The King addressed all grandees as '*mi primo*': 'my cousin.'"

But of course, thought Ino.

Abuela moved to a marquetry cabinet made of walnut, ebony and painted wood. The top half had doors that opened to reveal five drawers to either side of another locked central compartment. Within this inner space was yet another door. It reminded Ino of the gaudy matryoshka doll Veronica had brought back once from a trip to Russia. The bracelets on Abuela's slim wrist jangled as they twisted and turned a small gold key. When she had found the last compartment, she fished out a velvet pouch. It seemed an awful lot of trouble was involved in keeping such a tiny object safe.

"For you." Abuela had taken Ino's hand, then opened it palm upwards.

Ino felt the soft velvet before Abuela dropped several coins into her hand. For a moment, Ino's heart skipped a beat. She sincerely hoped they wouldn't number thirty pieces of silver. But no – these coins were old, and they were gold.

"*Arras*. It literally means 'earnest money.'" Abuela's face couldn't have been more earnest itself. "Passed down from generation to generation. During the Spanish Civil War, they were hidden in the very walls of Salto."

"And they signify?"

"They signify, *querida*, a bridegroom's promise to his family. When the time comes, they will come to you."

Ino didn't want to spoil the moment by pointing out that when the time came, hopefully she would be a bride, not a groom. Before she had a chance to say anything, though, Abuela scooped the coins up, replacing them in the pouch, and then the hundred or so little drawers were opened and closed all over again.

"But this is for now."

Another little velvet pouch was pressed into Ino's hand. Ino stared at the gold signet ring embossed with a crest.

"It belonged to that countess." Abuela flicked a look over her shoulder towards the portrait. "Catalina. It can only be handed down to women in the family. We are a matriarchal society, *hijita*." She slipped the ring onto Ino's third finger. "Mmm… a little big, but not terribly so. I told you yesterday, this is a family run by women. You are not and should never be defined by a man, or anyone for that matter. You are you. You come from a long line of strong women. I am confident that you will not forget it."

Ino felt the unfamiliar weight. It was uncomfortable and would certainly get in the way. She didn't usually wear jewellery and wasn't sure that she wanted to start with this piece. She wasn't sure that she even liked it. The ring made her feel 'owned'; the very thing Abuela had counselled against. She smiled weakly. "Thank you. *Gracias*."

"Good. You are one of us now. You are the newest countess, but it's not something we talk about. To other people."

Then why mention it at all? It was irrelevant.

"So that *you* are aware." Abuela answered her unspoken thought.

"And are 'people' aware?"

Abuela's nostrils flared. "Of course. No need to say anything here. Everyone knows who we are."

Ino still didn't see the point, but it was clearly important to her grandmother. She looked up, not at Abuela, but at the portrait. Catalina's eyes were on her, but in a benign way; not in a malevolent, haunted-house kind of way. On the contrary, Ino felt emboldened. Her ponytail swished from side to side.

"Yes? You want to ask something?"

"My cousin Rafael? Where does he fit in?"

Abuela's eyes narrowed. "He doesn't. Rafael... plays polo. And talking of which..." She glanced down at Ino's shoes. "Very good choice. But we're running late. We must go."

The heat of the city was overpowering, seeming to rise from the patterned pavements, enveloping everything in a steamy veil. It was suffocating, dulling Ino's mind already made sluggish by jet lag. Strange to think, but even in this short time Ino wished they didn't have to leave cool Salto with its vaulted high ceilings, cold marble interiors and shaded groves. She wished fervently that she could creep into her linen-draped bed (where lolling was so clearly discouraged), press her face into the smooth, scented lavender pillow, and sleep. This trip to the city was alarming; full of the unknown all over again.

Edu deposited them directly in front of the clubhouse. He rushed to Abuela's side. Gesticulating to a small man who had shot from under the guard's shelter, he began shouting in Spanish; short, guttural words that seemed to Ino far easier to pronounce than anything she had heard so far. She made a note, running them up and down a mental keyboard of sounds, storing them for future use. They were surrounded by parched yellow hills. Abuela led Ino through the main building, open on all sides. Giant ceiling fans made up of old airplane propellers shifted warm air from one side of the vast vestibule to the other. Ahead, the brilliance of green fields contrasted violently with the aridity of the landscape. Just visible from where they stood were the twenty or so stables that looked to Ino like a large slab of chocolate. Abuela said that there was even a small chapel.

"Why a chapel?"

"Because it's a dangerous game, *hijita*. Players get injured all the time. Occasionally spectators as well."

"Surely a hospital would be more useful?"

"Well, yes, and we cater for that too."

Ino followed Abuela's line of vision outside to where three ambulances were parked in a row by the field.

"Sometimes players die. And rather like in a *corrida* – a bullfight – the men get nervous; they like to pray before a match."

Ino was jolted from her listlessness. She had watched ice hockey, but in that game no one – at least as far as she knew – made a formal thing of praying first.

Abuela was dismissive. She understood the associated danger of polo, but did not respect the player when the addiction got out of control. "And I love horses, but this game…" She shook her head. "A bottomless pit."

"Of what?"

"Why, of money, *hijita*, of money."

With every step they took, Ino felt increasingly cowardly, smaller, and more homesick. Salto had seemed strange only the day before, but this place seemed even stranger. For one thing, there was the love of horses. Ino had not grown up with pets – Veronica didn't like them, and the fact that she travelled so much made owning one impractical. The strong smell of manure and heat and dust was everywhere. The palm trees were ramrod-straight. There wasn't a whisper of a breeze. Ino turned to position herself under a fan, but Abuela popped on oversized black sunglasses and led the way outside.

"Don't talk to the grooms," she said, alarmed by how men were staring at Ino. "In fact," she caught one of the patrons giving Ino the eye, "don't talk to anyone."

"Well, unless they speak English I can't, anyway," said Ino, unaware of the attention she was attracting. She was dark and willowy in her white dress, and a novelty at the club.

"Mmm…" said Abuela, unconvinced. "Stay with me for the moment, whatever you do. The thing is that I have to leave you here for a few—"

"What?" Ino squealed, utterly terrified at the prospect of being without Abuela. In Montreal, she was capable of going to school alone, boarding buses, negotiating downtown, but the thought of being without her grandmother paralysed her with anxiety.

"I was going to say 'hours'. I have to run a few errands and I thought this was the best place for you to be. Now I'm not so sure."

Neither was Ino. "Can't I come with you?" she pleaded. "I can stay in the car with… with Edu? I-I don't know anything about polo. I don't even like horses!"

"Don't you?" Abuela was genuinely shocked. "But all Monte Alegres are fine horsewomen."

"Yes, well, not this one. I've never ridden a horse in my life. I'd… I'd rather be with you."

Abuela frowned; pursed her lips. She hadn't foreseen this. She fingered her pearls, knotting and unknotting them. "Let's find the boys," she said then, striding towards the fields. "We'll find your cousin Rafael and then we'll see what we do. Look! If I'm not mistaken…"

She loped down the steps leading from the restaurant area to the lawn below, where two deckchairs were positioned as close to the fence as it was safe to be. Ino noticed the chairs because not only did a steady, thin stream of smoke curl upwards from the striped seats, but from time to time a steward passed by, telling the occupants to move back – which they did, but once he'd gone, crablike, the deckchairs moved forward again. But she was surprised Abuela could tell it was 'the boys' – one of them presumably being Ino's cousin Rafael. All she could see was a booted foot protruding from either end of the chairs.

It was only when Abuela stood virtually in front of them that the two men jumped to their feet. Riding gear – whips, helmets, knee protectors – and cigarettes tumbled to the ground. As ponies were walked back and forth in front of them, they paused to watch them go by, barely heeding Abuela. Ino hung back, shy, uncertain. The air was crackly with heat and adrenaline. She had never seen polo being played, but even she began to feel the contagious beat, the quickening of the pulse as players thundered past. The sun's rays bouncing off the metal hardware of saddles and bridles made them shimmer in the heat.

And then something Abuela said must have resonated, because 'the boys' glanced in Ino's direction. But a quick glance was all it was – they seemed largely disinterested. Abuela paused for a moment to watch the game in progress and then took one of them by the forearm. She had called them '*muchachos*', but clearly they weren't 'boys' at all, but young men of around twenty-five. Ino made an idle guess as to which of them was her cousin, but they seemed identical except that one had startling blue eyes; the other brown. The latter gabbled something Ino couldn't understand and then suddenly, spinning on his heel, took her hand, swooping down as if to kiss it. Ino pulled back in alarm. Now! Now was her chance to show them what she was made of. She rattled off the words she had heard Edu say earlier. There was a stunned silence followed by a smirk of amusement. The brown-eyed man actually *laughed* before turning to Abuela to kiss *her* hand. He threw Ino a final look before striding away. Abuela apologised on Rafael's behalf. *So, that's him.* Ino was surprised. She had been certain the blue-eyed man was her relation; he seemed altogether kinder. So if that was her cousin, who was this?

'This' turned out to be Rafael's *other* cousin Emil; no blood relation of Ino's. He and Emil had been inseparable since… well, ever since they were small.

"It'll have to be you." Abuela addressed Emil.

"Me? What do you mean, me? You are joking, *verdad*?"

Abuela was losing patience, and Ino realised with a start that the heated discussion had been about her. Except now she was hot and thirsty and bored. She hadn't *asked* to come here. Maybe they should remember that! Once again, just for fun, Ino used those pretty words that seemed to have produced such an effect earlier.

Both Abuela and the man stared at her.

Ino used the words a final time, and was pleased with herself until she realised that they'd not helped change Abuela's mind. Not one bit. In fact, Abuela seemed more determined than ever to abandon her. She blew Ino a kiss, before Ino could call, *Espera! Wait!* But Abuela had moved away more quickly than a woman her age had any right to. *Just great*, thought Ino. *Just darn wonderful.* She glowered at the man, who, to give him his credit, didn't look particularly happy either. For a moment they stood awkwardly together, but his attention was soon diverted by the game going on behind them. He motioned to the deckchairs and they sat, Ino taking the seat vacated by her cousin.

"We'll just finish watching the game," he said, already engrossed.

It was clear that wild horses weren't going to drag him away (she'd have liked to see them try, though), so Ino made herself comfortable, kicking off her shoes and shading her eyes from the sun's glare. She felt like a lump of lard in this heat. Every bit of her was clammy, her dress clinging to her skin. And if she felt that uncomfortable, she couldn't begin to imagine how the riders must feel. The horses too were lathered in sweat, snorting in protest as they galloped up and down the field.

"You ride, of course." It wasn't a question. He wasn't even looking at her, and she smiled.

He thinks he has solved the problem of what to do with me! How to while away a long, boring afternoon. Well, she would soon scupper those plans! *Why 'of course'? Why so many assumptions?* Ino was becoming irritated. She had been parachuted into this ridiculous world of castles and outdated snobbery and expected to fit in. She didn't want to. It had been fun last night in a weird, zany way, but now she'd just as soon go home, thank you very much. Home to Canada, that is. To Ontario and summer camp. *Ahora mismo.* "Nope," she said firmly. "I know nothing whatsoever about horses."

Emil looked at her properly then for the first time. She was suddenly as much of a curiosity to him as he was to her. He'd been leaning back, rocking in his chair, but he sat bolt upright on hearing this arresting piece of news. "Really?" He had never met anyone who didn't ride. His gaze swept over her; rested a little longer on her signet ring.

Suddenly self-conscious, she sat on her hands, pretending to concentrate on the game, and didn't meet his eye. She was beginning to hate her ring. It was too big and made her feel as though she'd been chained by an invisible link to an equally obscure, padlocked ancestry.

But Emil didn't leave it at that. His head moved this way and that, watching the riders. "*Figúrate!*" (Which, she guessed, meant something along the lines of 'Imagine that!') "A Monte Alegre who doesn't ride!"

Ino scowled. She knew the score, thank you.

"So, what *do* you know about?"

He was still watching the game, his whole body tense. She noted the taut muscles of his neck as he craned to understand a sequence of play from the tangle of riders and sticks. She watched too but none of it made any sense, and just when she had grasped which team was shooting at which goal, they changed ends. She blinked. At home, no one usually asked her anything; not even if she had finished her homework, which she always had. Maybe it was a rhetorical question. Emil was completely captivated by the polo. With any luck, if Ino waited long enough, he might forget that he'd asked her anything anyway. Adults generally did.

But he didn't forget. There was a lull. Spectators poured onto the field, stomping about on the grass. Even the beautiful, well-shod women with their sleek, streaked locks and immaculate little summer dresses smoothed down their clothes to traipse from the stands. In their pretty colours they looked like butterflies fluttering about the grass, but Emil made no effort to join them.

"Shouldn't we?"

He shrugged. "You can if you want." His position didn't change: legs stretched out, heels digging into the ground. He reached for the cigarettes tucked under her deckchair. He lit one, waving away the smoke; removed a shred of tobacco from his lips. Every movement was slick, confident, carefree. He inhaled, drawing deeply. "Well?"

She could tell him about... She racked her brain. What exactly *could* she tell him about? Her school that had been founded after a great sea battle? Her books? Her recent, slight and new obsession with historical romances with stirring titles like *Sweet Savage Love*? In fact, a man on the flight over had asked her what she was reading, and when she'd told him he'd answered, "Guess that's the only kind there is", and gone back to sleep. She was silent.

Emil shook his head. "Then you are not your father's daughter."

Ino was startled. "Why do you say that? Did you know Santiago?" It was her turn to really look at Emil. His colouring was striking: dark, almost navy-blue eyes in a tanned face, and black hair. He had a long nose, a wide mouth, even white teeth. His expression was genuinely puzzled. She watched as his elegant hands moved to his mouth, then tapped ash from his cigarette.

She felt an odd tightening sensation in the pit of her stomach, and looked away. Maybe she didn't dislike him quite so much.

"Well, we all knew Santi."

"I didn't." And suddenly, there it was. A stupid, traitorous tear which she wiped away quickly with the back of her hand. She would *not* cry in front of this man, not here, not ever!

The riders reappeared on the field, their grooms tracking them with fresh ponies.

"Tell me about my father," she said, almost angrily. "He was a good rider? Obviously he was. Silly me. He was a Monte Alegre!" She had just remembered something else. "Tell me. Are you also a Head of a Cow?"

"Excuse me?"

"A Cabeza de Vaca? A grand… whatever?"

"Grandee?"

"That's the one."

A long horn sounded. A final blast.

"Game's over."

"Well, that's a relief."

"Yes."

"What? Yes, it's a relief the game is over? Or do you mean you are one?"

Emil made an apologetic shrug. "Both."

"I thought they were really rare."

He shot her a sideways, amused glance over a smoke ring. "Once, maybe – not any more. Don't concern yourself with any of that. It doesn't matter."

"It does to Abuela."

"Yes, well. She's a different breed."

"Of cow?"

"I didn't say that!"

"And my fa… Santiago?" She was angry again. The fact that she hadn't known him and had to ask a stranger. "Did that kind of thing matter to him?"

Emil took a final sideways puff, stubbing out the butt with his heel. He picked up the end, though, slipping it into his cigarette box. Getting to his feet, he reached down, holding out his hand. For a moment she grasped it; it was warm and dry and all at once an anchor – the only certain thing in this… insanity. But he pulled away. There was nothing meant by the gesture other than one motivated by natural courtesy.

"To him least of all. You really don't know?"

She wouldn't be asking if she did. "I know absolutely nothing about him," she mumbled. "But I want to know. I want to know everything."

Emil gave her a strange look. "Okay… So, we could start here."

"Here?"

"As good a place as any. *Sígame!* Follow me." Emil left his helmet and whip by the chairs. "They'll be fine," he said to her unspoken question as they moved towards the clubhouse. "Would you like something?" he asked politely as they passed the bar.

Waiters polished glassware. Huge bowls of sangria were filled to the brim with slices of orange and ice cubes floating on the top. Platters of tortillas, olives, bread and other tapas were lined up ready to be offered to the guests.

"What's that?" She pointed.

"*Pulpo en su tinta* – octopus in its ink."

Ino shook her head vigorously.

Emil laughed. "You should try it sometime. It's very good."

They bypassed the dining room through a corridor that led to the main hall. Emil stopped before glass units displaying photographs, silver plates and trophies.

"There, do you see?" He pointed to the wall where the names of former presidents of the club and winners of the Villapadierna Cup were engraved in gold. "Santiago Monte Alegre de Cabeza de Vaca, Count of Salto al Cielo. That's him – that's your father."

Ino swallowed, suddenly overcome with an emotion she couldn't explain. She felt hollow, while everything else felt horribly overexposed. The sunlight was excessive, sending rays through the open-plan building like flaming arrows. She should have felt pride in her father's achievement, but it would have been misplaced and false. The more information she was given, the less she understood. No sooner had she recovered tiny vignettes of his life than they vanished just as quickly. It was so strange to think that he had played here at this club, had been part of this club, but that others were privy to an even more selective one: the club of having known him.

Emil brushed her arm. "I'm sorry."

"No need. It's not like I knew him."

"But you still feel it. Maybe that's worse."

"Do you suppose…?" She grabbed Emil's arm. Something had suddenly occurred to her. It might explain everything. Her voice dropped to a whisper. "Could I be… you know… *adopted*?"

Emil snorted a "No!" with such force that she knew he was being truthful.

She wasn't sure why, but she was relieved. She needed to belong here.

"How about *una* Coca-Cola? A Coke? Would you like one? You'll feel better."

Ino laughed. He looked so worried. "It's okay, really. I just have so many questions. I just can't believe…" She shook her head. "I'll understand it all, I guess, one day. But *cuéntame*," she raised her green eyes to him, "tell me, did you ever meet him?"

"Why, yes, of course."

"Of course…" she echoed.

"He was a Monte Alegre… That, and apart from being Rafael's uncle and mine by marriage, he was the one who got us started on polo – Rafael and me. Didn't Abuela tell you that?"

"No, no, she didn't. Maybe she meant to. We've been catching up on a lot. I only met her for the first time yesterday… I only arrived yesterday."

"Yesterday?"

"Yes. Although it feels like I've already been here… Anyway, she's been telling me about Santiago when he was a small boy. She likes telling me about the cute things he did when he was little, but she hasn't said so much about later."

"Maybe because later, things weren't so cute."

Ino was startled. "What do you mean?"

"Nothing. It was a retort. Nothing was meant by it."

For a moment they looked at each other, but he remained silent.

"So, don't tell me what he did – tell me what he was like."

Emil took her arm. "Come – we'll go over there." He nodded in the direction of the number three field.

"Let me guess. More polo?"

"No… well, yes. It's more pleasant, that's all. It's stuffy here."

They went outside, brushing past spectators, leisurely moving from stand to stand. It was too hot to move any faster. Emil seemed to have forgotten how old she was, because he gave her a glass of sangria, which this time she accepted. She was so thirsty she drank quickly and the drink went straight to her head. They walked past tethered horses, and tents where all manner of equestrian paraphernalia was on sale. Players relaxing after a match watched Emil and Ino with open curiosity. He took her by the hand as though she were little, guiding her to the empty pitch. Which was just as well, as she began to feel as though she were floating.

"Well?" She just hoped she wouldn't start hiccupping.

"Well." Emil stopped to lean against the white picket fence. He rested a foot on the first rail looking at the ground, his dark hair flopping into his eyes. She touched his arm to focus his attention back on her. He smiled at the intensity of her look. "It's hard to describe just how attractive your father was. It wasn't just that he was good-looking; he had this magnetic personality – both men and women were mad for him. When you were with him you just wanted more – even if he wasn't saying much, being with him was enough. You must know that *aquí*," he stamped the ground for emphasis, "looks are everything. You can be a child molester or a murderer but if you are *guapo*, then the world forgives you. Of course, it had trouble forgiving…" He stopped short.

"Forgiving?" Ino felt suddenly cold in the merciless heat.

Emil shook his head. "That… your father was so glamorous, so gifted."

"Oh." She breathed out, relieved. She could retreat to her dreamy haze.

"Santiago was good-looking, but on top of that he had *duende* – you know the word? It's that *chispe*, that spark or charisma that exists for both sexes. It's a kind of magic in a person."

"Ah… so people were jealous."

"No, they weren't jealous. That was just it. Everyone loved Santi. He was such fun to be with, but he was also clever at judging his audience. He could just as easily spend time in a downtown bar in the Petritxol as he could at an embassy party. Everything and everyone was of interest to him. He was popular as a result. *Basicamente*, he was good at everything he did; anything he wanted to do. Apart from being a brilliant linguist, he was also a great musician. Again, that ear of his meant that he could hear a piece of music once and then just play it. He was tremendous company. There really has never been anyone like him. I knew him first simply as my cousin's uncle, extended family that we are, but then he became a friend."

"Did Rafael feel the same way?"

"As I say, Santiago was a friend to everyone – people of all ages, from all walks of life."

"I feel there's an 'and' somewhere, or even a 'but'?"

Emil was silent.

"Is there?"

"Everyone has their demons. All you need to know is that Santiago was clever and sporty. A rare combination – certainly around here." Emil gestured in the direction of the clubhouse. "I mean, look at Rafael and me!"

"Well, I hardly know either of you, but I can tell already which of you is the kinder."

Emil pulled her ponytail. "It's not kindness," he said gruffly.

"No?" She was coquettish; emboldened by the sangria. "Then what exactly?"

"Why, you'll grow up."

"And then?" Her voice was embarrassingly throaty.

"And then I'll be waiting."

Her heart was pounding. She felt (or perhaps she only imagined) the tip of his finger on her cheek. Her heart jolted. She couldn't breathe.

"But in the meantime, *pequeña*, it's time for a riding lesson."

"Have you finished with the paper?"

"I'm sorry?"

A man with a disability badge hovered in front of Ino. He motioned to the newspaper by her laptop. His eyes, through bulbous glasses, were impatient and unfriendly. He was used to reserving her spot and didn't like the fact that he would have to find somewhere else to sit. And all at once Ino was pulled back to the present, to the Discovery Centre, and to the million and one chores that awaited her.

"Don't worry," she said, "I'm just leaving."

"About bloody time," he muttered under his breath.

Ino smiled agreeably, refusing to completely abandon the sweetness of her reminiscences. *You were the one great love of my life*, he had said once.

But was it true still?

Archie

Cedar Avenue

I could have loved you completely. I <u>did</u> love you – no holding back, no reserve, no games, no malice or guile. But now this!!! I am winded; gutted. I honestly don't know what to say. There is still love – there will always be that; after all, you can't switch off feelings just because you have changed; have acted as you have. But – and there's a big, agonising BUT! – how can you do this to someone you love? I don't understand. Help me to understand. I really am asking you to, because without understanding, I'm not sure I can continue.

You've taken something from me. If I were innocent, I'd call it that: innocence. Faith. Belief. You've taken it from me. And for that I can never, ever forgive. I thought we would write our future in the stars – me in you, remember? You in me.

25

Rafael
Barcelona
August 2017

If Rafael associated Ottmar Liebert's *Barcelona Nights* with polo, he would always think of Elgar's *Chanson de Matin* (even if it was now evening) with Salto al Cielo. The music had been running on repeat in his head all day, and with it an urge to visit his childhood home. When by late afternoon he knew that no amount of *brazos* or Unamuno or even a visit to Emil was going to shake this mood of his, he grabbed the keys to the communal parish car (a Seat circa 1970) and headed for the parking lot. It was out of curiosity, he told himself; to see what had become of the place – nostalgia at best for what he remembered as a simpler time. Wrapping the skirt of his soutane around his ankles as he drove through the city in rush hour, and then stopping at a petrol station to remove it altogether, he was still justifying reasons for the three-hour drive even as he approached the turn-off for Salto.

And, as the name suggested, he couldn't suppress the leap his own heart made at the sight of the familiar sign. Accelerating as fast as the crusty old car could manage, he played a game with himself to see if he could again find that particular place where the castle, shrouded in mist, would suddenly appear from across the lake. He pulled the handbrake, rolled down the window, and closed his eyes only to open them again quickly. He wanted to savour that first glimpse that could never really be repeated; not now, not ever.

And then, there it was: the one-time Roman outpost, the fairy-tale island, Salto. Salto… the Salto of his imagination; the Salto of his dreams, his youth, his undoing. In the evening sun, its four turret roofs gleamed pink and muted and lovely. Once, the reflection of its whitewashed exteriors would have glistened on the water, while the earlier structure with its arrow slits, battlements and ramparts, would have been every bit the fortification it was built to be. From here, though, the castle formed a perfect oval and was sweeping and graceful.

Rafael felt exhilarated in a way that he hadn't in years, but as he reversed into muddy undergrowth, his conscience pricked him. Rather than indulging a trip down memory lane, shouldn't he be spending time devising novel ways to apply the gospel message to the lives of his parishioners? What exact message was that, though? At times, he was perfectly perplexed as to what he believed in; what he was trying to achieve. And coming here was only going to make it more confused – of that he was certain. "Keep it simple," one kindly priest had advised him in the seminary, "and everything will work out. Be a priest, not a buddy; a man of authority, but never an autocrat; a spiritual father, but not a biological one." Rafael frowned. Was that what all this was about, then? The continuation of a line; the planting of seed? *'May you live to see your children's children'* and all that, then possibly… Maybe. Yes.

He was still feeling buoyant as he made his way on foot along the shallows of the lake. He loved to walk across the old drawbridge and think of his ancestors' jealously guarded licence which had given them the right to crenellate.

"Right to *what*?" Ino had asked, astounded, when Rafael had expanded on some of Salto's history (the parts omitted by Abuela) on her first visit to Spain.

He'd agreed that the old-world traditions sounded ridiculous, but all it had meant was that, once upon a time, Alfonso I had permitted a Count of Monte Alegre to build his castle.

"Was that necessary?"

"Well, yes – for one thing, we were always fighting the Moors."

Ino had shown interest, and for a brief moment there had been something akin to affection in their kinship. Encouraged, Rafael had pointed out the family crest which, he explained, could be seen everywhere, engraved everywhere – on wood and stone and leather – a constant reminder of who they were and how they belonged. From where he'd been standing, just there, he'd also pointed out the dungeon, which had been built deliberately at water level rather than below it, its access door leading directly onto the lake's banks – a kind of emergency exit. And in recent times, during the Civil War, it had come in handy too, once or twice. But archaic or not, there was no denying the history; *their* history: a Monte Alegre had lived on this spot from 1150 onwards. Until now.

Until now. Rafael frowned. How was it that Salto was vacant? It should be alive with the sound of children's voices; the bustle of family life. Once again, he felt that familiar tightening in his chest. He'd not exaggerated when he'd recounted Salto's history to Ino all those years ago. The castle had survived some twenty-five sieges, withstood being captured seven times, and yet now its greatest enemy was neglect. Like a woman who was still beautiful, but not loved. Breathing in the cool air, he realised with a visceral shock just how much he'd missed the place, how he'd longed for it, and how no church could give him the serenity or the peace he craved. At the same time, he felt invigorated; every nerve alive with the thrill of being home again. With boyish delight, he felt as though he were playing truant. He had removed his soutane earlier; now he took off his dog collar and shoved it into his jacket pocket, which he carried slung over one shoulder. Here, he desired to be neither priest nor penitent, and especially not count – only himself, home again, walking backwards even as he moved forwards to recapture the steps of his youth.

But the pleasure of his return soured when he saw the padlocked gates ahead. Getting through the portcullis had been a doddle, but gaining access to the second courtyard was going to be more of a challenge. Where once gardenia and camellia had woven their pretty heads through the wrought-iron posts, waist-high weeds now formed a protective barrier. He shook the gates, but the lock was rusty and unyielding. He stood back, considered their height, then confidently placed a foot on the first rail. Time was when he'd have been up and over in a matter of seconds. To his amazement, he wasn't able to propel himself up at all. Breathless, he tried again, but without success. Surely his physique hadn't changed all that much?

And then he remembered. Patting the head of the lion statue to his right, he wedged his foot into one of the rungs for balance while he rooted around in its mouth. It was worth a try, although he really didn't think the key would still be there after all this time. But it was. A thrill coursed through his body at its discovery, happily replacing the shock of his lack of fitness. At first he thought that the lock might have been changed, that it was the wrong key, but after a few more attempts the gate, if not exactly swinging open, eventually creaked apart. He set his shoulder against the heavy iron, pushing with all his strength and managing at last to squeeze through.

Panting from the exertion, Rafael palmed a packet of cigarettes. He really should try and give up – cut down *por lo menos*; at the very least. This latest little jaunt had certainly demonstrated that he wasn't as fit as he used to be. He tapped the box, ignoring the horrendous notice cigarettes now carried. Gone were the days when the Marlboro Man or even Gitanes positively encouraged the habit. Now, if he actually read the warning, he'd never light up in the first place. Which was the point, he knew, but the pictures of aborted babies were positively damaging. He *needed* a cigarette after seeing that kind of stuff.

Puffing gently, he immediately felt calmer. He sat on a tree trunk in the cobblestone courtyard where there'd once been a well. He remembered huge containers of potted orange trees lending colour to the pebbled paths, and tobacco plants scenting the air. He wasn't sure what he'd been expecting exactly. In his mind's eye he'd imagined, fancifully, that the place would be untouched; that, as in the fairy tale, he would discover that the castle had merely been sleeping. But even in the benign evening light, nothing short of a million euros was going to bring *this* castle to life. He stubbed out his cigarette in the gravel – more weeds and self-seeding flowers than pea shingle – and began walking along sandy paths and up stone staircases, while keeping to the perimeter of the inner tower. He made a mental note of the broken windows, the tiles that had slipped from roofs and outbuildings, and where only wisteria seemed still to thrive.

Rafael had no desire to enter the *castillo* itself – for one thing he didn't have a key, and for another, well, if he was honest (and he'd decided this visit was going to be all about honesty), he was frankly afraid of what he might find in those dusty, boarded-up rooms. Nuria had died the same year as Abuela and as far as he was aware no caretaker had been hired to fill that vacancy. He didn't want to see the devastation that moths or small rodents or quite simply abandonment had wrought upon the place. Ignoring signs, too, for the mill and granary, he walked down once neatly mown terraces and through chaotic orchards to the pretty stone bridge, which thankfully seemed to have been spared erosion. It was as romantic as ever, with water passing beneath, ever clear and clean.

As if drawn by a higher power, his feet seemed determined to take him south, through fields of sunflowers to the one place he had not been brave enough to revisit; not since that summer, not since… He paused, hesitated, his heart doing that jittery spasm thing. Maybe he had the beginnings of an irregular heartbeat? Or worse, an arrhythmia? He should probably get it checked out. He shifted his jacket to his other shoulder, mopping his perspiring forehead with his dog collar. And still something stronger than the voice of reason drove him on. He knew he should turn back. He knew nothing would come of dredging up painful memories – memories that were best forgotten. But even as the path narrowed – a small hedge on the one side with the river behind it, and on the other a row of cedars lending leafy shade – he could see the folly in the distance and he was overcome with emotion, with excitement, with joy.

There it was: a nineteenth-century summer house (and therefore the most 'modern' structure in the whole of Monte Alegre), built in the time of another Alfonso – eleven Alfonsos down the line, to be exact – for the King to honeymoon with his bride, the beautiful Mercedes. Said to be his one first and best love, she would die six months into their marriage at the age of eighteen. But who could foretell any of that when the pretty wooden pavilion was built? It was on two storeys with a wrap-round veranda. The King, delighting in what he saw, had called it *Sospiro*. Abuela had said that it was a sigh for the life that was already slipping from the only woman he would truly love. Who could say? But what Rafael did know was that the name had been prophetic. As it would be for himself, for Emil, and for Ino. It would become a sigh for what might have been.

Rafael walked completely around the folly, before retracing his steps and coming back to the front. Under his touch, a broken banister threatened to split completely, a dislodged bird's nest spilled its shrieking offspring onto the wormwood-infested timber, and his feet crunched on shattered pottery. Too late to turn back, he was here once again as if for the first time. He hesitated only briefly before gingerly mounting the rotten wooden steps. Mindful of the gaps in the floorboards, he edged towards the balustrade, folding his jacket over the handrail. In the distance, grey hills were an idle brushstroke in the darkening sky, and far beyond the natural boundaries of water and wheat. Crickets chirped, the cicadas began a cacophony of sound, and then came a kind of silence... And then splitting that silence came sudden laughter, or the memory of it;

the sound of gorgeous Argentine tango; then the not-so-gorgeous Catalan *cobla* with its distinctive *flabiol*, that bagpipe-esque ear-splitting flute that makes up one of the ten wind instruments in the band. Rafael almost started to keep time, knowing that his mind was playing tricks.

And as if suddenly conscious of the reality of it all, after all these years, he slumped heavily on the low, rotting threshold. Again there was that uncomfortable tightness in his chest. He watched as a salamander slithered between the rocks on the path in front, eschewing the warm stone for the cool shade of mint and lavender. He followed the reptile's trajectory as it re-emerged on the path to the unplayable tennis courts. Beyond that was the long-dried-out swimming pool with its crumbling concrete surround and broken diving board. Doors hung off their hinges in the changing-room huts, and peeling paint hung as thick as shower curtains. But from Rafael's elevated position, ragged shafts of light blurred the decaying edges of the *castillo* and, for a few hours at least, returned it to being the enchanted place of his youth; to twelve years before; to the night of Ino's eighteenth birthday.

It was all very different then. There was no whisper that evening of what lay ahead; not the slightest hint that this night wouldn't be like any other, that day after languid day wouldn't follow as it had always done, fluidly and without incident. Everyone and everything was assured; confident of their place in this well-ordered, affluent and most of all predictable world of theirs. The evening was warm, fragrant with the heady scent of mimosa; the heady scent of love. Every possible path leading from the principal courtyard was lit with lanterns. Fairy lights were strung like a giant's jewelled necklace interlaced through the olive trees, connecting formal and informal gardens, and around the swimming pool. Hired staff rushed to and fro, replenishing tables with tapas: large plates of *pa amb tomàquet*, whole legs of *jamón serrano*, and stuffed squid. There was a rainbow collection of salads, artichoke, celery and baked tomato flans. Waiters ferried large buckets of ice and champagne and glasses from the *castillo* kitchens to the pool house against a background buzz of conversation and laughter and the tinkle of crystal. Pretty girls flitted among the trees like beautiful, sparkling fireflies (or *cuca de llum* as they were known in Catalan), never staying long in one place. Many of Rafael and Emil's polo friends were there too, fresh from a late afternoon game, still in their sporting whites. Some had arrived by helicopter, the putt-putt of their engines audible from across the lake. The frisson caused by the arrival of these young warriors was palpable with an excitement that accompanied them wherever they went. They were all young and beautiful and carefree.

So far, Rafael would have said the party was a success. Apart from the choice in music. Abuela had stopped the DJ playing Rihanna's 'Unfaithful' for the umpteenth time – she didn't like the tune, she said, never mind its title – but no one was drunk, nothing had been broken, and as yet no one had ventured into the pool.

"None of that skinny-dipping," Abuela warned. "Or at least not until us oldies have gone to bed."

Rafael had never seen Abuela nervous, but on this occasion she was an anxious hostess. She wanted the party to go well – after all, she warned 'the boys', it was as good as Ino's 'coming-out' party.

"Her *what*?" Emil had wanted to know.

"Oh, you explain," she had said, gesturing to Rafael as she always she did when anything cultural, historical or educational required more detail.

But Rafael had more pressing matters on his mind and, like the salamander, had slunk off as quickly and quietly as possible to the shade and quiet of Sospiro. As he sat smoking on the porch, he tried to calm himself, to will away his preoccupations. And then in the gloaming he spied her pink Dior dress; a vivid splodge of colour amidst the white gardenia bushes. He sat absolutely still, hoping to remain hidden.

"I can see you!" Her voice rang out gaily. "I can see your smoke, so you can be as quiet as you like but I've found you!"

Blast and double blast. "Ah... hola... Sol?"

The voice was coming closer and becoming tetchier with every step. "You don't sound very sure. Who did you think it was?"

If she were smart, she'd be asking who did he *want* it to be? But she wasn't, so she didn't. He, on the other hand, *should* feel elated, excited, something – *anything* but the increasing apathy that crept over him every time he saw her. Half of her attraction had been *her* attraction to Emil. It was always titillating for Rafael to go after a girl that Emil had met first and make her fall in love with him instead. But the truth of it was that ever since Emil had lost interest in Sol, so had Rafael. They were both fond of her, of course – she was part of their gang – but if Rafael wasn't in love with her any more, he was pretty sure Emil wasn't either.

Sol held up her gown, picking her way along the edge of the path, exposing dainty, tanned ankles above beautiful custom-made Ferragamo shoes. And in those few seconds before she reached Rafael, thoughts careered through his head. Those silk shoes alone reminded him that she would be wealthy in her own right; that she was pretty much perfect in terms of beauty and background; that, having grown up with the game, she wouldn't mind a bit about him playing polo. She tossed back her sleek blonde hair, one graceful hand resting on the banister, mounting the step, searching for him. She was exquisite all right. There was nothing whatsoever to fault except that... except that... Except that she was, well... *boring.* There was no other word for it.

He frowned, frustrated at his reaction but it couldn't be helped. Boredom was the one hurdle he constantly battled (and never conquered) when dating any girl, not just Sol. In fact, he'd always been fascinated by Tolstoy's *Anna Karenina*, and not for the love story. It was Vronsky's character with whom Rafael identified. There was a part in the novel that resonated with him. Vronsky, on finding himself at last in Europe with Anna – the two of them having overcome so many hurdles, the least of it being Anna's own guilt at abandoning her husband and young son for him – is described as being quite simply bored. What was it Tolstoy had said about Vronsky? Something along the lines that men (wrongly) imagined happiness lay in the gratification of their wishes. *How true*, Rafael thought, looking at Sol's clear, flawless, blank face. *How true.* He didn't want to see Sol now or ever. He wanted to discuss tomorrow's game with Emil. He wanted to talk about polo and women. Women other than Sol. In fact, he'd told that gorgeous Costa Rican girl to meet him later. So what was Sol doing here instead? What was going to happen when Miss San José turned up? He began sweating gently.

"*No bailas?*" Sol asked.

Rafael blinked. Had her voice always been this tinny? As though already anticipating his reply in the negative, as if… "I've danced enough," he said sternly.

"I don't feel like dancing any more either," she said easily. "I could just sit with you."

No, please don't! "All right…" Maybe his lack of enthusiasm would show, and she'd get the message. "But wouldn't you rather be at the party?"

"I'd rather be with you."

Christ! Rafael shot her a suspicious look. Music was coming from the pool house. The Chinese lanterns swung invitingly above paths lit with flares. It wouldn't be long before people started swimming. And then what? He couldn't bear the thought of Sol clinging to him in the water… "Have you seen Ino?" he asked.

"Why?" said Sol sharply.

"No reason." Rafael shrugged. "Other than, it is, after all, her party."

There was an uncomfortable silence. Sol took the two steps required to join him on the veranda bench. Rafael stole a glance. Even her profile was near-on perfect, with her straight little nose, full upper lip, and her hair in its Alice band brushed neatly away from her tanned, smooth face. He could see the hint of equally tanned breasts rising above the bodice of her expensive dress. Was it his imagination or did they look fuller, more pert than usual? Whatever the reason, she did nothing to excite him. Emil (or any man) could have her if he wanted her. Rafael lit another cigarette from the end of the one he'd just finished, drawing on it deeply, but even blowing smoke out of the side of his mouth (he was careful that it went nowhere near her hair) seemed to bother her.

"What's the matter?"

"I feel sick – the smoke makes me feel sick."

"Oh, I'm so sorry. Perhaps you'd better go in."

"Here?"

God, not here! He'd never get rid of her here! "I was thinking of the *castillo*."

"Will you come with me?"

Rafael looked towards the pool house. "I will in a minute. I'm just waiting for Emil, but you go – I'll catch you up." Not very chivalrous. Not what Santi would have done – he caught himself thinking about his uncle's impeccable manners.

"Always Emil!" she said, stamping her foot. Except that from a sitting position it wasn't much of a stamp.

"Now, Sol," said Rafael, surprised, even a little amused, in spite of himself. Maybe she could *learn* to be livelier company. She really was very pretty.

"Don't look at me in that tone of voice!"

Humour at last!

"*Mi amor—*"

"I'm not *tu amor*."

"You're not?" Well, that was a relief.

"And I haven't been for some time."

"Oh?"

He could tell she was sulking. She began to list his faults. He took too much time getting dressed (true), he didn't like to stay up too late (not before a match; true again), he preferred his cousin Emil's company to hers (we-ell…).

"And we never go out!" she finished triumphantly, tilting her chin.

Rafael motioned to the lights behind her. "Well, we're out now."

Sol fiddled with the bracelet on her left wrist and suddenly her voice went quiet. "Yes, but it doesn't feel as if we're out *together*. It feels as though we're here separately. It feels as though we've been playing cat and mouse all evening."

"And which are you? The little mouse?" Rafael thought that quite good, himself.

"Not funny," said Sol grumpily. "Not funny at all."

Rafael took another puff, crossing his legs patiently. He supposed this was as good as any conversation he was going to have this evening. "So, what is it you want?"

She leaned against the pavilion wall. "I don't know," she said, so quietly that he had to lean in to hear her. "Nothing feels right."

He couldn't agree more. "Maybe you're right."

Her head snapped up. "What do you mean?"

Rafael shrugged. What did she think he meant?! "*Tal vez*, maybe we're just not suited. Oh, it's not you," he said hastily. He always laid the blame at the door of his character… or polo, or the summer, the winter, being a Monte Alegre, whatever.

"Are you saying that we should… *end* things?"

Hallelujah! God, this was easy. He nodded slowly, keeping his gaze lowered while figuratively punching the air. There was an uncomfortable pause. The music seemed to be getting louder, then softer as the DJ began playing Julio Iglesias. "So the older ones can have a slow dance and go to bed," Rafael joked joyfully. He was feeling very, very good at this moment. Surely this would turn out to be one of the easiest endings to any relationship he'd ever instigated? His only regret was not having brought out a bottle of cava with him – and where *was* Emil? Oh boy, would they celebrate now!

"Maybe we should, but—"

She'd got it! *Oh, yesss! Thank you, Providence!* "You might at least *pretend* to sound sorry," he said, making his tone sulky, as though he actually minded.

"Oh, I'm sorry all right."

The weak trickle of tears had dried (Sol was a crier, but she never allowed her make-up to spoil), so why was she sounding angry? Especially as they were reading from the same page, so to speak. Why was that beautiful bosom beginning to quiver all over again? Give him horses any day. He would never understand women!

"Sol?"

"You really don't get anything, do you?"

Rafael inhaled this time, taking extra care not to annoy her with his smoke. He made a helpless gesture. "No…" What was there to get?

Sol gave another angry sniff, then tossed back her pretty blonde head. "I'm pregnant," she said.

"Come again?"

"Not funny."

"What? No! I mean, it's not… I'm not… What did you say?"

Sol's blue eyes were flints of sapphire stone. "I said, I'm pregnant."

Pregnant? *Pregnant?!* She didn't say that. She couldn't have said that!

"*Joder!*" swore Rafael, spluttering, and all at once – lights, camera, action – his world, the world he'd thought to be so much in control of, imploded.

"And I'm keeping it," she said defiantly.

Rafael felt a pounding in his ears as though someone had clobbered him with a mallet. If only that were the case and the sum of his problems. He took another deep puff, then, dropping the butt on the floor, ground it into the decking. Catching her accusing look, he hastily brushed it over the edge with the toe of his shoe.

But slowly, playing for time. "Well, don't expect me to marry you!" he said coldly. She might be feeling nauseous, but he could turn and vomit the entire contents of his stomach right now, *ahora mismo*.

Sol blinked furiously. "But you have to!"

Something about her tone irritated him. "I don't *have* to do anything!"

"What don't you have to do?" said Emil chirpily.

Neither one had heard him approach. Rafael could hardly believe that only a little while ago, the sight of his cousin carrying a bottle of cava and glasses hooked in his left hand would have made his heart sing.

"Cause for celebration?" Emil asked, blue eyes dancing with his usual easy-going merriment. Rafael had never seen him on such good form. He opened the bottle with a flourish, placing glasses and an ice bucket on a rickety old table just around the corner against the wall. "Sol?" he said, offering her a glass.

"Oh!" she said, bursting into tears.

"No?" Emil gave Rafael a questioning look. "But, *tu cosí meu*, you'll have a glass?" He looked astonished. He too had envisioned all kinds of scenarios for the evening – this glorious, balmy evening – but he had not anticipated the grumpiness of these two. He shrugged. "Suit yourselves, my friends – all the more for Ino-Bambino. Come to think of it, where is she? She was right behind—"

Sol suddenly swooped behind him and grabbed a glass. "Actually, *idiota*, changed my mind. I will, and don't tell me what I can and can't do."

"Wasn't going to," said Emil amiably, pouring Sol a glass. He took a quick swig himself. "Ah, delicious. I do love our Salto cava. Much better than the French stuff, don't you agree? Lovers' tiff?" he added pleasantly, after being met with stony silence.

Rafael made a disgusted face. Emil could feel his tension; the unpleasant tension he – or rather, *they* – experienced when a match hadn't gone according to plan.

"It's more than that," spat Sol, tossing back her beautiful hair and pointing her pretty little shoe.

"Don't!" warned Rafael, half-rising.

"Don't what?" she taunted.

"I mean it."

There was a menacing moment's silence. Emil looked from one face to the other before Sol, tilting her chin provocatively, took a swig of champagne.

"I'm pregnant and *tu primo*," she enunciated the words 'your cousin' as if they were dirt, "*tu primo* says he won't marry me."

Emil choked on his drink. "Did you say *pregnant*? As in…?"

Rafael got to his feet and, brushing past Emil, also reached for a glass. Ordinarily, the shocked look on Emil's face would have amused him. *Ta-da*, he might have teased, *don't say I haven't surprised you!* But this was no joking matter. In fact, in a burst of rage he wanted to punch Sol, Emil, anyone; punch his way back to a few moments ago when everything still seemed *normal*. His hands were shaking as he drank cava. He didn't give a toss what it was – French or otherwise. He would get as drunk as possible, just as quickly as possible, and hope that this… this *pesadilla* – nightmare – would go away. The music had momentarily stopped, and they could hear exuberant shrieks coming from the swimming pool.

"Yes," snarled Sol. "As in."

"Good news?" Ino's unmistakable voice was, like Emil's, positively joyous. Everything about her that night emanated delight: the thrill of being young and beautiful and the toast of Salto. Of being in love. Even Rafael had noticed a change in her; an additional radiance that didn't emanate from the light behind her. Her aqua silk dress clung to her slender form, and the tiny jewels that made up the straps of the bodice twinkled in the light. Her hair was held in place with a diamond comb, and there were diamonds at her ears and throat. The jewellery were gifts from Abuela, passed down through the female line. The first countess,

Catalina, had worn them on her wedding day and had chosen to be painted in them for the portrait hanging in the great hall.

For a moment Rafael was distracted by Ino's beauty, while Emil's eyes darkened with desire. He held out a hand to help her climb the steps. Her hand stayed in his, and had he not been so absorbed in his own drama, Rafael would have seen that another story was unfolding before him.

"No!" said Sol and Rafael, in unison and with such force that both of Rafael's cousins hesitated.

Ino looked questioningly at Emil, who shook his head but, still keeping her hand in his, led her to the table so that they were partly in shadow. He poured her a drink, his fingers lingering on hers. Rafael couldn't be certain, but he thought he saw Emil's lips brush Ino's temple. She stood so close to him that their shapes became blurred; their single silhouette outlined on the painted wall behind. As far as Rafael was concerned, Emil didn't seem to be taking the news as seriously as he should. Rafael made furious gestures in his direction, which Emil either misunderstood or chose to ignore.

"Then you'll have a lot to talk about," he was saying now, backing away. "Come, Ino-Bambino, let's leave them to it. You promised me a dance."

And she, giggling foolishly, said something like, "You're not still calling me that? Not now that I'm eighteen?!", or some such nonsense. "Now that I have a right to crenellate!"

"What *is* she talking about?" said Sol.

Rafael shrugged. "Family stuff."

Emil, misunderstanding, nodded in Sol's direction. "So… um… it *is* congratulations? Maybe?"

Rafael ignored him. "Ah, Ino, *cariño*," he said, wanting a bit of sport and noticing with a flicker of pleasure how Emil's face became sombre.

"Let's go, Ino," was all Emil said. "Bring your glass."

"Ah, Ino," mimicked Sol unkindly, but Ino, in her happy bubble, didn't pick up on the sarcasm. Didn't pick up on anything.

"Are you happy?" asked Ino sweetly. "I mean, about... you know..."

"Happy?" snarled Sol. "*Eres tonta?* Are you completely stupid?"

There was a stunned silence. Emil rounded on Sol, but Ino laid a restraining hand on his arm. His arm went around her slim waist, pulling her close – too close, thought Rafael. She nestled into him and he bent his head to her, and in that moment, Rafael felt an uncontrollable surge of jealousy. Their bent heads, his cousin's shoulders turned protectively to his other cousin's, spelled a harmony and contentment that Rafael had never before experienced, and by the sound of things wasn't going to either. Fury suddenly engulfed him. Who did Sol think she was, trapping him like this? Well, he wouldn't be trapped! He refused! She could have the kid if that's what she wanted, but it was nothing to do with him.

"You stupid girl!" Sol repeated icily.

"*Sol!*" This time, both men rounded on her.

"What? You think she shouldn't know?! You think you are all so superior, you Monte Alegres, you pathetic Salto cousins! Your ridiculous '*duendes*'. There's nothing magical about you lot. And *she*, you – you are all bastards, just like she is; just like—"

"Enough!" said Rafael, grabbing her arm roughly.

But Ino turned. "No, I want to hear. What do you mean? What did she mean, 'just like she is'?"

"She doesn't mean anything," said Emil gently, stepping in front of Ino as if to ward off any more harmful words.

"Don't I?" said Sol, shrugging off Rafael's hand and moving to pour herself another drink. "Why don't you just tell her?!"

"Tell me what?" Ino moved from behind Emil to stand in front of him, but he held her firmly against him, his arm across her chest. She rested her chin on his wrist, holding him with both hands.

"Sol," said Emil, "not now. I know you're upset but you need to sort out your... situation with Rafael. Nothing else is important; certainly not now—"

"Ah, no." Sol's eyes were slits; her cheeks flushed from drink. "I think here and now is perfect." She pointed one pretty little foot, tracing a figure of eight on the painted timber. She held her gown behind her so that it stretched across her belly. "What if…" Her eyes narrowed. "What if I were to say the baby was yours, Emil?"

Ino let Emil's arm fall away. "What?" she whispered, horrified, turning to him. "Emil?"

"*Amor meu—*" he said in Catalan.

"*Mi amor!*" scoffed Sol. "*So* much love in this place!"

"Sol!" warned Rafael angrily.

"Oh my, all this attention suddenly! Well," demanded Sol, "if I said the baby was yours—"

"What are you doing?" said Emil gently. "*Venga*, Sol."

"Hypothetically, if the baby were yours, what would you do?" Her voice rose shrilly.

Ino looked up at Emil. He glanced down at her, brushing the top of her head with his lips, shaking his head faintly to reassure her. He wasn't really paying attention. It was attention-seeking, that was all, his look seemed to say – and a bit of jealousy too, perhaps, that Ino was having such a splendid party.

"I said, what would you do?" repeated Sol.

And suddenly all eyes were on him.

Emil shrugged. "Well, it's not difficult. I'd marry the mother of my child. But—"

"*Ves?*" said Sol smugly. "*Cerdo!*" she directed at Rafael. "Pig!"

"Rafael, take her into the house," said Emil sternly.

"The *castillo*?" said Sol. "No, thanks. I'd rather be anywhere than there."

"Then I'll take you home," said Rafael, and then changed his mind. "Actually, Edu can drive you."

"Oh, pass the buck, why don't you? Wipe your hands of the problem."

"Sol," said Ino gently, "nobody means anything unkindly. We all care—"

"Care?" said Sol sarcastically. "And who are you to care about anything, Little Miss Muck? You think you're so grand, so full of all these airs and graces with Abuela wrapped round your little finger, when you are nothing but a bastard, just like this." She hit her stomach, so that they all jumped towards her. "Nothing but a bastard!"

Ino's eyes were full of tears. "What do you mean?" she asked, hardly above a whisper. "Why do you say that?"

"You might be at your fancy Oxforrrd," said Sol, rolling her 'R's, "but you really are *tonta*. I can't believe they never told you. Never *showed* you—"

"Okay," said Rafael, taking Sol's arm. "That's it – I'll take you home."

"No," said Ino. "Wait. Tell me, Sol! Showed me what exactly? What haven't I been shown?"

Sol broke free from Rafael, the delicate strap of her dress breaking in the process. Her mascara was smudged (though only slightly) and her hair had come loose from its band. "You mean you've never looked in the graveyard? A *castillo* with its own chapel and graveyard and you've never *looked*?! Wow, that's *nobleza* for you."

"That's it! *Basta ya*. Enough!" Rafael took her wrist, yanking her down the steps of Sospiro.

"See for yourself!" screamed Sol. "See for yourself what your precious father was! Better still, ask *how* he died!"

And just as suddenly, the music, the voices and even the *cobla*, having started up again, all stopped. Rafael's memories had seemed so real that for a moment he was disconnected, and then he was left with an overpowering sense of loss. How he wished his older self could go back in time and correct the mistakes of his youth! How much he regretted: his callous cruelty; his casual regard (or *dis*regard) for life. Dazed, he left the summer house with its ghosts and its sadness and made his way back over the little bridge. There was one more place that he wanted to visit before he went back to the city. He had saved it till last, to see if now, all these years later, it would still have that same hold; that magnetic pull that had called him in the first place.

A barn owl flew out as Rafael entered the beautiful chapel with its vaulted ceiling and twelfth-century frescoes. The place was as cool and peaceful as ever, but he genuflected before an altar covered in debris. Bird nests were grouped along the beams; twigs and leaves and cobwebs sprung from paned-glass windows. In a sudden shaft of light, the paintings were illuminated and Rafael offered an impulsive prayer of thanks that their colours were still intact. There were the usual muted ochres and pinks but there was also azure; that most precious and coveted blue made from mountain stone which the Germans called *bergblau* and which was mined locally in Spain. It was the blue used for clothing of the Virgin Mary, the wealthy, the nobility, the King; the blue of medieval manuscripts. While Rafael's sight was filled with the wonder of ecclesiastic worship, a familiar, unwelcome aroma began to invade his senses. Sneezing from the incense that still clung to the pews, he went out into the twilight and the tiny graveyard.

And there under the cork tree – the same tree from whose bark he and Emil used to scrape their little boats – he found the grave. Unlike the rest of the cemetery, the small patch of grass around the simple slab was newly mowed, and someone had left a posy of mimosas. He had no trouble reading the inscription:

Santiago Monte Alegre y Cabeza de Vaca
Duke of Salto al Cielo
Grandee of Spain

There was no date. Because it wasn't important. Rafael knew that there was more. He knelt on the ground, running his fingers along the base of the gravestone where grass and hibiscus met just enough to camouflage what remained of the English:

*'And when the sudden impulse came
I acted, and my action made me wise.
And I regretted nothing.'*

Beloved companion…

It had been left at that. Neither Rafael nor Emil had ever been brave enough to fill in the gap; to set, for posterity, a stranger's name in stone.

Archie

Cedar Avenue

I can have any woman I want, but I want you.

Damn you to hell and back. I will never forgive you for what you've done. Why didn't you just say you weren't coming? Is it possible to hate you this much and want you this much and yearn for you and always, always miss you when you are gone?

I am being driven mad. If only you had just come. One week; it's all I asked for. It's all I've ever asked of you.

There's nothing wrong with you! What the hell do you have to be depressed about anyway? You have always done exactly what you wanted; you have what you want now, don't you? Why else would you stay away?

Go to hell and die a nasty, horrible death. Die.

26

Veronica
Geneva
August 2017

Another flight, another speech, another memo, and here she was again. Home. Well, home at the UN, with Leila shooing away yet another wardrobe team and fluffing up her hair. Veronica frowned; she wasn't entirely convinced by her outfit, although it was definitely an improvement on the last. Even she was in agreement that the first option of gold Chanel with thick fringed braid was a little too suggestive of haberdashery. The second (Leila had persuaded her into a Christian Dior shirt dress in stiff gabardine), while also off the catwalk, still managed to remind Veronica of Abuela. *Abuela?* Veronica hadn't thought about the woman in years! Were all paths leading to the past rather than – fibre-optically, as they should be doing now, at this very moment – to the future?

Veronica squared her shoulders and, arms hanging nonchalantly by her sides, stepped out of her office. Almost at once the long corridor seemed full of people: secretaries, officials, journalists, visitors, all nodding and talking and buzzing or walking, heads bent over mobile phones. For a moment a glimmer of pride shot through her. She wasn't proud of many things in her life, but she was proud of her work, and prouder still of her colleagues. These men and women were part of grandiose organisms created to enhance communication, and all in the hope that the world might achieve a longer-lasting peace.

She pushed her way through revolving doors, swiping her security pass when required, heels tapping on marble floors. And as she walked, fingers occasionally trailing the painted walls of rooms decorated as a result of the collaboration of many countries, it never ceased to astound her that less than a good twenty years before the whole area of the Porcupines was even founded, signals could be sent through cables between Ireland and Nova Scotia, and less than a decade after that, the number of voice channels that could be sent through a copper cable of twisted pairs was six. And today? Well, today that same cable could send thirty-four *thousand* channels. It blew her away that currently there were more phones in the city of Tokyo than in all of sub-Saharan Africa, while almost two thirds of the world's population still did not have access to a telephone.

"They're in the Council Chamber today," said Leila, appearing at Veronica's elbow as if from nowhere; a sleek, smooth shadow dressed from head to toe in Gucci.

She's earning more than I am... Veronica started. "Are you sure?"

Leila's eyebrows arched; never a good sign. Like a cat's, the hairs seemed to flick upwards. "Of course I'm sure."

"'Kay, 'kay, just checking." *Keep your hair on!* Veronica would have liked to say, but Leila wasn't someone you ever teased. Nor was Veronica, she thought wryly.

Veronica almost ran past Leila. She was uncharacteristically weary; travelling so much had finally caught up with her. Either that, or she was getting old. No, never that. And although she was ten minutes early, she headed in the direction of the 'chamber', which really wasn't a chamber as such but a square-shaped room without a podium. Instead, a large table for twenty-one people was placed in a semicircle in front of the five windows overlooking the park. It was a room Veronica knew very well, although she hadn't been in it for a long time. Now, as then, she looked up at the gold-and-sepia ceiling. Why was this coming back to her at all? And yet the tape running in her head continued unbidden, unwanted, unloved...

"The murals are by Sert."

Veronica had thought herself alone in a room where, given the large windows, and in order to preserve the murals' ink, the lighting was deliberately subdued. She had started, recognising the man from earlier that day.

"Santiago," he said, bowing formally and taking her hand before she'd a chance to offer it. "De Monte Alegre." He gestured at the murals. "Just before and at the beginning of the war—"

"War?" she breathed.

"Our war – our Civil War," he said, barely glancing at her. "The Catalan artist José Maria Sert painted these. They are supposed to depict the progress of mankind through health, technology, freedom and peace. A gift from my government to the League of Nations."

She breathed out. She thought for the first time in many, many years of the church in Northern Ontario, St Jakub; the beginning of her conversion to... well, to this life. 'Santiago' was 'James' in English, which was 'Jakub' in Polish. It was only a coincidence. *There are no coincidences in nature, only consequences.* A consequence, then; a sign. The missing link.

And it struck her now, with a further irony, that these murals dedicated to peace were actually constructed in the midst of war. Sert's depictions concentrating on sculptural figures incorporated the limitations of space, as though emphasising the notion that even within apparently limitless nothingness, humanity imposed its end. Yes, it was certainly ironic, but then so much now struck Veronica as paradoxical. Not least the fact that, in a life dedicated to communication as hers was, she should have virtually none with her only daughter, nor her former family in Spain, nor with the person who in theory should know her better than the other two put together: Leila Silamni. But the truth was that she, who was never afraid of anything or anyone, could be reduced to an inward jangle of nerves by the notion of intimacy.

Enjoying being alone for the few minutes before the circus began, Veronica perched on the edge of the long table; not at the one from which she would later speak, but the one directly facing the interpreters' booths. The six sleek, indented boxes, discreetly positioned beneath the first of the enormous murals, had hardly changed since she'd first begun working at the UN, though the internal technology naturally had. She swung an elegant leg. Intermittent moments like these gave her cause for reflection. She had certainly come a long way. But then, she had known when to seize a chance and squeeze it for all it was worth. Certainly the fluent French gleaned at the endless hockey games Mr Bickell had dragged her to all over Canada had unleashed in her an almost freakish linguistic ability. This extraordinary gift (Veronica hadn't gone to university, nor formally studied languages) had secured her first interpreting assignment. Still, she would have said that her greatest gift was not that, but a talent for chasing opportunities.

And then there was Santiago. Although, if she remembered correctly, he had done most of the chasing. Perhaps she'd sensed that things would be different with him, or perhaps she'd been simply out of her league, but whatever the reason, she was unusually cautious. They could so easily not have met.

It was a cold day in January, and Veronica, in one of her last interpreting roles before she moved into the secretariat body of the UN, was only a 'second' in the booth that day. In fact, she wasn't even due to be called until the afternoon.

The conference was not only of a high-profile nature, but riveting stuff, and a far cry from the endless grind of disarmament talks. Giving evidence before the United Nations Ad Hoc Working

Group for the Commission on Human Rights was Dr Sheila Cassidy. With time to spare, Veronica had read up on the doctor caught up in the violence of the Pinochet regime. Having given medical assistance to a political opponent of the new regime, Cassidy had been arrested by the Chilean secret police and tortured.

As during any 'session', the silence within the booth was deafening. Veronica, though, noted nothing untoward. She watched the delegates in the chamber below, heard the vacuum of thundering quiet in her shared tiny space above them, and awaited her turn. She wasn't sure what prompted to her to glance at her colleague when she did. Either it was her expression or the palpable stillness in the chamber below. Whatever the reason, Veronica grabbed a headset just in time to hear Dr Cassidy's testimony for herself. With painstaking attention to detail, the former medic described the events that took place that infamous night at the notorious Villa Grimaldi, as the DINA (secret police) endeavoured to make her disclose information about her patient and other contacts.

"I have already given evidence to tribunals in Helsinki," Dr Cassidy was saying. "I think it is particularly important for the families of those who have died, who have been tortured…"

Veronica did a few mouth exercises; took a sip of water. Okay, it was obviously bad, but not *so* bad. She was dying for a coffee. There was still time to grab a hot beverage. But now Dr Sheila Cassidy was describing being tied to a metal bunk frame, being stripped naked, the picana being used on her to deliver electric shocks, and the internal injuries she sustained as a result. And just like that, Beatriz, Veronica's Peruvian colleague, slumped forward onto her desk. Her line went dead.

Veronica leapt to her feet, as had a sea of Spanish-speaking delegates. Fiddling with their earpieces, they gesticulated towards the booth, making helpless gestures of incomprehension. In one swift move, Veronica leaned forward, grabbing her own ear defenders. She switched on the levers and resumed the interpretation. She breathed out; sipped some more water. It was okay; the momentum of the meeting was resumed. Beatriz came to, motioned to Veronica that she was leaving, and stumbled out of the booth. Looking down, Veronica's eyes met those of the Spanish delegate whose face, in that brief moment, was looking up at hers...

"Bit dramatic, wasn't it?"

"You guessed what happened, then?"

"Guessed? My dear, we saw it all! One minute that sleek Indian head was babbling away, and the next it had slid from view, only to be replaced by," he made a 'ta-da' gesture, "by you. And you are, I might add, by far the more beautiful."

Veronica was secretly pleased, though not about to show it. "It's incredible, the impact her testimony still has after all this time," she said evenly.

"Cigarette?" A silver case appeared from his breast pocket. "Du Maurier," he added, in case she needed reassuring.

She barely hesitated. Her hands shook from the adrenaline coursing through her body (as they always did after a stint in the booth), but also from excitement. She could feel the chemistry between them, a bolt of electricity, and though her eyes sought his (almond-shaped; khaki with specks of yellow), peering (she hoped) deep within, his remained watchful, detached, and therefore all the more alluring. She cupped his hand oh-so-casually while he lit her cigarette. His skin was cool to the touch. He bent his head back, smoke escaping through the side of his mouth. He was effortlessly elegant, languid, patrician. Every pore in her skin tingled. He embodied everything she had ever wanted; everything she had worked towards. She closed her eyes momentarily, allowing them to reopen, wide and clear and blue. Now it was her turn to throw back her head – that thick blonde mane of hers. Now she had his attention. She noticed how he watched her, eyes narrowing but mistaking (not for the first time) appreciation for desire. But she was blind; blind to everything but her ambition. This man could give her an identity, a pedigree, a family. This man was the answer to her prayers. And she would do everything in her power to entrap him.

Archie

Cedar Avenue

A year? Goodness, is that how long it's been? Whose fault is that, exactly?

Yes, well… they say time heals. Like hell it does! It certainly adds a certain perspective, I'll grant you that. As if we need perspective, my love, my demon. But getting back to that article you so thoughtfully sent me from the Boston Journal I will say it set me thinking…

In one of our more interesting discussions, you've asked me about evil – the difference between it and mental health. And I've said that evil strikes me as a religious concept, but in its absence, would there be a judiciary? Answer that, my temptress. There is right and wrong. As judged by others; not by me. You believe in a kind of morality more than I do. I believe in opportunity.

Which you have taken away from me. Don't you forget that.

For Christ's sake!!! What do you want me to say? Why didn't you do what you said you would? Why couldn't you have waited?

I don't want the other woman – she's just a diversion. But she's unemotional; not a passionate streak in her body, thank God. Ice-cold. Like you are now. TO ME!!! Frankly, it's a relief.

27

Ino
Winchester
August 2017

Hoping to drown out the stress (or distress, more like) of the day, Ino lay in a cool bath, a gin and tonic wedged in the soap dish. From her tub, she could look up at the sky, where a single plane blazed a path through the cloud. It looked like a huge fish; its tail a shark's fin. For a moment she imagined she was lying at the bottom of a giant ocean, looking up at it.

The peace of this strange sensation was soon disturbed by someone down the lane playing the ever-popular 'Despacito' (made even more so by the Bieber remix) at top volume. The music video had garnered twenty million views within the first twenty-four hours of its release, so she guessed the craze for this catchy tune wasn't going to wane any time soon. Every muscle ached; every nerve screamed in response as much to discomfort as to the music.

It was still light out and heat steamed off the thatch as though the cottage were a massive pudding boiling dry in a cauldron. It had been an unusually hot day, with temperatures nudging thirty-six degrees. It had been an unusual day in all kinds of ways. Ino slowly sank under the water. Exhausted after her party, Calypso was asleep, and Archie was still out. After today's performance, Ino thought it extremely unlikely that he would come home at all.

All the windows and doors were open; Ino was so hot she needed the breeze to blow through the house and through her tangled thoughts.

Today was Calypso's birthday, and Ino had worked hard to make it special. Pink balloons tied to the gate had welcomed a bevy of little girls to a *Frozen*-themed party – though, given the heat, nothing could have been climatically further from the film. The table under the pergola was also set with *Frozen* plates; pictures of Olaf and Elsa staring up from skating scenes etched onto matching cups. Calypso wasn't the only child dressed as a Disney Princess. Soon, twelve other Disney Princesses were squealing and skipping round the garden as Ino tried to engage them for long enough to play Musical Statues and Musical Chairs. Chivvying them down to the lower lawn was another matter, and her head was already on repeat, throbbing to the strains of 'Let it Go'.

Calypso was beside herself with excitement, her chubby little hand clasping her wand as though it were a lightsabre. From time to time she ricocheted back to Ino, hissing, "Don't let them near Oreo!", but otherwise she was happy to join in with her playmates.

To begin with, things had gone relatively smoothly, although the little girls did race about screaming ever more frenetically – the heat, the sugary drinks, and the music all revving them up so that after only an hour they were at fever pitch. Ino herself was perspiring heavily, but her ponytail, feeling like a damp squid down her back, was nothing to the now-grubby psychedelic costumes and the wilting plastic jewels hanging by a thread off the little girls' netted skirts. Then, at the same time, two or three wanted to go to the loo. Seizing the opportunity to go into the house, others began tearing upstairs, wanting to see Calypso's bedroom. Celia lost her wand, another her crown, while yet another said she was going to be sick. Ino settled that child in the cool drawing room, wishing she could stay with her and bury her own head in a pillow. Eventually, she herded the rest of the panting, tearful little girls to the orchard where it was coolest, getting them to sit cross-legged on a rug, and went up to the house to fetch the parcel for the next game.

To her surprise, Archie was home early. He had parked in front of the house and not in the drive as the gate was closed and he couldn't be bothered to open it. Ino soon realised why. Initially she was relieved he was back: another adult – any adult – would be a help with the children. But relief was almost instantly replaced by disappointment, followed in short order by anger. Archie was in no condition to help with anything. On the contrary, he had begun helping himself to the children's tea, which Ino had left carefully wrapped in cling film, laid out on the kitchen table. He had demolished most of the icicle-shaped sandwiches and licked off the icing from the fairy cakes. He was now carefully unwrapping the Pass the Parcel present so as to get at the little chocolates and sweets hidden among its many layers.

"*Archie!*" cried Ino.

Archie merely blinked as he stood, swaying, by the sink. His stained shirt was hanging out of his trousers, his hair was damp with sweat and his face was very red, but whether from heat or drink Ino couldn't tell.

"Archie!" she repeated, this time in dismay.

And he merely echoed, "Archie! Archie! Archie!", continuing to tear through the parcel until all that was left was a few layers of pretty pink tissue paper.

Ino gritted her teeth, her heart pounding with the familiar feeling of dread as though she were standing on the edge of a precipice, bracing herself for a fall. She pushed past him to go into the little pantry where she had hidden more prizes, and picked up the one she had intended to use for Pin the Tail on the Donkey. Her mind was racing – she would have to improvise quickly. She grabbed some chocolate bars as consolation prizes and went back through to the kitchen. Archie was standing by the open fridge, trying to carve an uncooked chicken with a spoon.

"Change of plan, darlings," she cried gaily, going back to the children… and then stopped short.

Calypso was straddling some child on the grass, holding her arms pinioned. Except it wasn't 'some child': as she got closer, Ino saw to her horror that it was Marion's daughter Celia.

"I told you not to touch her!" hollered Calypso pulling the girl's hair, while Celia (always Celia!) kicked her legs hysterically. Her princess skirt was ripped and her crown was broken.

"Calypso!" cried Ino. "That's enough! Get off her!"

"But she touched Oreo, Mummy!" Calypso's little face contorted with fury. "She actually got into her hutch!"

"I only wanted to stroke him!" sobbed Celia.

"Her!" screamed Calypso. "It's a *her*!"

"Oh, for goodness' sake," said Ino impatiently. Beads of sweat had gathered between her breasts and her dress clung to her stomach. Leaning down, ignoring Calypso, she hoisted Celia to her feet, brushing out her ripped dress. "You'll be okay," she said quietly. "Calypso's really very sorry, aren't you, Calypso?"

"I am *not*!" said Calypso. "And if you touch Oreo again, I'll smash your face in."

"You'll do nothing of the kind," said Ino sternly. "Now apologise immediately."

Calypso stood defiantly.

"Now!" said Ino. "Or there won't be any cake and you won't have any of your presents. And all your friends will go home." *If only they would…*

"Sorry!" muttered Calypso unconvincingly.

"I want to go home anyway," sniffed Celia.

"No, you don't," said Ino brightly. "I know! Let's play Pin the Tail on the Donkey."

"I thought we were playing Pass the Parcel," said Amelia's chirpy little daughter.

"Change of plan," said Ino tightly.

"Pin the Tail is for babies," said the American mother's child.

"Really?" said Ino. "I *love* it! Come on, who's going first?"

That game lasted all of twenty minutes, and with still another hour and a half to go, Ino was at her wits' end. "Tea!" she announced desperately, only to discover that all that was left of the children's tea: the sugar mice, flapjacks and sandwiches was the cake itself. Luckily, the little girls were too exhausted and hot to notice.

During the only lull of the afternoon, Archie came out to the pergola, a Hula Hoop hooked on every finger. "I have a game," he suggested.

Ino looked up in gratitude, only to brace herself almost immediately, ever thankful to be the only one in earshot.

"You can all suck Hoops off my fingers. One by one."

Ino closed her eyes. "Go!" she said fiercely. "Go now or I'll call the police."

Archie's eyes were wide. "You'll *what*?" he said, making a grab for her, but instead tripping and landing, dazed, on the ground.

The little girls squealed in delight, thinking it part of another game. Only Calypso frowned uncertainly, still gently hiccupping over a sodden Oreo.

"*Now* can I go home?" cried Celia.

"Yes," said Ino faintly. "Now, yes. I'll text Marion."

"And I'm going home too," announced Archie.

"You *are* home, silly!" said Calypso, the last of her sobs subsiding.

Archie looked at her as if she were retarded. "Christ, not here!" he said, turning on his heel and stabbing out balloons with his key as he stumbled to his car.

"You shouldn't drive!" Ino called uselessly after him. For a moment she thought he would turn back, but instead he hurled a half-eaten chocolate bar at her and flicked a V-sign for good measure.

Ino sponged herself. It had been a helluva day all right. She knew very well that things were getting worse. So why was she still here?

Especially after the trip to the Discovery Centre when she had resolved to change her life. She took a swig of her gin and tonic. There was Calypso, of course, but she – *they* – would be better off on their own. It wasn't as though Archie loved Ino. She was very clear on that score. Funny; it wasn't being beaten or kicked but the fact that he couldn't – *wouldn't* – help her when she needed it most. *That* had been the coup de grâce. So what on earth was she doing? The truth of it was that she didn't know where to begin. She should initiate a conversation with Archie, of course, but he was never sober enough.

"You are who you love," he – not Archie – had said once. "One life; you have one life…"

Ino poured shampoo onto her head, not bothering to lather it into her hair. She held her nose and submerged her head. Coming up for air, her ears still full of water, she heard a dull thud. She shook her head, closing one ear to clear it, and then stopped. There it was again. A pipe? The Aga? She patted her other ear with a sponge. Another thud. She froze – the thudding was still there because someone was knocking on the bathroom door! The bathroom door which was to her left and a mere three feet away from her! Her mind went into free fall, imagining all kinds of scenarios. She held her breath. It sounded as if someone was actually trying to break down the door. Ino kept very still as she reached for a towel, her gaze travelling to the open window. It *was* possible to get out through the window, but what then? This was a cottage so the ceilings weren't high, but even so, the bathroom was still on the first floor. Could she jump? And what about Calypso? Her bedroom was on the left of the landing, tucked away round a corner. That was a small mercy; it wasn't immediately obvious to a person coming up the stairs. Ino's phone, though, was in her bedroom. No use whatsoever at this moment. Suddenly, she felt very isolated and afraid. Dormer Cottage was the only house at the end of the lane. Even Michael was half a mile towards the village but in the opposite direction, and he was hardly in a position to do anything. The thumping was much louder now; impatient.

"Hello?" Ino croaked, deciding to confront her fear. "Who's there?"

"Police," said a female voice.

"*Police?*" squeaked Ino. How did she know it really was the police?

As if reading her mind, the voice replied, "It's your PCSO Jane Leeming, from the other day. Your alarm has gone off. Every—"

Ino grabbed a towel, wrapped herself in it and sheepishly opened the bathroom door.

"Your alarm went off again," said Jane Leeming, clearing her voice.

Ino tightened the towel around her, toga-style, and shook her head in disbelief. "But that's impossible – as you can see, I'm here."

"Mmm…" said Jane Leeming. "Well, something is triggering it. You might want to check again with the alarm company. By the way, I walked around the property a couple of times."

"I didn't hear you," Ino mumbled.

"That's kind of the point. Every door and window appears to be open."

"It's a hot evening."

"Yes," agreed Jane Leeming. "A perfect one for a burglary. Someone could have been in and out with half your stuff all the while you were up here soaping yourself."

Ino flushed, getting ready with a witty retort, and then thought better of it. She wished Jane Leeming had turned up a couple of hours earlier when she'd needed her and given Archie a fright. But then, nothing would probably have upset Archie. "Okay," she said compliantly. "What do you suggest I do?" She took a step forward, feeling awkward in her towel. She'd got the message.

"Get the alarm checked out ASAP – we've discussed this before – and don't leave everything open like this, no matter the weather.

Furthermore, I could have been halfway up the lane with your kid and you'd have been none the wiser."

"I wish you had," said Ino under her breath.

"What was that?" Jane Leeming turned sharply. Strange noises seemed to emit from the various devices strapped to her body. Distracted, she bent to talk into her pager.

"Nothing," said Ino quickly.

Jane Leeming moved to the staircase and Ino padded after her. The front door was indeed wide open. After Calypso's party ended Ino had simply walked up the stairs, not checking on anything.

"Cup of tea?" she added, hoping to sound conciliatory.

Jane Leeming shook her head, pocketing the mobile she'd been tapping, and spoke into her airwave radio. Ino idly wondered what she put in all her other pockets. "This isn't *EastEnders*," she said, as if reading Ino's mind.

"No, of course not, no." Ino leaned against the heavy oak door, fiddling with the enormous old-fashioned lock so that Jane Leeming would take the hint that she fully intended to lock up properly. Water was dripping from her hair down her back. She would have to hop back in the bath and rinse out the shampoo. "By the way," she said. "There *is* something I've been meaning to ask. I was going to email, actually."

"All ears," said Jane Leeming. Ino could tell she was curious; preparing herself to share a confidence.

Ino took a breath. "Did you know Catherine Parish?"

Jane Leeming half-turned.

"You know?" said Ino quickly. "The previous occupant? The one who mu—"

"I know exactly who you mean," Jane Leeming interrupted curtly. She plunged her phone into a back pocket. "But no, I didn't, not personally."

"So, you never met her?"

"Well, not when she was alive."

Not funny.

"Look, I was the officer on duty," added Jane Leeming more gently. "Not pleasant, okay? But it's not really the problem here."

Except it sort of is, thought Ino. "No, you're right. Of course it's not."

"You need to sort out your alarm." Jane Leeming gave her a look as if to say, *And the rest…* "Lucky your kid's a heavy sleeper."

"It was her birthday party today," said Ino, mentally grimacing. "We're exhausted."

"Yeah," said Jane Leeming. "I have a three-year-old. I know what that's like."

Ino looked surprised. "Wow, you look so young."

"I *am* young." Jane Leeming rooted in her jacket for her car keys. "As are you. There's still a life to live." She gave Ino a pointed look from which she shied away. "Right," she said. "That's me done for the day. Now, I don't want to be coming up here again."

"I'll see to it. Promise," said Ino, impatient herself now to be back in the bath.

Jane Leeming turned. "There's help out there, you know." She appeared to be studying the pretty rose bush to the right of the footpath. "Don't be so proud; it won't do anyone any good."

Ino blinked. "We're fine," she said tightly. "But thanks."

"*Pasito*," she muttered to herself when Jane Leeming had finally gone. Slowly. Just take things slowly…

Archie

Cedar Avenue

Weather has never affected me before, but it does here. Just knowing I can't go out makes me yearn for light and heat and sun. Barbados it is. You said that's where you wanted to go; that you'd never been to the Caribbean. Well, I've rented a house from a friend. He won't be there so we'll have the place to ourselves. They hold a music festival there every winter. You'd like that too. Pavarotti is booked for the season. Who knows, you might even get to meet him.

We'll meet in New York. You've not been there, either. Actually, you've not really been anywhere, have you, little mouse? Never travelled further than Fort William. But that's why I'm good for you: to show you the way; to take you to all those places you've dreamed of seeing. We'll go up the Empire State Building; to Staten Island, Block Island. Hell, all the islands!

*I've always had money but not time, and now I have both. And I want to spend it – to lavish you with all the things you've never had. Spoil you. I hate the women here. **They** are spoiled. As if it's their right to demand; to have. You were never like that. If anything, you're too humble. But that will change once you know what I like; what I need. Then you'll know how to please me. Absolutely. You'll learn.*

28

Ino
Winchester
September 2017

Despite the warm weather, Ino felt shivery, as though she were coming down with the flu. It was mid morning. She had dropped Calypso off at school early and, after the debacle of the birthday party (the horror of which was all too fresh in her mind), was reluctant to face the other mothers.

There was still no sign of Archie. Not a word. She had tried messaging him only because his secretary had called wondering if he was running late. He had apparently scheduled a patient follow-up for that afternoon but hadn't as yet put in an appearance at the hospital. The secretary had questions about X-rays; wondered if Archie had called in sick and she'd not been informed? Ino was candid. She couldn't help as she'd not seen him. Nor did she care what the secretary might deduce from that information.

Ino had restored the house to order and, ignoring the policewoman's advice of the evening before, the windows and back door were all wide open again. There was a delicious scent of jasmine coupled with the strange, unexplained chill every time she walked through the kitchen. It succeeded in making her feel strangely anxious. She kept hearing that baby too now – the baby Michael said must live nearby. Today, despite feeling unwell, she wanted to be outside – the cottage made her feel claustrophobic.

Ino made a cup of tea and was just taking it out to the garden when she heard an ambulance. Stepping onto the patio, she was just in time to see it rush past. She was surprised that the driver had come down the cul-de-sac. The 'no through road' was clearly marked at the entrance to the village. Dormer Cottage was the last house before the open fields. Ino waited as, sure enough, the ambulance turned and then barely slowed. She walked to the little side gate between the thatched barn and the clump of Japanese anemones. A man, who looked no older than fifteen, leaned out of the window. He was chewing gum, had an earring in one ear, and both arms were covered in tattoos. She nodded before he had time to complain.

"I know," she said sympathetically. "It's a dead end."

"Willow Cottage?" he said quickly. "Man called Michael?"

Ino's heart skipped a beat. "You've passed it. It's closer to the other end, just after the corner on your left."

The driver nodded his thanks as the ambulance screeched off, taking a clump of overhanging yew with it. The lane wasn't designed for large vehicles. Ino pursed her lips, her stomach clenched with anxiety. She wasn't sure if she should rush down to see how Michael was – she assumed it was Michael – or whether to wait helplessly for news. She would only be in the way, she argued, and besides, she knew Michael better than she did his wife, whom she'd only met a handful of times.

Ino decided to wait until later in the day before walking down to the village shop; headquarters of all information and gossip. Nonetheless, her hands were shaking when she went back to her tea. She was too agitated to sit, so meandered through the garden to the oblong pond. Surrounded by topiary shapes and a high yew hedge, it was a wonderful place to play hide-and-seek with Calypso and her friends. Chubby rose and lavender bushes bordered the worn flagstones and velvety white peonies gave off their fleeting, delicious perfume.

Moments later, there was another crunch of gravel. With sinking heart, she knew even before she saw Archie's car that he was home. Peering through a gap in the hedge, she heard the familiar fumble as he emerged from the car. Actually, 'emerge' was too benign a word to describe the manner in which he was catapulted from his seat. More impactful was the fact that he appeared to be wearing nothing more than – she blinked – a plastic Sainsbury's bag in lieu of trousers. Her stomach clenched with apprehension. Foolishly, she had hoped… hoped what? That he would return bearing gifts and promises of reconciliation? That he would proclaim undying love; that he would change? Or none of the above – that he would simply return sober?

"Where are your clothes?" was all she managed, appalled, when despite her misgivings, she went to meet him.

Archie giggled, hiding his mouth behind his hands in an infantile gesture. "I have no idea," he whispered.

"And… and…?" She could only gesture to the plastic bag that did little to cover his nether regions, above which his flaccid belly hung like a bag half-full of icing sugar.

Archie shook his head as though he were having an imaginary conversation. "Clever, clever…" he said in that soft, ridiculous voice.

Now that she looked more closely, his plastic 'pants' were rather ingenious. He had thrust his legs through the two handles of an ordinary plastic bag, pulling the rest up around his bottom. In any other circumstance, with any other person, the whole effect might have been comical, but Ino felt only despairing tears and the familiar tension in her belly.

"Oh, Archie," she said sadly.

Archie's eyes sharpened, suddenly sober. "Oh, Archie, Archie," he mimicked cruelly. "That's the best you can do? 'Archie, *Archie*'?" He made a violent swiping gesture as though she were a shower curtain he were pulling clear. "Well, all *I* can say is, she was a darn better fuck than you are – a damn good fuck, actually."

Ino blinked, tears sliding down her cheeks. Was he saying that he'd *slept* with someone else? Was he *actually* saying that? Her head began to spin in shock, and then anger welled up inside her; all-consuming and extreme. She wanted to punch him in the face. She now understood the expression 'seeing red', because that's what she was consumed with: nothing but red-hot anger. Her eyes filled again, but this time with tears of anger. There were beads of perspiration under her arms; on the back of her neck. Her temples throbbed as if her entire body's blood had rushed there. She was deranged herself, then, anger pumping through her body as though she were being attacked from within. It was as though her entire being were being battered about by an invisible force. She was powerless to tame it; powerless to calm herself. She felt as though every vein in her head would burst; her heartbeat was outside of her body completely. Her breath was ragged. Had she had a weapon to hand, she would have used it. She was shaking, sweating, dizzy with anger. And the worst bit of all was that she was powerless with it. Powerless to change him or their circumstances.

And yet… and yet… there *was* something she could do. Or not do. The only person she had power over was herself. The only person she could change was herself. Somehow, from somewhere deep within, a steady voice of reason told her not to react viscerally; to wait, to stay calm, to find out the facts. Not to meet anger with anger. As on the occasion of their first date, Ino began to count slowly. *One. Two…*

"Can't you see what's happening? Can't you see?" she said at length when her breath was a little more even; when her voice didn't crack. When she could face looking at him.

Archie halted, swaying on his heels. The pupils of his eyes darted in super-quick time as they always did when she spoke to him; as if, already bored, he were following an imaginary tennis match. This time, she seemed to have caught his attention. Then the pupils homed in on her. He held his chin in his hand like Rodin's *Thinker*. "Are you serious?"

Surprised that he should even answer, Ino began talking

rapidly, afraid there wouldn't be another opportunity to talk. She dived in clumsily, but it didn't matter. She had wanted to talk to him for so long. *Three...* "We're in trouble," she said. "We need help. Both of us. I admit I do, as much as you. This can't go on." She motioned to his naked body, and now that she came to think of it, was that *nail polish* on his toes? "I mean, you're a highly respectable professional!"

But he was losing interest; his mouth creasing as it normally did if she ever voiced a concern or complained about anything.

She tried a different tack. "You may not care..." She swallowed. *Four...* "You may not care about us, but surely you care about your work? You care about that, don't you? You are needed. You—" Her voice whined unattractively.

"Oh, do shut up," said Archie savagely. He made to go into the house, and as he did so, the plastic bag split and he stood stark naked.

"Oh my God, Archie!" she said, anxious now. "What if someone sees you?! What if Cal—" *Five...*

"What?" Archie looked at her in genuine amazement. "You actually think I care a damn what people think? What 'people'? I don't care who sees me! Who are these so-called 'people' anyway?!"

"Okay, okay." She regretted having spoken now.

"You know something? You really are such a snob! I always thought you were, *Condesa*," he said, spitting out the title she never used, and Ino winced. "*Christ*, let them see me! Bring it on! This is such a boring place anyway! I bet the village would be thrilled to have something to gossip about. Nothing has happened here since Cather..."

Ino closed her eyes. She felt like sticking her fingers in her ears and shouting, *La la la, not listening*, as Calypso sometimes did. Except that now she was absolutely listening, and her eyes shot open. "Not since?" she demanded.

Archie swiped away an imaginary fly. "Nothing."

"No, it's not 'nothing," persisted Ino. "Not since what? What were you going to say? *Catherine?*" There – she had said it. "Is that what you were going to say? Not since Catherine?" She knew she should leave it alone. That this really wasn't the moment to antagonise; that neither one of them was in any state to talk sensibly. She knew she should walk away, but Archie swivelled on his heel in the gravel and lunged towards her. She turned to face him but then, in a split second's instinctive move, stepped neatly aside.

With a surprised giggle that rapidly turned into a moan, Archie fell heavily onto the gravel. For a few seconds he lay prone as if relaxing on a comfortable bed.

"Archie?"

He grunted, turning over so that he was lying face down, but he stretched his legs, his feet pointing inwards. Small pebbles were stuck to the hairs on his back. *Six. Seven. Breathe!* How had it come to this? How had *they* come to this? Instead of kicking him in the ribs as she would have liked to, she went into the house to fetch him a glass of water. She ran the tap for a long time, stealing a glance from time to time out of the window and hoping that he would move, but he continued to lie on the ground, his face resting on his hands. She turned off the tap and went back out, hunkering down on the gravel beside him.

"Archie," she said quietly, placing the glass in his hand. "Surely this is a wake-up call? You lying here while your department is wondering where you are? Never mind the fact that you have confessed to sleeping with…?" She shuddered. God only knew with whom.

At first there was no movement and Ino wondered if he'd even heard her, but moments later there was a nod of the head. Bits of stone still clung stubbornly to his skin and hair.

"Look at me," she said, but he shook his head. "What's that?" she said, gently this time.

"It is," he mumbled gruffly into his hands. "It *is* a wake-up call!"

She sighed deeply. *Eight… Oh, thank God, thank God.* She sat back on her haunches. She could feel the tendons taut in her ankles. Maybe at last things would change. "You really think so?" she said, ever so gently.

Again, he nodded.

Ino wanted to sob with relief. She took a sip of his water. "I knew you'd get there," she said. "I have confidence in you. You're an intelligent man; it's just a blip, it's—"

"Get where?" In one extraordinary move, Archie jack-knifed to his feet so that Ino had to avert her eyes from his dangling penis, which was now at eye level. "You bet it's a wake-up call!" he said fiercely. "To *you*!"

Ino slumped sideways in shock.

Archie then went on a tirade, calling her a sociopath, a slag, a liar. Round and round in circles he went, repeating himself and making no sense. He said he had recordings of her telephone conversations. He said he had heard her arranging lunch dates. That he had proof. He asked her to answer him honestly. Good grief, no wonder he drank! "Wouldn't you? If you had to put up with this shit?" But… (heavy sigh) he could forgive her; he *wanted* to forgive her, if she would only promise never to lie to him. Could she do that? He was happy to draw a line and move on, if she could do that.

She nodded wearily.

"So," he said, "did you have lunch with So-and-So?" He couldn't actually remember the name; "Some man, anyway."

Ino blinked. She'd had crazy conversations with Archie before, but this took the fantasy to a whole new level. And where was this supposed lunch?

Aha, so she had!

No, she was just curious as to where he thought she'd been.

Well, he didn't know where, but he absolutely knew she had. He repeated the question.

"This is insane."

"So, you lied!" Triumphant. "See, I knew it!"

And then they began all over again. He accused her of lying, of seeing other men, of arranging clandestine meetings, of having sex. As if she had the time! When had *he*?! Ino couldn't help the silent retort. On and on he raged with his repeated, bitter tirade. Ino felt the blood pounding through her body, felt her heart hammering painfully against her ribs, her mouth went dry, her hands shook. Silence. A roar. *Breathe!* Oh, who cared? *Ten.* The walls of her mind were closing in to protect her.

"Your silence is an admission of guilt!"

"No, it's a denial of this lunacy!"

Walk away, said a voice. *Walk away.*

Ino got to her knees; felt herself being hurled sideways. "Enough! Enough!" she screamed. And only because he was drunk was she able to push him off her. Tears streamed down her face now, and not tears of anger. She knew she shouldn't pay attention to any of it, shouldn't take it personally, that it was all part of his illness, that she should know herself and her own truth. She should be strong, but the unjustness of his tirade got under her skin; the false accusations stung. She also knew that she felt a sick, masochistic desire to continue listening. And in continuing to engage, she understood that in a strange way it was because it would also fortify her. With every physical and verbal punch, it was the only way she would finally be empowered to leave.

The sound of the ambulance stopped them both. Once again, it appeared to be using the end of the lane to turn around. And then quietly, the blue light went out. Did that mean…? She didn't dare hazard a guess. As if in a trance, she walked away from Archie and down the narrow path by the thatched barn and onto the lane. She was aware that her clothes were dishevelled, her hair a mess, her face tear-stained and bloody. All she knew was that she had to get away. The sun was bright and high in the sky, a wood pigeon cooed, a fat robin sat on a neighbour's fence. Somewhere a lawnmower drowned out the buzzing sound coming from a wasps' nest embedded in a corner of the thatch. Wasps spun a figure of eight above the chimney stops, darting this way and that in their intricate dance. Normal. Everything appeared so normal. As she walked down the lane past the neatly kept houses, Ino couldn't help wondering about the lives lived behind those doors. At the same time, who on earth would have guessed the ugly scene that had just taken place at her house?

Ino was tucked away in her favourite part of the garden. A bench had been hollowed out of an enormous yew hedge and was completely camouflaged by overhanging branches. An unopened package lay on her lap, and she turned it over just as she contemplated the surrealness of recent weeks, turning them over in her mind. Tears had long seeped back into her heart and she was spent. The package had been left to her by Michael, and before he died, he had entrusted it to his wife. Ino had come to her hiding place every day now for over a week. It was time. In the moonlight, she unwrapped it slowly; not that the brown paper warranted such care, but Ino was almost fearful of what she would find within. The blue-gold embossed cover was battered from use; the spine torn to reveal the yellowing threads beneath. She examined the title page:

One Day at a Time in Al-Anon:
The Steps, Traditions, Slogans
and Serenity Prayer

She read the first 'step': 'We admitted we were powerless over alcohol – that our lives had become unmanageable.' And then she read the Serenity Prayer: '...to accept the things I cannot change, courage to change the things I can, and wisdom to know the difference'.

And wisdom to know the difference. That was the crucial part; the part she struggled with. She ought to have understood that there was nothing she could have done – no angry reaction of hers would ever have made a difference. The emphasis was on changing *things*, not people. Unless *he* wanted to change, he wouldn't. What change she *could* effect, however, was in her response to him. She hadn't done so well earlier; she acknowledged that. She'd quite possibly even aggravated the situation and, if she were honest, almost enjoyed that particular fight. She had thought (misguidedly) that if her reaction was strong enough, Archie would register the impact of his drinking. And then he would stop.

But he wasn't going to stop; not at present, anyway. There was no way of telling what his rock bottom was going to be, but she couldn't create one for him. What she *could* do was better organise her life; change her response. She had stayed far longer than she should have – *her* rock bottom hadn't been anything dramatic. It wasn't a miscarriage, nor domestic violence. It was something small; trivial. It was seeing him in his plastic underpants; it was being left alone to deal with Calypso's party. It was any number of daily thoughtlessnesses. People had tried to help her – that PCSO, for one – but Ino had been too proud, believing that if she could somehow cover up the cracks, the fissure would disappear completely. How wrong she'd been! But now it was time – time to go back to work; time to leave.

Brushing away tears – not of self-pity but of relief – she picked up her mobile. At first, she couldn't even see the numbers. Should she text? No, she would call. He didn't have to pick up. Her fingers tapped out a number that was once as familiar to her as her own.

"*Sí?*" He answered almost immediately.

You are who you love… You come from a line of strong women; something stronger and more important…

She could hardly speak. What had she been thinking? The story she'd played out in her head a million times was nothing like the reality. But the comfort of hearing his voice, of hearing her blood, of knowing what she should always have known and yet had forgotten – that she had a choice – made her silent. Where were the words now? She was glad she was hidden away, far from the house; glad that she was alone in the dark. Glad that it was 2 in the morning.

"*Sí?*" He was insistent, firm, not sleepy at all. She had the impression that she hadn't woken him; that he might even have been expecting her call.

"*Rafa? Soc yo*," she said at last in Catalan. It seemed that now more than ever it was important to use their language; to show him that she was still her. "It's me, Ino."

She heard the sharp intake of breath. "Ah, Ino-Bambino, *sí*," he said, as though it were the most natural thing in the world that she should be calling him in the middle of the night after so much time, so many years. And then the cosy, inviting command: "*Cuéntame.*" *Tell me; tell me all about it*, knowing what his response would be.

And I shall tell you the truth at last… You are who you love.

Rafael was saying it again: "Tell me" in Catalan. But unless she was honest with herself, what *could* she say? Unless she could talk about *him*, she would never move on. Unless she could fix what was broken, then she would never make sense of any of it. That was, after all, the crux of the matter. Or rather, *he* was. And as she spoke, the years between disappeared, memory after memory washed over her, and she saw his face.

For now we see through a glass, darkly; but then face to face: now I know in part; but then shall I know even as also I am known.

29

Ino
Oxford
June 2005

The sound of stones peppering her window interrupted Ino at work. She was writing up notes from a lecture on the *Novelas Ejemplares*, those twelve short stories full of adolescent angst, the desire for freedom from parental authority, and the nascent attraction to the opposite sex. Given that the novellas were printed in the seventeenth century, they struck Ino as being remarkably modern, as was his macho boast that he was a genius for doing so! Was someone actually *throwing* stones at her window? Why didn't they text or phone? Or ring the buzzer? Like any normal person would? There it was again: the staccato sound of stone against glass – subtle yet persistent.

Ino threw down her book, pushed away her chair, and went over to the window to open the casement, pulling her hair over one shoulder to it keep clear of the wrought-iron fittings. "Oi!" she said.

"*Oi?*" The echo that came back was decidedly Spanish.

She leaned out further, catching a flash of white jeans and a tanned forearm. "Oh my God," she giggled. "It's the Hardy Boys!"

"Er... *sólo uno*; just the one."

"Shh!" someone called crossly from across the quad.

"Come up!" stage-whispered Ino. And then, when he began

to hoist himself up a drainpipe, she said in alarm, "I didn't mean *literally*! Wait! I'll come down and let you in."

She banged her head as she straightened. Jumping to the mirror, she checked her reflection. Her eyes were bright; her cheeks flushed. She tucked her shirt into her jeans. Her heart was pounding. She ran down the stairs and unbolted the staircase door. Emil, stubbing out a cigarette with his boot, grinned at her. He hadn't changed out of his polo gear, and every bit of him seemed to glow under the quad lights.

"Where's Rafa?" she asked, peering behind him.

"Why?" said Emil suspiciously. "We don't go everywhere together, you know. Were you expecting him?" he added worriedly, his confidence suddenly diminished.

"No, no, I just assumed... and, well, actually, yes, I *did* think you went everywhere together!"

Emil smoothed his unruly hair, attempting to pat the front locks into place. "Not this time."

"How was the game?"

"We won! I've left Rafa with Sol. Better that way."

She stood in the doorway, arms crossed, legs crossed, feigning total ease, while all the time she was acutely aware of the pulse at his neck, the hair rising above his polo-shirt collar, and his smell – that clean grass-linen smell of his, despite time spent in the saddle. "Should we wait? Are they coming?"

Emil had moved closer; one arm stretched above them both, leaning on the architrave. "God, I hope not!"

And something in his voice made her look up. He watched her intently as if waiting for some signal, some sign, his eyes charged with so much emotion she caught her breath.

"I hope not too," she said, hoping to sound casual, but her voice broke. And as she flattened herself against the wall to let him walk past her, to lead him upstairs, he caught her by both arms just above the elbows, pulling her to him.

"*Ino, espera*," he said hoarsely. "Ino, wait – there's something..."

His lips were close to hers. Too close. She could almost taste the sweat, the horses, the hay. His thigh against hers was rock-hard. If he hadn't already been holding her, she would have fallen. Instead she grabbed the back of his head, holding him still, her mouth opening under his.

"Yes, Emil?" she breathed.

"Ino, *cariño*, my cousin's cousin," he said.

For a long time afterwards, she could feel the imprint of his arms on hers, folded in the blanket of his embrace. It dawned on her that she felt safe, perhaps for the first time in her life. Not that she had felt physically *un*safe in her mother's home in Montreal, she chided herself, but this was an entirely different feeling. Living with Veronica was unsettling. Ino never knew when her mother would be absent on another business trip, nor for how long, or indeed if she would come back at all. Sometimes, Ino had the impression that given half a chance, Veronica might choose not to! Emil made her feel truly wanted. It was a seductive feeling. She felt that wherever she went, he would always find her.

She rubbed her face against his chest. Hair tickled her nostrils, and she laughed. For that moment at least, her lungs, her sight, her touch were full of him. She was smothered by him. She could barely turn her head in the crook of his shoulder without her lips brushing his skin. Later, they both sought that constraint, unable to be away from each other for long, that first day following that first night. They were intensely aware of each other, even when surrounded by people. Every time she looked up, Emil was looking at her.

In the quiet of another Sunday morning in college, the sound of the phone sliced through the leaden silence. Emil only answered because of Rafael and the match they were scheduled to play in the afternoon. But it was an irate Rafael wanting to know where the hell Emil was, as they were supposed to be exercising the horses. Rafael muttered something about exercising something else, and Ino giggled. And in her tiny bed, Emil reached for her again.

Much later, they arrived at Kirtlington. It was another warm summer's day. Ino had donned one of the dresses Abuela had sent from Barcelona. This one was green; a chartreuse green that Emil said matched her eyes. It was her favourite. It had oversized buttons on each shoulder and side pockets, and, being almost mini in length, accentuated her longs legs. She wore the emerald earrings Abuela had given her for her real birthday. They would celebrate it officially that summer with a big party at Salto.

"What?" she asked, noticing his frown.

"The only thing I don't like about being with you is the way every man and Argentine dog stares at you."

Ino laughed. "Maybe it's because I am with *you*," she answered sweetly.

"No," he said. "That's absolutely not it. One more," he pleaded, pulling her under the shade of an oak tree to kiss her. "Just one more."

"Emil!" she protested, laughing. "Emil!"

"Let's skip the game," he said gruffly. "Let's…"

His hands were in her hair; at her waist. Her body became liquid and gold and smooth under his touch. The muscles of his arms were like iron bands behind her back, and yet she felt his gentleness and his love.

"Can this mean I am more important than your horses?" she teased.

As they strolled across the field to meet Rafael and Sol, Emil's hand protectively poised on the small of her back, Ino thought back to the first time she had met the three of them, and how different it all was now. She'd been such a child, and 'the boys' and Sol had all seemed so grown-up. Now, three years later, it was she who had grown up; she who had changed the most.

"Are you sure?" she whispered as they drew near. "Are you sure you don't mind Rafa knowing?"

"*Mind?*" echoed Emil. "Why should I mind? I want to tell the world!" He stopped abruptly, pulling her to him, kissing her hair. "I'm not ashamed! Ah…" He raised his head, looking at the sky. "I know what it is. You think I'm too old!"

Ino pulled away. "Or that I'm too young?"

"Well?"

"I'm completely happy."

"So am I."

Hand in hand, they approached the hospitality tent. Ino quickly discovered that Kirtlington wasn't the Real Polo Club of Barcelona, nor was it Smith's Lawn, but like the other places it had its own fair share of polo groupies – lots of young girls who spent too much time in the fake-tan department. They all seemed to have uniform platinum-coloured hair, hoop earrings, tiny skirts and white heels. There were others who considered themselves to be a cut above the rest. These sported blazers, shorts and Hunter wellingtons – "Slutty preppy," whispered Emil. There were shrieks as they balanced pint-size glasses of Pimm's; splashed drink down bare thighs, calling to each other loudly across the bar area.

Emil guided Ino through the designated eating area onto the terrace and lawn. Sol, seated at a small table shaded by an enormous sunshade, was lovely with her hair swept up in a neat chignon and dressed in a prim navy dress with a white collar. Rafael leaned against the back of her chair but did not move as he watched his cousins approach. His head was cocked to one side and his eyes narrowed as realisation dawned.

"Tell me, no!" His eyes darted from Emil's face to Ino's.

"Yes," said Emil, defiantly, proudly.

"*De qué hablas?*" Sol, of course, was oblivious. "What are you talking about?"

Rafael raised his eyes. "Doesn't matter." He caught Emil's look; shook his head as if to say, *Don't! We both know Sol isn't known for her brains…*

Sol crossed her legs, one pretty ballerina pump dangling from a slim, tanned foot. "Ah, *hola*, Ino," she said carelessly.

Ino, sweeping down, kissed her cheek. "Glorious day, isn't it?"

Sol blinked. "I s'pose." Her eyes appraised the badly dressed girls. A sudden breeze lowered the temperature, and she shivered. "Relatively."

Rafael sprang forward. "What can I get you little lovebirds? Champagne? Pimm's?"

Neither Emil nor Ino appeared to have heard him. Ino was aware of Emil's breath on the nape of her neck; his lips hovering by her ear. Again, she savoured the solid, comforting shape of him; a barrier against the rest of the world.

Sol pursed her lips in frustration. "You never look at me like that," she said sulkily.

Rafael Rafa, eyes on the game that was about to begin, had lost interest in all of them. "Don't I, *mi amor*?" he answered vaguely.

"No, never."

"It's only the polo," said Ino happily, leaning against Emil. Her head just scraped his chin. He played with a strand of her hair, and she closed her eyes.

"That's not what I meant." To attract his attention, Sol tapped the back of Rafael's leg.

Birds were singing, the field was bright green after earlier rain, and the sky, though a tepid blue, was cloud-free. Ino's spirits soared. As Emil ran his fingers down the length of her bare arms, she felt desire tilt the pit of her stomach. He moved her hair so that it cleared her neck to kiss her.

"I meant what I said before," he whispered. "Let's skip the game."

Ino turned, horrified. "But you're playing!" she protested. "You can't let your team down."

Emil shrugged. "I can. Easily. There's *always* an Argie waiting in the wings."

She shook her head against his chest. "*Ni habalar*," she stated firmly. "Don't even think about it."

He turned her to face him, holding her by both forearms. "Are you defying me?"

"Yup."

He brushed her hair away from her forehead, pulling her close. "Well, don't make a habit of it."

"Oh, for God's sake," said Sol, giving Rafael another well-aimed kick.

"*Para!*" he said sharply. "Stop that!"

"Why?"

"*Why?*" said Rafael, still not looking at her. "Because it's annoying for one thing, childish for – *joder*! Did you see that?" He turned to Emil. "Why didn't the umpire call it?"

"Wasn't looking," muttered Emil.

"No, you weren't," chipped in Sol.

"But the other umpire didn't call it either – they must have been distracted."

"By you, *amor*," whispered Emil.

"Oops! Duck!" warned Rafael suddenly.

At first it looked as if the ball flying through the air was headed towards the spectators. Rafael brushed Sol's foot away, instinctively bending to protect her. But at the last moment the Argentine pivot tapped the ball in the air and, with a single motion, put it through the goal. A show-off move if there ever was one.

"It's seven to five."

"You're kidding."

"I don't think Kirtlington has ever seen such a shot; certainly not in living memory."

The teams swapped ends, cantering to the centre. The players lined up and the number four ran out to take the lead, his horse stretching out at full gallop. Now even Emil was paying attention. Another goal: seven to six. The horn sounded and they were at half-time. The commentator then invited all the spectators to tread in the divots with the very tired joke to "Watch out for the steaming ones."

"You can see Sol struggling with that one," hissed Rafael. "Come on; we might as well join in."

Sol was ahead of them. She actually liked that bit, which for her was more about people watching than actually being useful. She darted about the pitch, a frothy navy confection in her little-girl dress and shoes. But she was disappointed. Kirtlington's finest could hardly compare to Saint-Tropez or Pilar. She identified a mere handful of Chanel bags, the ubiquitous Tod's, and a couple of women wearing the on-trend Gucci 'pyjama bottom' pants, but that was as fashion-forward as it got. She shrieked delightedly having spotted a man wearing Louis Vuitton fur slip-ons. She picked her way delicately across the grass, not wanting to soil her new shoes by allowing them anywhere near a divot. From across the field Rafael called to her, gesturing that she should move off the field. But Sol ignored him, and in frustration he turned back. She had always made an irritating habit of wandering what was essentially the area of nine football pitches and then being one of the last to scurry back to the safety of the stands.

In the corner, far away from the game, Emil bent his head to Ino's. They were united in their desire for one another, reassured by the notion that they had all the time in the world. The prospect of endless days at their disposal made them relaxed and content. In a sudden rough gesture, Emil pulled Ino to him, and she laughed.

30

Emil and Rafael
Barcelona
October 2017

Emil tied on an apron and propped open the door with a patio chair. He turned the 'MA' shop sign to 'closed', although it was hardly necessary. The destruction of the cake counter was there for all to see. Sweeping up the broken glass, he knew that he should be angry, but he wasn't. He was vaguely annoyed at having to get someone in to replace the pane, but it was an inconvenience; nothing more. He knew what it was to feel frustration to such a degree that violence might seem the only release. A broken window was nothing in comparison to the injuries sustained in yesterday's demonstration.

It was hot for October; October 2nd to be precise. Emil, along with every Catalan of his generation, would never forget the events of the day before. October 1st would only become – in time, if not already – a shameful, bewildering blight on Spanish history. The sight of black-clad troopers armed with batons beating up the elderly and the very young was not something that should be associated with a democratic government. Such images, together with those of women being dragged by the hair or tossed like so many sacks of tomatoes down concrete steps, had been shared around the world. So much for *pa amb tomàquet*. The media had done more to further Catalan separatism than any Barcelona politician. He lit a cigarette and crouched on all fours to sweep up the remaining detritus.

"*Pero qué haces?*" said his cousin in a tone more irritated than sympathetic.

What did it look like he was doing? "Ah, *hola*, Rafa," said Emil as Rafael's dusty Tod's came to a stop in front of him. "No Mass today?"

"Said it," said Rafael curtly. "What are you doing?"

"Someone smashed our windows last night during the riots," Emil replied calmly. "But for all I know, it might have been the *Guardia*."

"Can you blame them?"

Emil got slowly to his feet and took a drag on his cigarette. His cousin looked uncharacteristically riled; or rather, as riled as he would have done when they were young. Dusty shoes aside, his hair was dishevelled and he was sporting a black eye. "What, the police or the rioters?"

"Both."

"Well, I don't blame the rioters. We all, I hope, are appalled by the show of force. The world has seen the nasty side of our *Spanish* government."

Rafael stepped over the mess and flopped down in the chair. "And all we want is peace. Yeah, yeah. Well, at least we agree on that."

"I hope on more." Emil took another puff. He had the feeling that dealing with Rafael today was going to need more than tobacco. He had not seen his cousin this agitated in years. "*Venga*, don't sit there; sit here." He darted into the shop and returned dragging out a more comfortable chair. "Let's have a *trago*. I could do with one."

Rafael wiped his forehead. "*Dios mío!* So could I."

"Sit, then; I'll fetch a bottle." Emil went back into the shop and this time brought out a carafe of wine and glasses and placed them on the little table under the canvas canopy. "This way, we can also keep an eye on the shop." He poured his cousin a *vino tinto* and handed him a plate of olives.

Rafael took one but winced.

Emil nursed his wine. "What happened to your face?"

"I was on The Ramblas yesterday."

"I thought priests were supposed to be apolitical."

"Well, I'm not feeling particularly priestlike. As Unamuno once said, there are moments when 'to be silent is to lie.'" Rafael downed his glass and poured himself another.

"'You will win through brute force but you will never convince, for to convince you must persuade,'" Emil finished for him.

Rafael shot him a look. "Exactly. And now the initial question of breathing life into a flagging cause is no longer remembered, not even relevant – you have those who genuinely believe in separatism, those who don't, and those who are anti-establishment and will fight anything and anyone for the sake of it."

And because, although Emil agreed with him, he didn't want his cousin to think they were politically on the same side, he volunteered, "What happened was still unconstitutional – a betrayal."

"Pah!" snorted Rafael. "In this country national unity has become almost *spiritual* – the slightest concession and Madrid becomes hysterical!" He made a fluttering gesture with his fingers. "*Dáme un cigaro.*"

"Certainly, being told you *can't* leave ensures that you do." Emil handed him his packet and a lighter. "You don't smoke any more, do you?"

"No," said Rafael, lighting up. He crossed his legs at almost the same moment that Emil crossed his. For a moment they felt the old camaraderie between them as they had all those years ago when they played polo together. "And never mind the sentiment behind it all!" he added, drawing heavily on his tobacco but feeling a sort of calm descend. "In purely economic terms, as of today, some five hundred businesses have moved their offices out of Barcelona. Madrid will have no choice but to cut our funding, the stock exchange will collapse, and bingo – euro crisis all over again."

"Volkswagen went today, and CaixaBank."

"If Puigdemont ignores Madrid then Madrid will have no option but to invoke our autonomy." Rafael was thoughtful.

"I really don't know how it has come to this. I mean, apart from the usual rumbles about further devolution, supporters of a break have been in the minority. Even I have to concede this. We had everything, and we are at risk of losing it all. You know what this means, don't you?"

"Well, they've already arrested two of the politicians from the far left, holding them without bail – then again, Puigdemont needs the support of all ten MPs from that party to secure a majority. With Madrid threatening to activate this famous Article 155 of the constitution, more arrests are a certainty. Including Puigdemont's."

"They'd never dare!"

"Maybe, maybe not. Of course, Puigdemont is caught between a rock and a hard place. The Popular Party is now pressing to form a republic, but any deviation will cost Puigdemont their support, and without it he cannot win. Madrid is running out of patience. It too knows that whatever it does now will be held to account, and not just by Spaniards. The world is watching us."

"Mmm…" Emil rubbed his chin. There was a couple of days' hair growth – it was the closest he'd got to growing a beard since his days on Easter Island.

"What?"

"Someone, I think, may be watching – watching me in particular."

Mirror-fashion, Rafael now mimicked his cousin, feeling *his* chin thoughtfully, although, in his case, his fingertips came up against the needle-thin ridge scar tissue of an old polo injury where he'd been struck in the face by a mallet. He was lucky not to have lost his teeth. He'd got his revenge, though, thumping the Argentine bastard in return, although he'd been sent off for his trouble. "You mean all of this," he made a circular motion, "wasn't because of rioters?"

Emil stretched. "I don't know. Maybe."

Rafael leaned forward, his arms on his knees. "You know you can tell me," he said.

Emil considered his cousin's cassock. "You, or Padre Rafael?"

Rafael leaned back again. "Both."

Emil tapped the edge of his glass. "So, pour us another."

Rafael tilted the carafe, filling their glasses. "Of course, you know what would go so perfectly with this?"

"No, what?"

Rafael went through a mental inventory of cheeses. "I think, I think... yes, some of that Salto Manchego. But cut up into tiny pieces. You don't have any of that?"

Emil considered his cousin before taking another sip of wine. "Well, I have some big Manchego," he said. "And a really big knife."

"Really?"

"No."

"Oh." Rafael was genuinely disappointed.

"You've eaten quite enough. Anyway, there's this girl—" began Emil.

"Oh, boy."

"No, girl."

"Yes, yes, I heard you. *Joder*, what do you take me for?!"

"And it's not like that, either... Look, do you want me to tell you or not?"

What Rafael *really* wanted was that Manchego. The slightly nutty flavour would complement the smoothness of the wine quite perfectly. "*Perdona*; sorry," he said vaguely. "*Cuénta.* Tell me."

Emil took another swig of wine, shoved his hands in his pockets and stretched out his long legs. The wine was beginning to warm him pleasantly. "I felt sorry for her – I mean, she's just a kid. She was hanging around here. Trouble at home. You know the deal."

Rafael nodded. Did they hell.

"At first I minded the intrusion, then I didn't, and then I did." Emil didn't mean to say the words, but they came out anyway. "I don't need a kid."

May you live to see your children's children to the second and third generation... There was a pained silence.

"And you're not having an affair?" Rafael didn't intend for his words to be spoken either, but he couldn't have the other conversation. Not now, not ever. Not since Sospiro.

Emil made a face. "She's a kid. No, she really is. She must be sixteen, tops."

"So legal, then."

"Oh my God, are you even listening?" Emil glared at his cousin, then shook his head. "What she did do is this." He jumped up and went into the shop, fishing out a folder from behind the counter. "She thinks we should change the logo; update things." He placed loose sketches on the table in front of Rafael.

Rafael pushed aside the carafe, glasses and ashtray, and leaned forward, sliding the papers round, examining them carefully, looking at them through half-closed eyes, then landscape, then getting up to fix the corners between bits of broken glass before standing back. He thought of his recent visit – the thousands of years of history; the abandoned castle slowly decaying into the lake. "They're good," he said at length. "Actually, better than. I like them. I really do."

"Yeah, so do I."

"So, what's the problem?"

Emil grimaced. "She doesn't know I have these. She forgot them the last time she was here. When I sort of lost my temper."

"Sort of?"

"No, I did. She took to hanging out here... I don't know. It was awkward. Like I said, I don't want a kid. I'm not ready to be anyone's papa."

Rafael patted Emil's shoulder. "It's okay, *cosí*, it's okay. But you know, I think this... person... this girl—"

"Gemma."

"Gemma is on to something. Maybe it's time to put our hearts into this."

"You mean mine."

Rafael pushed aside the drawings, sitting down once again. He leaned back in his chair, hands behind his head, for all the world as casual as any well-to-do public servant in the chic Sarrià barrio. But when he at last straightened, his tone was anything but. "Okay, yours," he agreed. "Don't ever think I don't feel responsible for… for what happened," he finished gruffly.

"Ugh! No one forced me," he said. "I did what I did."

"To help *me*," said Rafael quietly. "*Lo reconozco*. I will always be indebted. There's an irony, you know. You did the more priestlike thing and yet…" He gestured to his robe. "Except that I think I'd not have become what I have if it hadn't been for what *you* did."

Emil made an impatient gesture. "We are where we are."

"Yes. But…"

"But?"

Rafael frowned. "I still don't understand how you think that this… this Gemma had anything to do with your windows being smashed?"

Emil placed the drawings carefully back in their folder before setting it aside. "I may have exaggerated. It was just a feeling."

"*Bueno pues*." Rafael hesitated, gauging his cousin's mood change. "Emi?"

"Yes?"

"Are you certain you don't have a slice of Salto Manchego hidden somewhere?"

31

Veronica
New York
April 1987

It was a whirlwind romance. Well, perhaps 'romance' wasn't quite the right word. Shortly after that initial 'encounter', Santiago had suggested dinner. It was like no other she'd ever had. Unlike meals with Mr Bickell, where she'd done well to eat two mouthfuls, he was that keen to get into her panties, Santiago appeared to want only to continue their conversation about the Catalan muralist Sert.

"You can see those vast scenes of swirling humanity not only on churches but in skyscraper lobbies," he had said, spreading his beautiful hands – long, straight fingers with immaculate nails emerging from equally pristine white cuffs. His skin was naturally tanned; his hair jet black. "Imperfect and humanly beautiful bodies against a perspective that magnifies space."

Yes, that's you all right, she thought. He had pushed aside his plate, ignoring the delicious lobster and champagne. He hadn't drunk a drop, while she was already giddy.

"And the colours are worth noting: he used blue and green." He looked into her face. "Like your eyes at this moment."

She held his gaze.

He turned away. "But it was uncharacteristic. Sert was more accustomed to utilising a limited range of dark and sombre tones, layering them atop a gold base coat. He resumed his use of chiaroscuro images..."

Chiaroscuro? What was Santiago talking about? The only chiaro-whatsit Veronica wanted him to see was the exquisite silk of her new Dior dress; a dress that had cost an entire month's salary – well, if you included the Ferragamo suede shoes that matched so perfectly. She had never been in love before. Mr Bickell had been her ticket out of the Porcupines, the other casual hook-ups sexual gratification, but Santiago was sophistication and glamour personified. And an entirely other world.

"You should go blonder," was all he said at the end of the meal. He touched the shoulder of her dress. "And the blue, less electric."

The next time they met for another uneaten meal on his part and far too much champagne on hers, she knew exactly what 'chiaroscuro' meant. And more.

"His later work changes," she was able to say. "Now the overflowing masses of workers inhabit a shallow foreground, seemingly ever in danger of falling right off the walls and into the arms of the viewer."

Santiago started. He lit a cigarette, leaning back against the wall, watching her thoughtfully through a cloud of smoke. Her hair was much blonder; her dress was dove grey. As a result of these subtle changes, her eyes appeared to change colour; bright jewels in an already flawless face.

"If you've been to Rockefeller Center or the Waldorf—" She got no further, for he leaned over and kissed her.

And that was that. He had taken her directly to the Waldorf in New York to see those very murals. They had had separate bedrooms and he had not kissed her again. But she hadn't minded. She'd been so excited by the city, by the shopping at Bergdorf Goodman, by the Empire State Building, by The Frick Collection, by Santiago himself, by his stories of his family and of everything that she herself did not have – or had had once, but had turned her back on firmly and forever the moment she signed that statutory declaration. On the second night he proposed. There was even a ring – well, he didn't have it on him as it was a family ring, but he knew it would suit her perfectly. Veronica thought she would stop breathing with happiness.

"Is there no one you would like present?" Santiago had asked, but she had shaken her head vehemently.

Besides, she added sweetly, at such short notice, who could possibly arrive in time? She had thought fleetingly of Mr Bickell – she'd have given anything to see the look on his face when she told him she was going to be a goddamn countess – but she didn't know if he was even still alive. And now more than ever she wanted to forget that entire period in her life. She never wanted to step onto an ice rink again, and every ghost that ever was at Rockefeller Center made her backbone unhinge when Santiago suggested she try skating.

"My mother will be so delighted that you are a Catholic," he had said when they were finalising details for the wedding.

Veronica had smiled weakly. She had thought he was going to say that his mother was going to be so delighted to meet her. Either way, she thanked her lucky stars, if not Providence, that once again religion had furnished just the right opportunity.

She went to Saks for her wedding dress, not letting on for a moment that she understood the words the Serbian sales attendant let slip while pinning Veronica's figure-hugging sky-blue gown and little Juliet lace cap. She carried a bouquet of white roses. She had no maid of honour. Santiago had, as his best man, the Marquess of Pescara, the Spanish Ambassador to the UN. There was one other guest. Santi's dear friend who happened to be in New York at the time, Martin Ranger.

32

Emil and Rafael
Barcelona
October 2017

"So, what's the matter?"

Emil ignored his cousin. He was busy clearing the tables Gemma and her friends had used at breakfast, then straight after lunch, and then at *merienda*. After a month's sulking, Gemma had slunk back to the *pastelaria* and Emil was certain now that she wasn't responsible for the brick-throwing. He was ashamed that he should have ever thought her capable of such violence in the first place. Rafael's bulky figure seemed to fill every corner of his line of vision. He could feel irritation and resentment fuse in him. Rafael never considered that Emil might be busy; nor, God forbid, would it ever occur to him to lend a hand.

When Rafael repeated the question, Emil was incredulous. What did he honestly *think* was the matter? The city was collapsing! Catalonia was collapsing. A general strike was scheduled for the next few days, and there were roadblocks throughout the province stretching to the Pyrenees. It meant that any goods coming from France were blockaded. It meant that the *masa* for his pastry goods couldn't be dispatched. It meant all kinds of complications for the bakery. For all his cousin's so-called priestliness, Rafael couldn't be so oblivious to recent events, could he? Weeks had slipped by, and every new one seemed to herald some fresh, seemingly insurmountable challenge. Sometimes, Emil didn't even try to keep track of the days, punctuated as they were by the endless fiestas for the hundreds of saints that no one believed in any more. All he knew was that there was predictable consistency in the infrequency of visits to his *pastelaria*. The intensity of the political climate was altering the way people shopped and spent their leisure time. More importantly for Emil, it was affecting the way they *ate*. They scurried from his bakery, a loaf of bread tucked under an arm, no longer lingering to chat or comment on banalities. The antics of the King's brother-in-law that had kept them all entertained for so many years were long forgotten in the wake of the sheer panic that gripped Emil's neighbours and was palpable as the days stretched into late autumn. Where colours had typically been hoisted to support Barça's football team against Real Madrid, today there was a fight-to-the-death sentiment behind La Estelada. With rhetoric all too familiar to Franco's generation, Albert Rivera, the leader of the Citizens Party, was likening (just as Franco had) nationalism in Spain to a cancer. But he had gone further. Catalunya belonged to Spain, Rivera declared. It did not belong to its acting leader, Puigdemont. And this from a former member of the parliament of Catalunya! But then, Emil felt allegiance to both and to neither. What he did feel every day, more keenly, was that the world as he knew it was slipping away, along with the aspirations of his youth.

Rafael was humming '*Els Segadors*' ('The Reapers'), the song of 1640 that had become the Catalan anthem. "*Catalunya triomfant, tornarà a ser rica i plena*" (*Catalunya triumphant will once again be rich and bountiful*), he was singing now.

So, thought Emil, he was hanging out in La Rambla Catalana where most of the demonstrations were taking place, and where this song was being sung night and day.

"*Endarrera aquesta gent tan ufana i tan superba. Bon cop de falç!*" (*Drive away these people who are so conceited and arrogant. Strike with your sickle!*)

Emil came to a temporary halt; his cousin had just walked over his newly mopped floor. "Yeah, yeah, *bon cop de falç*. You're in my space."

Rafael whistled a few more bars through his teeth. "And you're so busy."

"I am, actually. I mean," another pause, "not that you'd know. I mean," again Emil pronounced the words with exaggerated slowness, "not that you'd know what went on here other than to eat my *brazos*."

Rafael inhaled, attempting to flatten his *slightly* heavy body so that Emil could pass. What was it with his cousin? Emil was rushing back and forth in much the way Abuela's manic housekeeper Nuria used to at Salto. A lot of energy for – Rafael lifted a foot – not much return. "Are we quarrelling?"

Emil shrugged. "Dunno, are we?"

"Look, I came because you haven't been picking up *and* the shop has been closed."

Emil flipped the sign to 'open'. "Voilà – closed no longer." He whipped past Rafael to switch on the counter lights and remove the covers from platters of fresh food. He reached into large canvas bags to gather up the small bread rolls that he lobbed into the baskets lining the wall. The action reminded Rafael of the tennis lessons they'd had when they were small.

"I've not had a decent *bocado* in weeks," Rafael complained cheerfully. "At a push, I'd even consider some of that zealously healthy rye stuff."

Emil considered his cousin coldly. "Yes, well, you know why that is. Not so many people fancy sitting in front of a boarded-up window."

"Y-yes, but you had that fixed."

"There are other things that need fixing."

For a moment they stared at each other frostily, but Rafael hadn't been joking about missing out on Emil's confectionery. He could put up with anything if it meant a decent dessert at the end of it. He scraped a chair to one of the little wrought-iron tables and sat down determinedly, an incongruous figure in his cassock alongside the doll-sized furniture. "You're right, of course, and now that you mention it, I *will* have a *brazo* and a *cortado*, and then you can stop sulking and tell me what's really bothering you."

Emil glared at him but nonetheless set aside the bread bag. He switched on the coffee machine and carefully unwrapped his cousin's favourite cake. Rafael waited patiently, then, taking a pad from his robe pocket, began jotting down notes for his Sunday sermon. *A lo que salga*, he thought – well, actually Unamuno had thought it before him. It roughly translated as 'Whatever comes.'

While Rafael scribbled and the coffee brewed, Emil got out his broom and began sweeping the outside paving stones. From time to time he offered a casual "Sorry" as he biffed Rafael's ankles.

Rafael, knowing it was deliberate, mouthed, "*No importa*", though secretly wishing he could biff him back. Nor did he dare draw attention to the fact that the coffee had been brewing for some time.

After what seemed an age, Emil finally sliced into the cream dessert before banging it and a cup and saucer onto the table.

'*And gives to every power a double power*,' wrote Rafael.

For his part, Emil contemplated his cousin with rather less compassion. Rafael was getting chubby, he thought gleefully; actually *chubby*! *Eat away, dear cousin of mine!* Surely gaining weight must be the only blemish on his simple life? For what worries could he possibly have, this priest with his designer shoes and lofty theories? Not that Rafael seemed remotely troubled by his expanding girth. Not remotely! Well, Emil had something to tell him that should pierce his exasperating good humour. He put away his broom and from behind the cash till removed a new packet of cigarettes, peeling away the thin red plastic ribbon before scrunching up the cellophane and throwing it in the bin. Slowly, he peeled back the silver paper and carefully removed a cigarette. He loved the feel and smell of a new package of clean, smooth tobacco. He tapped the box so that one slithered to the fore and offered it to his cousin. When Rafael delved under the folds of his robe to find his lighter, Emil felt the returning warmth (albeit a tepid one) of their habitual companionship.

"Exactly how many pockets does that thing have anyway?" he asked when they had both lit up and savoured the first few drags.

A thin line of smoke escaped from the corner of Rafael's mouth. "Enough."

Emil nodded, stretched, and looked at his cousin directly. "Did you know," he said at last, "that the *pa de pagès* Salto so prides itself on is made from flour imported from France? That we – *I*, more precisely – pay a thousand euros per ton for it, whereas other bakeries pay two hundred?"

Rafael blinked rapidly. *Aha... now we're getting to it.*

"And in case you're wondering, that *brazo* is made with the imported stuff." Emil gestured to Rafael's half-eaten dessert.

No wonder this *pastelaria* had always been Rafael's favourite even if he was, of course, biased. He could taste the residue of burned sugar on his lips. He let his cigarette smoulder, a thin black line eating into the white paper as it balanced on the edge of an ashtray. "I did not know that," he said, feigning interest. "Our *coca* as well?"

Emil leaned against the outside wall; the bricks warm behind his back. He finished his own cigarette, stubbing it out beneath the sole of his shoe. "No, our sweet *coca* – *that* pastry we make here. But our bestseller, and what we sell across Spain, is the other."

Rafael took a sip of coffee with a satisfied groan. His cousin really did make an excellent barista. He crossed his legs, a gleaming Prada shoe peeking from under his cassock. Emil couldn't help noticing. Since when had his cousin switched designers? Rafael and Emil had both been Tod's men ever since meeting Diego in Capri so many summers ago. Emil was certain that on that same trip, because of some petty argument about astrakhan fur, Rafael and Miuccia had never jelled.

"So, you understand what this means?" Emil's indignant face

was inches from his. Too close. He was (in the manner of dear old Nuria) 'hovering'. It was a habit that always made Rafael nervous. Without allowing his cousin time to reply, Emil added quickly, "Well, I'll tell you what it means. It means that without that particular flour we can't make the same recipe; without that recipe we have no *pa de pagès*. It's what we're famous for. We don't make money on this." He gesticulated to Rafael's sweet pastry. "The cakes can be bought in, but not the bread."

"I see. It's jolly good, though. I've always liked the *cremat* flavour—"

"Rafa!"

"Just saying… and…" Rafael struggled to think of something relevant to say. "And other suppliers?" he managed at last.

"I'm working on that. But we're in the minority. Most chains are just that, and use other formulas. We're in the same boat as everyone else, though, with regards to the strike action and resulting transport difficulties." Emil frowned, and Rafael noticed the dark circles under his cousin's eyes; the lines etched from nose to mouth. When had he grown so much older?

"I'm sorry. I didn't realise. I should have done, but you rarely talk about this place. You always seem to manage…" Rafael held out his arms in the manner of *Christ the Redeemer* as seen from the Corcovado.

More on a sugar-loaf rush than a sympathy one, Emil couldn't help thinking but his expression which had begun by raging, with eyes that blinked rapidly and nostrils that flared in much the way his favourite horse's had once, were calm again. His testiness gave way to humour as he contemplated Rafael. The guy could be such an idiot! And he might not be the person Emil most loved in the world, but he was certainly the one he had known the longest. Cousin, brother – it was all the same to him. Emil could not remember a time when the other had not been in his consciousness.

To begin with, neither one of them had wanted Salto or anything to do with the place, and certainly not the *pastelaria*, but

Emil had, rather strangely, developed a great fondness for bread making. He certainly had never considered what he would do without it. Not since polo, that is. He glanced at Rafael's bored face. But where to begin? They were in the midst of a general strike. With paralysed imports and the banks freezing accounts it was only a matter of time before the shop began to suffer irreversible setbacks. More than setbacks – Emil would be amazed if they didn't fold completely. And he didn't mean the empanadas.

"There is something puzzling me." Rafael was frowning as he got to his feet and began pacing, coffee in hand. But Emil might have known it wasn't simply to ward off cramp. He watched in amazement as Rafael moved behind the counter to fetch a refill. Rafael always waited to be served, something people including himself, always seemed happy to oblige.

"What's that, *cosí*?"

"I find it a little sorrowful," said Rafael, still standing and stirring several teaspoons of sugar into his coffee, "that we offer a bread made with *French* flour. Maybe we need to rename it. *Pa de pagès* – country bread – should be *pa francès*."

Sorrowful? Did Rafa think they were in the confessional? Still, Emil had to admit that he appeared to be trying. After a fashion. "I agree," said Emil, also standing to talk across the counter. "But that's because the ancient grain varieties have largely disappeared here in Catalonia. That's the EU for you. Competitive prices plus pre-frozen dough (which is, frankly, more economical) have pushed traditional small businesses out of the market. *We* could make so much more if we went down that route."

Rafael contemplated the mouth-watering selection of pastries. The portion of *brazo* Emil had given him had really been very small. "We may have to."

Emil looked astounded. "Absolutely never."

Rafael reached over the counter to sample another cake, but Emil swiped away his hand.

Annoyed, Rafael puffed out his cheeks. "Well, I have no idea what should happen. How are you – sorry, *we* – to find the kind of flour we need, if it's only to be had in France? And then how are we to get it here in time, bake the bread and distribute it? If I can't have another piece of cake," his eyebrows raised, then fell, "I'm going back to my church."

"No, you're not." Emil turned away and grabbed the folder of drawings from behind the register, thrusting it in front of Rafael. "Yes, of course we can find flour elsewhere, but that's only part of it. I've been back to Salto," he said.

Rafael recalled the fresh flowers on Santiago's grave. He wanted to say that so had he, but remained silent. Emil didn't elaborate, intent on searching through Gemma's drawings. Loose papers fluttered to the ground, with Rafael bending down to pick them up in a lackadaisical kind of way, until Emil found the one he was looking for. He smoothed it out. A gold (but not too gold) sheaf of wheat was intertwined with the Monte Alegre coat of arms. The background was an elegant pale grey.

"Very pretty."

"This is a solution – *the* solution."

Rafael looked blankly from the paper to Emil's animated face.

"A baker doesn't *create*, he transforms," said Emil, with more passion than Rafael had heard him speak with in years.

"I don't understand."

"Bacteria and yeast are what create bread. It's the baker who transforms the mix into something beautiful."

"O-kaay."

"You aren't with me."

"Like a… potter with… er… clay?"

Emil scowled. "I can feel you're going to piss me off."

"No! No! At least, I hope not! I'm listening, really I am." Rafael gathered up more loose sketches from the floor; the exertion causing him to pant for his trouble. "Are these new ones also Gemma's? So, you patched things up?"

"What? Yes. Look, that doesn't matter."

"They really are lovely drawings. I like this one with the wheat with 'M' and 'S', and the grey is modern but…" Here Rafael's cousin looked genuinely perplexed. "Don't we… um… already have a coat of arms?" Rafael thought of one of the four great halls at Salto, where an entire wall was covered in crests embossed on leather shields.

"*Rafa!*"

"What?"

"*Joder!* If you'd only listen! God, you can be so annoying!"

"I'm not trying to be," said Rafael pleasantly. "Look, why don't you just settle down and tell me what this is all about?"

Emil took a deep breath, spun on his heel almost 360 degrees and reached behind the front door to flick open the small fridge with his foot. He whipped out a San Miguel, offering one to his cousin which Rafael declined, gesturing to his unfinished coffee. Emil tapped the beer cap on the edge of the table and drank straight from the bottle. The thought – a whisper of a memory no more – came to him that the action used to drive girls wild at the polo club. They said it was manly and sexy. For a moment he was distracted by the idea that there was anything sexy about the two of them now. "You know how I like to bake bread."

Rafael's reaction was predictably blank, his taste buds fizzing with espresso and *brazo*. *Not this again…*

"I can see you aren't listening."

Rafael felt a surge of childish pleasure at his cousin's irritation. "I am!" he protested. He stole a glance at Emil's tetchy face. Oh, this was fun! This was worth it! Maybe he could just grab a chocolate truffle when Emil's back was turned; the ones with the dusting of darker chocolate shavings as light as powder… Or not.

Emil was all businesslike again. "Then you'll remember," he was saying in that obsessive way, "that we produce only a small amount… well," he shrugged, "small by local standards, due to lack of space. The current political situation has forced me to rethink. I wasn't sure what I was going to do about next month's supply until..." He paused and took another swig of beer.

"Until?" prompted Rafael mildly. *Ahora!* Now! If only Emil would replace the wretched drawings...

"Until I went back to Salto. At first it was to, you know, look after Santiago's grave. But then when all this Puigdemont/separatist thing blew up and the banks began to play silly buggers, as the English say, I went back to see the *forn*."

"The *forn*?" The incredulous expression on Rafael's face made Emil pause.

"Yes, the *forn*."

"But that old thing hasn't been used in years! Half a century at least." How different they both were: Rafael had gone to see Sospiro, the summer house; his cousin, the old oven.

"Not quite as long as that, Rafa, but yes, some years. And guess what? It could work! I want to go back not only to cooking our bread in a wood oven, but to using ecological flour ground in a stone mill. *Our* stone mill, with cereal raised from dry farming. I want to produce flour from the Salto mill. I want to call it Salto al Cielo bread. So good you've died..."

"...and gone to heaven. I get it." Rafael pursed his lips. The only dying and going to heaven he could envisage was in consuming one of those small chocolates. "There's a lot of 'wants' in there, amigo."

"Maybe, but it makes perfect sense. Do you know how many coeliacs there are in Spain?"

Rafael, having resorted to cleaning his plate with his finger, stopped midway. "Dazzle me."

"Seventy-five thousand."

Rafael emitted a low whistle.

"Uh-huh... and do you know why?"

Rafa licked his thumb. This was ridiculous. This was his *pastelaria* too, after all. He should be able to have just a *little* more of anything he fancied, quite frankly. All this self-control was overrated. "Too much time on their hands?"

Emil knocked back the rest of his beer and bared his teeth. "Now you're officially pissing me off." He collected the sketches together, shuffling them in order.

Rafael grabbed his arm. "I'm sorry, I'm sorry," he said quickly. "You know I'm kidding. It's just that, honestly, with what you've just told me I could be as panicked about the business as you are."

Emil nodded. "It's okay. Except that I'm not. I *was*. But I think you've misread me. I'm actually excited. *Escucha*. Listen, the flour produced from over-fertilised wheat is *una mierda*; complete shit. It's not surprising so many people get sick. If you think back to the bread *los avis* – our grandparents – had on the farm, do you remember how delicious; how aromatic? How you could smell the birds and the—"

"Bees?"

"*Rafa!*"

"Sorry, sorry." Rafael put a finger to his lips. "I promise. Not a word."

"You could smell the beech wood from the ovens in which the bread was baked. But in their day, it took *days* for fermentation to take place. Not the hours it can now. Everything was done by hand. The wheat grew this high," Emil touched the back of his chair, "not the mere centimetres mass-produced crops do. I want to go back to that, and I think there's real demand."

Rafael nodded slowly, once again eyeing up the pastries in the cold display unit. What if he had a very, very small bowl of *Crema Catalana*? Nothing; just an espresso cup size… "I think there is too," he said smoothly, reaching for a serving spoon. If he just kept talking; yes, that was the way to do it. Emil was so engrossed in his train of thought that he wouldn't notice if Rafael simply scooped up the cream in one quick go. "But you're forgetting one thing…" (Eureka! He'd done it! Ah, the creamy deliciousness of it…) "There might be the slightest, tiniest *problemo* with this plan of yours."

Emil frowned. "What's that?"

Rafael had the spoon halfway to his mouth. "Ino," he said.

33

Veronica
Salto al Cielo
May 1987

Veronica knew she had made a mistake even before Santiago placed the ring on her finger – except that, if she remembered correctly, he hadn't exactly 'placed' it anywhere. A whirlwind wedding was his idea, and given their busy work schedules she'd been more than happy to comply. They both had forthcoming conferences they were expected to attend. He was expected in Port-au-Prince, she in Copenhagen; yet there was still time, he said, in that grave, measured way of his, for a short weekend break before the wedding and before he took Veronica to meet his mother in Spain.

Veronica's heart had soared further when he'd said in the same breath that he'd booked the ridiculously romantic Manoir Richelieu at La Malbaie. The name, which literally meant 'Bad Bay', had never resonated before. Perhaps it should have. The hotel was in the Charlevoix region – that strip of land that runs east of Quebec City along the St Lawrence River; an area of Canada Veronica had always wanted to visit. It was where the waters of the Great Lakes flowed down to the sea. It was where people like her grandparents had sailed up that stretch of river for their first look at the New World. Veronica fervently hoped it would be her last.

The hotel – an old-world place with a wood-beamed lobby

known as 'the castle on the hill' – had some of the charm, Santiago said, that she would find at his own castle, Salto. "And look out for Harry," he had whispered when they were checking in – separate rooms, as only befitting a couple of their social standing.

"Why?" She had given him that wide-eyed look, although now there was nothing contrived about its artfulness – she felt like a deer (or moose, given their location) caught in the headlights.

Placing his hands on her shoulders, he had turned her bodily (but away from him) in the direction of the empty hallway. Veronica placed a hand on his in an attempt to hold him but he slid away, his touch as though it had never been.

"Rob too – he might be here."

Later, she realised the 'Rob' Santiago spoke of was Robert de Niro; the 'Harry' Harrison Ford, and this hotel was a favourite of theirs. And not only of theirs, she quickly learned from the pictures of other movie stars and heads of state that lined the entrance walls.

Veronica felt out of place for the first time in her life. The hotel, built on the designs for a French chateau, was exquisitely comfortable – her name, Comtesse de Monte Alegre (a premature move surely designed to awaken the Furies), was even printed on the toiletries in the bathroom! But the delight of what she was a hair's breadth from becoming was countered by an uncomfortable voice of caution. And after all, what was instinct other than self-preservation?

She was being foolish, she scolded herself when, after kicking off her shoes, she sank onto the gloriously comfortable feather bed for a 'siesta' before cocktails. The siesta was Santiago's idea. It was only mid afternoon; the sun a fireball mid-horizon, the river a thick blanket of ever-changing blue and grey and silver cutting through emerald-green forests. She hoped Santiago was being playful. And more.

It was wishful thinking. Knowing the little Veronica now did of her husband-to-be, reclining anywhere in close proximity to the other wasn't on the cards. Santiago seemed agitated, but not with passion – at least, not the amorous kind. He was heading off to watch the whales – there were thirteen different varieties, apparently, and the fishing boat he had hired would sail past the famous Tadoussac Lighthouse. Heart sinking, Veronica didn't even suggest joining him.

He gave her a weak smile. "Wear the palazzo pants," he advised. His lips kissed the air above her hand, though she had offered her cheek.

Whitney was belting 'I Wanna Dance with Somebody' through the music system, the words splicing Veronica's thoughts, when she saw them. She'd spent the past hour waiting by the fire, staring out of the bay (Malbaie) window that overlooked the thrusting, throbbing, mighty St Lawrence. With every passing hour the rushing waterway seemed to intensify and alter. At twilight, rays bouncing off its snow banks made it all glittery translucence. Now it had become metallic and dense. Veronica's right foot jigged, the kid leather ballerina shoe dangling from her slim foot in time to the music. She had not worn the palazzos, but a much tighter-fitting pair of velvet cigarette pants teamed with a vibrant scarlet silk shirt. Her lips had started out the same hue, but after two Martinis there was more colour on the glass than on her lips. She flicked through a magazine. The alcohol was coursing through her veins nicely – she'd not eaten all day. One more drink and she'd be quite tipsy. She wanted to be tipsy. She needed something to stem the rising panic, the doubt, the fingers of resistance springing up like a spiked gate guarding her inner soul.

What was wrong? Why wasn't it perfect? It should all be perfect! Veronica's reflection in the floor-to-ceiling windows showed an elegant, expensively dressed young woman. The rise of her pert, firm breasts accentuated her tiny waist and long legs. She shouldn't be on her own! Santiago ought to be sitting with her, sharing a drink and a joke following an afternoon's lovemaking. After all, they were in a gorgeous, plush hotel; two good-looking – no, correction:

beautiful – people about to get married. She bit her lip. And not from the old habit to give it colour. Then again, she reasoned, why allow emotion to get in the way now? She had (or soon would have) everything she had ever dreamed of; everything she had worked so hard to attain. For a fleeting moment she thought affectionately of Mr Bickell and his penchant for florid Victorian novels. She had certainly felt petted in his company. She had felt desired.

As Veronica tried to attract a waiter's attention, peering round the wing of the high-backed armchair, two men came through the revolving door. The man in front was laughing; an odd, effeminate laugh, punctuated by a rather theatrical toss of the head. When the taller of the two inadvertently caught the shorter man's ankles, the laughter intensified. Happy – oh, so happy! – relaxed laughter. Veronica sprang back, grazing the tip of her nose on the chair's rough fabric. But too late. Santiago had seen her. Or perhaps he hadn't? She held her breath; considered staying exactly where she was.

But then footsteps approached. She caught whiffs (along with opulent cologne) of "I want you to meet… it'll be all right. Come, my dear." (The last not directed to her.) And then there he was. Santiago's polished moccasins, the ones with the black tassels, came to a standstill in front of her. Shoes that were pristine. Shoes that had clearly not stepped out of doors. "Veronica," he always pronounced it 'Beronica', "I want you to meet a dear friend of mine – or at least, I hope he will be as dear to you as he is to me."

Santiago's introductions were always suave, utterly enchanting, but this time 'Beronica' was truly mesmerised. She was especially mesmerised by her husband-to-be's arm slung so casually around the younger man's shoulders. In a way it never was around hers. She stared, transfixed, at the black hairs peeping from the white shirt cuffs on Santiago's wrists, the Omega wristwatch, the animation in his eyes. She felt her heart beat uncomfortably as she tried to stem the growing anger, the sense of frustration, and the even stronger desire to slap them both.

There was nothing 'dear' or endearing about Martin Ranger. From that first introduction there was rivalry for Santi's attention, let alone heart. But 'rivalry' suggested an uncertain outcome, when it was quite clear to them both who had won. To say that Veronica and Martin hated each other on sight was putting it mildly. At first, she had wanted to laugh hysterically – the man was decked out in more jewellery than she was, and his was real! Martin hadn't wanted to laugh, though. He looked as though he would have cheerfully biffed her one (she would have done the same, given half a chance) right there and then. *Well, we'll see, won't we?* She thought defiantly, not budging from her chair. She stared at him rudely, forcing the short, chubby man to bend down to her while she continued to wriggle her leg and look beyond him for the waiter. She had behaved childishly, peevishly; she recognised that then and accepted it now. Exasperation and fear all encapsulated in that moment of reckoning. And surprise. Surprise that a man as appreciative of beauty as Santiago was should be so enchanted by a man as coarse as Martin Ranger. They appraised each other, each in that harsh electric light upon which too many sharp objects and surfaces threw back an unflattering sheen, and understood exactly what the other was about.

In that moment (despite every instinct telling her to walk away), Veronica decided, and only for the hell of it, that she would accept the challenge; she would engage. She flicked Santiago her most winsome smile and rose in one fluid movement to mould her body to his. Her fingers moved behind his neck to kiss him on the lips; to bite them and hold them. "Did you see the whales, then?" she murmured in as husky a voice as she could make it.

"No whales," stammered Santiago when he had got his breath back and flung look after apologetic look in Martin's direction.

"Oh?" Veronica's eyes narrowed.

"No," said Martin, his face inscrutable. "Only seals."

Later, at dinner à trois, the jewellery box landed with a thud on her lap. It was so heavy it almost disappeared within the velvet crevice between her legs. Through the haze of alcohol, indigestible food and Martin Ranger's simpering giggles, she felt a leap of excitement. *This will make it all worth it*, she decided. Was she becoming blasé? Had she so quickly forgotten the Mr Bickells of this world? How only a few years ago she'd have given anything to be here with anyone, quite frankly, just to be warm and fed? Except that she was more than that. She was exquisitely dressed in grown-up clothes and drunk on Martinis, Montrachet and rosé champagne. She was exactly where she'd wanted to be all her life. Santiago was the most elegant, sophisticated man she'd ever met. And she was certain the ring would reflect this. Really, what else mattered? Once she'd set her sights on him, there wasn't a man she'd not been able to have – Santiago was no exception.

Veronica glanced at Martin animatedly describing some art gallery they'd visited (obviously together) in Berlin. A jewelled pin he'd been wearing on the front of his shirt had slipped. He attempted several times to reposition it before Santiago, brushing away his hand, gently re-pinned it himself. Did either of them speak German? Martin's withering look was so dismissive, Veronica went back to playing the guessing game in her head. What would it be? A diamond solitaire? A square-cut emerald; an aquamarine? But the latter only if egg-sized, otherwise it might look fake. The women in Schumacher certainly would consider it a cheap alternative – a place where size, status, *show* mattered. Her gaze flicked sideways – this was where Santiago should be looking at *her*. Actually, there were a lot of 'shoulds'. They should have seen the whales (or seals) together; they should have had a romantic dinner together. They should be alone now.

Oh, to hell with it. She flipped open the leather lid. A tiny brass knob with a flimsy arm held the thing in place.

"You had to have your own," said Santiago.

"Oh." She couldn't help the shock of disappointment. The horrible urge to cry; the surge of anger. She scooped out the hideous, large gold signet ring with the central blue stone that looked frankly ridiculous on her slender, pale little hand. It slid straight off and back onto her lap. Not that Santiago had noticed, or Martin for that matter. Her fiancé's dark eyes were ablaze all right, but not with love for her, while Martin's burned with a different kind of passion; hatred, if she wasn't mistaken. Veronica felt sick with the realisation. *Walk away!* screamed every cell in her being. *Walk away!* "Oh," she said again. She met Martin's gaze now. "How divine!" she taunted. "How simply divine. I think this calls for more champagne, though, Santi, don't you?"

"And I was thinking it was bedtime for all," said Martin combatively.

Veronica blinked, giving him the full blast of her clear anthracite eyes. "Oh, by all means," she said sweetly. "You're excused; you must be so tired! Besides, there is so much that Santi," she flicked her tongue around her lips, "and I have to discuss. Obviously, with the wedding next week..."

It was Martin's turn to look startled.

Aha! So, you didn't know, did you? Dix points, she thought, *à moi*.

But, far from amused, Santi was ashen; he could look at neither of them.

Christ! thought Veronica. *Talk about the reluctant bridegroom!*

"Tell me," Martin was saying now. "Where did you say you grew up again?"

"I didn't," said Veronica. But two could play this game. "Goodnight, Mr Ranger."

Furiously, Martin threw down his napkin. "Santiago?" His tone was imploring; wimpish.

Santiago sighed. "It's for the best, my de… my friend," he said. "Get your beauty sleep."

Veronica's eyebrows raised. Nothing, in her mind, would ever make Martin beautiful. He was too short, for one thing; too stocky. He had a bulldog neck and head. He was Sancho Panza to Santi's

Don Quixote without any of the former's humour or common sense or touch. But perhaps madness?

Martin tossed his head. "See you at breakfast?" He wasn't looking at her.

Veronica leaned into Santiago suddenly, straddling one of his legs with hers. "Breakfast?" she echoed. "Oh, I don't think so. Santi and I have so much catching up to do. I don't plan on letting him get up all morning."

Veronica was, frankly, surprised that Santiago had still wanted to get married after that; after the fight they'd had in the morning. Mentally she prepared herself for the inevitable dismissal; had even placed the little box with the hideous ring on the bedside table. To be honest, she wasn't altogether disappointed. A large part of her was actually relieved. But he hadn't wanted to call the wedding off – far from it. To her astonishment, he had wanted to bring the day forward. If anything, it was the weekend he wanted to abort.

And so it was that, married, Veronica found herself staring across the lake at Salto, the other castle on a hill. She should have felt wonder; delight, even. She should have gasped at the way the building appeared to be floating beneath the clouds, suspended in the trees; queried how they were to arrive there when between them and it was nothing but water. Above all, she should have felt intense relief. Financially she was secure in a way she could never have imagined: she had a name, she had background, she had a wonderful job. Everything was strange and new, which should have given her the biggest thrill of all, but absent was the excitement of being in love; of being loved in return. Not that she had expected love, but on meeting Santiago she had dared to hope. She wondered now if he were even capable of such an emotion. Not hope; love. She wondered if she was. She wondered at the reason why he had really proposed marriage. She wondered in a different way, even more ardently, why she had accepted.

Veronica stole a glance at him. Her husband of four days sat in the front seat, talking animatedly to their driver. Not beside her, holding hands, but beside him, Eduardo – no, Edu. Santiago called him Edu. If Edu was good-looking (Veronica glanced at him from time to time, marvelling at his capacity for listening as her husband had hardly drawn breath since they left the city), Santiago, with his long aquiline nose, full lips and tanned skin, was beautiful. His arm rested along the back of Edu's seat, inches from the back of his head. The shirtsleeves of his fine Egyptian cotton shirt were rolled up; his suit jacket slung over his shoulder like a matador's cape. (Veronica would learn shortly from Abuela that even his boxer shorts were handmade by a tailor in Barcelona.) He was the very image of the sophisticated European diplomat. There was something so inherently dashing about him, so glamorous, that even now, unconsummated as their union still was, just looking at him made her backbone unhinge. She felt a tingle in her loins; a visceral yearning.

And yet... and yet, there was also something else – something she couldn't quite articulate; something unsettling. During all the years (never mind effort!) spent hiding her background, her origins in Schumacher, and living with the constant fear that someone or something from that time might find her, she had never experienced this apprehension. So why should that be? The air was gentle on her face; the ring ghastly, yet reassuringly heavy. All should be well, but anxiety flooded through her.

By the time they finally arrived it was almost dark, and Veronica wasn't certain who was the more exhausted: she (shaken and dishevelled), or their antiquated vehicle. Her full-skirted rose linen dress with its Peter Pan collar that Nadja at Saks had assured her would be perfect for a honeymoon abroad was now crumpled and soiled. What had seemed uber-chic in the air-conditioned changing room of the Fifth Avenue department store was ridiculously childish here. Spanish women appeared to favour earthy colours in stiff silk faille or shantung. Little-girl pink was definitely the wrong colour. Santiago clearly thought so too. No plus points awarded, either, for changing in the plane's minute toilets, balancing wash kit and handbag on the sink and praying their contents weren't flushed down the disposal unit. She had thought, cleverly, to roll the dress in tissue paper, carrying it all the way from New York in her hand luggage. But to no avail. Santiago had frowned, perplexed, when she emerged from the toilet, red-faced with the exertion of changing in such a confined space, the noise of the airplane engines drowning out some but not all of his comments. "Grey, blue, aqua are your colours. Why this?"

Why indeed? It occurred to Veronica as they rounded the last bend (and only then did the outline of the *castillo* come into view) that her impulsive purchase might not have been her only rash decision. What did she know of any of this? Of Spain? Of the aristocracy, of *Santiago*? But then she pinched herself figuratively. She was a countess now! That had to count (ha ha) for something. She glanced at her husband, willing him to look at her, catch her eye, even, if only for a nanosecond. But, as seemed his wont, if their eyes did meet, his look conveyed such bemusement that she was the one to look away first. They didn't do much better conversing. Throughout the entire journey he had talked animatedly to complete strangers, as he was now to Edu, only lapsing into silence with her.

"Mama will have turned in," he said to no one in particular.

But as Edu slid from behind the wheel to open Veronica's door and help her out, and Santiago repeated himself, Veronica realised that the information was actually intended for her. She felt her stomach contract in a way it hadn't done since she was a kid, and it wasn't with excitement. She smoothed down her dress. The skirt seemed to have acquired a life of its own, refusing to lie flat, and was sticking out at odd angles. To her surprise, Santiago was suddenly at her side. For a moment, she thought he might even take her hand. She wanted only to snuggle into him for reassurance, feeling suddenly cold in the humid night; cold and tired and afraid. But already he was moving away from her. They had parked in front of a pebbled path leading to an arch, a flight of stairs and a covered walkway. On the left-hand tower, a beautiful illuminated clock struck the hour.

"You'll meet her in the morning."

Who? Again, Veronica turned to him, but already he was on the top step, making his way through another arch. She craned to see where he'd gone. Over the archway was a coat of arms. His footsteps sounded ahead, and she shot after him, lost in the dark. *Wait for me!* she wanted to cry, feeling as small and infantile as she had never done as a child. She watched his tall shape narrow, then elongate, a shadow dipping this way and that along the covered walkways. His pace quickened until he was virtually running across an Arabic courtyard with the tinkling sound of water coming from a central fountain. Without it for reference, Veronica would have stumbled in the dark.

And then she heard him. Them. "Welcome, dear friend." His voice low, passionate, floating above her.

Dear *friend*? Was that what she was? *Strange words with which to welcome a bride*, Veronica thought irritably, though there was no denying the warble in his voice; the way it cracked with feeling. But no – this warm greeting was not for her. Of course it wasn't! There was another man standing directly under the arch of the double doors. A single lantern shone above him as he sidled towards Santiago. Although 'sidled' was probably the wrong word to use for someone with his unfortunate… what was it Mr Bickell's tailor would have said? 'Configuration'? Veronica's breath was strangled, her heart constricted, her palms sweaty. And what was Santiago doing now? Arms outstretched, Veronica felt for him as though playing blind man's buff, her hand suspended in the space where the shape of his body should have been, but Santiago was bent from the waist, *bowing*. Actually bowing! And in that supremely graceful action he was gesturing to his heart, his lips, the ground. She heard the word 'welcome'. But who was welcoming whom?

"My house," Santiago was saying again, touching his lips, his heart, in the way in which Veronica had seen Arab leaders greet newcomers. "My house, dear Martin… All at your disposal."

The 'house' (a misnomer if there ever was one) might have been at Martin's disposal, Veronica thought testily the following morning, but it sure as hell didn't feel as though it was at hers. Why, oh why had she been so *stupid*?

She had slept fitfully, exhausted by the journey, upset, bewildered, and out of control for the first time in her life. Her entire body was clammy with perspiration as she kicked off the fine linen sheets. The room was silent, and so dark she had no idea what time of day it was. A thin fluorescent line of light, however, beamed from under the closed shutter. She pummelled the soft pillow. She was quite alone. She doubted Santiago had been near. She certainly had no idea where he had spent the night in this vast castle. At length, hunger propelled her out of bed and she padded towards the window. After a bad-tempered wrangle with the latch, she punched open the shutters, delighting as they banged against the outside walls. The air was sultry, the sky cobalt blue, everything still but for the cicadas in the bush and the occasional rustle of dry grass. The mountain range across the valley turned brown then yellow as the sun's rays streaked a path across its horizon. The fields stretched endless from there; endless and serene.

Veronica blinked. She had wanted adventure, she had wanted security – well, she had both in spades, and if she now found herself in a foreign country married to a virtual stranger then she had only herself to blame. She looked around her. The room was sparsely furnished with the large double bed she had slept in, a table and chair against one wall, and an armchair in the corner. The en-suite bathroom was old-fashioned by Canadian standards, the marble cracked, the plugs rusty. The towels too had seen better days. Someone had unpacked her clothes and her dresses hung neatly displayed in the large, rickety free-standing cupboard. There was a faint, lingering smell of dried lavender amid the wooden coat hangers, the empty ones knocking against each other. This castle was considerably less luxurious than the hotel they'd just left. She wished fervently that they were still there, even if Martin... Ugh, Martin. Was the man destined to pop up *everywhere* they went?

She turned on the shower. A thin trickle of lukewarm water began to spurt and hiss. Still, she was grateful for any means to shampoo her hair, letting the droplets run off her face. If she trusted her instinct, if she listened to what an inner voice was screaming at every turn, she would accept that her husband of a few days was far more excited at being with his friend Martin than he was with her. But how was it possible that Santiago, who was such a perfectionist, such an aesthete, could find Martin Ranger remotely attractive? How could he find him more attractive than *her*? Was she missing something?

Veronica let the water run cold, but she was barely cool as she dried herself. She stood before the cupboard with its peeling painted doors and stray wood splinters. There was going to be nothing demure about her choice this time. She pulled a fuchsia-pink silk dress off its hanger. She had chosen clothes for her honeymoon with such excitement, such care, and now she'd have happily burned the lot if it meant attracting her husband's attention. She frowned. She wasn't going to admit defeat just yet. She almost smiled. Veronica liked a challenge; liked to rouse herself when the chips were down.

She whirled in front of a mirror speckled with black spots. Cut on the bias, the skirt pooled around her ankles; as she twirled, it clung to her thighs. Tiny mother-of-pearl buttons nestled between her breasts. Hair drying in blonde tendrils around her flushed face, she knew she was desirable. To just about anyone, she thought bitterly, except the person who should desire her the most. Surely, Santiago couldn't keep this coolness up for long? There wasn't a man she'd not been able to seduce, and her husband was not going to be the exception!

Fastening the tiny gold buckles of her Roman-style sandals, she straightened, breathless, flung a final glance at herself in the mirror and ventured from the room. Where *was* Santiago? The place – this *castle* – was massive. It felt just as big as the Manoir Richelieu, but the hotel had had staff there to show her around. This place seemed deserted. And in virtual darkness. All the shutters on the top floor were closed. Against the heat, she supposed. She peered down the circular stairwell and felt dizzy. She descended slowly, noting the huge oil paintings that covered the walls, virtually frame to frame. Everything here was oversized – unflatteringly so. Veronica had never seen such a collection of ugly men, women and dogs. She appreciated now the care with which museums curated collections. No one in their right mind would pay to see this lot.

She skipped down the stairs, not because she was feeling in the least light-hearted, but out of a desperation to be outside. Her hand trailed polished wood as she passed dozens of shiny suits of armour, heavy oak chests covered with embroidered silk shawls, stuffed birds that made her shiver, and discarded polo mallets. What *was* this Salto? And who ran it? Did Santiago? His *mother*? What sort of people lived here? Were they happy? Could she be, in a place like this? Veronica's mind buzzed with questions, each more unsettling than the last.

She jumped the last step, emerging into the great hall. Here was yet another enormous space dominated by a stone fireplace so colossal she imagined entire hogs being strung up there to roast. There were more hideous portraits, more tables crammed with silver-framed photographs of men in uniform with unbecoming moustaches. Weaving its way through this crowded collection was a herd of white china horses. Their extreme plainness contrasted with the rest of the decor. Fascinated, Veronica lifted the smallest foal, holding it carefully between thumb and forefinger. About to compare it to another figurine, she heard voices coming from outside.

She stood completely still. She heard her name spoken several times. Or was she mistaken? No: the man – her *husband* – was definitely talking about her. Her body tensed; her heartbeat felt laboured, having as much difficulty pumping blood through its ventricles as the car had earlier changing gear. She wondered if it would ever retain a steady beat. Try as she might, she couldn't will herself to be calm; her heart and her throbbing temples had become a single pulsating mass. She *should* make a sound. She *should* move, but instead she remained rooted to the spot, incapable of action. Santiago's voice dropped to something like laughter (actually, something that sounded more like that squeak, that *giggle* she was beginning to find incredibly irritating), and then Martin – she was sure it was Martin – murmured something in response. Then there was silence. Veronica pressed her hand to her heart, feeling it pulsate under her palm as though it were a live, separate creature. Her mind was as jagged and alien as the rest of her, instinct attempting to unscramble the jumble of confused messages that seared through reason. It was *un*reasonable to respond like this, she knew. So why was she? Why did everything about Martin and her husband…?

Still clutching the china horse, she circled the table twice. What was wrong here? What was wrong, dare she say it, with *Santiago*? She would ask him, right now. She dropped the china horse a little too hastily. With a domino effect it caught the tail of one of the other horses, sending the china legs tumbling down, and with them two of the smaller photograph frames. She froze, but thankfully they hadn't broken and no one appeared to have heard. Hastily she stood the little figures back on their feet and tiptoed away. Still on tippy-toes, she went onto the veranda where her husband and his friend sat huddled over a breakfast table evidently set for two people. Their heads were almost touching.

"Oh, good morning," said Santiago, springing back, and in a tone that suggested he wished her anything but.

Martin, of course, remained silent. Veronica kept her expression blank as she waited for Santiago to stand; to greet her, his bride, his wife, on this, the first day of their honeymoon. He scraped back his chair so slowly that she was already seated by the time he had got to his feet. She flushed, but restrained herself from commenting. She would give neither of them the satisfaction of seeing her riled. Santiago leaned back in his chair and lit a cigarette. Breakfast was clearly over for him, then. Ever elegant, he wore slacks, a linen shirt with the sleeves rolled up, and espadrilles. She stared at his feet. She'd never seen a man wear that kind of footwear before. The feet emerging from black canvas were tanned and smooth and as elegant (she could only imagine) as the rest of him.

"I suppose you want to look around?"

She looked up, startled. Her stomach was beginning to growl. She couldn't exactly remember when she'd last eaten. It must have been on the Air Canada flight from New York, but with the different time zones she'd lost track. "Yes, I'd like to," she said tightly.

"Fantastic!" said Martin, suddenly alert. "It's been ages since I've been here. Love to see what you've done to the *forn*."

"*Forn?*" Veronica looked from one to the other in disbelief. Was she never going to be alone with Santiago? What had happened to the suave, impeccable manners that had so captivated her when they'd first met?

For a moment Santiago held not hers, but Martin's gaze. "We have an oven, yes, of course. A baker—"

"*Bakery?*" interrupted Veronica, incredulous, as hysterical laughter bubbled within her. Pent-up nerves, fatigue from the journey, and tension at the onslaught of so many confusing emotions threatened to overcome her.

"Yes, what's so funny?"

"N-nothing." Everything! Everything was funny. Too funny, actually. Here she was, a skater from Schumacher, Ontario, married to a baker from some remote village! Furthermore, a baker who couldn't give her a roll, let alone a bun in the oven! She had tears in her eyes. Scratch that – it was freaking hilarious.

Santiago looked genuinely affronted. "Of course, we are not *bakers* – whatever gave you that idea?! But there *is* a farm on the estate, just as there is a chapel and a school."

"Great," said Veronica sarcastically when she had strangled her last chortle with an unladylike hiccup. She reached over to help herself to Santiago's cup, feeling Martin's dislike bore into her. She swigged it down. She hated tepid black coffee. She smiled sweetly. "Good to go. Let's get going, then…"

Veronica had no idea how long she'd been walking. Her 'good-to-go' smile hadn't lasted long. By the time they'd left the covered walkway that led onto the long drive, her husband's girlish titters had driven away any resolve to be patient. She'd hung back, pleading fatigue – not that he'd noticed. Anything she said was disregarded. Her skin crawled with prickly heat, annoyance and frustration. Her heartbeat was erratic.

She held back, lingering in a small courtyard beneath the castle until she could no longer hear Santiago or Martin Ranger at all. After a while, she followed a path that led from there to the fortified side of the castle. She passed stone fountains, following the heady scent of roses to orchards laden with pomegranate, apricot and quince. The burnt orange and lemon of the exuberant fruit was gorgeous against the purple of liriodendron and a brilliant blue sky. When she closed her eyes her senses were assaulted by the tangy aroma of cypress and spruce. But she longed only to escape, and she quickened her pace now, sprinting down stone steps to terraces laid out with miniature yuccas. There were vegetable and fruit gardens too, featuring ornamental clusters of exotic varieties.

She paused to catch her breath under a large plantain, and then again later under a spreading poplar. By the spruced cork trees whose bark (she was later informed) supplied the champagne growers of Val Negra, she shook out a stray stone from under the sole of her sandal. And still she pressed on, losing all sense of time and direction. Nestling in the valley, the Montseny mountains rose steeply. There was no view of the lake from there; no expanse of open space to turn her face eastward and home.

Yes, home. Canada. It was only by the stream that headed God only knew where that she came to a stop. Tucking her skirt between her legs and crouching down on all fours, she cupped her hands to drink from clear, cold water. Exhausted, she sat back, lost and bewildered. She'd spent her whole life running away from her past, and yet here she was thinking about it more and more; clinging to it with a fondness she would never have thought possible. She kicked at stones, pushing small pebbles into the water's edge, tears streaming down her face. What had she done? She had striven to be financially independent, beholden to no one, had sworn she never would be, and now here she was, trapped. What was she doing with a man (well, *men*, actually, and yes, there were two of them) she hardly knew? The person she had met in North America and then Geneva, with his exquisite manners and beautiful clothes and diffident, reserved air, once home seemed to have become someone else entirely. He had promised glamour, sophistication, connections. He had the roots and family she had never had. She had been blinded in her purpose to acquire them, but now she had, a terrible suspicion was growing that she had sacrificed something far greater. And all for what?

Then there was the other matter. 'The love that dare not speak its name', or a love that wasn't even whispering in her direction. There, she'd said it. She'd said it in her head. She began walking again, then running. She considered herself worldly and yet the possibility that Santiago might be homosexual had never occurred to her. What other explanation could there be?

The river wound its way through a narrow gorge before converging on a quiet, elegant waterfall. *Like Santiago*, she thought. *There, but not there.* She turned away from its trajectory, imagining that the way back to the castle was ahead. She moved through dense vegetation and waist-high thickets of gardenia and camellia. After a while, she reached a clearing of olive groves and peach trees; clumps of sweet lavender, mimosa and syringa. Momentarily becalmed by the delicious scent, she paused before setting off again at a run. She wanted to be tired, so tired that she couldn't think, wouldn't *feel*, and soon she was struggling through a jungle of the very wheat that supplied the blessed *forn*. She felt the breeze caress the tops of her arms; prickly tips of the golden blades scratch her thighs. She felt the meadow grasses tickle her ankles as she picked up more speed, running as fast as she could as though being chased; as though she were skating, moving forward to turn on her heel. And fall…

With a jolt, she concertinaed headlong into the greensward. Winded, she coughed, before turning slowly to lie on her back. Nothing hurt. She thought about sitting up, but was suddenly spent. Well and truly depleted. And, lying still, she contemplated a sky that was as seemingly benign and blue as any Canadian sky. She closed her eyes. She had lost track of time and all sense of direction. She had no idea where she had got to. She had run past stables and a mill, smallholdings and cottages, woods and glades, and now here she was lying on her back with no idea how to get home. *Home?* It certainly wasn't that. She could never imagine it would ever be that.

"*Condesa? Señora?*"

And suddenly the world stopped spinning, and the compass of her ambition began pointing steadily, unwaveringly north again. *Countess.* Yes, indeedy, she *was* a goddamn countess. Oh boy, if old man Bickell could see her now! If those old bitches in the community laundromat in Timmins, Ontario could see her now. Well, obviously not *now*, now. Not lying on the ground on her back. But in general, now. That had to be worth all this upset.

She looked up. An old man with kindly eyes was peering down at her. He wore the soft felt hat she associated more generally with Frenchmen on bikes brandishing wheels of Camembert and baguettes. He also wore the black espadrilles that not long into the future would be fashion statements everywhere. The same espadrilles she had seen on Santiago. A canvas bag of freshly sickled wheat was slung over a shoulder and his stained suede singlet swung loose. He reached down and pulled her to her feet.

Despite his age, he was surprisingly strong. When she swayed, he held her easily.

"I... *quiero*," she said slowly in her halting Spanish. "*Quiero* get back. I want to get back." She made a walking motion with her fingers. "To Salto?" she said hopefully, this time making a circle to denote the castle.

"Salto?" echoed the old man, puzzled. Any moment now, she imagined, he would remove his beret to scratch his head. But he didn't.

"Yes. *Sí, sí*."

The man smiled. "*Sí entiendo*. I understand." He smiled warmly, and this time copied her too, only his gesture was bigger, more expansive. His embraced sky and horizon alike. "But which part? *Qué parte de Salto?*" he said. "*Todo Salto*. It's *all* Salto."

34

Emil
Barcelona
October 2017

Emil hesitated only once before calling the familiar number. It was one (even more than Sol's) he'd had trouble deleting. Deleting Sol's had been medicinal; for the sake of his mental health. But the other... to delete the other was to cut off a still-healthy limb, and so he never had. He never looked at 'P' for 'polo' anyway. For some reason he'd needed Dutch courage just to make the call, and had taken refuge in a bar across the road from the *pastelaria*. Now he wished he hadn't. It was noisy – lots of businessmen in shiny suits worn not as in his day with moccasins, but with platform trainers. Men! He sniffed mentally. They looked half Emil's age. But here they were knocking back beer and wine and happily tossing toothpicks, olive stones and scrunched-up bits of tissue paper – the kind Emil wrapped up his croissants with – onto the floor. Absent-mindedly, Emil took a fistful of roasted almonds, cramming them into his mouth.

"*Sí?*"

Emil almost choked. He hadn't really thought anyone would answer. Now he motioned to the bartender to get him some water as, coughing and spluttering, he put a hand to his ear. "Diego?"

"*Sí, Señor Conde.*"

Emil couldn't believe it, and yet here was his groom answering in just the same brusque fashion as he had ever done. And, as before (as if twelve years hadn't elapsed since his last phone call), he didn't skip a beat before asking, "You want me to bring the horses? You want me to arrange a game?"

Emil mouthed a "*Gracias*" to the waiter who brought him a glass of water, which he gulped down. "Not a game," he said, washing away the last of the nuts. "But I do need all the grooms and at least two horseboxes if none of the lorries is available. I need gasoline to be delivered to our Salto petrol station. Er… and I need catering staff."

"All this for an… *asado*, Señor Conde?" Diego asked, deadpan, but Emil could hear the perplexity in his tone. Barbecues were not usually so complicated. You ordered the meat; it was delivered and cooked. *Asado completo.* "Señor Conde? You still there?"

Emil took another gulp of water. He could feel a hysterical tickle at the back of his throat. "Yes, my loyal friend. And not just any BBQ. It's going to be more of a Great Spanish Bake Off."

Archie

Cedar Avenue

What's the point? It's my turn to be depressed. What's the point of any of it? The weather has defeated me. I've not opened my window in three months. We've had forty centimetres of snow. A pastry shop handed out free bagels for those who made it to the store, but there was a catch! You had to be wearing snowshoes or skis. Cute, eh? Sickly, I say.

I'm going home.

35

Rafael
Salto al Cielo
October 2017

"You're late."

Rafael saw, rather than heard, the intake of tobacco before the car door was wrenched open. Given half a chance, he was certain Emil would have hauled him out by the scruff of his neck as well.

"Yes, all right. *Despacito*, no?"

"On the contrary, we have to hurry."

"But it's not even light!" Rafael gestured feebly to where he imagined east to be. Squinting, he could just make out the bulk of stone statuary against hedges so overgrown they were almost taller than their heads, and the glow of *cuca de llum* – glow-worms – scattered peripatetically along the upper reaches. He was dying for his own cigarette. A return like this warranted pacing; his body was awash with anxiety.

"And what on *earth* are you wearing?"

Marginally thrown by the sudden shift in tone, but pleased all the same that Emil had even noticed, Rafael lifted up the skirt of his soutane in much the way Mammy does when Rhett Butler asks her to show him her red flannel petticoat. Coquettishly, he turned his tanned ankle this way. His Gommino Tod's in soft-as-butter honeysuckle suede really were exquisite, but probably not ideally suited to Salto's red clay paths. He was happy to admit that a short flirtation with Prada was over and he'd gone back to his first love, although the thought did cross his mind that vanity (yet again) just might have got the better of him.

"Not *those*!" Emil dismissed Rafael's footwear, flicking (except it felt like a pinch) his cousin's cassock. "*This!*" There was another hiss of tobacco before he threw away his cigarette.

Rafael longingly followed its trajectory, while at the same time hoping that a spark wouldn't set fire to the crisp undergrowth. They were standing by one of the many wrought-iron gates that fenced off the estate, and the one closest to the mill. Behind it, the sun was beginning to rise just as it did in North Africa: suddenly, without fanfare, bursting onto an azure sky to announce the merciless heat of the day to come.

"How on earth do you expect to bake in that?"

"Bake?" echoed Rafael, perplexed. "Am I supposed to be… baking?" One look at Emil's tetchy expression made him reverse the thought. "I mean… of course I am." He cleared his voice. Several biblical quotations involving bread or bakers sprang to mind, but he checked himself. In a quick, elegant move he lifted the offending article off his shoulders, shaking out his hair and sunglasses. "See? Gone!" He tossed the robe through the car's open window onto the back seat and swung round, pleased with himself. He tucked his shirt into his sparkling white jeans and adjusted his Hermès belt. Or rather, he let it out a notch. Must have been last night's little *postre*.

"Oh my God!"

Rafael blinked. "What?"

"How is that better?"

"I'm sorry?"

Emil really did pinch him this time, taking the aqua linen shirt between two fingers.

"*Ojo*, you'll stain it!" protested Rafael, taking a step back.

"*Ojo*, my point exactly. We're here to *work*, in case you hadn't realised." Never mind the undergrowth, Emil's face was ready to ignite *pero ya*.

There was a rustling and a murmur of voices as a bevy of young people appeared at the top of a short flight of stone steps where terraces and patios divided the castle grounds. The diversion was just in time too, thought Rafael, giving his cousin a questioning look, especially when one of the girls stepped forward. He did a double take, and it wasn't because the half-light behind her was playing tricks with his eyes. She appeared to be wearing a corset and very little else. On closer examination the strange garment seemed to consist of a pair of high-waisted shorts cut away to simulate a corset, but retaining the dangling stocking suspenders. A tiny black bandeau top revealed a tanned midriff. It was a decidedly sexy look, a distracting look, and one that in all his years of not inconsiderable experience, Rafael had never seen before. Emil was a fine one to criticise his attire; at least *he* wasn't half naked.

"It's okay," said the girl, reading his expression. "We've got aprons, or…" She turned back to her friends. "I'm sure someone can lend you a T-shirt."

Rafael was amazed at the self-awareness (or rather, lack of) in the young. *He* wasn't the one who needed covering up. There were more giggles as he turned in their direction, beaming. "You must be…"

"Gemma," said the girl, swooping over to him, all white teeth and bouncy hair. Rafael liked that instantly about her. Although he didn't think that generally American girls had much taste – he glanced at Gemma's shiny platform trainers that completed her extraordinary get-up – he couldn't fault their personal hygiene. Her cheek brushed his with the customary greeting.

"*Encantado*," said Rafael, genuinely charmed. "And these are your friends?"

Tall, skinny girls, all wearing the peculiar corset shorts, stood flamingo-like, hugging the stone walls.

Gemma nodded. "Yeah, from the Spanish school."

"Aha…" Rafael was beginning to think that this was going to be almost as good as being in the pastry shop.

"That'll do," said Emil, standing between them. He prised a notebook from the back pocket of his jeans. Chewing a pencil, he glanced at his list. "Okay, let's get going. Let me remind you that we're here to work." He shot his cousin and the boys in the group a meaningful look. Most of them wore jeans that seemed to be falling to their knees. He could see a band's width of Calvin Klein boxers, and wondered if they would consider wearing a belt, if only for the duration of the job. Swatting away a cloud of mosquitoes that had suddenly appeared like a dandelion in front of his face, he thanked Providence that he'd been able to call on his grooms to do the heavy work. "The *mozos* have spent the better part of a week repointing and lining. They've swept the chimneys; the dough has been rising over the past few days so everything is ready to go. The rest is—"

"In God's hands?" volunteered Rafael in a stage whisper. There was a titter among the youths which he played to, raising his eyebrows in solidarity.

The dramatic screech of brakes as horseboxes scraped through rusty gates, and the accompanying expletives heard above the dust and ensuing chaos, announced the arrival of the '*mozos*'. Rafael remembered some of the grooms from his polo days – indeed, some had even travelled with him to England on occasion. They jumped from the moving vehicles, landing on the balls of their feet like cats; or as the acrobats they were, from the bare back of a polo pony. Within a short while, chattering, sucking on yerba maté, making lewd comments about the girls, they had nonetheless organised themselves, unloading boxes of tray liners, general packaging, and cast-iron paddles. Rafael felt a nostalgic pang seeing their iconic felt hats and the bright kilim embroidery of their gaucho belts. *Gemma's friends could do with a couple of those*, he thought ruefully. The Argies were in high spirits, at one moment forming a human chain as they passed condiments, chicken wire and what appeared to be the carcasses of two whole lambs down the line. Soon they were perspiring freely. The rest of the young people hung back, talking in a cacophony of foreign languages.

"It's for later," said Emil curtly. "When the baking is done, the Argies insist on cooking us an *asado*."

Ho ho! Things *were* looking up. Rafael's mouth watered at the thought. The way the Argentines cooked meat was second to none. The cut they chose was different from any he'd seen anywhere else in the world, and the manner in which it was prepared: the animal splayed on a crucifix and tied with wire over a simmering fire, slow-cooked until velvet flesh melted away…

Emil jerked his head in the direction of the river. "But if you're really going to help, it's this way."

For a moment both he and his cousin hesitated, acutely aware that while one path led to the mill, the other, unkempt and shaded by overgrown fruit trees, would end at Sospiro. Swatting away whatever memory lay before them, Emil strode ahead and Rafael followed, a sudden tightening in his chest rendering him speechless; pinholes of melancholy pricking through any earlier resilience. He also felt like the Pied Piper. Behind them snaked the column of Gemma's friends and helpers for the day.

They walked for some thirty minutes before Gemma came to a stop, leaning over to catch her breath, hands on her knees. "Is this really a castle?" she panted.

Rafael held a thorny rose branch away from her face so that she could pass as they clambered through waist-high lavender and gorse. Her bare legs and arms were criss-crossed with scratches. He hesitated briefly before offering her his cashair sweater. "It's hot, I know, but it's better than nothing."

She accepted the sweater gratefully, draping it over her shoulders. "So, is this a castle?" she repeated with the same sceptical edge.

The path was bordered by shrubbery; the view obstructed by cork trees. Abuela had once been proud of the fact that Salto used to produce the best-quality cork in the world. What Gemma couldn't see, though, and what Rafael knew lay beyond, were orchards of every conceivable type of fruit. Apple, pear, peach, fig, grapefruit, plum and cherry would give way to the hectares of olive groves until finally, rich arable soil farmed for lentil and soy unfurled into a vast carpet of sunflowers. Gemma might not be able to grasp the magnitude of the place but she would certainly be able to smell it: the scent of pine trees hung heavily in the air and the path was blanketed with their needles.

"It's a castle, but I think of it more as a…" As a what? What *did* he think of it? Suddenly what Rafael thought was that he'd not felt this off-kilter in a while. To some extent his previous visit had even been cathartic. Trudging up this path with Emil, within a hair's breadth of the summer house, was different. Rafael felt as though he were the target for some invisible sniper determined to obliterate him with unsettling memories. He wondered if Emil felt the same way. His cousin was certainly on edge, but then that might just be on account of getting his precious bread baked in time.

Gemma was looking at Rafael expectantly.

Once, he replied silently. Once he might have said that Salto was home. *But now?* "Sorry," he said aloud. "*What* did you say?"

Gemma ducked under his arm, holding the branch clear for her friends to pass in front while she and Rafael continued to amble along the narrow path. "You were saying that you thought of this place as more of a…?"

Emil, overhearing, threw Rafael a look over his shoulder; an eyebrow raised.

In response, Rafael pulled down his sunglasses. "I don't know what I was saying," he replied truthfully. "I guess what I meant was that you've not really seen the castle bit. So far, you've seen the Salto back roads and this way round the estate, but when we've finished we'll go up to the 'house'. Technically, it's not a *house*, house. It's more of a monastery."

"Monastery?" Gemma was frowning.

"*Technically*," said Emil, half-turning. "I'd say it's more of a fortress."

"Is this a tongue-twister?" she teased.

"Could be," said Rafael evenly. "Emil is just being pedantic." It was strange talking about his – their – family like this and trying to be objective. It wasn't something he usually had to do. The family was virtually a household name; it didn't need explaining. But all this talk made him feel doubly connected to the place in a way he hadn't for a long time. It made him think, as he had been doing ever since they'd got there, of Ino. "But Emil's right," he added. "Once upon a time, Salto was the most important stronghold in Catalonia. Not wanting to boast," Emil's shake of the head only egged him on, "but our family came second only to the royal family. The Monte Alegres were called 'kings without crowns' because they owned so much land; not just here in Catalonia, but in the whole of Spain." Rafael nodded in his cousin's direction. "I bet *he* didn't tell you that."

Gemma shrugged. "Not in so many words. I kinda guessed… but I never imagined." Her eyes were bulbous.

"And our flag—"

"You mean the Catalan?"

"Yes, I mean the Catalan. La Senyera."

Gemma nodded, smiling confidently, remembering what Emil had told her. "Yeah, I know. The white star on a blue triangle was inspired by the Cuban Revolution."

Rafael shook his head. "No, that's La Senyera Estelada."

"I thought—"

"Look, all '*La Senyera*' means is 'flag,'" explained Rafael patiently. "And the original one belongs to us."

Emil called to the young people who had forged ahead in the wrong direction. The overgrown path had emerged onto a clearing, but the way to the mill was not along the less dense of the two. The youngsters were headed to Sospiro.

"Tell them to come back!" Rafael's tone was harsher than he'd intended.

"I have," snapped Emil.

Gemma looked from one to the other. "What do you mean, 'to us'?" She stopped to take a water bottle out of her rucksack. She looked cool enough in her extraordinary get-up, but her hair was damp. Rafael's once-pristine cashair hung like a dishcloth around her neck. She was using its sleeves to wipe her face.

Rafael tried not to wince.

"Ah, well now, that's interesting," volunteered Emil. "Less a question of when Harry met Sally than when Hairy met Baldy."

Gemma looked suitably blank, but her friends began making the same orgasm-simulating noise Meg Ryan did in the film. When the hilarity ended, Rafael took over the explanation.

"The flag is known as Els Quatre Dits de Sang," he said, holding up the four fingers of his right hand. "The Four Fingers of Blood."

There was still a general titter, with the boys jostling each other and punching the air. Some of the girls were fake-groaning and whispering to each other, throwing back their heads.

"Ignore them," said Gemma. "I'm interested even if they're not! Go on, tell me more."

"Yes, we want more!" sang the boys.

"Oh, buzz off!" said Gemma, calling after them. "Really, I'm interested. Tell me."

"Well," said Rafael as he and Emil began to continue walking, but slowly and at an angle so they could still talk, "as our ancestor – well, mine to be precise – lay dying—"

"Dying?"

"Oh, not recently," said Rafael reassuringly. "This all happened around the ninth century when the wounded Wilfred the Hairy gained his colours. You see, before that battle he didn't have any. The French King, except technically it was West Francia then, Charles the Bald, was so impressed by his bravery and, realising that Wilfred's men would need some sort of banner to follow, offered his own copper shield. Wilfred dipped his fingers in his wound and ran his hand down the shield."

"And that's how we got La Senyera," finished Emil.

"Wow," said Gemma with a sigh. "This is all too weird."

They had emerged onto a clearing, where they were greeted by the unmistakable smell of woodsmoke crackling in the dry air and the galumph of small toads. A cobbled courtyard and arched stone outbuildings comprised the mill and ovens. The young people spread out, shading their eyes in the sudden glare. The *mozos*, who had arrived some time earlier, were already hard at work preparing the ground for the lamb spits.

"This," said Gemma, pulling at her suspenders, "is awesome! I've never seen such a grand-looking mill."

Rafael adjusted his sunglasses, trying to see the familiar buildings through detached eyes. Structures dated from the time of his hirsute ancestor. Moorish arches, Romanesque and Gothic made up what they at Salto loosely dubbed 'the ovens', while the mill was exactly the kind to be seen in illustrated editions of *Don Quixote*. "I suppose…"

"*Hola, Señor Conde*," said the man who had once been Rafael's main groom, darting out from a doorway to greet him. Other stable boys from the polo club emerged from one of the paths leading to the old mill. They were sweaty; their faces covered in soot.

"Just tell me it's working," said Emil anxiously.

There was a pause while Esteban the groom lit a cigarette.

"Oh, give me one, will you?" said Rafael, but Emil restrained the groom as he rooted round in his overall.

"It's working, it's working," Esteban announced.

Emil clasped the man around the shoulders. "*Por fin!*" he exclaimed. "At last!"

Esteban scratched his head under his felt hat. Despite the heat, none of the Argentines ever took off their hats. "Nothing to it," he said evenly. "The ovens were rusty, dirty, full of all kinds of garbage. You wouldn't believe the skeletons: tiny heads—"

"Yes, all right—"

"So, what you're saying is, the bread will bake?" interrupted Gemma.

"*Sí, Señorita,*" Esteban answered her gravely. "The bread and anything else you want will bake."

And it did. By late afternoon, under a sun high in the sky – a round, brilliant orange ball of contoured light – the loaves were all warm and neatly lined up on trestle tables. The only tins available (they'd not brought ones heavy enough for the old ovens) had been the ancient cast-iron moulds bearing the Salto coat of arms. But that couldn't be helped. It added a kind of cachet, Gemma said, proposing that those loaves be set aside, marketed as a luxury item and priced accordingly. Emil readily agreed.

Rafael did too, but delighted in a more subversive interpretation. In this climate of national independence, with Catalonia once again struggling to assert itself, Salto would be associated with resistance and opposition to Madrid. Every man, woman and school-age child would not need reminding that Salto had been the backdrop for the main political and military events that had occurred on the Iberian Peninsula – eternal conflict then, as now, between Catalonia and Spain. There was a delicious symmetry in the fact that then too there had been resistance to another king; another Felipe. Salto, even before recent events, had represented the last stronghold of Catalan freedom. Once again, she could play her part. How utterly delicious it was that, with the simple breaking of bread, this message would be consumed again and again! Amen to that. Yes, the day had turned out surprisingly well.

Rafael felt a welcome lethargy invade his limbs. Through the archway, along the grassy knoll, and on spikes shaped in the form of a cross, dripping in garlic and citric juices, the lambs were splayed on mesh wire. Vigilant Argentines kept watch, poking the resistant meat, while others attached chorizo sausage and offal cuts to hooks, suspending these in metal *tachos* or cylinders. Succulent pieces of pork belly and sweetbread were roasted on the *parilla* which was laid atop mounds of ash left over from the main fire and set aside for the purpose. Rafael found a secluded corner of wall and sat on the ground. Some of the youngsters played cards, sprawled on the dusty courtyard, languid and relaxed, lulled by the heat and the heavy air spliced with the rich aroma of meat and freshly baked bread. Others dozed; others had gone back to the castle cellar to see if there was any wine remaining and returned carrying a crate between them. Rafael felt a gut-wrenching lurch when he saw the date. It was the cava reserved for Ino's eighteenth birthday. One of the *mozos* began playing a pan pipe; the haunting music of the Pampas not so very out of place in this strange, ethereal Salto of theirs. Rafael felt his eyelids droop. His limbs, so tense at the start of the day, were mellow now; merging into the ground, the mosaic history that was Salto…

"*Compadre*."

It was a while before Rafael identified the voice. He must have dozed off, as he was no longer propped up against the hacienda dwelling but slumped, almost lying prone, his feet splayed out in front of him. He'd long ago stopped worrying about getting his shoes or trousers dirty. He sat up, still groggy from sleep, looking about him. There was a cheerful air. Gemma and her friends had made a long, continuous dining table by assembling several ones together. It appeared to extend along the courtyard and beyond the inner archway. Green glass bottles glinted in the sun, and wild flowers arranged in jam jars were splashes of colour against the Byzantine stone. There was also, of course, bread, over which Emil presided like a protective mother hen, swiping away any rogue insect that dared settle on his wares.

"*Compadre*," repeated Esteban. "*Es que…*" he stuttered in Spanish.

"What is it?" Rafael's mouth felt like straw. He could do with some ice-cold cava, and something sweet…

Esteban was twisting his felt cap in one hand while smoothing what looked like a white napkin in the other. "No, no! Nothing bad," he continued in English. "*Es que…*"

Not this again… Rafael felt light-headed. Maybe he needed

sugar more than drink. Maybe he was diabetic, just as Emil was fond of suggesting from time to time? Rafael used to think it was when his cousin was feeling quarrelsome, but what if Emil had picked up on something after all? He'd read somewhere about the symptoms: unusual thirst; light-headedness… Panic seized him. It was entirely possible. He'd have to see a doctor pronto.

"*Compadre*—"

"Now, Esteban," said Rafael, getting unsteadily to his feet. "We aren't going to be ping-ponging like this all evening, are we?"

"No, no."

"Then what is it? Spit it out, man!"

And then he saw that the *mozos* had formed a circle in the courtyard; that one of the trestle tables had a cloth on it; that Esteban was holding out another. For him.

"Many of the *muchachos* are here for the first time," began Esteban. "You know, from Pilar and Pazos Kanki." He mentioned the poorer rural areas of Buenos Aires.

"Ah…" Rafael suddenly dawned. "They're homesick?"

Esteban nodded vigorously. "Yes, but they want – if you would, Padre, *Compadre*…"

"They want to go back?"

"No." Esteban held out the cloth. "They want to hear Mass. They want you to say Mass."

Rafael could not have been more astonished had his grandmother's ghost risen up from the chapel graveyard. "B-but," he stammered, "we have no wine or br…" *Which was a nice try even for you, Rafaelito*, he said to himself later, because of course there was an abundance of both.

A wonderful yeasty smell filled his nostrils even as he took the proffered cloth and *porrons* of Rioja were being passed among the young people. The girls were giggling as the boys tried to drink from the conical spout, with varying degrees of success. Those with white T-shirts looked as though they'd committed murder by the end of it. Rafael draped the cloth around his neck and followed

Esteban to the makeshift altar. Silently, the *mozos* removed their felt hats, falling to their knees – shadows against the setting sun.

Rafael had been reluctant, but now he was moved. In that moment, something shifted. Something changed. Never had he said Mass with such sincerity; never had it meant so much. Never had he really believed. His thoughts turned to the drama of electing a new pontiff – the '*Habemus papam*' moment after which white smoke unfurled towards the sky. Also in the manner of a newly elected pontiff, Rafael kissed the white garment before replacing it around his neck. He held out his arms to the gathered youths. *Acepto*, he thought silently, at last. *Acepto.*

36

Emil
Barcelona
October 2017

It seemed a simple enough favour. In exchange for all the work she had done on the logo, the drawings for the new coat of arms, and the extra hours she'd put in helping out at the *pastelaria* and then of course at Salto itself, Gemma had said there was only one thing she really wanted. That 'thing' turned out to be Emil agreeing to a blind date with Gemma's mother. And much sooner than he'd anticipated. Initially, he'd blithely agreed; the proposition so hypothetical, so far into the future, he'd not given it another thought. Not really believed it would actually happen. Gone were the days when he'd had to deal with anyone's family. He treated Gemma as a young adult, and so he'd been doubly taken aback when she announced the impending arrival of a parent; a somewhat feared one-who-must-be-obeyed kind of parent at that. More importantly, the said parent was in town that very weekend and was free to meet. There was no point in pleading bakery commitments: Gemma knew only too well just how busy he was. He felt the noose tightening even so, but a promise was a promise, and besides, maybe, just maybe, it might be fun to go out with someone in a dress for a change, who wasn't Rafael.

Nevertheless, he was apprehensive entering the lobby of the newly refurbished El Palace. To him it would always be simply the

Ritz – the glamorous hotel frequented by Abuela's mother and King Alfonso XIII in the 1920s. It had undergone many transformations since. It had been a Red Cross shelter during the Civil War before becoming a place of congress for politicians and celebrities from all over the world. Its most recent makeover, however, had also resulted in a name change.

Gemma had chosen the time; Emil had chosen the place. Although not as on-trend as The One, and certainly (God forbid!) not encapsulating the romanticism of the Neri (personally, his favourite), El Palace was the stomping ground of his youth. He knew the staff (or at least, some of them were the *children* of people he'd once known); he could escape if needs be. Sensing his last-minute nerves, Gemma had assured Emil that he would like her mother. Her mother (*Mom*) was super clever and dynamic. And *young*. (Which didn't mean much – these days, everyone looked young to Emil.) There was another thing. Gemma's class attendance had been poor – actually, 'poor' was an understatement. She'd not signed in for a month. Emil was to plead her case, emphasise her natural creativity, say that she was better suited to a career in art rather than languages. It wasn't blackmail exactly, but they both knew just how much time Gemma and her friends had given to saving the *pastelaria*, to baking bread, to turning out the little loaves onto the long metal sheets as they cooled in the sun…

Emil spotted 'Mom' before she saw him. And for a moment, for a split second, he thought he was in a time warp; that, moving through the hotel's revolving doors, he had stepped back twelve years; that the woman waiting for him was Ino. She was undeniably beautiful. He'd always fancied brunettes, and there was something of the Ino that was in this older Indian woman. There was also a sleekness and confidence to Nancy Skinner that had been absent in the young Ino. Emil wondered fleetingly if Ino too had since acquired this maturity. He rather hoped not. Nancy was dressed in a simple V-necked dress with a diaphanous asymmetric overlay that managed to be both demure and sexy. She wore Hermès slides

– the season's latest must-have – and an Hermès Birkin in the same tan colour conquered the ground at her feet. She was exactly the kind of woman he would have homed in on when he was young, and precisely the kind of woman he now found about as attractive to be with as a coiled python. If he could have turned on his heel and fled, he would have done. He desperately needed a cigarette, and while he was willing to wing it in lesser establishments, he knew that lighting up in this hotel would guarantee him being thrown out. The manager was a friend, and Emil didn't want to upset him either. He was on the verge of visiting the little boys' room – there used to be an exit onto the street where he could have a smoke – when Gemma appeared from behind a pillar.

"Emil!" she cried, her face alight with genuine pleasure. Her cheeks were flushed; her eyes danced. She looked different, and then he realised that she was wearing a dress for once and her normally messy hair was brushed out – a bit lopsided, but still becoming.

"Am I glad to see you," he said with feeling.

"Have you met my mom yet?" She tugged at his hand and he could feel the weight of expectation through the pressure of her fingers. He knew how much she wanted him to like her mother. He knew in that moment that she wanted it to be more.

"Is that her?" he said, motioning in the direction of the lounge area, knowing full well that it couldn't be anyone else. She was the only Indian woman there. Besides, she looked like Gemma. The lobby was filling with tourists: young people in jeans, exposed midriffs and – horror of all horrors – flip-flops! (Emil had a complete aversion to feet.) There were older American men sporting baseball caps and trainers, but no other Asians. For a moment he had a vision of earlier times, when women wore pretty frocks and men starched linen suits (not the wrinkly, wilting English variety either) just because it was, after all, the Ritz.

Gemma nodded proudly. "She's great, isn't she?"

"What?"

Gemma blinked, and Emil sensing tears, was quick to reassure.

"Oh yes... yes," he said uncomfortably. With every passing moment, though, he was having second thoughts. He hadn't been on a *date* date for years. There'd been women, of course, but none of the relationships had lasted very long.

"I mean, she looks so young, don't you think?"

Emil was momentarily distracted by the names engraved on the wall above Nancy's head. The list of famous people who'd visited the hotel read like a who's who of the twentieth century. "I'm sorry?"

Gemma was looking at him. And so too, from across the room, was Nancy, probably wondering what was taking him so long. There would never be time enough was the truth of it. He felt panicked – worse, exhausted – by the prospect of dinner, and just as nervous as when he'd cantered onto the field on a skittish pony. He also felt caught between the two of them: the girl standing in front of him (making the idea of scarpering wishful thinking) and the mother perched on the sofa with those aggressive Hermès sandals trained in his direction. Like a sniper with a target in her sights. He'd never liked Hermès, although come to think of it he did like Patrick; a scion of that god of trade. They'd played polo together on several occasions in Sotogrande before the... Gemma was looking at him now with that *Don't you dare!* look; the *You promised!* look.

Emil resorted to a lame, "She's very beautiful."

Gemma beamed. "Well, I'll see you guys later, then."

Later? He caught her arm. "What? Aren't you staying for dinner? Aren't you coming too?"

"Are you kidding?" Gemma winked. "What would be the point of that?"

Oh God! Every point! If Emil was going to go a step further, he would *have* to have a cigarette. "I guess we'll survive without you," he heard himself say, with a brightness he was far from feeling.

But something in his voice made Gemma soften. She patted his arm. "Just let her talk about her work."

"Apart from her best production, of course?" *Ouch!* He waited for the withering put-down, but to his amazement Gemma seemed delighted.

"Well, you'll find out, won't you?"

Nancy, looking up at that moment, caught his eye. And didn't look away.

"Catch you later," Emil mouthed to Gemma, who, smiling broadly, turned on a tattooed ankle and disappeared through the revolving doors. A passing waiter gave him a knowing look which Emil ignored and, giving up on the lifeline of a smoke, valiantly crossed the marble floor.

"Emil," said Nancy without moving.

Her voice was tinny; American. It sent shivers through his teeth but his old self kicked in. He found himself bowing over her hand and kissing the air above it, languidly settling into the deep sofa opposite her. Adopting a pose of supreme calm, he raised an arm, ordering... *Champagne? Yes, champagne – not cava. God, no!* And being... well, being what was expected of him.

"Ooohh!" said Nancy. "Gemma said you were one of those old-fashioned types."

"We can have drinks here," he said, unbuttoning his cream linen (and, truth be told, somewhat tight) Ermenegildo Zegna jacket. "And then we can go to a place I know. Barcelona has a lot of fun bars." *And then I can smoke!*

Nancy dropped her mobile into her bag – the bag that had probably cost more than a small flat in Sarrià – and uncrossed her legs. Loose veils of chiffon fell about a toned, taut body. She shook her fringe; a smooth curtain of hair that skimmed perfectly arched brows. From every angle her face was beautiful – there was no 'bad' side. She grinned, showing lots of teeth. She was clearly up for it and until she opened her mouth he might just have been tempted, but her too-loud laugh seemed insincere – he *knew* he wasn't that funny – making him uneasy. Every sentence ended on a question mark, which confused him. And when it came, she drank most of the bottle in double-quick time. "So, what are we waiting for?" she said when he'd barely finished his own single glass of fizz.

She jumped to her feet like a gymnast coming off an exercise bar. He half-expected her to do a backwards flip. But she didn't. Instead, she yanked him to his with such force she stumbled against him. For a hideous moment he thought they'd both go down, but he managed to steady her, holding her firmly at arm's length. An eternity seemed to pass as they grappled silently. She wasn't giving up so easily, though. She managed to duck from under his arm and position herself in the crook of his shoulder. In a direct triangle of sunlight, he could make out the fine down on her cheeks. And all at once, he lost his appetite – appetite for everything. His expression was determined as he walked her as quickly as he dared towards the hotel lobby, guiding her past open spaces that seemed to consist entirely of cut glass, mirrors and black marble. The scent of gardenia reminded him of Monte Alegre.

"Señor Conde," said Sancho the doorman, who'd known Emil all his life.

"*Conde?*" echoed Nancy.

Emil grimaced. "For my sins. It's not important."

She smoothed the immaculate linen of his sleeve. "Oh, it is to me, honey, it is to me."

"Vallvidrera," Emil instructed the driver of a waiting taxi, when they were out on the busy pavement of the Gran Via de les Corts. He muttered something about it being the longest street in Catalonia, cutting across the entire city proper, and that its name had changed several times depending on the government in power.

But Nancy wasn't interested. "Vallvi-*what*?" she said, tripping over her Birkin.

"You'll see." He grabbed the offending handbag and bundled it and Nancy none too gracefully into the back.

Despite his initial misgivings, he felt a heady rush as they left the city, leaving behind thoughts of the *pastelaria* and Salto, and sped towards the mountains. For the duration of the drive, at least, Nancy seemed intent on garnering her wits, and was silent.

"Tell me about your work," Emil said, remembering Gemma's advice, when they were at last installed on the rooftop terrace of one of Emil's favourite bars. Located within Tibidabo Amusement Park, it commanded spectacular views of Barcelona. Tibidabo was a corruption of the Latin 'I give you', he told her, and said to be the place where Satan had tempted Jesus.

"Uh-huh?" said Nancy in response to this apocryphal tale, more intent on cleaning her knife with her napkin and then examining her teeth in its reflection. "So… it's another road trip, yeah? From San Fran down to Louis Obispo," she was saying now, her head nodding in agreement with herself. "God, I love this dinnerscape." Her neat brown hands caressed the shiny mosaic tabletop.

Emil suppressed a wild desire to laugh out loud. He'd never heard a place setting described in such a way. But now that he looked around him, he realised that this place too had changed since his last visit. Glassware in cool hues of green, purple and blue followed a Moroccan theme, while synchronised lighting enhanced the bar area itself. He was barely able to identify the jewel-size canapés hidden among the tiny cacti.

"What's so funny?" She smiled broadly, but he could tell she wasn't at all sure why he was smiling. She made small blowing gestures (her fringe got in her eyes), and her foot brushed his repeatedly. She had ordered – rather than allowing him to – another bottle of Rioja. The wrong bottle; the wrong year. She was already directing the waiter, telling him about her company.

"Where did you say?" Emil said out of politeness, attempting to resume their conversation.

"San Luis Obispo." She pronounced it as an American might, not a Latin.

"The sainted Luis…"

"What? Yeah, I guess, yeah."

Emil sat back in his chair, shoulders at right angles to her and the rest of the terrace. This way he could appear to be listening to her while keeping an eye on what was happening *behind* her. But he was bored. He frowned. Almost everything about Nancy grated now. Not only her question-mark punctuation, but her lacquered nails, and the way she held her cutlery. "Don't conduct the orchestra!" was what Emil and Rafa's *niñera* (or nanny) used to say. Nancy had two orchestras going on. Emil leaned forward to remove the knife that she wasn't using from her hand. And then, so as to appear less rude, covered her lips with his finger. Briefly. Almost at once, he realised his mistake. For a terrifying, heart-stopping moment he thought she might suck his finger.

She downed another glass of wine and let the curtain of hair fall over her face. "So, I was thinking, yeah?" She shovelled a slice of Manchego onto a crust of *pa amb tomàquet*. "Gemma's been talking about this place of yours. You could go big – *real* big. I mean, there are loads of Hispanics where I live. And you could expand. Why not bring out a skinny bread?"

Emil's glass was halfway to his mouth. "A *what*?"

"A skinny bread." Her tongue caressed her lips.

"How would that work?" Emil's tone was harsh, dispelling any idea that this was some sort of foreplay. And now, much to Nancy's irritation, he positively welcomed the reappearance of the waiter, asking him all kinds of silly questions.

"We have partners in different cities in the States," Nancy was saying, pulling at Emil's arm to draw his attention back to her. Unlike her face, her strong, lean forearms were completely hairless. She was certainly into perfect grooming, which was something he always appreciated, but her demeanour seemed at odds with the masculinity of her delivery. There was nothing soft nor cosy about her. Despite the outward trappings to the contrary, she wasn't feminine. "We can pass the rebranding over to them. Yeah? I can see the billboards already!" Her fingers spread, fanlike. "You remember that ad for Coppertone or whatever the hell it was called then? With the dog pulling down the kid's pants?"

Emil did remember. He'd also thought it incredibly tacky, on a par with the enormous bulls advertising Jerez sherry that could be seen beside motorways all over Spain. Nancy bared teeth that were so exaggeratedly white they could have lit the way to their table. He imagined them detached from the rest of her face like a dentist's anatomy model. He idly wondered what sex with her would be like – vigorous, no doubt; *devouring*. The thought was distracting. Perversely, might it be therapeutic, though, to be devoured whole; reduced to nothing; obliterated? He allowed a flicker of attraction to fizz between them. Could he forget? That was the question.

"We need something equally provocative," she said suggestively. "But it has to be clean."

"Sure. Yeah." *Yes, yes!* He'd say anything if it meant forgetting once and for all. Forget the whole damn thing. And perhaps this was the woman to make him do it.

"Yeah?" She seemed startled by his spark of interest, red nails tapping against her wine glass. Emil glanced at them too. Like her shoulders, they were also square, as though the manicurist had got bored and just hacked across them.

"Yes." He shook his head. "No – I mean, no." It was his turn to pour more Rioja – the one he'd ordered and not yet finished. Nursing the glass, he took a sip, savouring the richness and earthiness of the grape; the result of patience in a process unaltered in centuries. And something else. An understanding of temperament.

"We need to shout difference," she was saying. "As a female CEO in a male-dominated industry, it feels right to own the brand. Adding the old lady dough—"

Dough? What was she talking about? "*Perdón.* I'm sorry," he said. "What did you say exactly?"

She blinked, scratched her head, her hair extensions sticky in the heat. "What? Which bit?"

"Were you referring to *Bocado de Damas*?" He was incredulous, taking another sip to steady himself. *Paciencia… calma…*

"Yeah… yes, I was. I was talking about the old lady stuff."

"Is that what you call it?"

Nancy also took a sip (except it was more of a wine-glass gulp), emitting a throaty laugh. "Well, yeah… it is, though, isn't it?"

Inwardly, Emil recalibrated his thoughts. Outwardly, he poked in his cactus for a thimble-size dollop of cauliflower mush. What *was* this country coming to? These anorexic-enabling portions weren't tapas! And you couldn't call this a date! What was he doing here, listening to this drivel? What was she talking about? She hadn't really called the jewel in his crown an 'old lady dough', had she? "I don't know where to begin. How to answer."

But Nancy wasn't interested in helping him do that. "So… yeah…" she continued. "It reflects the current vogue for embracing vegan and organic products." She was warming to her subject, her head wagging from side to side in a decidedly Indian fashion. And she had kicked off her shoes – or shoe, at least; her toes were tickling his bare ankle. Like all style-conscious European males in summer, Emil wore shoes without socks. Her nails scratched his shin. "At the moment, we offer witty eco packaging. Your stuff needs to be just as sexy and playful as the rest of our products, and of course, given the general climate, intergenerational and non-binary."

Witty? Non-binary? Emil rubbed his chin. "You want to do all that with… *bread*?"

Nancy regarded him oddly, as though he were an oversized teen. Give them another couple of hours and Emil suspected she'd have said, "Well, *duh*." She was nodding again. Everything she said appeared to be a two-way process, as though she were running everything by an inner competitor first. "Yeah. Bread is just a product like any other," she explained patiently. "I've done it with beverages; I'll do it with this." She tapped her glass, motioning to the waiter to fill it up, as the bottle from which she'd been liberally helping herself was now empty. "Same again, amigo."

"A she-wolf," Emil said aloud, but thinking to himself, *That's what women like her were called in medieval times.* Rafael would be proud of him. Something from all those church visits had stuck after all.

"Pardon?"

Emil took a swig of ice from his water and began crunching it. An irritating habit of his, he knew. Rafael would be less proud of that. He spoke, ice melting on the tip of his tongue. He hoped he didn't choke. A distant cousin of his (neither Ino's nor Rafa's) had died choking on an ice cube at a cocktail party. Would he tell Nancy that? "A she-wolf is a female grey—"

"I know what a wolf is!" snapped Nancy. "What the hell has that to do with bread." This time, it wasn't a question.

Emil took in the bundle of fury she was fast becoming and once again suppressed a terrible boyish urge to laugh. The Rioja, on the other hand, was a good year. Smooth and understated. "With bread? Why, nothing; nothing at all."

"Then…?"

"I was just thinking about – well, women, for example, like… well, like Isabella of Anjou."

Nancy's head jerked up. "Who? Isabella who?"

Emil smiled; he knew where this was going. The wine had taken the edge off his appetite. Just as well, given the doll-sized portions he'd seen coming out of the kitchen. "It really doesn't matter."

"No, it does." Nancy gulped down half a glass of the newly poured wine. "Does this Isabella live in San Fran? More importantly, *should* I know her? Can you get your sec to call mine? What's her Twitter feed like?"

Emil set his glass down carefully in front of him. Secretly amused, he kept his tone neutral. "Dead, I believe."

Nancy's eyelids flickered violently. "What? How can the feed be dead?" (Flick, flick.) "Don't you *want* this to work?"

She reached for his hand; except he wasn't convinced she wasn't going to pinch him. They began to play a cat-and-mouse game across the table until her hand, moving, crablike, towards his, pounced to hold his hand in a vice-like grip. But the more he wiggled his fingers, trying to edge sideways, the tighter her hold became. For a moment they played a feeble (feeble on his part, anyway) tug of war until he gave up and let her hold him. It was only when he rather desperately motioned to the waiter that she released him.

Emil pulled out his wallet and, dismissing the younger man's attempts to offer them more tapas or even the dinner menu, said curtly, "Just the bill. I can settle right away," he added, as the waiter looked as though he might disappear for another half an hour.

"'Just the bill'?" echoed Nancy incredulously. Her dangly earrings were bobbing frantically. "Are we going someplace else? We haven't had... like... *dinner*?"

The waiter had returned in double-quick time, leaving a fat leather pad with a piece of paper pinned to one end. Emil tucked a wad of banknotes under the clip.

"You're kidding, right?"

Emil hesitated only briefly. "Nope. Sorry, I mean, no." He reached into his pocket for change. "It's contagious." He motioned to her mouth. "The American way of speaking, that is."

He anticipated a sharp intake of breath, but not the slap. All at once, her attractive features rearranged themselves into a snarl.

He got to his feet, making a small bow. "I've paid for your taxi back to your hotel," he said. "But you should know, my bread isn't just a product. And the *Bocado de Damas* aren't either. At least, not to me. It may not be the most unique thing in the world but it has cachet, even if only in Catalonia."

Afterwards, hopping into a cab of his own, Emil reflected on the disastrous date. He felt a pang at the thought of Gemma's disappointment, but no regret for anything else. Nancy was brash and he'd been harsh, and somewhere in between had been a flicker of base attraction. But somewhere along the way, too, the evening had turned competitive; in the context of dating it was not something that ever excited him. On the contrary, it chased away desire. He'd found her attractive enough to begin with, but by the time he'd said goodbye, any chemistry between them had completely dissolved.

He patted his jacket pocket. "Mind if I…?" he began.

The taxi driver shook his head. "I'll join you."

Emil tapped the packet, sliding a cigarette towards the driver, who reached over one shoulder to pull it from the box. Emil lit the man's tobacco and then his own. He leaned back in the car, his elbow resting on the open window. "Nice evening," he said inanely.

"Yes," agreed the driver, inhaling so deeply Emil thought he'd swallowed the cigarette *entera*; whole.

"Trying to give up, by any chance?"

"I *was*. I blame the politicians. They've got me smoking again. The stress they've put us under – the stress they've put our *families* under! Everyone's at each other's throats. The wife has moved out of the bedroom. Says she won't sleep with a *Spaniard*. Have you ever heard anything so stupid? And don't get me started on those pigs from Madrid!"

Emil smiled. Madrileños would always be viewed with distrust by Catalans, and recent events had only fanned old grievances. Soon Carlos (the *taxista*) and Emil were on a first-name basis. The tobacco appeared to have loosened Carlos's tongue. He lamented Puigdemont's decision to flee the country after promising to lead the people in their struggle. Yes, agreed Emil, it was a great shame. He didn't like to add that it was also cowardly – having left his deputies to face the music, they had promptly been arrested and refused bail. Carlos didn't have the vocabulary to express what he thought about that! Emil did, but didn't want a heated discussion now either. The cigarette had calmed him and he wanted to remain that way. After all, it was still a lovely evening, even taking into account the Nancy debacle.

"Agreed," he said. "I agree with everything you say – *con todo lo que usted diga.*"

"So, my friend, *you* should be a politician." Carlos caught his eye in the rear-view mirror. "Would they all could be so diplomatic."

Emil was silent. Being called diplomatic was a first. They were zipping along at breakneck speed, dodging motorbikes and only just slowing down when they came to a red light. But Emil's thoughts had slipped far away: not to reliving the evening at all, but to acknowledging why Nancy's comments about his *bocados* had so riled him. And in understanding why they had, he appreciated the confectionery's sentimental importance, and how it was that he'd come to develop them in the first place.

37

Emil
Bourg-Madame
No Date

Once upon a time, in order to forget what had happened, Emil travelled the breadth of Europe, and then when the distance between him and Salto wasn't enough to abolish the remaining traces of residual emotion, he went further, taking a train from the Urals to Kazan. But not even freezing in Kamchatka or suffering frostbite in Alaska had numbed his mental anguish, so he pressed on eastward. From Anchorage he flew to British Colombia and then, knowing instinctively that he would be more comfortable in Spanish-speaking Latin America, headed south for San Francisco. Feeling the familiar cadences of language beat down the barriers of self-preservation, he crossed from California into Mexico. In Tulum on the Yucatán Peninsula, far beneath the Mayan ruins and with the crashing waves of the Caribbean Sea whipping away his only pair of sunglasses before knocking him to the ocean's bed, he found, if not peace, then a kind of resignation. But still he was not ready to return home. Instead, armed with a borrowed copy of a biography of Simon Bolívar, he retraced the Liberator's footsteps, attempting to understand the violence, courage and terrible boldness of his ancestors.

By now with a penchant for border towns, he found himself visiting three in one day, criss-crossing Paraguay, Brazil and

Argentina before flying to Paris from Buenos Aires. Having intended to fly direct to Barcelona he experienced a last-minute panic at the thought of seeing Abuela, of seeing Sol's family, and at the absence of beloved others. Changing his flight for Paris instead, he decided he would return to Salto on foot and through the Pyrenees. Except that when, so many months later, Emil finally reached that funny little place called Llívia – a Spanish enclave surrounded by France – he lingered, isolated from his memories by the 1.6-kilometre corridor that separated it from the rest of Spain. Until, that is, one morning when, sitting in a small coffee shop in Bourg-Madame, exhausted from his hike through the mountain range near Port de la Selva, he ordered bread rolls and *jamón iberico*.

For months now, he'd not been hungry. Since he'd set off on his travels two years before, he'd lost some fifteen kilos and was the lightest he'd been since he was a teenager. But there was a certain aroma in the shop – the smell of freshly baked bread; the bread of their own Salto – that attracted him. He ordered at the small counter from a cautious middle-aged woman who eyed him with curiosity. She placed a cafetière on the table alongside a basket of piping hot rolls. He poured the steaming coffee and bit into a roll, and there it was. Not quite the Proustian madeleine, but something just as meaningful. Suddenly, all the summers of Emil's youth came rushing back to him: the long, boring days of Easter when he and Rafael were supposed to be studying for exams they failed on a regular basis; longing only to be on their ponies and on the polo field. And then later he could almost taste the romance that was Ino, the scent of her skin and hair. He could almost feel her under him once again, her hands on him. No woman subsequently had ever moved him in the same way, nor ever would. He almost choked.

"*No està bueno?*" The woman behind the counter scurried forward with a glass of water. "Is no good?" Although her hair was grey and deep lines on either side of her nose cupped her mouth, she was beautiful. Her voice was beautiful even when sharpened by intrinsic concern.

Emil shook his head, tears spurting. "No, it's good – almost too good," he stuttered. "The bread is delicious." Actually, it was more than delicious. It was the best food he'd had in the entire time he'd been away.

"Ah." She looked confused. "*Pues?*"

"*Pues?*" *Pues* what? He could still taste home on his tongue, that's what, even after swallowing the last crumb. He could taste the robust crust; the dewy, soft *mie* that was never the cardboard, fabricated, pre-frozen stuff he'd had everywhere else.

"You like... bread?" she said. And he knew the question was complex.

Emil nodded.

For a moment her mouth twitched halfway to a smile, halfway to expressing the growing excitement she was feeling at stumbling across a fellow bread aficionado. "Come, I show you."

He tore the end piece from another new roll and, coupling it with *jamón*, crammed both into his mouth before kicking his rucksack into a corner. He was experiencing an unassuageable hunger.

"*Poc a poc!*" she chastised in Catalan, but chased with a smile in much the way Nuria had scolded him when he was a child. *Slowly! Eat slowly!*

Knowing that something was about to change in him; that whatever he had been looking for over the past few years was, in part, to be found here in this small village, he scrunched up his paper napkin, grabbed another quick gulp of coffee and followed her past the white-tiled lobby to the area at the back. Outdoors was a wood oven with a cast-iron door that threw off heat and cooked neat, uneven loaves.

"This is our mistress," she said proudly. "She has governed through dictatorships, republics, civil wars, times of hardship, times of success – most importantly, she has fed the hungry. She endures."

Emil felt the warm metal as though touching the flank of a horse. "The same?"

"The very same." The woman held out her hand, flicking her hair over one shoulder at the same moment. "Carmen." She introduced herself.

"Emil," said Emil, bowing and holding her hand an inch from his lips. It had been a long time since a salutation had been required of him.

When she smiled there were traces of the beautiful young woman she'd been once. "Your hand is still warm," she said, before adding, almost to herself, "I don't think I've ever had my hand kissed before." She turned back to the enormous stove. "But it's not just about the oven," she continued, her voice businesslike once again. "In this case, an original one. No." She moved to the little shelves where dough was slowly rising. "It begins, most importantly, with the wheat. We use ancient varieties, indigenous to Catalonia. But that's not all. It's a process – a long fermentation at mild temperatures – and above all it's about time; it's about *paciencia*. To make great bread you must have patience. There is the baker and then there is the creator. They are different things. Not everyone succeeds."

She spun, suddenly girlish, on her heel and held his forearm. She seemed to be peering into his very soul, and yet he was not embarrassed. On the contrary, he needed this woman, this stranger, to know just how lost he really was.

"Do you have time, Don Emil?" she said, and he knew that because he had kissed her hand, he was now 'Don'; that, unwittingly, he had revealed something about himself. But he didn't mind. In fact, he wanted her to know everything about him. He was tired of pretending.

He hesitated only briefly. "All the time you need," he said, and meant it.

Carmen grabbed an overall that was folded over a rack beside the oven. She handed it to him. "Then let's begin."

"*Now?*"

She smiled, amused. "You said you had time, no?"

"Yes," he agreed. "You're right, I did."

"In that case," she said, "let's go. You'll need these too." She kicked a pair of plastic overshoes in his direction.

Emil looked blank.

She smiled, moving ahead. "Oh, don't look so alarmed! We begin at the beginning; we follow the source…"

Scrambling into the overall Carmen had provided, Emil, with still one leg to go, followed, hopping on one foot.

Hunkering down, she lifted a trapdoor, under which rushed a natural spring. "Outside." She dropped the lid within inches of his toes. "*Sígame.* Follow me."

Emil shoved his feet into the overshoes and followed Carmen through a narrow door, as though following Lucy and her siblings through the wardrobe to Narnia. And, like Narnia, they appeared to have stepped into another world. A collection of outbuildings surrounded a cobbled courtyard. Neat canvas bags lined stone walls, bursting with wheat. Water carried through channels powered the hydraulic mill that stood turning its giant sails above them. Emil shielded his eyes, watching the blades slice through segments of blue sky.

"Do you know the process?" asked Carmen, grabbing a handful of what Emil thought looked like grass.

He was about to say that he did, although not well, but something made him stay silent. He would wipe his mind clear of everything and learn from the beginning.

"First you must separate the chaff – you see, we want only the wheat berries." She ran her hands through a sack-load of prepared kernels. "In the old days it was done by the wind; that's why we call it winnowing: the wind would blow away the chaff, leaving the heavier berry to fall to the ground…"

He let her talk on; her voice was soothing. How many times had he heard Rafael leaf through the Bible for references to farming? It must be every novice's favourite sermon. *Behold, he winnows barley at the threshing floor...* Emil's attention did not waver as Carmen showed him the old-fashioned grinder with its huge stone disc. He listened, too, as she explained once again the importance of slow fermentation, how the quality of the water itself mattered, how the wheat was still selected by hand, and that there were two varieties to be found in Catalonia.

It was only as they sat in the sun many hours later, sharing a bottle of *tinto*, and munching on more bread because Emil couldn't get enough of it, that he allowed himself to think of Salto. In telling Carmen about his place of birth, he did not describe the *castillo* itself, with its vaulted ceilings and patios. He did not elaborate on its history as a former Visigoth settlement where excavated Roman baths still meant the soil was naturally irrigated and fertile. He did not recount a single anecdote involving monks and robbers and Civil War brigands. His mind skirted the chapel, stables, wine cellars, water fountains, olive groves, and wonderful orchards bursting with fig, orange and *níspero*. It did not once, even momentarily, alight on Sospiro.

In answer to her questions, instead it found purchase as it hovered over and then settled on Salto's abandoned mill. He felt his heart kick-start, jolted into a semblance of its former life. So just maybe, he was alive after all. He took another swig of wine, a fistful of black grapes, and stretched his long legs out in front of him. They sat companionably, their backs against warm brick, discussing bread making, Pablo Neruda, and unhappy love affairs. It was certainly then that Emil felt the first stirrings of a different kind of passion: a love for and with bread making. Later in the evening he took pleasure in describing *Bocado de Damas*. He tried to evoke the daintiness of their slender cinnamon stripes, brushed all over with the faintest dusting of icing sugar. He confided that some months before, while contemplating the Torres del Paine, he'd vowed that one day he would create his own version, made from his own wheat. Sitting with this French Catalan woman in her ancient mill, he also recognised something else: that his journey was coming to an end; that before too long he might even be ready to go home.

Archie

Montreal General Hospital
Cedar Avenue

You say that you still care; that we are friends. No 'friend' does to me what you have; no lover treats the beloved as you have, as you are treating me. You're scared I'll be angry!!! Of course I'm angry. This is on you. Remember that. You and you alone. 'Alone'; 'uncertain' – those aren't excuses! I'm alone; I'm uncertain. I'm in another country with hideous people I can hardly understand and who certainly don't understand me! You have the advantage of being in your home town. You have a husband. There. I've written the damn word. Husband and child. When did you think I'd find out? When were you going to tell me?

What do you want from me now?
Leave me alone.
A.

38

Rafael and Emil
Barcelona
October 2017

"Now..." said Rafael.

"Now?" echoed Emil, surprised at the energy behind his cousin's usually languid voice.

There were spreadsheets and bank statements strewn all over the tiny table. Emil's laptop sat precariously beside a pot of coffee and packs of coloured ink pens. He still preferred to work things out by hand. On another table, Gemma and her friends were happily mocking up the new logo for the printers. To his immense relief, Nancy hadn't disclosed much to her daughter. For his part, Emil had explained as diplomatically as possible (maybe there was something in the *taxista's* compliment after all) that as much as he liked Nancy, it would never be 'that way'. Given Gemma's initial enthusiasm, she had taken the news remarkably well. In fact, Emil had been a little miffed at how well. It didn't matter, she had reassured him, as Nancy was in a long-term relationship anyway, with some guy in New York who'd set up his own investment house. Emil was secretly pleased that the man was in a profession he had never respected. In his head, he was already one of those bogeymen who created easy pickings for amoral speculators.

The 'closed' sign tapped against the open door as the balmy breeze wafted through the shop. Emil was chain-smoking, an ashtray full to the brim with cigarette butts nestled on a chair all to itself beside him. Rafael sat facing him – in theory to provide moral support, but in reality Emil's cousin seemed to be on a mission to eat him clean out of stock. But Emil was in a forgiving mode. After all, the cousins had pulled off the extraordinary. And they couldn't stop talking about it: what they'd done, how they'd done it, and the aftermath. It was by far their favourite topic of conversation – actually, it was their *only* conversation. They congratulated themselves on restarting the old ovens at Salto, marvelling at how, when baked, the *Bocado de Damas* had been delivered on time, repackaged and rebranded. Best of all had been the sight of some twenty Argentine grooms who had never led anything more volatile than a skittish pony, suddenly in charge of thirty schoolkids (mostly girls), seven hundred loaves of bread (not including the *bocados*) and ten altar boys.

"You know we must have broken every law in terms of health and safety, never mind child protection."

Emil shot Rafael a withering look. "So sue me."

"Just saying. You have to admit that Nancy…" Rafael threw Gemma a sideways glance. "She was *fantástica*, no? The way she coordinated everyone. Put appeals out there on Facebook and Twitter."

"No!"

"No?" Rafael's antenna was spiked. He sat up.

"I mean, yes – in that, yes."

"What do you mean, 'in that'? Was there something more? *Joder*. There was, wasn't there?" Rafael's eyes were positively ablaze with curiosity.

"For God's sake, keep your voice down." Emil nodded in Gemma's direction. "And no, nothing happened. And yes, she was amazing. But you know all that. The YouTube clip was especially useful." Actually, why Nancy had decided to help him he would never know. But he wasn't about to divulge anything to his cousin.

"Now…" began Rafael again.

"Not this again."

"Well, I've been trying to tell you."

"Okay, so spit it out. And it's no to any hot food, in case you're asking," Emil added testily, eyes swivelling to the door. *Closed means closed even to you, hermano!*

"No, not that."

"What, then?"

Emil was vaguely aware of Rafael rifling through his trouser pocket. He wriggled some more, straightening his legs under the table and lifting his bottom clear of the chair. He knocked the table.

"*Cuidado!*" said Emil, irritated. "Isn't it time for matins or whatever?"

"*Joder!*" Rafael swore.

"*Rafa!*"

More wriggling; another thump. It was like having a small child. Gemma and her friends were less trouble.

"Okay. Okay."

Emil looked up, pausing in his calculations. "You've lost something?"

"Aha!" Rafael sat up again. "I've never prayed so hard – well, relative to the problem." Managing to steer a course through the obstacle course of paraphernalia, he slid a jewellery pouch across the table. "*Qué susto!* I've rarely been so afraid! Couldn't remember what I'd done with it. I even began to doubt that little Maltese nun who does the laundry. Mea culpa."

Emil rolled his eyes and began laboriously filling in a spreadsheet. He had half a mind to get one of Gemma's mates to do the work; *they* typed so much faster.

"You know, you could just do that directly."

"Thanks, but I prefer to do it my way. What is this?" Emil barely glanced at the pouch. "The bishop's ring?"

There was a pause. "No, Ino's," said Rafael. "She… er… misplaced it once." *Ha! That's got his attention*, he thought, noting the way Emil stopped typing; the way his eyes narrowed with suspicion.

But the tic flickering in his cheek was a giveaway. Had Emil always cared so much? Rafael felt a pang of envy – a venial sin if ever there was one. He might dress it up as something else, explain it away, but it was envy all right. Rafael was envious of his cousin's ability to feel or care so passionately (even if the feeling was painful) about *anything*. Did *he*? Had he ever? He had entered the priesthood with intentional ignorance; a hardened heart more to do with apathy than conscience. It had not increased the voluntary character of sin as defined by Thomas Aquinas. In Rafael, *all* feeling had been neutralised. How very puzzling. Perhaps it *was* time for matins.

"Ah!" was all Emil said now, much to Rafael's disappointment. Didn't he even *want* to know how Rafael had come to have Ino's ring in his possession?

Emil shrugged again, carrying on with his typing. Apparently not.

Okay, cosí, you can pretend disinterest all you like but I have something else tucked up my sleeve! Rafael reached for Emil's half-smoked cigarette and took a drag.

"*Oye!*" said Emil.

"*Ojo*," countered Rafael with a sharp intake of tobacco. He coughed at its strength and his unfitness. "Pay attention. The '*problema*' we spoke of recently has become reality. I've booked flights. Ino needs us. We're going to England."

Archie

Cedar Avenue

Yes, I am calmer now. A bit. Not sure why. **Maybe I am just resigned.**

This is a brave new world with a climate not unlike the one we have known, briefly, together. The harshness despite the modernity does not fail to surprise me. If <u>I</u> find it difficult, how much more so must the early settlers have done?! I am in awe when I think of those people leaving everything they had known, everything they had loved, to brave the fierce, merciless seas and arrive here in this godforsaken, relentless cold.

You say you are experiencing frosts like no other; that you are cut off from the nearest village and the one snow plough can't get through. Well, that's bonny Scotland for you. Let me tell you – we've had the worst winter here in years. Here's something to mull over when you're tucked up with hubby and kinder: it's colder here than in the Gale Crater on Mars! It was minus thirty-five – everyone has flu; staff have called in sick.

I'm living at the hospital at the moment – it's easier that way. Besides, what's there to go home to, eh? And why would I want to live any more underground than I already do?

The winter here is lived in the dark. No darker than my thoughts; no darker than you have made them. Two thousand snow blowers are out on the streets and not one can chase away the greyness in my soul.

39

Emil and Rafael
Winchester
October 2017

As they sped along the M3 towards Hampshire, leaving London by the same route as he had done on that last momentous day, Emil couldn't help feeling both excited and apprehensive. But it was a different kind of emotion from the one he'd experienced prior to his date with Nancy. He knew exactly why he should be feeling anxious now. He was only surprised that Rafael should be feeling just as nervous. They had both virtually chain-smoked since arriving and the car rental was already beginning to smell like one of those seedy bars in the Carrer Petritxol, its ashtray overflowing with cigarette butts and discarded matches. Normally finicky to the point of obsession, Rafael hadn't hesitated in throwing his discarded coffee cups on the floor and, because he needed fortifying for the drive, had bought a packet of Jaffa Cakes – a stranger concoction Emil had yet to taste – and half-eaten biscuits wrapped in cellophane were newly ground into the rubber mat as well.

It was a bumpy drive. In addition to the repeated flicking of ash and crumbs from his lap (which meant the car lurched sideways), Rafael seemed to think that the only way to tackle roundabouts was to circle them twice or even three times. With no prior warning, he kept veering off suddenly, changing lanes (to the extent that they kept to any) at an alarming rate. Most of the trip was accompanied by the sound of other drivers beeping their horns at them and the irritating ping of the seat belt alarm. Rafael refused to wear his.

"Do you a*ctually* know where you're going?"

Rafael gave his cousin one of his unpleasant looks, but it wasn't nearly as unpleasant as the one a passing driver gave them before making a crude hand gesture. Smooth-as-silk fields stretched before them at last. But instead of pondering as to what lay ahead, Emil's thoughts turned inwards and to the past. It was impossible for them not to, with every horsebox exiting at Ascot just as his had done on that other Sunday, long ago. As he glimpsed Argentine grooms in their ubiquitous felt hats, sitting up front, smoking, the sight of them set off frame after frame in his head. But he couldn't bury the memory any longer. In order to go forward he was going to have to go back; push through to the beginning…

Sol's displeasure had dominated the mood that day. Emil hadn't been particularly diplomatic in telling her that there wasn't a lunch reservation for her in the Cartier tent. An oversight no more. It was neither a slight nor a reflection of his ranking among the players. He had simply forgotten to make the phone call, and now it was too late. She would just have to find bar food in any of the tents located alongside the number-one field. It was a sizzling hot day – the hottest (so the radio informed them) since 1976 – with temperatures already hitting thirty-five degrees. Apparently, whole sections of track had melted (resulting in travel disruption), the roads were vulnerable, and the very young and elderly were being advised to stay indoors. Already the heat had the same lacerating feel as Andalusia in high summer. Not that anyone would be mad enough to visit Andalusia at that time of year. Emil had once, wishing to burn memory from his mind, and had been shocked to see fields of sunflowers razed to the ground; the dry terracotta-coloured earth wizened and hard. The heat rising from the tarmac had the same impact now. Neither rider nor horse was going to be comfortable with it, either. It remained to be seen whether the game would even go ahead.

"Emi?" Sol's tone was sharp.

"*Sí, miamor?*" His reply was automatic. He was used to her demands.

As Emil edged his Porsche through the narrow Ascot lanes, his mind was not on Sol but on the forthcoming game. It was to be no ordinary game either, but the prestigious twenty-two-goal Cartier Queen's Cup in which he and *not* Rafa had been chosen to play. Not only that, but Emil would be opposite Adolfo Cambiaso, the world's number-one player. Given what he had done for Rafa, it seemed only *justo* – fair – that Rafa should allow him this one indulgence. But Cambiaso! *Ho ho*, thought Emil joyfully, mentally rubbing his hands with glee. What player in the world wouldn't pay a small fortune for the privilege of playing with him? Ah, yes, so he had; a lifetime's sentence, even… But *Cambiaso* – the god of polo! From the age of seventeen, Adolfo had been a ten-goaler. Twenty years on, he was still unstoppable, still unbeatable, still King of the Pampas. A few days earlier, when Emil and he had played together, Cambiaso had scored seven goals in seven minutes, winning the game by one goal in the last moments. The expectation was that today would be no different.

In the seat beside Emil, Sol fanned herself despite the air conditioning. She felt queasy nearly all the time now. Her beautiful hair hid her face and her tanned skin glowed. He found it hard to believe that she was so sickly when she looked the very picture of well-invested well-being. For a moment he was distracted by her beauty – for she really was beautiful – but then as she stretched a tanned leg and her straight, Prada-shod little toes flexed in resentment, he changed gear and sped forwards.

"I don't understand," she said now, puffing out her cheeks.

"What, *miamor?*" Emil had taken to calling her this: the two words rolled into one. She was too obtuse to realise that to him the endearment was meaningless, and yet to a stranger it was the very essence of devotion.

"I don't understand why we can't be with the others."

"We – or rather, you – will be, for the game."

"But not the lunch."

"Not the lunch."

A small frown puckered her flawless brow. She flicked her wrist so that her fan made snapping sounds as it opened and shut. "*Ay qué calor!*" she said in Spanish. "Aren't you hot? You don't feel the heat?"

"Not especially." Emil turned into Windsor Great Park, where rhododendrons lining the drive shone psychedelically bright in the merciless sun. Day trippers strolled in every direction and cyclists wound precariously in front of him. Forced to drive at a snail's pace, the adrenaline was beginning to surge through him and he was impatient to get to his horses. As impatient as he was to deposit Sol. "You'll sit with…" He swerved to avoid a man and his dog.

"*Ay, Emil!*" she complained. "With…?"

He didn't have the courage to say he'd not actually arranged for her to sit anywhere and she'd have to hang out with the other players' wives. At least until the game began. He, for one, never ate before a match. He was too nervous. He'd have a beer or two afterwards. But she would need to eat; he knew that. "You'll see the Queen," he offered brightly.

Sol threw him a scathing look. "With?" she repeated.

He frowned by way of an answer, parking as close as he could to the pony lines.

"I can't eat the Queen," said Sol, eyeing up the team tent with disgust.

Emil jumped out of the car, tucking his T-shirt into his white jeans. "If you don't want to wait here," he said, reaching into the back seat for his helmet and gloves, "you can sit in the grandstand with…"

"*Dios mío*, here we go again! *With...?* With the *petiseros*, you mean?"

"I was going to say the Argentines, actually."

Sol shot him a withering look. "No."

"No? *Miamor?*"

"I want to sit in the Cartier tent."

"Well, that's just not possible."

"Why not? You're playing, aren't you?"

"I am," he agreed patiently. "But today is a Cartier-*sponsored* day. It's nothing more than an exhibition game, you know that. You've seen dozens of them. It's just a bit of theatre." Emil gestured to a field past the clubhouse where Cartier's hospitality tent was sprawled by the end goalposts. "The glitzy lot up there don't know the first thing about polo. They're here because it's part of the season, or because they've paid a helluva lot of money for the day." He made a conscious effort to keep the irritation out of his voice, leaning sideways towards her. "You're a player's *wife*," he said, touching her arm. "You're worth a thousand of them. Cambiaso's wife and kids will all be on this side too. Besides, surely you're here... well, for... me?"

Sol's eyes widened. "Whatever gave you that idea?"

"No... well, yes. *Tienes razón.*" He straightened up. "Look, you'll have fun. Just go and sit down. Paco's wife will be along shortly, I'm sure."

"I don't care for her."

"Then don't talk to her." *Just go!*

Emil's groom came up to him then. A helicopter hovered above, causing the trees around the arena to spin in the sudden tornado. Dust kicked up from the exercise tracks but the horses were unfazed. "Cambiaso," said the groom reverently.

"Cambiaso," Emil agreed solemnly.

There was a minute's silence.

"*Y la Señora?*" asked the groom, who, like sailors with women on boats, regarded them all as singularly bad news and a bad omen.

"...is going to sit," said Emil, taking Sol by the elbow. "You'll be fine," he added in a whisper. "Wish me luck?"

His lips brushed air as she turned her face deliberately away.

"I would if I were sitting in the tent."

Nonetheless, she hesitated, and now in retrospect Emil wondered if her tough act wasn't just that: a touch of bravado. More than a touch. He had felt sorry for her. They had both married the wrong cousin, after all. But then, he was soon so caught up in preparation for the match that he didn't notice as Sol was swept up in the crowd. On this occasion, the clubhouse was closed even to regular members who hadn't purchased an additional ticket. With security guards posted at the entrance, Sol had no option but to sit in the stands and wait. Spectators hovered under makeshift canopies, trying to keep cool, fanning themselves with their programmes.

Emil surveyed the Queen's ground with a thrill. Despite the heatwave, the cropped grass was as brilliant a green as ever. Not a single blade was uneven or out of place, and the sky above was as unblemished as the ground beneath. Marching onto the field, the band began to play, and slowly spectators began to fill the stands. Not many emerged from the Cartier tent, though. Nor would they, Emil thought wryly. He could have told Sol this. Too much champagne and too many lobsters were being consumed, and besides, it was cooler there than anywhere else. He suspected that not many of the women were remotely interested in the game, being there only to see and be seen. He wondered vaguely where Rafael was at that moment; in which city or town. They'd not spoken since the wedding. Emil had wanted to kill him a few months back, and not in an idle way either. But for one day – just one – he was going to play polo. He was going to forget.

Emil's groom approached him with his weakest pony.

"You think?" said Emil.

Esteban nodded. "Jes, jes," he agreed. "You can recover with the better ones later."

Emil buckled his helmet, shoved on his gloves and leapt onto the grey. The air was still; voices an atonal barricade offsetting music from the band. And setting aside his personal problems, he decided to enjoy the game for what it was. On a purely physical level he was elated to be out in the sun and in heat that was so reminiscent of Spain he had to remind himself that it wasn't Sotogrande. Only the green fields and the sloping horizon of the Great Park were a reminder that he was not at home.

And then Cambiaso was there before him in his black shirt, a number four on his back. Not that this meant anything. Cambiaso was a law unto himself; a seamless, fluid player who was not incapable of swapping numbers after a chukka just to confuse the other team. "*Hola, Emil*," he said.

"*Hola.*"

"Watch Mercado; mark him."

Emil nodded.

"And we'll swap you – you play a better defensive when Polito is in a forward position. But no *te apures*," Cambiaso said, slapping him on the back. "Don't worry. We'll work out the kinks; we'll get used to each other by the last chukka!"

They rode out together towards the centre of the field, removing their helmets as the band struck up the national anthems. And then they were off. Except they weren't. Cambiaso's groom suddenly approached with a fresh horse, throwing the other team into an apoplexy of panic. Cambiaso, grinning beneath his mouth guard, leapt from one horse to the other without touching the ground. It was an acrobatic movement they could all do, and one that never failed to evoke ecstatic responses from the female spectators. Cambiaso was still grinning as the commentator introduced the teams. The umpires galloped up, throwing in the ball, and the game began.

Pounding across the ground, Emil felt on the edge of the world. Never had he experienced such exhilaration. Maybe it was playing without Rafa and with Cambiaso. Either way, he was in no doubt that this was the pinnacle of his polo-playing career. He knew it would never again be as good as this. The ball was his and then it wasn't, and then Cambiaso missed the goal. *Sería posible?* Was it possible? The ball was brought in from the back line with a long hit towards the centre. Cambiaso quickly took control, only this time the ball spun high, flying into the air and into the crowd. There was the usual predictable gasp followed by the gurgle of relief as no one was hit. A young boy caught the ball and, because he didn't know the rules, threw it back onto the ground. The umpire called the bell, and play was interrupted while an umpire from the other team knocked the ball into the boards. The game resumed and again Cambiaso – the great Cambiaso – missed. His long strides were fluid and elegant but he kept missing the ball completely. Emil galloped forward, hooking the ball from under his opposing player and notching the first goal on the scoreboard just thirty seconds after the first line-out. He was even more elated as, by half-time, he and he alone had established a two-goal advantage.

The horn sounded and spectators spilled onto the field to tread in the divots. From his vantage point at the furthest end point from the Cartier tent, Emil searched the crowds for Sol. There were thousands of people milling about the clubhouse, players and patrons alike, all enjoying champagne in the heat. There wasn't the remotest chance that he'd spot her. Irrationally, he'd imagined that her long blonde hair and baby-pink dress would stand out even at this distance, but they didn't. There were hundreds of pretty girls just like Sol, most of them more strikingly dressed, picking their way along the ground, giraffe-like, tall and sleek and aware of every male's attention.

But Emil had no time to ponder the social aspect of the game. The spectators were a blur of colour against the vivid action in which he was at the very centre. His heart was pounding. Cambiaso called him over to sit with the other players to discuss tactics. And then they were out again. This time Emil was on his favourite horse, Cartridge, but the flow of the second half was interrupted by penalties, and a combination of stop-start action and penalty conversion opportunities brought the other team, Los Indios, back into the game. By the end of the third chukka the score margin sat at just six-four, and by the fourth they were tied. Tensions were running high as weeks of matches rested on a single golden goal. Emil dug his heels into Cartridge's flanks. This was on him, even if he died in the process.

But in the end, of course, it wasn't Emil who died that day, although parts of him did – his self-belief for one; his youth for another – never to be recovered. And later, in his dreams, it seemed that it was only ever there, in his subconscious, that he did hear the unexpected sound of the horn. With his back to the goal he charged, mallet held high as though it were a lance; as though he were leading an army. With his back to the Cartier tent, he galloped with Cambiaso and Nacho and El Negro, leading them onwards; leading them to victory. So wired was he that he was still shouting when the umpires galloped towards him, still shouting when the commentator called an end to the game, and shouting still when he realised that he was the only rider still astride.

All Emil knew was that once again someone – he would never know who – had hit the ball wide and far, and this time it had landed somewhere among a chattering group of women. And later he would learn that it wasn't just 'somewhere' at all, but a glancing blow to Sol's right temple. Somewhere else still, the band was playing that summer's new release, 'Boulevard of Broken Dreams'.

"Do you think we'll ever play again?" asked Emil as they passed roads signs depicting riders and their mounts. He didn't have to say at what. He knew Rafael understood just how far his thoughts had travelled.

Rafael inhaled deeply before chucking yet another cigarette out of the window and blowing out smoke through the side of his mouth. He was huddled over the steering wheel as though he were driving a racing car. "No."

"I didn't think so either."

"*Bueno pues.* Well, then."

Emil shrugged. "I know. Just wondering."

"Don't."

And that was how it had always been. Rafael taking the lead; Emil following, sweeping up behind them. Even then; even now. In the days that followed Sol's death, they had been too stunned to speak much about it. But Emil, already shocked by the quick succession of events that in just a few months had irrevocably changed his carefree world, was now doubly traumatised. He had married a woman he didn't love who was carrying a child that wasn't his, and all because…? Because? Even now he wasn't sure why exactly, except that at the time he knew it was the right thing to do and because he couldn't abandon a friend in the way that Rafael had been prepared to abandon Sol. Perhaps it was because his act of self-sacrifice was a gesture designed to atone for them both. Or maybe it was simply because if he couldn't be with Ino, it really didn't matter whom he was with. It was all the same to him. And in the end, a random act was all it had taken to snuff out the lives of the woman and her unborn baby; to liberate Emil and give him back the life he'd had.

But of course, it wasn't so simple. Emil was never going to be free again; not really. None of them were. Wrapped around their hearts and minds was the overwhelming, crushing burden of guilt. It was ironic, though, that Sol's wish, granted just as she was about to set foot in the Cartier tent, should also have been her last. And afterwards? Afterwards…

Emil tugged on his cigarette, feeling the tobacco shoot through his veins. He glanced at his cousin. Rafael was rubbing his eyes, muttering something about hay fever. There was something else. Emil wasn't used to seeing Rafael without his dog collar, but then he remembered how stunned he'd been when he'd seen him in it for the very first time. Deciding to live in Oxford to pursue a degree in theology wasn't all that surprising after all that had happened, but Emil had never for one moment imagined that Rafael would actually become a priest.

And Ino? Because, after all, that was why they were here now. Emil felt an overwhelming need for a drink, coupled with indescribable fear. In the aftermath of Sol's death, Ino had been as far removed from his world as she was now. He felt the metal in his shirt pocket, there against his heart. Would she even want to see them? He knew what it was to have moments of loneliness; impulse. Hell, he and Rafa were acting on impulse now themselves. Ino had called Rafael and he had comforted her. But perhaps everything was okay again between her and… and that asshole of a husband of hers. *Husband.* She was a married woman. Emil felt himself tense.

"What?" said Rafael, catching his eye. "What is it? You keep looking at me."

Emil gestured to his cousin's shirt. "Have you lost it? Is it dirty? Or is this symbolic of a crisis of faith? More important, is it permanent?"

Rafael, ignoring the side mirrors, twisted his entire body to look behind him before changing lanes. Which was something of a concession to highway guidelines, Emil supposed. "All of the above," he said. "I was tired of Padre Pio."

Emil shot him a look. "You're lucky you can change personas so easily."

Rafael snorted. "It's not lucky, *cosí*, it's a *maldita* curse."

"Ah, a crisis of faith, then."

"It's always that."

Emil hesitated. "Do you think we're doing the right thing?"

"What do you mean?"

"I mean, going to Ino."

Rafael changed lanes again without indicating.

"*Joder!*" Emil swore. "I mean, fuck, Rafa!"

"It's okay. I saw him."

"You drive like you play – *played*," Emil corrected.

"So, you can relax, then." Rafael patted his cousin's knee

reassuringly. "Of course we're doing the right thing," he added. "Aside from the business that cannot wait, you and she have other issues to resolve. You should have taken care of all that a long time ago. Now, I'm going to make sure that you do."

Archie

Cedar Ave

The imprint of you is still here: of you in me; of me in you. You are everywhere: on the sheets; on my skin. I never knew it was possible to feel so at peace; so completely in tune with another being. I don't want anyone else. My appetite for you and only you is gigantic. I want to consume and be consumed.

Why isn't it as simple for you as it is for me? What is there to stop us being happy now? You said you would leave; that you could. So... leave.

I am waiting.

40

Rafael
Oxford
October 2007

Rafael had been lying when he'd said that he'd never thought about playing polo again. Of course he had. For him, the sport had been a drug, and just as addictive. Incidentally, it was astonishing what the young got hold of these days in order to get high: bottles of cough syrup, hand sanitiser (from which to extract alcohol), and, incredibly, the seemingly innocent contents of the bakery. He wondered if Emil knew that nutmeg, when smoked in large doses, produced a natural hallucinogenic compound called myristicin. Well, Rafael had put playing polo down as being as addictive as the best of the mind-altering drugs, and withdrawing from it was no less challenging. Sometimes, especially lately, the desire to ride was so great that he'd had to dive into the nearest church and breathe in the asphyxiating dust of porcelain statues to rid himself of the craving.

But denying himself the pleasure of playing was part of his atonement for Sol and Emil and even Ino. His head understood it even if his heart rebelled. And he was also lying when he'd told his spiritual mentor that he never thought about the accident. He did. Every day. And he'd thought about it at Salto recently; was thinking about it now as they sped along the once-familiar road, past signs for Windsor and Ascot. *The Lord guides the steps of a man and makes safe the path of one He loves.* Well, God hadn't taken care of Sol that day. Not at all. Maybe that had been the problem. Rafael hadn't loved Sol. Or not enough. He had shirked his responsibility and been punished as a result. He shuddered.

Emil thumped the sluggish air-conditioning unit. A blast of tepid air rose up hitting Rafael's eyes. He rubbed his face aggressively. When his hay fever was this bad, he wanted to tear off his skin. He swerved.

Emil placed his hand on the glove compartment to steady himself. "You're making me nervous, *coño*. Do you want me to drive?"

"No, I'm fine."

"You don't look fine." Rafael's face was pasty; his cheeks hollow. "Then what? A ghost run over your grave?"

Rafael looked at him pointedly. "Several." He covered the next involuntary shudder with a derisory snort. Another cigarette; another face-rub. They were doing well, the pair of them. But out of consideration for his cousin, Rafael made an effort to drive more carefully.

Part of the road had been resurfaced, and with the move towards smart motorways, this hitherto congested section of the M3 moved swiftly and was unusually quiet. Rafael would have welcomed the more familiar noise to drown out the turmoil of his thoughts. Where exactly was the compassionate God who lifts and carries his people through the dangerous passages of life? Rafael frowned. And what about this particular journey now? He knew very well what Emil was hoping for, but what about him? What did he want out of this? Forgiveness? Redemption? *I was young and now I am old but I have never seen the just man forsaken.* He had removed his dog collar and yet the habit of thinking in terms of biblical references was not as easy to set aside. Why couldn't he think about life... well, in terms of football like other normal people? But no – there it was again. Psalm thirty-six. Had he *ever* striven to be the 'just' man of the psalm?

Rafael didn't have answers. All he knew was that after the accident he had endeavoured to find meaning in the chaos he had created. For so long he and Emil – no, correction: *he*, not Emil – had behaved impulsively, immersed in their hedonistic lifestyle, living solely for women and polo. And for Rafael that carefree existence had continued even when Sol got pregnant: even when he'd refused to marry a woman he did not love, his cousin had.

The accident had ended all of that. Rafael acknowledged that his behaviour was reprehensible. He had not loved Sol, but he did love Emil, and so with a practicality previously unknown in him was galvanised into action. He had managed lawsuits – two of them, and neither one successful. The first against Cartier itself (tenuous by any stretch: Sol's Chanel-clad foot had barely crossed the tent threshold); the second against the Hurlingham Polo Association. An offshoot ruling of the latter was that the association's governing body decided that it would no longer offer its three thousand members insurance to cover accidental death among players. Not that Sol had been playing, obviously, but the HPA wasn't going to risk any more adverse publicity. In a preventative measure, going forward, playing members (and for that matter spectators too) would be required to take out their own personal injury insurance. Not a popular move, and one for which Rafael was consequently vilified.

He was even less popular with Sol's family once it was established that in attending the game she had assumed the risks of the inherent dangers, including balls and 'other objects... which may come off the playing field and cause bodily injury or even death'. It had not helped a jot that two deaths had resulted from this random act; not just the one.

After that, he gave up trying to comfort Sol's distraught parents and shied away from an increasingly fretful Abuela. Instead, he set up memorial funds, he funded Masses – endless *misas* for the dead – and he listened with mortifying patience as he was slandered and slated and accused of everything under the sun. But then, he didn't expect absolution. He had only to take one look at his cousin's stricken face to understand the effect of his selfishness. *Calm your anger and forget your rage...* And then he thought of his other cousin. And Oxford. And in the midst of it all, in the eternal turmoil of his soul and madness and grief, there was one idea alone that gave him solace.

Rafael began by going to Salamanca in the footsteps not of pilgrims, but of his beloved, fictitious San Manuel, who, like him a non-believer, was prepared to enter the priesthood. And there he deliberated the 'unbearable lightness of being' and learned how to manage his organic boredom. And, like Manuel, Rafael was always busy, terrorised by the idea of having nothing to do – of having too much time for contemplation. At the end of two years, Rafael compiled a collection of his quotidian reflections in a book called *God Helps Those...* It was the kind of thing he'd never have read himself: a glib, tongue-in-cheek (or so he'd intended) self-help book into which he channelled as much beautifully crafted sarcasm and as much unpleasantness as he could muster. He never expected to get either a publisher or an audience, and so no one was more astonished (or appalled) than he when virtually overnight it became a bestseller. Translated into thirty languages, the book was especially successful in South America. There they were fascinated (or so his publicist said) by the tragic, good-looking seminarian. He had become not so much the pious padre as the popular one. Tourists to Salamanca came not to see the thirteenth-century university (the third oldest in Europe), but to camp outside his small apartment, hoping to catch a glimpse of the dashing Don. But this kind of attention was just what he had come to the ancient town to avoid. Craving anonymity, he fled, a few years ahead of schedule, to Campion Hall, home to the Society of Jesus in Oxford.

And so it was that, on a crisp, beautiful autumn's day, he had found himself on the steps of the awe-inspiring Sheldonian Theatre, designed by his favourite architect, Christopher Wren. During his time studying with the Jesuit academic community,

Rafael had acquired, if not faith, then patience – well, patience up to a point. That point was fast approaching. *Según él* (in his opinion), he had waited long enough for his interviewer and, more crucially, the opportunity to smoke. He glanced up at the dome and the newly restored colours of the building – colours last seen in the 1720s. He marvelled (not for the first time) at a country in which the importance of conservation was taken so seriously, and in such contrast to his own. He thought with regret of the Old Town in Barcelona, which was being ripped up right, left and centre to make way for modern construction. Soon, very little would remain of the Barrio Gótico of his youth. These Brits knew how to do it. He had always loved Wren, and it amused him to think that Sarah Churchill had wanted the great man for Blenheim Palace but her husband had chosen Vanbrugh instead; a man better known as a dramatist.

And as Rafael's thoughts vaulted through memory, zigzagging across time zones, he remembered that first visit to Tom Quad and, of course, Ino. He wondered if she was still even in Oxford. He rather doubted it. She would have long finished her degree. The need for tobacco (having replaced polo) was the overriding impulse of the moment. He remembered feeling increasingly desperate and yet not wanting to be caught on camera with a fag in his hand. He was to be interviewed by the feisty female president of the Oxford Union prior to the evening's debate, the title of which – *Belief and Non-Belief: Is God Irrelevant?* – filled him with horror. He didn't doubt that his argument would be sufficiently rigorous – he would pose a more interesting question (at least to him) as to whether or not Christian ethics could survive the death of religion – but he feared he might give the game away. Maybe he'd better have that smoke – purely medicinal, of course. But just as his fingers felt in his trouser pocket for his box of matches, a swarm of screaming Spanish-speaking schoolgirls swirled around him and a mic was thrust in his face. He retreated mentally – he hadn't expected this. He ran a finger under his dog collar. It felt tight and scratchy.

"Please tell us, Señor – *perdón*, *Padre* Monte Alegre, why do you think your book has been such a hit; a bestseller in Latin America?" said an attractive journalist with a Media UK pin on the lapel of her poppy-red jacket.

"Well, I'm as surprised as the next man," said Rafael candidly, for the upteenth time since promoting the book. Mind you, he'd got his deprecating demeanour down to a fine art. "Or woman," he added artfully.

"*God Helps Those...* is certainly a provocative title," the perky journalist from Oxford South said with a smile. She was blonde and plump and twinkly. "And have you?"

Lots of titters there. Was she flirting?

Rafael gave her the benefit of his languid look; the one that used to make any female (and maybe a few males too) fall in love with him. "Have I what?" There was a delightful pause as he considered the woman. "Oh, I see… Now, really, I would never compare—"

"Are you excited about tonight's debate?" This from some spotty-faced youth at the back. Rafael looked again – it was a boy, not a girl, wearing one of those knitted tea-cosy hats. Completely unflattering, in his opinion.

"Of course."

"Why?" This new voice was sharp; not so friendly.

Rafael blinked. He'd begun to enjoy himself; relax a bit, even. He was suddenly alert. "*Why?*" He paused for effect, while at the same time rapidly scanning the crowd, trying to pick out the interlocutor, but could only see a row of smiling schoolgirls. "Well… for one thing, I'm happy to be here," he began, aware of the mobile phones suddenly thrust before him; the pens poised to take notes. "It's a great honour to be asked to speak at the union. And for another I believe" – *not* – "it's a question that we should all debate from time to time, don't you? I mean, whether it's the Christian God, the Muslim Allah, Total Overcomers Anonymous – no, really – or the evolution of the atheists, people will always argue about religion."

There was a murmur of approval until someone spoke. "You're joking, right?"

Of course I'm joking! There she was again – that aggressive, *angry* voice. A *rude* voice.

"I'm sorry?"

"Isn't your book simply a Ladybird approach to therapy in a twee update?"

A nervous titter went through the crowd, although the references – certainly the one to the Ladybird book series – were not understood by so many of the Latin Americans. Rafael couldn't agree more, but he wasn't going to admit it. Actually, being compared to the Ladybird books was a compliment! But this woman clearly wanted more. He rocked on his heels, shoulders square on. The sky was clear and bright. It would be even more perfect if he could smoke. Again he searched the sea of heads, but it wasn't obvious who had spoken. Never mind. He could be armed and dangerous when required.

"I'm flattered to be considered in the same breath as either…"

There were sniggers; a palpable frisson among the crowd as it surged forward, trying to get a closer look. At him. He flashed his Hollywood smile as though he was being photographed for *Polo Today*.

"As a final question – as we all appreciate how busy you must be – what advice would you give us students?"

"And you are?"

"Oh…" A slight, fragile-looking girl in a hoodie with her hands shoved in her pockets blushed entrancingly. "I represent the gay community at Oriel," she said.

Rafael blinked. She really was very lovely.

"Dr Montealegre?" It came out as one word.

"Yes?" Except in his relative shock it came out as 'Jes?' Well, what the hell was he supposed to say? Yay? Hallelujah? Bully for you? Congratulations? God loves all creatures? But then he admonished himself. *You came in search of the last, the least and the lost…* was what he should be thinking. "I'm sorry, what was the question again? Oh yes, advice…" He suddenly felt exhausted. Advice from *him*? "Well, what I would say," he said, clearing his throat as several spectators whispered, "Shh!" and silence fell on the group. Somewhere a wood pigeon was cooing as though mocking him. "What I would say," he repeated, "to the teachers among you – something that probably sounds obvious – is teach students *how* to think, not *what* to think; and students, be patient – especially the postgrads. Wait a while before writing." He hoped this wouldn't sound too pompous. "Wait until you've actually got something to say."

There was a brief silence, then the scratch of pens, the tapping of phones and iPads. And then, from the back, amidst the blurred faces, another question.

"Is that what you did?"

Rafael looked up, frowning, peering into the crowd. Who had spoken? That *voice*; so familiar and yet not. Out of place, that was why. The only reason it wasn't immediately recognisable. Was that… was that… *Ino*?

"Padre, Padre!" shouted someone else, literally throwing herself at his feet.

"*Que Dios te bendiga*," he said solemnly. *May God bless you.* His hand rested on the crown of the girl's head, while at the same time his gaze swept over the crowd.

And that was when she caught his eye, or rather, he caught hers. And in that instant, she fled.

"If there are no further questions…" Rafael descended the steps rapidly, sideways, pushing through the crowd. "*Espera, Ino!*" he called after her.

She hesitated briefly.

He could feel the surge of energy from the crowd gathering behind him as though he were the Pied Piper of Hamelin. "No, no!" he said to no one in particular. "It's over now. *Misa*," he blurted. "I have to say Mass."

Ahead, Ino darted down a narrow alley that led to Blackwell's bookshop. Rafael followed, managing to dodge the journalists, TV crew and hysterical teens in the process. He was pretty confident they assumed he was headed for the Catholic chaplaincy. Suddenly, Ino looked over her shoulder and he caught up with her; caught her as she turned.

"*Por Dios, Ino!*"

"*Por Dios?*"

He dropped her arm in alarm. He'd known she'd be angry, but the contempt was something else.

"What are you doing here?" she hissed, walking past him.

He caught his breath by lighting a cigarette. As her pace increased he had to almost run to keep up. "You mean you haven't seen me on the billboards? There's a really good one at the station just as you exit – slow down!"

"Oh, please."

"You mean you don't like it?"

"I don't like *you!*"

"Ouch. I'm taking it you aren't pleased to see me," he said, inhaling quickly. Ah, that was better. Now he could cope with this prima-donna cousin of his.

"I'm not. Just please tell me the other Hardy Boy isn't with you."

"He's not."

"Then I should be grateful for small mercies."

"Ino, Ino. Stop!"

"Why?"

"Because I want to talk to you."

"And you couldn't before?" She looked away in disgust. She was older than he remembered and the lightness in her eyes was gone; replaced by a determination, a wariness. Well, he and Emil, or rather, he alone was responsible for that.

"And what's with the priest thing? You aren't really?"

Rafael shrugged. "As good a job as any," he said, trying a different tack. Which backfired.

"Like you actually have to work."

Well, you don't have to either, but that's not the point... But he didn't contradict her.

"Is that what you think?" she added, everything in her demeanour combative, hostile.

"Of course not! Look, meet with me. Have a drink. Oh, don't be so naive," he added, irritated by her disapproving face. "I haven't given up everything!"

"Have you given up *anything*?"

Rafael ran a hand through his hair, thick and luxuriant and long. He knew women still looked at him with open interest. Open desire. "I know you're angry."

Ino paused then. "Do you?"

He had an uncomfortable feeling that, given half a chance, she'd punch him senseless.

But her voice cracked; her lips trembled when she said, "Actually, Rafa, I don't think you have any idea how I feel."

"Okay, so why don't you tell me?" he said gently. "Why don't we go somewhere and talk? I'd really like that."

Ino shifted her bag, giving him a withering look. "I have a tutorial," she said. "You can buy me a drink in the Randolph at six, unless you have to... say Mass or something."

"Are you still studying?"

"I'm *giving* the tutorial."

Rafael considered her resentful, mistrustful face. "And I don't have to say Mass. I'll see you there at six."

Rafael had a short siesta when he got back to his rooms, and then set off to meet Ino at the Randolph Hotel. Here too there were life-size models of himself. He had to admit that he was incredibly handsome in his immaculately tailored suit (the Roman collar adding a certain sartorial elegance), and the Salamanca sun had toasted his skin to a wonderful chufa colour. He could completely see why marketing him was such an easy task. He caught a reflection of himself in the hotel windows. *What a waste*, he thought. *Still, Rafa, chico, you have only yourself to blame.*

He waited impatiently in the lobby until a gaggle of Japanese students asked for his autograph. And it was with pen in hand that Ino found him standing by his cut-out model, signing his books. *Oops!* he thought as he saw her turn to leave. But then again, perhaps the promise of the renowned Randolph cocktail made her change her mind. He handed back a signed book to the last student.

"This," he gestured to the group of giggling girls, "was impromptu. Really."

Ino sighed. "I believe you. Is it *so* good? I'm intrigued." She caught his eye. "And don't tell me to read it. I won't."

"That's okay; it's not."

And for a moment, he knew she wanted to smile. She had changed into a cashmere sweater and soft leather biker jacket which, together with designer jeans and over-the-knee boots, made her look international and… well, frankly, gorgeous.

"What?" She threw him a quizzical, unfriendly look.

His eyes flicked over her again. "You don't look like the average lecturer."

"Visiting."

"Ah… I wondered. I didn't know if you'd still be here."

"Not for long, actually. I've applied to complete my studies at McGill in Montreal."

Rafael was genuinely surprised. "What, and live with Veronica?"

"It's only an idea."

"You must really want a change."

She was silent.

"Don't know about you, but I could do with a drink," he said, guiding her to the hotel bar. "You can tell me all about it."

She allowed him to place his hand lightly on her arm. He could feel the tension in her whole body, and felt sorry for her. She seemed so wounded, so vulnerable. He stole a glance at her face.

She was as beautiful as ever (as he would love to have told Emil, had he known where to find him), but the trusting innocence was gone. He motioned to a seat by the window and let her settle herself while he looked at the menu and gestured for the waitress. His eyes flicked around the room. The building was an historic landmark. Over the years it had housed and fed academics, tourists, and of course families of students at the university. The waitress when she appeared was suitably tongue-tied, and blushed every time Rafael looked at her. He wondered if he should ask Ino to order in his place. Eventually the waitress concentrated on looking at his Roman collar, and in that way, they managed to get through the menu. The specials were a bridge too far.

"It's disgusting," Ino said softly.

"What is?" he replied, startled.

"You've reduced the poor girl to an almost catatonic state."

I know! Ino seemed a little more relaxed. Maybe this would go well after all. "Can't help the effect I have," he said lightly, but he was pleased all the same. "Heaven knows what she'll bring us. She wasn't listening at all, was she?"

"I'm not going to debase myself by commenting. Aren't you…" Ino spread her hands. "Aren't you supposed to be a little… *humilde*?"

"That *was* humble… wasn't it?" He feigned surprise. "*I* thought it was."

"You mean for you." The edge had crept back into her voice.

Rafael lit a cigarette and crossed a leg to reveal silk socks and exquisite leather shoes. He felt better already – the hit of tobacco, the warmth of the room and, when it came, the drink. He saw Ino's eyes widen in appreciation at the sight of small bowls of olives. Maybe she was just hungry. He would let the G&T sink into her. As it would in him. She took a sip and was about to speak, but he passed her the olives, stalling for time. A student sat down at the piano and began playing Cole Porter.

"This is nice," said Rafael lamely.

Ino almost choked on her drink. Rafael watched colour swirl round her face. Her green eyes became darker. He sat back in his chair, nursing his own glass. *Lastima*; shame, he might have spoken too soon.

"You really don't know, do you?" She tossed back her head; undid her ponytail so that her hair fell about her shoulders. She slurped her drink noisily like a child playing with a straw. "I'll have another."

"You haven't finished that one."

A final slurp. "Have now."

He allowed his gaze to linger on her a moment longer before motioning to the waitress. "All right, Ino, what is it? How can we resolve this?" The waitress reappeared, but this time Rafael didn't look at her. "And could we have some more nibbles… oh, I don't know – something with bread?"

"Not for me," said Ino rudely.

"I think you should eat something."

"Why? Because I'll get drunk if I don't?"

Rafael shrugged. "Suit yourself."

The waitress returned with Ino's gin and some chicken skewers. There was more banter and flirting until Ino banged her glass onto the glass-topped table.

Rafael caught her wrist. "*Tranquila*," he said gently, and for a moment he knew she wanted to believe in him; so wanted it to be Emil sitting there in front of her; so wanted the clock to be put back. Didn't they all?

She leaned over his hands, her hair touching his skin. "I didn't *ask* you to find me," she said at last, hardly above a whisper. "I didn't need for Abuela or you or… or Emil to come into my life. I was perfectly happy as I was."

Rafael released her, sitting back and lighting yet another cigarette. "We came into your life, as you put it," he said gently, "because Veronica – I'm sorry; your mother – asked us to."

"Maybe, maybe not," retaliated Ino, rearing up like a skittish pony. "Whatever the initial reason – I can – I *could* cope with that – but not the lies! *All* the lies, Rafael! One more fantastical than the next. Did you really think I would never find out?"

Rafael exhaled, blowing out smoke above their heads. "Do you mean about your father?"

"I mean all of it," she said fiercely.

"They weren't *lies*, lies," said Rafael. "Lies of omission, if anything, but they were only to protect you. It was only because we cared—"

"Is that what you call *caring*? Well, you of all people should know 'The road to hell is paved with good intentions.'"

"Racine."

"Pascal." She all but spat the word.

"Ah, yes."

"Look, I don't mind at all about Veronica and what she did before she met my father – actually, if anything I have *more* sympathy for her now that I know the truth. But I was led to believe that he was someone – some*thing* – entirely different."

"He was a good man; a great man in his way," said Rafael.

"How do I know that? Why should I believe anything anyone says? There's Veronica pretending to be so grand when all the time she was just some pathetic floozy from Schumacher, Ontario. Did you know that she's not really even Canadian? That her first language is Serbo-Croat?"

"That's enough, Ino," said Rafael firmly. "I am no fan of Veronica, but you've got it all wrong—"

"Have I?" Ino's voice rose shrilly. She gulped an olive rather than her drink and almost choked. Tears filled her eyes. "Well, how 'bout you tell me, now that you're such a pro at it, how it really was? If you're capable of distinguishing truth from fiction?"

Rafael's eyes narrowed. Any moment now she would be hysterical. If only Emil were here – he could handle this! Rafael wasn't sure this was the moment for family revelations anyway. Ino began crying quietly; small sobs. He didn't dare touch her. He smoked another cigarette, ordered another round of drinks – a mistake, no doubt, but this time he needed it more than she did – and waited for her crying to subside. There was a small silence between them as Rafael considered his next words.

"You have to understand that things were different then, and Abuela—"

Ino made an impatient gesture. "…was the biggest hypocrite of them all!"

Rafael frowned. "No. That's unkind. She was a product of her generation; of the Civil War – Salto meant everything to her. She had survived; the family had. She only did what she thought best and in your interests. You should know…" He wanted to tell her about Abuela's will, but thought it best to leave that to the lawyers. *That she left everything to you.* "You must know that she asked for you when she was dying."

"And *that* is unkind," said Ino fiercely. "How dare you try and blackmail me emotionally?!"

"All right," said Rafael, uncrossing his legs. "You want the truth?" he said. "You can have it! Are you grown-up enough to deal with it, is my question? This is…" He was going to say 'childish', but thought better of it. "Your reaction…"

This seemed to have an impact, and Ino wiped her eyes. "Everyone has been lying to me ever since I first met you. All of you."

"That's debatable. But you're upset… why, exactly?"

Ino looked at him, her eyes wide.

"I'm serious," he continued. "Why are you still so upset? Because the truth didn't fit the neat, romantic ideal you'd formed about us? Is that it?"

"No!"

"Then why?"

"I honestly don't know how to answer that," she said quietly.

"Try."

"You've all been so… dishonest. On every level. You, Sol, Emil

– that's before we even get to the accident! I truly don't know where to begin."

Rafael's chest tightened unexpectedly at the thought of Sol, his child, the dilapidation that was Salto, and of course Emil. His shoulders slumped. Ino had loved Emil. That was the biggest tragedy. Theirs had been a short but not insignificant romance. "I'm not sure, then, that I do."

Ino rummaged in her handbag for a tissue – a beautiful Loewe handbag, he noted – blew her nose noisily and pushed back her hair.

"Look," said Rafael, the conversation already drifting. "You're right. There's so much that was hidden, kept from you, but I promise it was because we loved you."

"*Loved* me? Will you stop with that?! Really?" Ino hissed. "Love again?" She slumped. "I thought – no: I *knew* Emil loved me. And look what he did!"

Rafael's head jerked up. Didn't she know what had happened? Didn't she understand that Sol's child was his and not Emil's? "But he did – *does* – love you!" he said forcibly, astonished.

"Then where is he? Why doesn't he ever get in touch?"

Rafael's gaze was steady. "I don't know." But what he meant was that he didn't know where Emil was; that he'd not heard anything as to his whereabouts in eighteen months.

That seemed to quieten her. She was crying again. He tried to touch her hand but she pulled away.

"Don't ever doubt—"

"What? That he loved me? Oh, come off it! How stupid do you think I am? *Loved* me? He *married* someone else! He got her *pregnant!*"

So, she didn't know. Good God. "It wasn't like that." Rafael uncrossed his legs; ran a hand through his hair. She really didn't know. How could she not? The sobering reality – the enormity of her grief – was overwhelming to him. But it was more than he was prepared for. There had been so many assumptions. Or maybe it was simply that, ostrich-like, no one had been brave enough.

"It's never like that," she said sarcastically. "Like my father wasn't gay." Her voice rose shrilly. "Like my father didn't die of AIDS!"

There was a stunned silence. Rafael was aware that hotel guests were staring at them with open curiosity; not helped by the fact that they were speaking a mixture of Spanish and English as they always did – more Spanish to English, which they did here, as opposed to more English to Spanish when they were in Spain. But there was no mistaking the word 'SIDA' – Ino helpfully repeated the word in both languages.

"You're right, absolutely." He was at a loss as to how to respond. Talking to Ino like this rated as one of the more testing experiences of his priesthood. The different issues were coming fast and furious, each one loaded and problematic. "We should have talked about it all. We've been geographically separated—"

"That is *not* an excuse!"

He glanced at her tear-stained face – green eyes glistening, hands shaking. What had he been thinking? He had spent so much time focusing on his own well-being that he'd not spared a thought for Ino's. He had taken it for granted that she and Emil had talked; had somehow resolved things. As far as they could ever be resolved, of course. He felt uncomfortable now speaking on behalf of his other cousin. He could only tell her his own side of the story, as shoddy as that might be. "No, you're right: there's a lot to discuss. Probably more than we can cover at one sitting. But before we go any further, let me tell you about Sol. And me, that is – not Emil. I need to tell you…"

Ino stared at him, scanning his face, looking at the high forehead, the thick hair, the wide yet fine eyebrows that swept above his warm brown eyes, the long nose, the even white teeth, the full lips. Rafael saw his reflection in her eyes and knew it was not pleasing to her. "And I need to go." She rose unsteadily to her feet. Her hair spread over her shoulders, her vivid beauty attracting another kind of attention.

He reached up and caught her wrist. "Oh, don't be so

melodramatic. Sit down, for God's sake. You want to talk? Well, I'm here now. Who knows when there'll be another opportunity? You can't just run again because the truth is uncomfortable."

Ino bent from the waist to finish her drink. "Actually, I can, and sitting here watching you smoking, flirting, drinking, and pontificating on the fantasy of truth—"

"'Pontificating'?" he said, confused. "'Fantasy of truth'? What on earth are you talking about? There's no fantasy! The truth is fantastical enough, believe me. Sit down!"

But Ino, swaying in front of him, was determined. "No – I've decided I'm done. This time I really am. I don't want to hear any more – not another word. I don't ever want to hear from *any* of you."

By which Rafael knew she meant Emil. And he also knew that she didn't mean a word of it. He also realised that this wasn't the time. One day she'd want to hear, but not now. It was too raw. Besides which, some of it should really come from Emil.

"All right, all right," he said quietly, standing and stubbing out his cigarette and motioning for the bill. He patted his jacket suit pocket, feeling for his wallet. "Can I at least take you home? Walk you to your college?"

"I've got my bike. I bet you don't have one."

"Actually, I do."

She seemed surprised by this, and for a moment Rafael thought she might change her mind and stay. But once he'd dropped a fifty-pound note on the table, miming to the waitress to keep the change, the mask came down again. He touched her soft-as-silk leather jacket, feeling her recoil – an unusual reaction in a woman. He buttoned his jacket and wrapped a navy cashmere scarf around his neck. With his Roman collar disguised, he looked chic and sophisticated. He could have stepped from any advert for Patek Philippe watches. He knew that, with her equally beautifully cut clothes, they made a glamorous couple. On the face of it.

"I'm at Campion Hall if you need anything. You can always leave messages with the porter."

"I know how it works."

"*Bueno pues.*"

"You always say that."

Rafael shrugged. "Only when I don't know what else to say – when I've run out of options…"

Ino threw back her head haughtily. "Is that what I am?"

Rafael breathed heavily. "Of course not."

She turned to go.

"Wait!" he said. "Before you go, I have something of yours; something you left behind." He dug into his jacket pocket, fishing out a velvet pouch. He placed the Monte Alegre family ring in the palm of her hand.

Ino looked at it as if he'd offered her a dead rabbit's entrails. "I didn't leave it behind. I don't want it."

"That's not something for you to decide, Ino. Like it or not, you *are* a Monte Alegre." *Like it or not*, he thought, *you've inherited Salto al Cielo, the mill, the church, the entire village…*

"You don't get it," she said coldly. "I don't want it. I don't want any part of it, or of the family."

This time he believed her. "*Vale, vale,*" he said in Spanish. "I surrender."

"No, *I* do. Here!" She all but threw the ring back at him. "Go on, take it."

He looked at his hand, and a shaft of pain struck his features. To relinquish their birthright, albeit in the form of a piece of jewellery, he found hugely symbolic. "You will find it, you know, one day," he said at length. "I promise you."

She frowned, half-turning. "Find what?"

"Forgiveness."

"*Forgiveness?*" she echoed. "From whom?"

"Not from, for. *For* the past."

Archie

Cedar Ave

You say you like Lawrence after all. Well, this is from 'Wedlock'. Yours, not mine.

> *Do you feel me wrap you*
> *Up with myself and my warmth, like a flame round the wick?*
> *And how I am not at all, except a flame that mounts off you.*
> *Where I touch you, I flame into being; – but is it me, or you?*

41

Emil
Winchester
October 2017

Emil – lost in thought, buried deep in his memories – was periodically catapulted back into the present by the jerky movements his cousin was performing in the name of driving. Short of taking control of the wheel himself, no amount of protest could make Rafael see how nervous his driving was making him. Emil stole a glance at his cousin's hunched form. It was a jolt seeing him without his dog collar. It had been a shock to see him wear it for the first time all those years before, but it was an even greater one to see him without it now. The removal of a simple piece of clothing made him seem both vulnerable and accessible. It also exaggerated all sense of the man as opposed to the office he represented. Either way, there was no escaping the fact that time had not stood still for either of them. Emil sucked in his own belly. Had he changed so much? Would *she* think he had? And yet as they drove past the lanes crowded with memories, the air felt alive with their former, youthful selves. And now that this moment was virtually upon them – a moment he had dreamed of but never really thought would come – his thoughts turned to the girl he had never stopped loving.

Part of him was calm. He was certain of his decision; of the steps he was prepared to take to ensure it. The other part tried, just as Rafael was also doing, to make sense of the past: of the accident and its aftermath and the intended journey of self-discovery upon which Emil had subsequently embarked, and to which end they were both arriving at now. It was hard to explain (even though he understood perfectly why they had) how it was that each man had felt compelled to act in the way he had: Emil to take on Sol at the expense of his own happiness, and later Rafael to become a priest when he didn't believe in God. Except that even that was open to debate. Emil believed that 'the hound of heaven' that had been chasing Rafa all these years might just have got to him at last.

Only Rafael's expletives interrupted Emil's thoughts as they turned off the motorway, following signs to what had once been the ancient capital of Wessex. And as they negotiated the remaining miles to Ino's home, Emil thought of the thousands more he'd travelled in the years following Sol's death. After the final inquest, he had left Spain wanting to put as much distance as possible between himself and Salto and everything he had once loved. With nothing left of his emotional life, he had wanted even more strongly to forget the physical one that had so shaped everything he had become.

Salto was so much more than a home. *Castillo* or otherwise, it was a complete world; beautiful and unique and self-supporting. But when the magic was dispelled it became claustrophobic and destructive. Its very remoteness overwhelmed him, inducing panic when once it had brought calm. The silence was deafening with the sound of her laughter. And increasingly the very idea of a 'castle' felt antiquated and ridiculous, as did Abuela's old-fashioned mode of conduct. Slowly, the life of the place withered along with the stonework and plaster. The fires in the *forn* extinguished and self-seeding plants allowed to creep within its walls. It became a macabre monument to a faded way of life; a relic best forgotten along with the bones of the unknown saints to be found in the velvet box beneath the altar.

If Emil was surprised by anything, it was the speed with which he had left Spain; or to be precise, Rafael – Rafael who had been more than a cousin: a brother, a twin. United in grief for their parents who had died when they were so young, they had been inseparable. They had looked to each other for support, too, in negotiating the strange world of Abuela's Salto with its romantic notions of chivalry and old-world manners. Treated like little princes, they were hardly equipped to deal with modern life. Up until the accident, the only stress in their lives came from wondering if they would get up in time (after being out all night) for a polo match; their heads cluttered with no more complicated a thought than the best feed to give a pony when even that could be delegated to a groom. And yet Emil had left it all behind with remarkable ease.

His starting point of Compostela and the Camino left him unmoved. Aimlessly, he moved east and off the mainland, following a haphazard paper trail to the original Santa Cruz. If that city (built on the grid system and before the opening up of the Suez Canal) was to be the blueprint for all cities in South America, then that's where he would go. Like another Valdivia or O'Brian, he would follow in the footsteps of the conquistadors before him and countless gap-year students since. His only remit was to achieve complete oblivion.

In Colombia he avoided visiting La Casa del Salto for that very reason – sharing the same name being the least of it. Pictures in the guidebook showed the same decay that would soon affect his Salto: the roof covered in moss, the curtains hanging in shreds, and the whole covered in a vast network of cobwebs. Neither place was any longer a symbol of joy and elegance. Similarly, the rubber baron's mansion in Manaus with its aroma of different jungle woods sent him stumbling into the humid air. In Rio he set out each morning to meet the violent heat which grew steadily more aggressive with every step he took. But memories of polo in Argentina sent him tacking across the continent, scurrying towards another Santiago. From Charles Darwin's garden, he climbed the Cerro Santa Lucia, pondering on the character of the Spanish explorers while inwardly cheering a race that has never been tamed. Only on Easter Island, buffeted by eighty-five-mile-an-hour winds, did he find peace; his mind at last reduced to sand. He'd sought this furthest, most remote island feeling himself bound by infinite space, yet yearning only to be king of a nutshell—

Rafael braked suddenly, reversed and accelerated, before turning down a dead-end lane. They had come to a quintessential English village full of rose-covered thatched cottages, and a church with gravestones clustered behind a picket fence.

"Another manoeuvre like that and we'll be *in* the graveyard!" protested Emil.

Rafael was again forced to brake heavily in the wake of the steady stream of cars leaving the village. The cars parked along the lane by the school jutted out at all angles.

"*Joder!*" Emil exclaimed, half in awe. "Respect, my coz."

"Don't mess with the priest." Rafael smiled, enjoying himself. At last, having given way to four cars in a row, he lost patience. "That's it!" he said, accelerating forward.

They passed playing fields, a war memorial, a village shop, then more cottages.

"I never understand how that works," said Rafael vaguely. "How water doesn't penetrate the thatch." And then he stopped the car and, almost in one movement, was reaching into the glove compartment.

"What are you doing?"

"My Roman collar."

"You mean your Linus blanket."

Rafael shrugged. "Maybe, but I need it."

"Not for… Ino?" Emil was incredulous.

"For myself."

Emil searched his cousin's face.

Unabashed, Rafael met his gaze. "I guess it's real after all."

"What is?"

"My faith."

Emil smiled to himself as his cousin twisted in front of the car's mirror, adjusting his shirt. He might not be the most conventional of priests, but Rafael was a man of God and always would be.

I fled Him, down the nights and down the days;
I fled Him, down the arches of the years;
I fled Him, down the labyrinthine ways
Of my own mind...

Emil squeezed Rafael's shoulder as he would have done before a game. "*Bueno pues*," he said quietly. He'd not thought it before, but all this time they'd *both* been running while standing still: his cousin from his vocation and he from the woman he loved. But now they had run out of track, there was nowhere else to go. They were here; they'd arrived. Annoyingly, as always, Rafael had got there rather sooner. Emil envied him that – his own destination was still uncertain.

They were here. In front of what he knew had to be Ino's place. They had stopped. And so had Emil's heart. He searched frantically for poetry with which to quieten himself. The hound of heaven had got to Rafael, but Neruda had Emil. He thought of that now.

Archie

Cedar Avenue

My dearest Catherine,
 I have made the greatest mistake of my life. There is no excuse for the way I have treated you – but I am paying for it; I have paid for it. In my separation from you I have been sorely punished. I am lonelier than I thought it ever likely I would be.
 Let's start again. Anew. Afresh. Leave him. Leave your child. You can have another. I'll give you another. Have no regrets; they don't do any good.
 How can you be so cruel? How…

42

Veronica
Salto al Cielo
May 1987

The room in the early morning was cold; her twin bed even colder. She looked across, surprised to see him.

"Come here," she said softly. She didn't know whether to giggle or cry at the panic on his face. "Only to talk."

He hesitated. Besides, he was already smoking. "*Bueno pues.*"

He stubbed out his cigarette in the thimble-size silver ashtray he nursed in his hand. He twisted, placing it carefully on the spindly bedside table, and then with equal care folded back the fine lawn. He was elegant as ever in his bespoke silk pyjamas. With precision, he placed his slender feet on the marble floor. Whatever hopes she had nurtured were gone, but from somewhere – yes, even from the depths of that black hole of the Porcupines – there came a glint of a former self. Hers and hers alone. Not someone she was trying to be. There was one more thing to be accomplished: he still had something he was capable of giving her. And she would take it.

He came to her bed, yet doing everything, she knew, not to touch her. But as he got in cautiously beside her, she slid out and in a single movement had jumped into his bed, diving under the immaculate covers, the beautiful lace-trimmed sheets pulled over her face. There was a moment's silence, and then from above there came the most glorious sound she would ever hear from him: laughter.

Archie

Montreal General Hospital
1650 Cedar Avenue
Montreal
Quebec
H3G 1A4

Oh, for God's sake.

You say you can't take much more. Well, I sure as hell can't. I'm exhausted by your demands. My hours are hideous – you know that; yet you whinge about sleep deprivation. Let me tell you about not sleeping. My shifts are forty-eight hours back to back and I make life-or-death decisions several times a day on <u>all of them</u>. You can have a nap whenever you like – get someone to mind the baby. But just back off. I need peace. Your screaming at me isn't helping.

Look, they say something pretty crass here but it's kinda true. Shit or get off the pot. If you want to jump, jump!

43

Ino, Rafael and Emil
Winchester
No Date

Tucked away under the yew hedge on her favourite bench, Ino had spent the past weeks while Calypso was at school, reading the letters that had tumbled from an unlocked, battered old briefcase she'd discovered while clearing out Archie's belongings. Well, 'letters' didn't adequately describe the stream-of-consciousness rant expressed on tattered fragments, newspaper, hotel stationery, beer mats – anything that had seemingly come to hand. And though it irked her to admit it, they were also love letters; letters imbued with pain. They were letters that had dispatched Archie's lover – this Catherine – into the arms of another man and then, when it was already too late, demanded her return.

There were press clippings too, the contents of which Ino already knew; had seen in the Discovery Centre. The final full stop in the tragic story. *Their* tragic story. Buying this house, she supposed, was Archie's way of remaining close to her; to Catherine. Or to torture himself. Why else would anyone want to live in a place where a loved one had committed suicide and murder? What kind of person would then bring his bride there to begin a new life? Except that they'd never had a chance – not at a new life, nor at happiness. They were doomed before they began, she and Archie. Did that make it any better? Should there be mitigating reasons for forgiveness? Would it have helped to know? Perhaps. If they could have talked; if Archie could have got help for his drinking. Perhaps. She wondered if the letters were even ever sent, as there was only Archie's side of things. There was nothing from Catherine.

Ino no longer cared. She no longer wanted the burden of trying to understand Archie's backstory. She wanted simplicity. To love and be loved. To be called 'beloved'. Pondering all this, she made plans, but mostly she just waited – waited because somehow she always knew they would come. Even so, when they did, she heard their voices as if in a dream – bickering, of course, and as competitive as ever. In her mind they were still the youths they'd been when she first knew them.

She saw them first: two grown men smoking as if their lives depended on it, both wearing jeans and Tod's – the one with a hand in his pocket, the other consulting his phone, both gingerly picking their way through the orchard, incongruous, international and completely out of place. The Hardy Boys grown up; grown middle-aged. And in spite of herself she felt tears in her throat and her heart hammered with longing and regret and confusion and desire. Papers scattered from her lap as she clambered from her hiding place. Now she raised an arm in greeting and tried to call to them, only no sound came.

But Rafael had seen her. "Ino!" he called. "God, this English countryside. I think I've been stung by nettles!"

She laughed almost hysterically, started to cry, then, laughing again, ran towards him, tripped, and fell into his arms.

"I'll take it that I'm forgiven," he said happily, steadying her.

For a moment her face brushed against his linen shirt, and the lime scent of his aftershave, the orange-grove aroma of fruit and gardenia, transported her to the past. Closing her eyes, it was easy to conjure up images of Abuela and Salto and the lovesick girl she once was. She wanted to howl in pain at the loss of it all.

In her sudden stillness, Rafael sensed that she was no longer looking at him, but over his shoulder at his other cousin. "I'm sure you'll give us tea and a chat and show us round your lovely place and all of that," he said at length to fill the silence. "But in the meantime, *si me lo permites* – if you'll allow it – I'm just going to take a look at your garden. I'll look for a dock leaf or something while you two, well, you know…"

There was more strained silence. Rafael looked from one cousin to the other but both seem rooted to the spot. It was not at all how he'd envisioned their reunion. He'd imagined two people running towards each other as they did in films, usually on a beach, but these green lawns – his gaze swept the grounds – would have to do. At a pinch. Except it wasn't like that; not at all. Neither one had budged. There was no running in any direction. Which, he supposed, was a good thing, but was he wrong to come? He hadn't thought twice about booking their flights, planning this great rescue, but maybe it was asking too much. Too much time had elapsed. They were different people. They were *all* different people now.

But then Emil, looking away as though reflecting on the countryside views, as though ready for the visitors' tour, took a step sideways. "Yes, do that," he said stiffly.

Still uncertain, Rafael hesitated. "Or—"

"*Vete!*" Go!

"Okay, okay, I'm going." Rafael suppressed a smile. *It will be all right*, he thought. *Emil is just nervous. It will be okay.* The nettle sting that had subsided moments before suddenly sprang into life and was prickly all over again. He rubbed an ankle with the side of his shoe. "God, it hurts!"

"There are dock leaves in the field beyond the orchard," said Ino. "They really do the trick."

"If you say so." Rafael was unconvinced, but Emil was sending him such villainous looks that he limped away, but slowly, hoping to overhear a drift of their conversation.

For a moment Ino watched her cousin's retreating back, uncertain as to where to begin, and suddenly afraid. The person standing before her was not the young man of memory. This person was a stranger. Of course he must be. But then so was she. She knew nothing about him, and now that the moment had come, neither seemed to know how to cross the divide. It had been twelve years since they last saw each other. Emil plunged his hands deep into his pockets; Ino touched her neck, playing with her hair out of habit, to cover the scabs on her face.

"Emi—" she began.

"No, Ino," said Emil once Rafael was out of earshot.

His 'no' was so decisive, she was startled. She didn't remember him being particularly forceful. Strong in himself, sure of what he wanted, but not bullish. She couldn't bear any more judgement; any more harshness. Especially from him. Despite the years of longing, of dreaming, she'd rather be alone if that was how it was going to be.

His next words interrupted her thoughts. "Before we say anything..."

"Yes?" She realised her 'yes' was overeager but she couldn't help it. She searched his face for the wonderful warmth he'd once had for her and for her alone, but it was closed; expressionless. Her heart was a hungry, pulsating muscle; one moment shrunken and small, the next so huge it seemed to fill her entire chest cavity. Skewering it now were ever-tightening slivers of fear.

"I have something – actually, more than one thing – that belong to you; things that I hope you will take back."

Ino wiped the tears that had come suddenly, quickly, like a child's. "What? Things of mine?" she said, her voice cracking. "You mean you came all this way..." Her attempt at lightness faltered.

"Uh-uh," he said, shaking his head. "Not so fast. Your answer isn't going to change how I feel, *por supuesto* – naturally – but it will help."

She nodded again, but the gesture was meaningless. She couldn't possibly know how he felt. How could she? Maybe it was all too long ago. Maybe he didn't feel anything any more. Besides, they – well, *she* at any rate – had been so young then. They were completely different people now. She imagined they had little in common. He was here out of politeness, because of the affairs that need settling. Rafael had been emphatic on that score. There was business to do with Salto that should have been dealt with years ago, after Abuela's death, but because of the volatile political situation in Catalonia the paperwork couldn't wait another month. She looked past Emil, scanning the grounds for their cousin. Rafael needed to come back. And then they could chat as he suggested and then the boys – the Hardy *Men* – could leave and then… and then Ino would carry on with the rest of her life.

"The suspense is killing me," she said drily, but her voice broke and so her intended lightness was unconvincing. She had begun to tremble with the shock of seeing him again. Besides, she wasn't sure what 'him' now meant anyway. Not exactly. It was a new version of someone she had once loved. She didn't know how to distil the memories, the emotions; how to make sense of any of it. What *should* she be feeling? Was he an answer to her prayers? Was this fate? A second chance? Or nothing at all? If she closed her eyes and he touched her, would she respond?

Emil looked away from her slowly, as though fearful that if he took his eyes off her, even for a moment, she might disappear. She, misreading his expression, thought it was because he was shocked at her changed appearance. Instinctively, she stepped back to the protective, forgiving shade of an apple tree, but he followed, so closely he could have stepped into her footsteps. Later, she understood the reason why his hands were shoved into his pockets. He would explain that it was simply because he'd been fingering the coins and the ring – her ring; the one that she had returned to Rafa all those years before. Although 'thrust *at* Rafa' was nearer the truth. Now Emil took her clenched fist firmly, but not to kiss it as she first thought. (Hoped? Was disappointed when he didn't? She wasn't sure.) He prised apart her fingers and placed her signet ring in the palm of her hand. But he didn't let go: he held her hand firmly, and at once his touch was overwhelmingly familiar and desirous and brought back memory after intoxicating memory, and all she wanted was to cling to him and never let go. But she was confused by him; by herself. She had dreamed of seeing him again, and now that he was here before her, his hands holding hers, she wished that he would give her a sign; some indication as to how he felt. Perhaps he treated everyone with such tenderness.

And just as she decided that he was only being kind, he pulled her to him. The ring was still in her hand, cold and uncomfortable, trapped between her body and his. His hands were on the nape of her neck, pressing her against his chest. He too emanated that same Salto aroma, and she was giddy with longing. Suddenly she knew exactly how she felt and the distance of years made no difference at all. She realised that just being with him was enough. That the love she had shored up for him all this time had never altered. And so because of this, to safeguard this, it took all of her willpower to pull away.

"And before we go on," she said, extracting her arm, her hair, "I need to know something too. That woman… and your daughter?"

Emil dropped his arms – slowly, reluctantly, she thought. "*Daughter?*"

Ino nodded, miserable all at once, swallowing hard, still clutching her ring. "I saw the YouTube clip. She looks like you. Dark colouring. You seemed such a happy family." She was talking rapidly. The words jumbled. "Your wife's American?"

"My *wife*? You mean Nancy?" His tone was the crack of a polo mallet on a ball.

Ino winced. She could picture it exactly. "And your beautiful daughter – she looks just like you too, with that dark colouring."

Emil frowned, then grinned. "Oh, you mean Gemma. Actually, I think she looks just like *you*!"

At least he didn't say 'a younger you'. It was on the tip of her tongue to retort so, but she wasn't in the mood for banter – and the flippancy of his replies was making her feel even less so by the minute. He continued to smile inanely.

"I'm confused. I thought that Sol... her baby..." Ino hadn't meant to start with that. What was she doing? It was going all wrong. *He* was all wrong. How could Emil treat the whole thing as some big joke? How could he stand there smiling so stupidly? Did he not understand the impact of his actions? That her life had come to an end on that sunny Sunday? Not literally, not like Sol's, but what she believed then and as now had, her one great love. Suddenly breathless, panic-stricken, she turned away, set only on escape – and she would escape. She could hide anywhere. She knew the garden; he didn't.

"Whoa!" It took Emil only a few strides to catch up with her. He grasped her forearm. "Wait a second! What are you *talking* about? I don't have a daughter and I sure as all hell don't have a wife!"

Ino's heart slowed to a steady thud. She so wanted to believe him. But then who...? Within moments she was confused and suspicious all over again. Her experience with Archie had made her doubtful, mistrusting. Except, said that little voice of conscience, *except* that she ought to have learned from what she'd been through. Going forward, she needed to take responsibility for her own actions and stop blaming others.

So where did that leave her? In the aftermath of the accident, she had wanted to put miles between herself and Emil. In the years after that she had sought to forget completely. Archie's shenanigans and drinking had certainly helped her do that! And then, of course, there'd been Calypso; her beautiful, wilful, adorable Calypso. But as the years passed Ino's thoughts had turned more frequently to her youth. Watching her daughter grow brought Ino's own childhood that much closer. Her half-formed girlhood had been arrested. She didn't want that for Calypso. Latterly, too, as hers with Archie had ended, Ino had thought more and more about her short relationship with Emil. For her, it had been the most powerful and important influence of her life. With the distance of years, it was bookended by tragedy; a before-and-after. And now here he was, standing before her. Suddenly his life experience was less important than the overwhelming sensation of simply wanting to be with him. To be enveloped by him. But also to be reassured that her feelings for him were genuine, not imagined.

"Then who were they?"

Emil smiled patiently. "Who were who?"

"The woman and the girl? You said Nancy? Gemma? You know, *Bocado de Damas*? The amazing creature who designed the logo? The one you think looks like me? Not to mention the uber-cool, smart, sassy New Yorker who has revamped the business? More specifically her super-white smile and pert bottom?"

Emil grinned broadly now. "Oh, *them*!"

"Yes," said Ino coolly. "Them."

"Well, 'revamp' is a bit of an exaggeration but I'll go with 'pert bottom'! 'Sassy', eh?"

Ino's expression was stony.

Emil was delighted. He cupped her chin. "Don't tell me you're *jealous*?"

Ino brushed away his hand. "No! I'm not jealous!" She took a deep breath. "Just answer the question. Are you with anyone?"

There was a splintery silence. "Aren't *you*?"

Ino's eyes were wide. "B-but I'm unhappy! It doesn't count."

"How do you know I'm not?"

"Well, are you?"

"Unhappy? Or married?"

"Both."

"Neither."

"Neither." Ino repeated the word. *Neither.* So that meant…

Emil crossed his arms, leaning against the trunk of the apple tree. He fingered a bit of bark absent-mindedly, snapping it in two. "Nancy isn't my wife," he said carefully, "nor did she ever want to be." He shot Ino an amused look which made her blush; made her inexplicably joyful. "Having said that, she *does* have rather a pert… okay, okay. Look, she didn't come to advise on Salto or anything remotely like – she came to Europe to sort out Gemma. There were a few hiccups. Nothing major. Just the usual adolescent stuff. Gemma's a kid who happened to come into the *pastelaria* one day. She reminded me of you, but she's not mine, and Sol's baby wasn't mine either, but surely you know this."

Ino's heart, which had begun galloping with hope and excitement, came to a thudding halt. Every rib ached with discomfort. She could hardly contain her shock. Not *his*? Consumed by grief and disbelief, she reached out to steady herself against the tree. How was it that he – that *they* – had never talked; that when she'd left that summer, never to return, no one in the family had ever tried to explain things to her? Something as monumental as that? That Emil hadn't? Had they *all* made senseless sacrifices?

Slowly the world stopped spinning. There was still this new Emil before her. There was a chasm of years and feelings… And yet again, surely it was simply fate or karma and just meant to be? Would she have forgone having her Calypso? The words from her father's gravestone came to her. Words she hadn't understood then but did now. *And when the sudden impulse came I acted, and my action made me wise. And I regretted nothing.* Ino had run out of the Randolph that night not waiting – not *wanting* to hear what Rafael had been about to tell her. Had she heard him out, would it have made a difference? Undoubtedly, but the guilt they all carried had to be expunged one way or another. In the end, everyone had their own journey to make. One that had to be made alone.

With determination, Ino met Emil's eye. She felt the tug of nostalgia as she noticed the lines around his eyes; the streaks of white in his once-dark hair. It didn't matter: he was still sexy, the bottom of her stomach still fell to her knees, the clock was turned back. He was still him. "I'm sorry. I am. I only—"

Emil threw away the tree bark in a definitive gesture. "Actually, I do feel responsible…"

And there, just like that, Ino felt the fragments of doubt all over again; logic no contest for emotion. Her lifting spirits stalled.

"Why?" she said in a small voice. "Were you involved? I mean, romantically?"

"No," said Emil patiently. He thought of the brash American with her dark beauty. Sliding doors... "Nothing like that. Gemma is a child. I am fond of her. She reminds me of you, actually, when you first came to Salto. Remember?"

"I remember," she said curtly.

"She's just a kid, but a talented one. She did the drawings for the new logo and for the flyers advertising our new *Bocado de Damas*, and then when there was the strike her girlfriends and my grooms..."

Ino looked at him stonily. She remembered what he'd always thought of Argentine grooms.

He ran a hand through his hair. "I know how that sounds! God, you're making this difficult! In fact, I'm just now remembering things about you—"

"Just tell me!" said Ino.

"Well, if you'd seen the *whole* YouTube thing you'd have understood. Incidentally, there was some amazing footage of Salto..."

Her eyes misted over.

Emil took her arm again, pulling her to him. "If you really want to know I'll tell you, but not now. It has nothing to do with us. You, on the other hand, have much more to tell *me*."

Ino didn't contradict him.

He touched her face, the bruises on the side of her face, the welts on her arm. "Did *he* do this?" Which was a rhetorical question. His eyes darkened.

"He's gone," she said. "In case you're wondering. And he's not coming back. You're right, of course. There's a great deal to tell you, but somehow it no longer seems important."

He held her even closer. This time, she didn't resist, but leaned into him. She was so tired. She wanted only for someone to take away the anguish and sadness. She wanted to be able to laugh again, carefree and joyful.

Emil caressed her face gently before standing back. He reached deep into his pocket. "There's something else." He dropped the ancient coins in her hand. "You left these behind too."

She stared at the *arras*. Earnest money. "Abuela never gave them to me the first time round."

"Maybe she knew something you didn't."

Ino swallowed. She was such a jumble of emotion she felt dizzy. She took a deep breath. "Are you giving these to me? As in, your family to mine? Or simply returning, as in giving unto Caesar?"

"What do you think?"

She was still holding on to the ring with her left hand. This time he placed it on her finger.

"There where it belongs."

She smiled, about to speak.

But he touched her lips. "'*And let me talk to you with your silence that is bright as a lamp, simple as this ring—*'"

"*A* ring," she corrected. "Neruda."

He shrugged. "*A* ring, then. You know it?"

Used to bristling, she bristled. "Of course I know it! I read modern languages, remember?"

But he touched her lips again; this time with his thumb. "The emphasis was '*with your silence*'."

She took another deep breath, ready to retort, and then was quiet. They had another chance to make things right – there might not be another. She should take it. There was only the small handful of now between them. All at once it didn't matter what he'd done in the intervening years, whom he'd been with, nor where he'd been. There was only his physical presence, his smell, his masculinity. She'd forgotten the overwhelming attraction they'd always felt for one another (and that had been reawakened now); the overwhelming realisation that only the other would do, that no one else would ever matter as much.

His hands moved to her shoulders; they traced the scars on her neck, then smoothed the hair from her temple. He pressed her head against his chest so that she heard the rhythmic beating of his heart. Her senses filled with the memory of something else, and she realised that her response was an imprint of that feeling over another – the rest was mere detail. And in that realisation came submission. His strength was all-enveloping and she opened to him, hurling her whole being before him.

And Rafael was right: not only did she forgive them both for stealing her dreams when she was young, but she also forgave herself for the part she too had played in allowing resentment to grow; for nurturing and fostering bitterness and allowing it to thrive. For a moment there was nothing but the immense power of the silence between them. And then, as it always would going forward, his shadow then hers, blocked out the house, the fields, the trees and everything that had gone before, everything that had ever been.

Epilogue

The crying bothered him again. Most nights he woke hearing the kid down the road, and recently it had been so bad that in order to get a good night's sleep he'd gone to a hotel in the centre of town. He'd had to come back to the house, though, to get some papers. He pulled up alongside the house, not screeching to a stop as he used to. The grass was overgrown; brown in patches. Honeysuckle tangled with a clambering rose, and a clematis shoot was a dangerously spindly spike poking through the pergola. Tulips were dead in their pots. Moss caked the staddle stones that flanked the short drive and the oak gate. He ran a finger over their furry surfaces but it would take a sharp knife and a bristle brush to make any difference.

He felt like a stranger passing through, marvelling that this had ever been – and still was – his home. Pondered what it was that mere humans left behind. Just ghosts; just the impression of a life. For a moment – but it really was only a moment – he felt an uncomfortable, awkward sensation. Something close to regret.

Objectively, he could see that it had been a cosy place; appealing, even. Not that either were words he generally allowed to infiltrate his selective vocabulary. He was aware that 'edgy' was the adjective most commonly associated with the good doctor, and 'good' was employed with sarcasm. Because he wasn't good, was he? He felt a twinge of an unidentifiable emotion. Why could he not feel as others did? At least he knew from the letters that he once had.

He was sober for once, and not enjoying the starkness it brought. It was quiet: no usual birdsong or distant lawnmower or barking dog. It was true that with sobriety everything appeared cleaner; somehow more antiseptic. A Hello Kitty figure lay discarded on the ground, as though its owner had left in a hurry or it had fallen from a bag. He picked it up and tucked it in his pocket. It must have belonged to Calypso. For a brief moment he thought about his daughter. His *daughter*? The name and concept were not overly familiar to him, and he attached curiosity to the notion rather than any latent affection.

To his surprise the back door was ajar, as though he were expected. He pushed it gently with his foot. And then again, he heard the baby – though this time it seemed much closer, and the cry wasn't so much a cry as a laugh. He felt warm breath on the nape of his neck; not alarming but comforting – satisfying, even – just like the rush of alcohol in the blood from a first drink. He turned.

"Catherine?" he said.

Acknowledgements

As ever, I am indebted to my Book Club: the wonderful Clare, Fenella, Jane, Marie-Louise, Nickey and Perry. Your support, dear girls, has meant more than you will ever know. My local book shop, P&G Wells, has been a constant in my writing life and I am grateful for theirs. Thank you too to Lynn and Lisa, my literary soul mates.

Faye Booth, 'my' copy editor has transformed this book into something readable. What is more, she is one of those rare creatures, an editor with a sense of humour. I am under no illusion as to the work involved and that the true talent in writing a book lies with the editor. Hers is a skill that has left me completely awestruck. Holly Porter and Jonathan White at Troubador have given invaluable professional advice.

Many years ago, I met a man whose courage in the face of terminal illness was the inspiration for the character of Michael. His wife's tenderness, patience and devotion were humbling. Claire, thank you for that example, that nobility of spirit.

There seem to be a lot of Clares in my life spelled in different ways! Clare Pelly read the very first draft of the very first novel I ever wrote. Thank you.

Pablo Neruda: "Poema 15" (poem XV), VEINTE POEMAS DE AMOR Y UNA CANCIÓN DESESPERADA
@Pablo Neruda, 1924 and Fundación Pablo Neruda

This book is printed on paper from sustainable sources managed under the Forest Stewardship Council (FSC) scheme.

It has been printed in the UK to reduce transportation miles and their impact upon the environment.

For every new title that Troubador publishes, we plant a tree to offset CO_2, partnering with the More Trees scheme.

For more about how Troubador offsets its environmental impact, see www.troubador.co.uk/sustainability-and-community